MORGANA MAGIC SERIES

AN AMULET THAT DISGUISES

A TALE OF MAGIC AND MYSTERY

ELERY KEENE

AuthorHouse™
1663 Liberty Drive
Bloomington, IN 47403
www.authorhouse.com
Phone: 1 (800) 839-8640

Published by AuthorHouse 08/29/2018

ISBN: 978-1-5462-5607-6 (sc)
ISBN: 978-1-5462-5606-9 (e)

Library of Congress Control Number: 2018909812

Print information available on the last page.

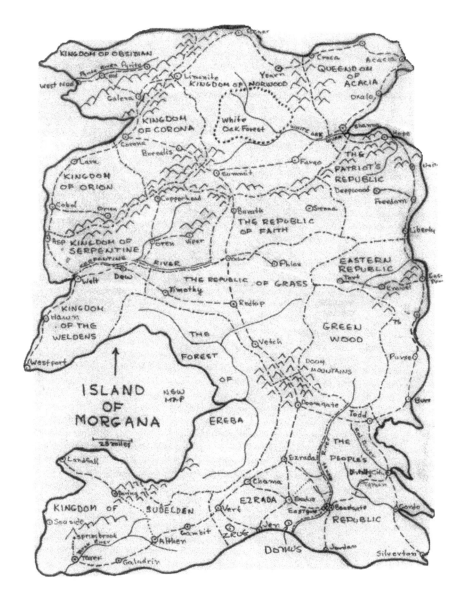

MAP OF MORGANA

PREFACE

Tiarra Galadrin, Johanna Morningstar, Eridana Silverdean, Aaron Ivey, Tamaranis Ri-ekm, and Reuben Huskins are on a mission. They have just spent two days in Exodus. They came here to find Robert Swift. His daughter, Sarah Swift hired them to find him. Robert Swift is a merchant trader who lives in the town of Althen, a town in the Kingdom of Sudelden. Each summer he puts his wares into wagons and carries them from village to village, hoping to sell them for a good price, or trade them for something that he can sell somewhere else.

The story takes place on the island of Morgana, an imaginary world. A map of the island is on page v. The people who live on this island have little to no communication with other parts of the world. The population is made up of several different races: Erebans, Eldens, Dwarves, Nogs, and Humans. All are considered to be Humanoids.

Family farming and logging are the primary occupations of the inhabitants. Farmers produce enough food to feed themselves and also the merchants, miners, soldiers, nobility and other who do not farm. Some fishing is done in the ocean, rivers, and lakes. Many hunt for food. Some mining and quarrying is done. Wood, stone, and adobe are the primary building materials. Wood is the primary source of fuel. Much of the land continues to be covered with virgin forest and wild grasslands. Food products grown on family farms include wheat, oats, barley, rye, flax, hay, beans, cabbage, beets, carrots, turnips, hops, apples, grapes, nuts and others. There are also sheep, cattle, pigs, horses, and poultry. Fish come mostly from the ocean but some come from rivers and lakes. Mining produces coal, iron, copper, lead, nickel, tin, clay, gold, silver, and gems. People make wool and linen cloth; iron and steel tools and weapons; lumber, leather goods, pottery, rope, and glass. They also make beer, wine, and whiskey. They use flint and steel to make fire. Magic is real, but only a few people know how to cast magic spells. Even fewer people know how to endow objects with magical properties. Some people have magic weapons, magic armor, magic jewelry, and other magic items.

Systems of travel and communication are slow. People use horses to ride and horses or oxen to pull wagons. Because few people travel more than fifty miles from home during a lifetime, most of them know very little of the customs of other cultures. There is often distrust of strangers who are of odd appearance and have unusual ways. Those few traders and adventurers who do travel, tell strange tales about what they have seen and done, but most people don't know whether to believe them or not.

Nations are governed by Kings, Queens, elected officials, and tribal officials. Some governments have dictatorial authority; some do not. Most governments treat their citizens very fairly; some do not.

The names of the months on the island of Morgana are Snow-fall, Ice-wind, Awakening, Quickening, Planting, Greening, Haying, Harvest, Leaf-fall, Bare-branch, and Darkening. The days of the week are Sun's day, Moon's day, Tyr's day, Woden's day, Thor's day, Freya's day, and Last day. Each month has twenty-eight days.

PART ONE

DISGUISES

CHAPTER ONE

WHAT SHOULD WE DO NOW?

Tyr's Day - Greening Ten *– Mid-Afternoon

It is mid-afternoon, and a very pleasant day. Tiarra Galadrin, Johanna Morningstar, Eridana Silverdean, Aaron Ivey, Tamaranis Ri-ekm, and Reuben Huskins, are in the courtyard of Sparrow's house in Exodus, a city in the eastern part of the island of Morgana. The eight foot walls around the courtyard are made of stone. The house, stable, and well are also made of stone. There are several horses in a pen beside the stable which is made of long wooden poles.

These six people came to Exodus to find Robert Swift and bring him back to his daughter, Sarah Swift who lives in the town of Althen which is located in the Kingdom of Sudelden which is in the southwestern part of the Island of Morgana. Her father had taken wagons filled with some of his merchandise on an annual expedition to sell them in other communities in the kingdom. Sarah was very concerned when her father did not return when he should have and she had stopped getting the daily messages that her father had been sending her. So Sarah asked her father's friends to come to help her try to find him. But her father's friends instead sent sons and daughters to do this. They are old enough, but not as experienced as Sarah wanted them to be. There were seven of them at the beginning but only six of them showed up at Exodus.

Tiarra Galadrin is a beautiful young woman with blonde hair tied back in a ponytail. Her pointed ears indicate that she is of the Elden race. Right now her ears are partially covered by a steel helmet. Otherwise she looks much like a human. She is twenty-five years old and five feet six inches tall. She is of noble blood because her mother is a daughter of the King. Her father is the heredity Thane of Galadrin, one of the nobles of the kingdom of Sudelden. She is wearing chainmail armor over a light orange long sleeved blouse. Her knee length, light green skirt shows that she is wearing tight fitting hose under it that cover the skin of her legs. She has brown leather boots on her feet. She is the only one who has had experience in combat before this mission. She does not use magic spells. She fights with a magic longsword and a magic self-loading one hand crossbow. She uses a shield. She bought a magic throwing knife, a gold ring that makes the wearer immune to poison and a Potion of Healing at Lady Lucy's magic shop. Just before leaving Ereba Queen Cassia gave Tiarra a Magic Leather Belt of Strength which will help her do more damage when hitting her enemies with her magic longsword. Because of her experience she has been the leader of the expedition but has listened well to the advice of the others.

Aaron Ivey is a male of the human race, not of noble blood. At five feet ten inches he is the tallest member of the group. He is twenty-five years old. He is of average build, not slender and not overweight either. He has dark brown eyes, curly black hair, and a slightly hooked nose. He is wearing a dark brown woolen hooded robe, or smock, tan trousers, and shiny brown leather boots. He has a heavy, ornately carved wooden staff in his left hand. He is a magic user. He would tell you that his spell energy comes from energy stored in the earth itself, not directly from God or other living things. His spells include Perceive Magic, Analyze Magic, Magic Beam of Energy, Snooze, and Blazing Hands. He has a ring of spell storing that was given to him by Queen Cassia of Ereba. Aaron bought a magic stylus that never runs out of ink and that cannot be broken and also a special hourglass that can't be broken and a Potion of Healing at Lady Lucy's at Lady Lucy's magic shop. Just before leaving Ereba Queen Cassia gave Aaron a Ring of Spell Storing. Its name is Zed. It can store no more than seven magic spells. When casting one of the spells stored in it he must say the ring's name and the name of the spell that he wants to cast from it, and say what he wants it to do. Queen Cassia had already put three magic spells into it. They are a Web spell, a Lightning spell, and a Fireball spell. Aaron has since added four Magic Beam of Energy spells because they are very effective when fighting enemies. Queen Cassia told

Aaron and the others that they should go to Exodus and find Sparrow, one of her helpers, at the Black Unicorn Inn. Sparrow would tell them where to find Robert Swift. Sparrow would recognize the Ring of Spell storing and know that the six of them are the ones that Queen Cassia has asked to find and rescue Robert Swift and bring him home. And it was because of the ring that Sparrow and Aaron's group were able to find each other. Aaron's home is in the town of Ezrada. Aaron would like to be considered to be the leader of the group instead of Tiarra because he is a male, but the group has decided that because of her experience she should be the leader. So far they seem to mostly agree that she is doing well and Aaron has pretty much the same assessment.

Eridana Silverdean is a woman whose father is an Elden and whose mother, who is now deceased, was a human. She has the same pointed ears that Tiarra has, inherited from her father. She is five feet six inches tall and thirty-five years old. She has a very nice female figure. She has a greenish tint to her eyes. She is wearing a green dress that is divided below the waist to allow her to easily ride a horse. Tight fitting green trousers cover her legs. Her soft brown leather boots come a short way above her ankles. She is a Druid spell caster. She calls upon nature for her spell energy instead of it to come directly from God. This would seem to be natural vegetation but it still seems to be available when she is inside a building. She does like to be out of doors most of the time. She likes sleeping in a tent. Her home is in Daring which is located about two days travel northwest of Althen. She can fight with a scimitar and a sling. Her magic spells include Perceive Magic, Ensnare, Glowing Target, Communicate with Animals, and Heal Minor Wounds. Queen Cassia gave her a Silver Chalice of Resurrection and a Silver Necklace that lets Cassia know where she is at all times. Her ability to heal wounds has made her very valuable to the group. The Ensnare spell causes vegetation such as grass, weeds, bushes, and even trees in a twenty foot diameter to entangle creatures so that they cannot move for a period of ten minutes. There is a chance that more than half of the affected creatures will not be fixed in place but will be able to move at only half the rate that they normally could. The Glowing Target spell, when cast by a Druid, outlines the target creature with pale glowing light. Except for quite small creatures only one can be outlined with one casting. Creatures so outlined will be easily visible in the dark, and will be easier to hit with a missile or striking weapons even in daylight. The outlining does no damage of its own. The maximum range is forty feet. The Communicate with Animals spell allows the Druid to communicate with animals within twenty feet in a telepathic way. This is a good way to gain information about an area and the creatures in it. Sometimes the animal will help the spell caster do something. The spell can be used with one animal at a time and it does not last for more than two minutes unless the spell caster has a lot of experience. The heal minor wounds spell can do healing when touching the wounded person and can be used repeatedly to completely heal a wound. It can be cast on others and also upon the wound of the spell caster. Eridana bought a magic gray cloak that changes color to match its surroundings and a Potion of Healing at Lady Lucy's magic shop. She thinks it will help her blend into the natural environment so that she may not be noticed by anyone if she wants to sneak through a wooded area to get somewhere. Just before leaving Ereba Queen Cassia gave Eridana a Silver Chalice of Resurrection and a silver bracelet. The Chalice can be used to resurrect up to two persons per week. To use it Eridana must have clean water in the chalice, ask a specific person to be resurrected, and let some clean water from the chalice touch the lips of the person to be resurrected. The silver necklace will enable Cassis to know where Eridana is at all times if she is wearing it on her neck. It has occurred to Eridana that she could let someone else wear it but this would not be what Queen Cassia told her to do. She feels obligated to wear it herself.

Johanna Morningstar is a human female from the town of Domus which is located in the southeastern part of the Kingdom of Sudelden. She is twenty years old and five feet eight inches tall. She has a nice looking, slightly plump, female figure. She is wearing a long brown, woolen, hooded robe, which covers her body loosely, without a belt. Her hood is hanging down behind her neck at this time. She has tough looking leather boots on her feet. She is not wearing any jewelry. She looks like a female cleric – a woman devoted to God who can cast holy spells. She is five feet seven inches tall. She has blue eyes and long blonde hair that hangs loosely down to her shoulders. She fights with a metal mace. She is wearing mail armor under her robe. She can cast Heal Minor Wounds, Cause Wounds, Illuminate, Perceive Evil, Empower Companions, and Demoralize Enemies. The Heal Minor Wounds Spell enables her to heal wounds by touching the wounded person or creature's body. She can use it to heal herself. Her Cause Wounds spell can cause damage by touching her opponent's body, but she almost never does this. The Illuminate spell creates magical light in the form of a fifteen foot diameter sphere of bright light at a distance of no more than sixty feet that can last for ten minutes. She can also use this spell to cast a globe of darkness for up to five minutes. The Perceive Evil spell allows her to detect the presence of an evil person and sometimes to recognize that a person or an object has been given an evil curse. The Empower Companions Spell is used to improve the morale of companion fighters within a twenty-five foot square the center of which must be within forty feet of the caster. It lasts for up to six minutes but it will not affect anyone already engaged in melee combat. The improved morale will make herself and her companions more effective in hitting their opponents. The Demoralize Enemies spell may be cast on opponents, which will lower their morale and make them easier to be hit by her and her companions. Her enemies will be more likely to surrender or run away. Just before leaving Ereba Queen Cassia gave Johanna a magic Crystal Bell which can be used to bring Queen Cassia's friend, Quicksilver, to help her. But Johanna can only use this once because it breaks into pieces when she uses it. Quicksilver has many very good magic spells that she can use to do this. Johanna's ability to cure wounds has made her very valuable to the group. Johanna has a cloak of invisibility and a Potion of Healing that she bought at Lady Lucy's magic shop.

Reuben Huskins is a male Dwarf from the town of Springbrook which is in the western part of the Kingdom of Sudelden. He is thirty-five years old and only four feet two inches tall, which is normal for a male dwarf. He has very strong muscles and a very rounded body which is also normal for a dwarf. He has long black hair and a black beard. His hair is wound up in a green turban that is held together with a blue topaz jewel clasp. He has dark eyes. His large bulbous nose, large ears, large hands and feet are typical of the Dwarven race. He wears a large bracelet on each wrist. He has a ring on the middle finger of his left hand that is set with a large amethyst. He is wearing a brown leather jacket covered by a shirt of chainmail. His dark green trousers are tucked into dark brown leather boots that nearly reach his knees. He fights with very sharp battle axe and uses a magic quick loading crossbow. He does not cast magic. He wears a chainmail shirt and uses a shield. Reuben has a bottle of perpetual clean water and a Potion of Healing that he bought at Lady Lucy's magic shop. It will never run out of water and the water is always clean enough to drink. He knows that sometimes the water from a pond or stream is not clean enough to drink without becoming ill. Just before leaving Ereba Queen Cassia gave Reuben a wristband made of electrum, an alloy of silver and gold. Queen Cassia told him that this wristband would help him to avoid being hit by an enemy in combat whether from a missile or a hand weapon. She told him that the wristband cannot be used when wearing his chainmail armor and his shield but it will provide better protection than that armor can provide. He also has a wristband of strength that he got from the fortune-teller that he consulted with during the first day that he was in Exodus. Reuben has very good carpentry skills and has brought some of his carpenter tools with him. He likes horses and usually leads his pack mule and the other two packhorses at the rear of the group when moving from place to place.

Tamaranis Ri-ekm is a human male who grew up living in a monastery after his mother died when he was only five years old. He has been trained and educated to be a Monk. He has been trained in the martial arts. He has intense looking light gray eyes and a small mouth set in a slightly fleshy face. He is dressed in a yellow ochre woolen robe that comes down below his knees. He has had almost no experience at all away from the monastery until becoming involved in this mission to find Sarah's father, Robert Swift. He is very much enjoying this opportunity to learn what it is like to live outside the monastery. He especially likes being able to communicate with women because no women at all live in the monastery. He is twenty-seven years old. He is only five feet four inches tall and somewhat overweight. He has no ability to cast magic spells. He is very agile. His only weapon is a hammer, so he fights in close combat. He also likes to kick at his opponents with his bare feet. He does not normally wear any shoes. He wears a tan colored wool cloth robe that comes down a little below his knees. His hair was always shaved away when he was at the monastery but he has been letting it grow for the last ten days. He acknowledges that he has not had enough experience away from the monastery to be the leader of this group. Just before leaving Ereba Queen Cassia gave Tamaranis a an ordinary looking black linen Scarf of Protection that will make it much harder for an enemy to hit him when in combat. She also gave him a pair of light brown soft leather boots that fit his feet very well. Queen Cassia told him that the boots are not magic but they will make his feet much more comfortable when riding a horse with his feet in stirrups and should help him do a little more harm to his enemies when he kicks them with his feet. Tamaranis has been wearing these boots ever since that time. He is reluctant to have anything to do with magic but he is also wearing the black scarf.

Sparrow is a young woman who owns the property where these people are talking together. She is a very good looking young woman with long, black hair. She is wearing a dark gray wool skirt, white linen blouse, and brown leather bodice, clothing typical for a middle class woman. She has blue eyes. Her warm smile reveals straight, white teeth. She is wearing a plain gold ring on the middle finger of each hand and a gold bracelet on her left wrist. A pendant hangs from a gold chain, centering itself in the area of exposed flesh just below her neck. She has a very good connection with Cassia, Queen of Ereba, who told Tiarra's group to travel to the town of Exodus and find Sparrow who would tell them where to go to rescue Robert Swift. Sparrow uses magic to communicate back and forth with Sparrow but does not seem to be able to use this magic to communicate with anyone else. Sparrow can also cast an invisibility spell. She used this spell to make herself and her companions invisible when they went to the house from which the rescued Wesley Stone. It also made their weapons and the rope that thy used to stay together as a group. But the people, their clothing, and their weapons became visible as soon as they attacked the Keepers that they found in the building. Tiarra and her companions think that Sparrow may be able to do other kinds of magic that they don't know about.

Also with them is Wesley Stone, an older man who looks like he could be Sarah Swift's father, but he isn't. Earlier this afternoon this group rescued Wesley Stone from a nearby building where he was being held captive by eight members of an organization called "The Keepers". The Keepers are a large group of soldiers employed by the government of The Alliance of Nations to promote their interests outside their own territory. The Alliance of Nations is a nation located in the eastern part of the Island of Morgana. This includes The People's Republic which is directly east of the city of Exodus, The Eastern Republic which is just to the north of The People's Republic, and the Patriot's Republic which is north of The Eastern Republic. These can be seen on the east coast section of the map of Morgana.

Wesley Stone was being tortured and interrogated by The Keepers. The rescuers believe that The Keepers were trying to obtain information about the people and government of Ereba, a nation located in the western part of this same island.

Ereba and The Alliance of Nations have been at peace for some time, but in the somewhat more distant past they were at war with each other. The government of The People's Republic realizes that their growing population needs more land to produce the food and other resources necessary to support their standard of living. The Ereban government leaders, and some of the other nations of Morgana are concerned that the recent peaceful relationship may be about to end.

The people gathered in the courtyard are communicating with each other, but most of their attention focused on Wesley Stone. He appears to be at least fifty years old, he has gray hair and a gray beard. His clothes are in poor condition, especially the back of his shirt because he has been whipped many times as part of the torture he has been forced to endure. But he is not bleeding now. Soon after they found him, both Eridana and Johanna used healing spells to cure the damage done to his body. Yet he seems to be quite tired. They think he probably hasn't had much chance for rest.

Eridana says, "Wesley Stone, I am so glad that we were able to find you and rescue you from The Keepers.

Wesley Stone says, "I am very glad that you found me and took me away from those terrible men who were torturing me. I'm also very glad that you killed them. They were terrible men. Thank you all."

Tiarra says, "Yes. We are all glad that we were able to help you. As you know, when we found you we thought that you were Robert Swift. That is who we are searching for. Sparrow told us that Robert Swift was in the building that you were in. When we found you and saw that you were being tortured, we thought that you were Robert Swift. You let us believe that until we had brought you back here to Sparrow's house. Then you told us who you really are. As you know, we went right back to where

8

we found you and searched the house more thoroughly. But we didn't find him. Sparrow used her magical system to tell Cassia, the Queen of Ereba, what we had done. Cassia did some investigation and then told Sparrow that Robert Swift is now in Divinity City, the biggest city in the land the Land of The People's Republic. We are going to have to go there, rescue him, and bring him back to his home at Althen. Robert Swift's daughter, Sarah Swift, has hired us to do this. Queen Cassia also wants us to do this. Have you ever been to Divinity City? Could you help us?"

Wesley Stone takes a few steps backward, while scanning the faces of the people with him. He says, "I have never entered into the People's Republic and I don't want to go there. You will have to do that without me."

Eridana asks, "While you were in the custody of the Keepers, where we found you, did you see Robert Swift? Did you have a chance to get to know him? When was he transferred from here in Ereba to Divinity City? How did they do it?"

Wesley Stone says, "I don't think I should tell you. Who are you? How do I know that I can I trust you?"

Tiarra says, "How do we know that we can trust you? You heard us say that we thought you were Robert Swift before we took you out of the dungeon. You didn't tell us then that you were not Robert Swift. Why did you wait so long to tell us?"

Wesley says, "I was afraid that if I told you then, that you might not help me get out of the house. I needed your help. I thought it would be better if I waited until we were at a safer place. As soon as we got here, I told you."

Reuben says, "Hold up your left hand. Let everybody see the scar on it. I saw your scar when I was unlocking the padlocks that fastened your wrists to the chain. We all have scars like that on our left hands."

Reuben holds up his own left hand so that Wesley can see it. Reuben says, "Everybody, show Wesley the scar that you have on your left hand. Then he will know that he can trust us."

Everybody does. Then Wesley asks, "Do these scars mean that you have all been inside the Forest of Ereba and talked with Queen Cassia?"

Tiarra says, "We all have. Have you done the same thing? Have you been helping Queen Cassia?"

Wesley says, "Yes. I have. That is why the Keepers kidnapped me, took me to their house, and questioned me about the Forest of Ereba. I don't know why they thought I might know anything about that. I told them that I didn't, but they didn't believe me. They kept asking. But I never told them anything about the Forest of Ereba."

Sparrow says, "You know that I have already told Queen Cassia that we have rescued you. Do you, Wesley, have anything that you want me to tell her for you?"

Wesley Stone says, "Tell her that I have some information for her. I don't think I should tell you what it is. Tell her that after I get some rest I will go to her and tell her. Right now I want to go home for a while."

Sparrow says, "I will go inside my house and try to communicate with her now. I must have complete privacy when I do this. You must all stay here in the courtyard until I get back. You might want to see if your animals have enough water and food. You can get water from my well. There are buckets in the stable. There is also hay and grain in the stable."

Sparrow goes into the house.

Eridana says to the others, "I know something about Sparrow's method of communication with Queen Cassia. I can communicate with animals that way. I know what they are thinking and they know what I am thinking. But I cannot communicate with people that way. No, I don't know what you are thinking unless you tell me. I don't think Sparrow knows what we are thinking unless we tell her either. I think her ability is special for communication with Queen Cassis. And it probably doesn't work unless Cassia wants it to happen."

Aaron, Tiarra, Tamaranis, Eridana, Reuben, and Johanna are not looking forward to going to Divinity City to try to rescue Robert Swift.

After a moment, Reuben says, "Let's feed and water our animals."

They go toward the stable. They see that there is a watering trough inside the corral. It appears to be empty. It is next to the fence so they can put water into it without even opening the gate. Reuben and Tiarra put water from the well into buckets and pour it into the trough. Aaron and Tamaranis bring armloads of hay from the stable and throw them over the fence into the corral. Eridana and Tiarra find the large grain bin. They put some grain into fairly large wooden bowls. They bring the bowls of grain to the corral, and dump it on the ground where the horses can eat it if they want to.

Wesley watches. He says, "I would help you, but it hurts so much for me to move, I really can't."

Johanna says, "It's okay. We know that you are hurting. Let me ask you. Did you see Robert Swift being tortured in the building where The Keepers were torturing you?"

Wesley says, "I saw another prisoner and heard his screams of pain when he was being tortured but I never had a chance to talk with him. It must have been Robert Swift. I didn't hear him yesterday. Maybe that is when they took him to Divinity City. I don't know how they did it. They probably took him in a wagon, he wouldn't have been able to walk or ride very well after all that torture. He would have been hurting just as badly as I am. But maybe they used magic. The people of The People's Republic are not supposed to use magic but I know that sometimes The Keepers do. Did you know that?"

Aaron says, "We have been told that The Keepers use magic but nobody else who are of the People's Alliance are allowed to use magic."

Wesley says, "The leaders of the People's Alliance wouldn't want their ordinary people to have the ability to revolt against their government."

Aaron asks, "Why would they want to do that? Doesn't the government treat all of their citizens fairly? If they have a good life, they wouldn't want to have a revolution."

Tiarra says, "From what I have heard they treat their own people fairly. The Keepers don't bother them. They bother people like us. They don't want us to come into their territory and bring any magic with us. They are afraid of what we might do, not what their own people might do. If they see somebody on their land with magic, they know immediately that it is not one of their own. The Keepers will immediately either kill us or put us in prison. They don't want that to happen to their own people. I am much more concerned about what the Keepers will do to us."

They all talk about this for a while. It is some time before Sparrow comes back into the courtyard. She walks briskly to them and says, "I have been able to communicate with Queen Cassia. Wesley, I want you to come inside the house with me. I will tell you privately what Queen Cassia wants you to know. She has agreed that it would be good for you to go home and get some rest before coming to see her in person in Ereba."

Wesley follows Sparrow into her house. When inside Sparrow says, "I now understand that you have been helping Queen Cassia get important information about what The Keepers may be planning to do, sometimes going into The People's Republic to do so. Is that true?"

Wesley says, "I can't talk with you about things like that."

Sparrow says, "I understand. But you must realize that I have a very close relationship with Queen Cassia. I would not share any information that you give me with anyone but her, Unless I have her permission. I am hoping you could tell me something that will help the people outside get to Divinity City and find Robert Swift"

Wesley says, "I don't have any of that kind of information."

Sparrow says, "All right. I can see that you are very much in need of better clothes. The ones you have are so badly torn and ragged. I have some in much better condition in my house that I think will fit you. You will be spending the night here. As soon as I can, maybe tomorrow if you are ready I will escort you to your home. I believe you live in the town of Jen. Is that right?"

Wesley says, "I do live in Jen. I will appreciate it if you can come there with me, but you don't have to."

Sparrow says, "We can talk more about that later. Right now I am going to get you some better clothes."

Sparrow leaves Wesley in the kitchen, eating an apple, while she goes into another room. When she comes back she has a shirt, trousers, and underwear of an appropriate size to fit Wesley. They are not new, but are in fairly good condition. While he tries them on, she goes back into that room and brings back some leather slippers that he can put on his feet.

Sparrow says, "This will have to be good enough for now. Perhaps you would like to get some rest while I go outside and talk with the others."

She takes him to a bedroom. He is lying flat on his back on the bed before she has even left the room and closed the door.

Then Sparrow goes outside. Her other guests gather around, very anxious to find out what she will tell them about Queen Cassia and Robert Swift.

Sparrow says, "I have given Wesley some better clothes to wear. He is now resting on a bed. He needs rest."

Then she says, "Queen Cassia wants you to go immediately to the prison at Divinity City in The People's Republic where Robert Swift is being held prisoner and rescue him. It won't be easy, but we believe that you can do it."

Tamaranis asks, "How does Queen Cassia know that Robert Swift is in the prison at Divinity City?"

Sparrow says, "I don't really know, but I suppose she has an agent or two there that she can communicate with in the same way she does with me. She probably asked them to let her know if they could find out where Robert Swift is. There didn't seem to be any doubt in her mind about where Robert Swift is being held. She was very definite about it."

Eridana says, "Then that is where we will go to rescue him."

Sparrow says, "Yes. But you don't have much time. Queen Cassia wants you to leave for Divinity City tomorrow morning, so that you can be there in time for the Festival of Light. This festival is the only time of year that people from outside The People's Republic can freely enter and leave Divinity City. At other times, no one enters or leaves without showing proper identification. This will make it much easier for you. The Festival of Light lasts six days. Many people converge on the city during this festival to celebrate and trade. Shops are open; many goods are bought and sold. The highlight of the festival is the execution of Fortune Tellers, Spell-casters, Spirit Healers, and people of the non-Human races who have been captured during the year. They will be burned at the stake. Those who beg for mercy may be killed with a sword, a less painful way to die. It is a horrible spectacle, but most of the people of The People's Republic believe that all such beings are evil. They celebrate these executions. The people who will be killed are kept prisoner in the large tower at the center of the city. It is very likely that Robert Swift is one of those who will be executed this year. If you are going to save him, you must do it now. And you won't be able to go dressed as you are. You can't look like a group of people going on a quest or looking for a fight. You have to look harmless."

Johanna asks, "So if I were to go I would have to wear different clothes?"

Sparrow says, "I don't think you should wear metal armor. Women of the People's Republic don't do that. And you shouldn't let them know that you are able to cast healing spells. The people who live there think that people who use magic are evil. Magic is not allowed."

Johanna says, "What I do is not magic. I am a Spirit Healer. I heal people. My ability to do this comes from God. It is a good thing. I am not evil, I am good."

Eridana says, "I am a Druid. My magic energy comes from nature, natural energy. This energy comes from God also. I am not evil."

Aaron says, "I am a spell-caster. I am not evil. My magic energy comes from the sun. Some of my spells do hurt people. It is my responsibility to use it only when justified. I know the reputation of the Keepers of The People's Republic. They are fighters. They do a lot of fighting. Killing people for a just cause is not evil, but I think some of what they do is evil."

Sparrow says, "I agree with you, Aaron. Queen Cassia and many other people of Ereba use magic. They are not evil. But the religious beliefs of most of the people who live in The People's Republic believe that magic is evil. They have laws to punish people who do it. If you look like someone who casts magic spells, or healing spells, you will be placed in custody, taken to the festival, and executed. I want you to go, but you can't look as if you cast spells. I can give you other clothes to wear so that you don't look like spell-casters."

Reuben says, "You said they also execute people of non-Human races. I am a Dwarf. Would that include me?"

Sparrow says, "Yes. You will have to wear a disguise so that you won't look like a Dwarf. Also, Tiarra and Eridana will have to do something so that their ears will not be seen. These people consider that Dwarves and Eldens are not Human just as they consider that Erebans are not Human. Dwarves and Eldens will be executed if found in The People's Republic. I have in my house what is needed to give each of you a suitable disguise. So don't worry. You will all be able to go into The People's Republic. You will be able to accomplish your mission."

Reuben says, "I don't see how I can go. There won't be any way to disguise me so that I won't look like a Dwarf. No matter what clothes I wear, I look like a Dwarf."

Sparrow says, "You might be surprised. I do have something that I think will disguise you. We can talk about that later.

Eridana asks, "When does the annual Festival of Light start? How long will it take us to get to Divinity City?"

Sparrow says, "I told you before, but I will tell you again. The first day of the festival is Greening sixteen. Today is Greening ten. You should try to be there before Greening sixteen so that you can rescue Robert Swift before the festival starts. The People's Republic considers Robert Swift to be one of their enemies, but Queen Cassia thinks that it is very unlikely that the Keepers would kill him before the festival starts. That means that you have five days to make the trip. The distance is between eighty and one hundred miles, depending on which route you take. You should be able to travel about twenty miles per day, so you should have no difficulty getting there soon enough. I suggest that you be ready to start early tomorrow morning. I will find places for you to sleep tonight.

Reuben asks, "Would you mind if I sleep in the stable with the horses? I like to keep an eye on them. When we are at an inn, I usually sleep in the stable."

Sparrow says, "You can sleep in the stable if you want to, Reuben. But you won't be sleeping with the horses. They will spend the night outside in the pen.

Reuben goes to the stable alone. He is thinking, *I don't see how I will be able to continue this mission. I can't go into The People's Republic. There is no way that I can be disguised to look like a Human. I'm short, but so is Tamaranis. The real problems are my facial features, especially my big nose. I also have huge hands and feet. I look like a Dwarf. No kind of clothing can change that. I might as well go home. But I don't want to. I want to go there. I want to help save Robert Swift. I'm a good fighter. They need me! Maybe Sparrow could make me invisible. But that only seems to work for about 30 minutes. Sparrow won't be there to make me invisible again. Well. Maybe she would let Aaron borrow her wand.*

Sparrow comes into the stable alone while Reuben is looking for a place to lay his bedroll out on the floor. Reuben says, "You said that you are a master of disguises. You can probably give my friends some pretty good disguises that make them look like humans that don't use magic.

But you won't be able to make me look like a Human, will you? What are you going to do for me? I want to go."

Sparrow says, "I can provide you with a disguise. I'll use magic to do it. You can go. You can help save Robert Swift."

Reuben says, "I know what you can do. You can use your wand to make me invisible, like a little while ago. If nobody can see me they won't know that I look like a Dwarf."

Sparrow says, "You know that spell only lasts thirty minutes. That won't work."

Reuben says, "You could give your wand to Aaron. He could cast the spell on me every twenty-five minutes or so.

Sparrow says, "No that's not good enough. I have something better. I have a magic item that will make you look like a Human. You will be taller and thinner. When you remove the item, you will change back to the way you look now. Don't worry. You'll be able to go. You will be able to help save Robert Swift."

Reuben asks, "What is the item?"

Sparrow says, "I'll show it to you later. Right now I need to communicate with Queen Cassia about all of the magic items that you all have with you. I want to know what she thinks about which items you should take with you into The People's Republic.

Chapter Two

A Farmer Family

Tyr's Day - Greening Ten – Late-Afternoon

Reuben is in the stable. Tiarra, Aaron, Eridana, Johanna, and Tamaranis are watching the six horses and Reuben's pack mule eating hay and grain in the corral that they brought to them from the stable just a few minutes ago. The animals are also drinking water that they brought water from the well to the trough just inside the corral. The large front door of the stable is open. They can easily see the saddles, pack saddles, Reuben's crate of carpenter tools, tents, blankets, cooking dishes, and food they had put in the stable earlier in the day. They also see a small vegetable garden nearby, where there is plenty of sun. They see beautiful flowers growing near the foundation of Sparrow's house.

They expect they will spend the night sleeping in Sparrow's house, but Sparrow has not yet showed them where that might be. While waiting for Sparrow to return they talk about the many things that they have done since being hired by Sarah Swift to try to find her father. They also talk about what they would like to look like when they enter the People's Republic to continue their search for Robert Swift.

When Sparrow returns she says, "Wesley Stone is still resting in one of the spare bedrooms of my house. He is very tired."

Eridana says, "We are tired too. We did a lot of fighting this afternoon. Do you have a place for us to sleep in your house? Or should we go back to the inn where we slept last night?"

Sparrow says, "I want you to sleep here, not at an inn. I don't want you to be seen going back and forth between here and your inn. The fewer people who have any idea that we are doing something together the better it will be for all of us. I will provide you with an evening meal and also breakfast. But I don't have enough beds for all of you to sleep in the house. I only have three bedrooms. One of them is mine. One of the others is being used by Wesley Stone. I noticed that you have brought tents with you. You can put up your tents and sleep in the courtyard. One of you could sleep in the bed in the other spare bedroom if you want to. I suppose it could be two of you if you are willing to both sleep in the same bed. Where do you want to sleep?"

Tiarra says, "I would like to sleep in the spare bedroom."

Eridana says, "I would rather sleep outside in my tent. I like being outside."

Reuben says, "I would like to sleep in the stable. That is where Tamaranis and I slept last night while the others were sleeping inside the inn."

Tamaranis says, "I would like to sleep in the stable as well."

Aaron says, "I don't want to sleep in a stable. I guess I'll sleep in one of the tents here in the courtyard."

Johanna says, "I would rather sleep in the house. But if the bed that Tiarra will be sleeping on is too small, I could sleep in one of the tents with Eridana."

Sparrow says, "I'm glad that you are all so cooperative. I'll show you the bed in the spare room when we go inside, in a few minutes. As I said, your presence here should be kept as secret as possible. So those of you who sleep outside should not wander outside of the courtyard where people might see you. And don't build a fire in the courtyard. That would attract the attention of my neighbors."

Eridana says, "We won't."

Sparrow says, "You should go to bed early and plan to get up early in the morning. You need to get a good start on your journey into The People's Republic to rescue Robert Swift. As you know, his life is in great danger. Cassia thinks he may be one of the first people to be executed during the special Festival of Light, but probably not before the festival starts. So your mission may be a very difficult one. But Queen Cassia is willing to increase your reward by one hundred gold pieces each if you succeed. If you choose not to go, you may return to her and she will give you each twenty-five gold pieces for what you have done already. If you do decide to go, I will help you with disguises. I'm very good at that. In fact, one of my rooms is full of clothing that can be used for that purpose. I can also help with makeup materials if that is appropriate. What do you think? Will you go?"

Aaron says, "I need to think about it. I would like to go. I want to keep my promise to Sarah Swift to find her father and bring him home. But the mission will be very difficult. We should spend some time thinking about it before making a decision."

Sparrow says, "You don't have much time to think about it. You need to be ready to go early tomorrow morning. You should decide before you go to bed tonight."

Tiarra says, "I want to go. We all should."

Aaron says, "I'll go."

Tamaranis says, "Before I decide I want to know what the plan is."

Sparrow says, "As you should. The next thing we need to do is make a plan. I think when you understand the plan you will all decide to go."

Eridana asks, "How long will it take for us to get there?"

Sparrow says, "I told you this before. The first day of the festival is Greening sixteen. Today is Greening ten. You should try to be there before Greening sixteen so that you can rescue Robert Swift before the festival starts. That means that you have five days to make the trip. The distance is between eighty and one hundred miles, depending on which route you take. You should be able to travel a little more than twenty miles per day, so you won't have any time to waste, but you can do it."

Johanna says, "We'll do the best we can. If we have to travel from dawn until dark we'll do it. I don't like traveling after dark, but I suppose we could if we have to."

Sparrow says, "I don't think you'll have to travel after dark, but you might need to if something happens that slows you down. I know that you can do it if you have to, but I don't think you will. But I do want you to get a good start tomorrow morning. You should spend the rest of today getting ready to go. You will need disguises. I will help you with that. I believe that I have the kind of clothing that you will need to use to disguise yourselves. Let's go into the house now. We'll go into my parlor where we can have comfortable seats while we talk about it."

They all follow Sparrow into the house through the back door. They go through the kitchen into the parlor. They are wondering what kind of disguises Sparrow might have in mind. Sparrow has been thinking about it too. She has made an assessment of the appearance of each and thought about what things she has in her house to make them look like something other than a group of magic users and adventurers. She thinks it would be best if they look like a farm family. Many of the people who go to the festival are farmers. While walking to the house she takes a look at each. She also uses her special psychic ability to understand some things about each that she cannot see.

When everyone is seated in the parlor, Sparrow says, "We must talk about what you will look like on your journey, especially when you cross the river and enter into the People's Republic. You must all appear to be of the Human race. If not, the government of The People's Republic will consider you to be evil and you will be killed. You, Tiarra, are an Elden. Eridana, you are a Half Elden, which they consider to be just as evil as a full Elden. Reuben is a Dwarf. They also consider dwarves to be evil."

Reuben says, "I'm not evil."

Sparrow says, "I know. But in The People's Republic you are considered to be evil. You will need a disguise."

Tamaranis says, "But the rest of us, Aaron, Johanna, and I, are of the same blood as they are. They should not consider us to be evil."

Sparrow says, "By their definitions, Aaron and Johanna are considered to be Spellcasters, also evil people who will be executed if found in The People's Republic. And you, Tamaranis, while technically innocent, would probably be found to be guilty by association with these evil beings. You would all be considered to be evil. If you enter The People's Republic as you are, you will be put in custody as soon as you cross the bridge across the Beast River from Eastgate to Beastgate. That is why you all need disguises, so that you will not look like outlaws to them."

Eridana says, "We understand. Tiarra and I can use our long hair to cover up the shape of our ears. We can look like we are of the Human race."

Tiarra says, "Yes. I will cover up my ears."

Sparrow says. "That would be a start. Aaron and Johanna, you are both dressed as Spellcasters. Aaron, your robe makes you look like someone who casts spells that hurt people. So you need to wear something else. Your robe, Johanna, is the robe of a person who casts healing spells. Neither of you can enter The People's Republic while wearing such clothing."

Johanna says, "My healing power comes from God. It is not evil. It is good. There should be no law anywhere against doing it. But I know. The people of my village and my religion all know that we are not welcome in The People's Republic. Give me other more suitable clothing and I will wear it."

Sparrow says, "I will."

Tamaranis says, "I know that you are going to tell me that my robe makes me look like a Spellcaster, even though I am not one. Give me something else that will fit me and I'll wear it."

Aaron says, "I think that Reuben will look like a Dwarf no matter what kind of clothes he wears. He won't be able to enter The People's Republic with the rest of us. That's too bad. He is a good fighter, and I know he wants to go. This isn't fair."

Sparrow says, "That's right, Aaron. They consider all Dwarves to be their enemies. But I have something in mind that I think will give him the kind of disguise he will need. I've mentioned it to him already. You will all be surprised when you see it."

Reuben smiles.

Sparrow says, "Also, all use of Magic is outlawed in The People's Republic, including possession of any magic items. If any of you are found to be carrying any magic item it will be taken from you, and you will be charged with a crime. The punishment would be execution at the Festival of Lights. So it would be best that you not take any magic with you into The People's Republic. But if you do, it must be very well hidden."

Tiarra says, "Our magic is very important to us. We need it. But we understand the problem. We'll hide it."

Sparrow says, "We'll talk more about that later also. I now want to tell you this. A successful disguise is more than a costume. You need to play a role. You need to pretend that you are somebody that you are not and have a plausible story that supports it. You all need to know what role each of you is playing so that you can relate to each other according to your roles instead of according to who you really are. You want to look ordinary so that you don't stand out in the crowd. You will be traveling together, the six of you. You should look like you belong together. What do you think would be the most ordinary looking group of six people traveling together to Divinity City for the festival?"

Tamaranis says, "It would be a family of farmers. We have been seeing mostly farmers along the road."

Sparrow says, "That's right. Good answer. Most of the people are farmers. There will be more farmers going to Divinity City than any other kind of people. How would farmers be traveling?"

Johanna says, "Most of the farmers we've seen were walking. Some had wagons, but the wagons seemed to be used mostly for carrying goods, not people."

Sparrow says, "You didn't see any of them riding fine horses like yours, did you?"

Tamaranis says, "We have seen some people riding horses, but not many. That was when we were traveling between Althen and Vert. We didn't meet anybody on horses when we were traveling between Ashua and Exodus. The only horses we saw were pulling wagons."

Sparrow says, "And that is pretty much what you will see on the road between Exodus and Divinity City. Most of the people will be farmers and most will have wagons. After all, most of the people who live on the island of Morgana are farmers. It is my recommendation that you disguise yourselves as farmers. You will blend very well with the other travelers. You won't be noticed. Nobody will ask you questions. You can leave your horses here. I'll take good care of them and give them back to you when you return for them, after you have rescued Robert Swift.

Tiarra says, "I would prefer to take our horses with us."

Sparrow says, "As you have already told me, a farmer family would not be riding horses to the festival at Divinity city. They would be walking beside a horse or two pulling a wagon. I have a one horse wagon you can use. You can take one of my horses to pull it. Use the gray one. It looks like an old plow horse. You must have seen it in the pen next to the stable. The wagon will be a place where you can carry most of your belongings. You can hide the things you don't want anyone to notice, such as your magic items and weapons, in a secret compartment under the seat of the wagon. You can also carry some goods from your fictional farm to sell at the festival in the back of the wagon. Lots of farmers take things to sell with them. I have clothes for you to wear that will make you look like a farm family."

Aaron says, "I don't think it will work very well to hide our weapons and magic under the seat of the wagon. That's the first place I would look for something hidden. It would be better if you could make our magic things invisible. You have a way to do that."

Sparrow says, "You know that my magic wand that makes things invisible only lasts for thirty minutes. That wouldn't make sense. Perhaps one of you can make things invisible. Aaron, you are a Spellcaster. Can you do it?"

Aaron says, "I have not learned that spell yet, but someday I will."

Eridana says, "I don't have that spell either, nor do any of the rest of us."

Johanna says, "That is not a spell that a priestess can learn."

Tamaranis says, "I do not cast spells."

Reuben says, "Neither do I."

Tiarra says, "And of course I don't either."

Sparrow says, "Then you will want to hide your magic in the secret compartment under the seat of the wagon. It's a very secure place. You will be able to get them out quickly if you see that you will be getting into a fight. It doesn't look like a secret compartment. The person I bought the wagon from told me that he had taken the wagon into Beastgate and returned with no trouble. The guards at the gate inspected the wagon going both in and out without paying any attention to it at all."

Tiarra says, "All right. I guess that is the best we can do. We do need to look like a farmer family."

Sparrow says, "There will be many, many farmers with wagons going to the festival. The officials won't want to take the time to look under the seat of every wagon. Their experience tells them that they won't find anything that would be a problem if they do. Don't worry about it. They will see you as a man and his wife with grown up children going to Divinity city, just like almost everybody else."

Aaron says, "A man and his wife going to the festival. That sounds good to me. I'll be the man, head of the household."

Tamaranis says, "No. That should be my role. I'm older than you are."

Sparrow says, "It should be Aaron. He looks more like a farmer head of household than you do, Tamaranis. You look more like a son than a father."

Tamaranis scowls.

Sparrow says, "You need to look like a typical farm family. You shouldn't wear any of your jewelry. Peasant farmers can't afford jewelry. Peasant women and children don't have any money either. The father would be the only one with any money. Give all the money you want to bring with you to Aaron. It shouldn't be a lot. If you have too much, I can keep the some of it for you and give it to you when you return. You can leave your extra jewelry with me too, and maybe some of your weapons that you don't think you'll need."

Johanna says, "We don't really have very much money, or jewelry either."

Sparrow says, "You need to think about your roles. Together, make up a story about your family history. Do it tonight. You all have to be able to tell the same story. People may ask you where you live. I suggest that you tell them you live in some out of the way place because no one will recognize you as a neighbor. Perhaps you live in a hut in the forest outside of Exodus, this city. There is a forest north of here. Aaron could be a woodcutter who has cleared a big enough area in the forest so that you can plant and raise a few crops. You probably would have a few cows, a few pigs, some chickens, and maybe some sheep. Sheep would be the source of the wool you women spin into thread. Tiarra and Eridana look old enough to be shepherdesses who take turns minding the sheep."

Eridana asks, "That sounds like a lot of animals that need care every day. Who would be taking care of them while we are away?"

Sparrow says, "You've got the idea. You have to be ready to answer that kind of question. Maybe you have another son and daughter that you left at home to take care of the livestock while you are away. That should be part of your story. You wouldn't come into the city very often, so the people you talk to won't think it's strange that they don't know you. Think about your story. Keep the concept simple, but you should have more details than what I have told you. I want you to tell me about it in the morning over breakfast."

Johanna says, "It will be Aaron, acting as head of the family, who will be answering the questions. Not me - or any of the rest of us."

Sparrow says, "That will be the usual case, but you can't be sure of that. What if he is injured in some way? Someone else will have to do it. Maybe you, Tamaranis, or whoever is playing the role of Aaron's wife."

Tamaranis says, "I could do it."

Sparrow says, "Let's take a look at the costumes. You might as well try them on now."

Eridana says, "Tiarra and I will need to disguise our ears."

Sparrow says, "You can both hide your pointy ears under your long hair. You shouldn't be wearing ponytails anyway. Let your hair down."

Johanna says, "It might be better if they wore bonnets. That would cover their ears very well.

Sparrow says, "That would work. Or you could put your hair into two nice braids, one over each ear. The wind wouldn't blow that away. Your ears would always be out of sight."

Eridana says, "I like that idea."

Sparrow says, "All right. Now, come with me into the next room. I'll show you the disguises. You can pick out something that you like."

Sparrow pulls a curtain aside revealing a door. They go into another room. Against one wall is a long rack of clothes of all different kinds. Men's clothes are at one end; women's clothes are at the other. They rummage through them, looking for something they would like to wear. Sparrow makes suggestions.

Reuben doesn't look at the clothes. He has little idea what size he will need after Sparrow makes him into a taller man.

Sparrow notices. She says, "Reuben, I'll help you find something later."

She turns her attention to the other five people in the room. "Try on your costumes. Aaron and Tamaranis, you can take some of the costumes you like and try them on in the parlor. The women will use this room. Reuben, you might as well go to the parlor and help the men. I'll stay here and help the women"

When the women are ready Sparrow calls out to the men into the parlor. "Aaron! Tamaranis! Reuben! The women are ready! If you are ready, you should come back in here so we can look at you! Then we can all talk about it!"

Aaron, Tamaranis, and Reuben go into the costume room where the women are. Aaron is wearing plain gray wool trousers held up by leather suspenders, an off-white wool shirt, and a tan leather vest. He has a brown straw hat, gray socks, and badly scuffed black boots. Everything Aaron is wearing looks nearly worn out.

Tamaranis has no shoes. His tan trousers only come about four inches below his knees. He has a yellowish-white shirt, a gray wool vest, and a gray leather cap that covers up his ears and hides the shortness of his hair. Reuben says, "I think you should wear the shoes that Queen Cassia gave you. They are not magic and you will like more like an ordinary person."

Tamaranis says, "All right. I'll wear my shoes." He puts them back on.

None of the clothes the women are wearing look new either. Johanna thinks that Sparrow might have acquired these costumes at a yard sale, or some kind of fund raising event where people donated clothes that they no longer wanted in an effort to raise some money.

Tiarra is wearing a low cut, clean white blouse with full sleeves a little below the elbows. Over this is a gray leather bodice laced tightly up the front. She has an orangy-red wool skirt that comes almost down to her ankles, and light tan shoes made of soft leather. A yellowish-white apron covers the front of her skirt, tied around her waist. She has undone her ponytail and arranged her long blonde hair into two long braids that cover her pointed ears. She looks like a farm girl except for the makeup she is still wearing on her lips and cheeks.

Eridana is wearing a similar outfit. Her skirt is light gray. Her bodice is tan. Her shoes are brown. She has also put her light brown hair into two long braids to cover up her ears. She never wears makeup. She looks like a farm girl.

Johanna has a dark gray full skirt, and a gray bodice. Her apron is yellow ochre. Her worn looking soft leather shoes are light gray. She has a white cloth sunbonnet.

Sparrow says, "You all look fine. Aaron and Johanna, you will need makeup to make you look a little older. Aaron must look like the head of the family and Johanna is his wife. Your beard, Aaron, is just right for the role. You should look as if you are more than forty years old. You don't need gray hair. Your hair is fine. You just need to have some dark lines that look like creases around the eyes, and something to change your skin tone a little. I will provide the make-up ingredients and help you put it on the first time, tomorrow morning. After that you will have to do it each morning yourselves. You may mess it up during the night. You can help each other. You may have to refresh it sometimes during the day too, especially if you perspire a lot."

Tiarra says, "I can help with that. I'm good with makeup."

Sparrow says, "I can see that; but you better not be wearing any on your trip to Divinity City. Farm girls don't wear makeup."

Sparrow looks directly at Tamaranis. She says, "I like the way your hat covers up your lack of normal length hair. You can pose as Aaron's son. You won't need any other makeup."

Tamaranis frowns. "I'm the son? I'm probably the oldest one here. I should be the father."

Tiarra, "You look young."

Sparrow says, "Tiarra, you will be Aaron's daughter. I like the way you have your hair. You could have a cloth cap that covers up your ears if you want to. I've got some of those around here somewhere."

Eridana says, "I suppose I'm another daughter."

Sparrow says, "You don't look like you are related to Aaron and Johanna. Your face and neck look wrong. I think you should pose as an indentured servant. Sometimes farmers have indentured servants who are treated very much like family members except that they are usually given the nastiest tasks that everybody hates to do. Just make sure your ears don't show. You could wear a cloth cap if you want to."

Eridana says, "I think I would like that. You know, I don't think Tamaranis looks enough like Aaron or Johanna to be their son, either. He should be an indentured servant too."

Tamaranis says, "Eridana's right. I would rather be an indentured servant."

Sparrow says, "That's up to you. It's your story. You work it out."

They all hear a bell ring five times from a distance so far away that the sound can barely be heard within the room. Reuben thinks, *That must be the town bell. If so, it must now be five hours since noon.*

Sparrow says, "It's time for me to get some meat at the butcher shop for our supper. When I get back I'll start cooking. Does anyone want to help me? There are eight of us. That's a lot of food to prepare."

Johanna says, "I'll help. I'm a pretty good cook. What are we going to eat?

Sparrow says, "I've got to go to the butcher's shop and buy some meat. I'll do that alone. You can help me when I get back."

Eridana says, "I'll help too."

Johanna and Eridana follow Sparrow into the kitchen to look around. They see a pretty good sized table, some chairs, a large fireplace with a big kettle hanging from a swinging rod, and many different kinds of dishes – some for cooking and some to eat food from when sitting at the table. There is a big wooden bucket with water in it sitting on a bench beside the fireplace.

Sparrow says, "While I'm shopping you could get the fire going good. You could also wash the big kettle. That's where we'll cook the meat and vegetables."

Eridana asks, "Where is your husband? I haven't seen him. Will he be surprised to see us all here when he comes home?"

Sparrow says, "I'm not married."

Eridana says, "I saw the swing in the yard and some clothes on the clothesline that look like they would fit a young boy. Do you take care of someone else's children?"

Sparrow says, "No. I have a son, but he isn't here. He's spending the night with a friend. It might be hard for him to keep a secret. He won't tell anybody that you were here if he doesn't know."

Eridana asks, "Did your husband die? I'm so sorry."

Sparrow says, "I was never married. Yes. I had a child out of wedlock, but I don't want to explain. Do you have to know?"

Eridana says, "No. I guess it isn't my business to know about that, but it must be difficult for you to raise a child alone."

Sparrow says, "I manage. I have a variety of skills. Helping people with disguises is only one of them."

Eridana brings wood from the wood box and puts it onto hot coals in the fireplace. Johanna starts washing the kettle. They also wash plates and bowls that they think will be used for serving the food. Some of the dishes seem to have been collecting dust for some time.

Sparrow picks up a pretty good sized basket, and goes out the door. She walks purposefully to the courtyard gate, opens it, goes through, and closes it.

When Eridana and Johanna feel that they have done what they can they join Tiarra, Tamaranis, Aaron, and Reuben in the courtyard. They are standing near the corral watching their animals.

Eridana asks Reuben, "What are you going to wear for a disguise? The rest of us have disguises. Where's yours?"

Reuben says, "I don't know. But Sparrow tells me that she has one for me."

The people wearing disguises walk around the courtyard, looking everywhere. This seems to help them feel more comfortable with the disguises that they are wearing. Reuben and Tamaranis go into the stable, looking for a good place to put their bedrolls and sleep for the night.

When Sparrow returns, Johanna and Eridana go into the kitchen with her. Sparrow has brought several pretty good sized chunks of beef, some bacon, eggs, dried beans, dried peas, and milk. She puts the ground wheat, dried beans and peas into her large kettle with some milk and water to make some porridge. She cuts the meat into smaller chunks, cooks it in several frying pans, and adds them to the porridge mixture.

When the food is ready Sparrow goes out the kitchen door and invites those in the courtyard to come inside and eat. Then she goes to the bedroom where Wesley is resting and brings him into the kitchen. Wesley walks into the kitchen very slowly showing that he is still in pain from the torture he was subject to.

Sparrow uses a very large wooden spoon to place a mixture of small chunks of beef, mixed with some porridge made of a mixture of milk, ground wheat, and dried beans and peas.

There are enough chairs for everyone to sit and eat. Water, milk, and wine are available for drink. Slices of brownish bread are available from a platter in the middle of the table. The bread must have been prepared on a previous day but there is enough for all.

While they are eating, Aaron asks, "What will Reuben be wearing for a disguise?"

Sparrow says, "I can't tell you right now. After we finish eating he and I will go into the stable and deal with that. That would be a good time for the rest of you to put up your tents. Tamaranis, you should sleep in one of the tents with Aaron. Reuben will want to sleep alone in the stable. He will want some privacy while he is getting used to his new disguise."

When they have finished eating, Sparrow says, "I'm going to help Reuben with his disguise now."

She looks at Reuben. "Let's go into the stable for that. You will want some privacy for what we are going to do."

Then Sparrow says, "I would very much appreciate it if Johanna and Eridana would wash the dishes and clean up the kitchen now. The rest of you should put up your tents and arrange your bedding. It would be best if you would bring your personal belongings into the house. You can put them into the room where the disguises are stored. They'll be safe there. Reuben, I want you to stay with me."

Everyone but Sparrow and Reuben go to the stable. Soon Aaron, Tamaranis and Tiarra are putting up tents. Eridana and Johanna are cleaning up the kitchen.

Sparrow and Reuben go into her bedroom. She puts several things into a pillowcase. They look like they are some of her clothes. Sparrow says, "These clothes will be for you. I am going to give you a magic amulet that will make you look like a Human woman."

Reuben blushes, "Me? A woman?"

Sparrow says, "I thought you might be embarrassed. That's why I waited until we could have some privacy before I told you about it."

Reuben's face is still red. "I thought you would make me look like a Human male."

Sparrow says, "I would if I could." She takes something from what looks like a jewelry box. It is an ordinary silver chain with a small figurine of a woman dangling from it. "This is it - an Amulet That Disguises. When you put this on you will look like a Human woman. You will be able to go into The People's Republic without any trouble at all. You will be able to complete your mission."

Reuben asks, "Isn't there something else you can do to disguise me? I don't want to do this."

Sparrow says, "I don't have anything else. If I were you, I would put the silver chain on when you are alone - in private. The best place would be out in the stable, after your friends have left it for the night."

Reuben says, "I need to think about this."

"Now would be a good time, then, for you to go to the stable and think about it. I'll join you with the amulet and these clothes when I think we can have some privacy there. Is that all right with you?"

Reuben says, "I guess so."

Sparrow says, "If you are going to do it, you should do it before you go to sleep tonight so that you can have chance to get used to your changed body. Go out to the stable now."

Reuben goes outside. He doesn't go into the stable until he thinks his friends have finished taking everything out of the stable that they might want for the night. He stands at some distance from where the tents are being put up and watches. He doesn't talk with anybody. He is thinking about the Amulet That Disguises.

Sparrow puts the amulet into a small sack and puts it on the bed beside the bag of clothes. Then she goes outside, finds Tiarra, and shows her the bedroom where she will be sleeping for the night. After that she goes back to the kitchen and helps Johanna and Eridana with cleaning up. She keeps checking on the progress of those who are putting up the tents.

When Sparrow sees that the people putting up the tents are no longer going in and out of the stable she goes back to her own bedroom, picks up the bulging cloth bag and the small sack she had left on the bed and goes outside. She sees where Reuben is standing outside the stable and goes to him.

CHAPTER THREE

REUBEN'S DISGUISE

Greening Ten – Afternoon

Reuben sees Sparrow walking toward him, carrying the large cloth bag. He thinks he knows what is in the bag.

Sparrow says, "Let's go into the stable now."

Reuben has noticed the wagon standing outside near the stable, a four-wheeled wagon with a canvas cover over the top. He asks, "Is this the wagon that we'll be using when we go to Divinity City?"

Sparrow says, "Yes. Take a closer look if you want to."

Reuben does. He sees that it has a seat at the front where someone, maybe two people, could sit and ride. He sees that there that there is plenty of room to put things in the back of the wagon. It is well covered by the canvas supported by curved pieces of wood attached to the sides. He also looks at the compartment under the seat where some of the things that they will be taking with them could be hidden, just as Sparrow had said.

Reuben says, "I just came up with a great idea. I won't need a disguise. We are going to have a wagon. It has a canvas cover over it. I could hide in the wagon."

Sparrow frowns, shakes her head side to side, and says, "Maybe. How long can you hold your bladder? When you get close to Divinity City there will be lots of other people on the road. You will only be able to come out of the wagon after dark. If the guards decide to search the wagon, and they will when you cross the river into Beastgate, you'll be discovered. You'll be in big trouble. I don't think it would be worth the risk."

Reuben says, "Maybe you're right. I don't know what to do."

The front of the stable has two large doors with hinges at the edges. Both doors are open. There is another smaller door at one side, very similar to the door of the house. Sparrow and Reuben go in through the large doors. No horses are in the stable.

Sparrow drops her bundle on the floor. She holds the amulet and chain up into the light coming into the stable through the wide open doors so that Reuben can get a good look. Reuben sees the same silver chain and figurine of a woman that he saw before in the bedroom.

Sparrow says, "When you put this around your neck you'll be magically changed into a Human woman. The change will not be permanent. When you take it off, you'll be a male Dwarf again, just as you are now. It's easy, a lot easier and more effective than trying to hide in the wagon. No one could possibly think that you're really a Dwarf."

Reuben says, "Are you sure that I'll be able to change back into a male Dwarf when I take it off?"

"Yes, but you don't have to, if you don't want to. You can remain Human as long as you want to by continuing to wear the chain on your neck."

Reuben asks, "Will I be taller? Will I have longer arms?"

Sparrow says, "Of course. It's magic. You will look like a normal Human being. No one will think that you could have ever been a Dwarf."

Reuben says, "I don't very much like the idea of being female."

Sparrow says, "I'd make you look like a Human male if I could, but I don't have an Amulet that does that. This Amulet is the only thing I have that will disguise you well enough so that you can go into Divinity City."

Reuben asks, "When I take the amulet off, will look the way I do now?"

"Yes. You will be exactly the way you are now, a male Dwarf. Will you do it?"

Reuben pauses for a moment, thinking it over.

Sparrow says, "You don't like the idea of looking like a female do you?"

Reuben says, "No. Would you like the idea of looking like a man?"

Sparrow says, "It might be all right for a little while. It might be kind of interesting to find out how the opposite sex lives. Don't you think?"

Reuben says, "I don't know. This is a big decision. Let me think about it."

Sparrow says, "Don't take too much time. You can't wait until morning. Your leg and arm muscles will have to stretch when your limbs get longer. There will be a lot of pain in your muscles. Your arms and legs will get much longer. They will have a lot of adjusting to do. That's why you should put the amulet on now. It will take quite a while for you to get over the pain. You may feel a little awkward moving around at first, but that won't last long. I think you'll like having longer legs. It may also take some time for you to adjust to walking around wearing a long skirt. That's why you should put the amulet on now. Don't wait. Either you do it now or you don't do it at all. If you don't, you might as well go home in the morning. It makes no difference to me. I can easily understand that you might be afraid to do this."

Reuben says, "I'm not afraid. Are you sure that I'll change back to my normal self when I remove the Amulet?"

Sparrow says, "I'm sure of it. You will only need to wear it for a few days."

Reuben says, "All right. I'll do it then. I don't like magic very much, but I've always had a Magic Crossbow, and I've been acquiring a lot of other magic during this expedition. It seems okay. I'm committed to this mission. I must go. I'll do it now."

Sparrow says, "All right. Listen carefully; you have to do this right. Before you put on the Amulet, you must take off all of your clothes, including any jewelry you are wearing. Take off your ring and those wristbands."

She kicks the bundle at her feet. "This bundle has all the female clothes you'll need. Put them on as soon as you can, after some of the pain has gone away. You will pretend to be a peasant woman, Aaron's daughter. I'm going to leave now. You don't want me to watch. I assume you won't want anybody to see you with your clothes off. I'll be back in a few minutes to make sure you're all right. I also want to make sure these clothes fit you okay." She puts the Amulet in the pocket of her apron.

Reuben says, "I'll do it as soon as you leave."

Sparrow says, "Before I go, I'll help you close these big doors. Then I'll go out the side door."

Reuben swings one of the large doors closed while Sparrow closes the other. Each door has two prongs about four feet above the floor. They both pick up a long wooden bar that can be placed horizontally behind the vertical wooden prongs. The ends of the long bar extend to intercept two additional prongs attached to the wall on each side of the door. There is no way that either door could be opened without removing the bar.

Reuben says, "My father's stable at home can be locked this same way."

Sunlight comes through the large window at the other end of the stable. It is much too high for anyone standing on the ground to look in. Smaller windows on the side of the stable next to the pen are also too high for anyone to look inside. Reuben sees no need to light a lamp.

Reuben has an apprehensive expression on his face.

Sparrow asks, "Are you ready?"

Reuben tenses, clenches his fists, shuts his eyes, looks down, and grimaces. "All right. Give me the Amulet."

Sparrow says, "Good." She gives the Amulet and chain to Reuben.

She goes out the small door, closing it behind her, and walks to the house thinking, *I have done my best. What happens next will be up to Reuben. If he doesn't use the Amulet, he might as well go home in the morning, but I think he's going to do it.*

Reuben shakes and stretches his muscles, trying to get rid of his tension.

He says aloud, "She says to do it now. All right. I will."

He lays the Amulet and chain aside for the moment and takes off his clothes. The turban comes off first. His long black hair falls naturally to the middle of his back. He removes both Magic Wristbands and the Garnet Ring that is supposed to protect him from fear.

A sudden wave of terror courses through his entire body. *What if Sparrow is lying? What if I can't change back? She says I'll feel pain. What if the pain is unbearable? Maybe I shouldn't do this.*

When he takes off his shirt the light coming through the window shines on the bulging muscles of his biceps and forearms, which are typical of male Dwarves because of the heavy work that they do. He also looks at the short curly black hair on his chest.

He thinks, *I can't look like a woman with muscles like these. I need strong muscles for fighting. This can't possibly work. I'll be an ugly looking woman. I shouldn't do this.*

He puts the shirt on top of the nearby grain box and stands there for a moment, thinking.

But what if I don't do it? I'll have to abandon the mission. That would mean dishonor. I would be too ashamed to go home and face my mother and father. What will my companions think? I'm not a coward. I'm a little apprehensive but I'm not afraid. I don't need my Ring of Protection from Fear. I can handle this. Putting on this disguise requires lots of courage. I can do it. And it doesn't really matter if I'm an ugly looking woman. It will probably be better if I am.

But he hesitates, pulling a skirt from the bundle of clothes near his feet. Looking down, he holds the skirt in front of his body, the top of the long skirt at his waist.

I don't want to wear a skirt. I like women, but I don't want to look like one. I don't think I know how to behave like a Human female. I don't even like Humans very much. I don't think I can do this. Not even for a few days.

He looks at the glint of sunlight reflecting from the Amulet and chain.

I'm weakening. It's hard, but I've got to put the Amulet on before I change my mind. It will be painful but I can stand pain. I'll be all right. I'm not afraid. Maybe I can wear the clothes of a man. Then I can behave as a man.

He grits his teeth, puts the skirt back into the pillowcase, and takes off the rest of his clothes, putting them on top of the grain box beside him. He picks up the chain. It has a fairly large loop at one end and a hook at the other. He unhooks the chain, tips his head back trying to get the loop of the chain with the Amulet on it under his beard, and threads it under his ears between his long black hair and his neck. He pauses in this position.

My hands are shaking and I can't see what I'm doing. Maybe I am afraid. But what if I am? It takes real courage to do something that you are afraid to do. I've got enough courage to do this. I can. I will.

By feel, he manages to hook the chain together. As he starts to slide his fingers along the chain toward the Amulet to make certain that it is properly arranged around his neck, he experiences a flash of warmth. It affects his entire body, feeling much like the flash he felt when crossing the bridge into the Forest of Ereba, but this is more intense and lasts longer. At the same time, he feels sharp pains in his arm and leg muscles. They feel as if they are being stretched farther than they should be, as if they might snap from the strain. It is unbearable. Involuntarily, he lets out a long, loud scream. It starts with a guttural growl and ends in a high-pitched shriek.

"Ooh my Gaw-ud!"

The clothes on the box seem to be about a foot lower than they were a moment ago. *No, it's me. I'm taller. My legs are longer. Ooh how they hurt! My arms hurt. They are longer too. And much slimmer.* He stretches them forward to get a better look, also hoping to ease the pain.

"Ohh!" The involuntary groan is so high pitched that it sounds almost like a scream. It hurts worse to move his muscles than to hold them still. So now that he has his arms out straight in front of him he holds them there and looks at them.

There's no hair on my arms! Or on my hands either. I had dark curly hair on the backs of my hands. They look so small and slim. My arms are longer but they're all stretched out. They look so thin and puny. They look – girlish! My fingers are shorter – and so thin – and there is little width to my palms. Yes, this is what Johanna's hands look like, Human female hands.

He drops his hands and arms down, jiggling them, trying to relax his muscles as much as possible. But the jiggling hurts and his muscles still feel tight. All his muscles feel tight. All his muscles hurt.

I can feel the movement of every muscle in my body. They all hurt, but my legs and arms hurt the most. I still feel warm. I wonder what my legs look like.

He looks down. There is no bushy black beard snuggling against his chest. Instead he sees a pair of bulging female breasts. Below his breasts he sees a tummy covered with hairless white skin. Bending slightly forward he manages to get a look at his legs, feet, and the floor of the stable. It seems to be a long way down.

My feet look awfully small. My legs are long and thin like my arms – no, not as thin. They still look strong, but I can't see any hair on them either.

He lifts each foot separately, flexing his leg muscles. They are already stretched thin but they are able to stretch some more and contract as necessary to move his legs. It hurts more to move them than to hold them still, but he can do it. He squelches the impulse to cry out from the pain while taking a couple of steps forward.

Good. I can walk.

Bending further forward he looks for his genitals but he can't see them. All he can see in this area is black curly hair. He puts his right hand there and feels flesh under the hair and a vertical crevice.

I didn't think about this happening. I've lost my manhood! She said I would look like a woman but it didn't have to go this far. It's too much. Nobody would have seen my male parts under a skirt. Sparrow should have told me this would happen. I wouldn't have done it. She tricked me.

Reuben straightens up. The pain from moving his muscles seems to have diminished, but he can still feel it.

I've lost my muscles. I've lost my beard. I've lost my... I'm not a man any more! I better take the Amulet off right now, and change back.

He puts his fingers on the Amulet and starts working them along the chain toward the clasp at the nape of his neck, under his long black hair.

I can be a man again. This is just a disguise. I'm still me inside. My memory didn't change. I can take off the Amulet any time I want to. I don't have to do it right now. I've got time to think it over.

He stops moving his fingers along the chain. Standing still, the pain has diminished. His muscles feel pretty good.

Reuben suddenly feels compelled to urinate and have a bowel movement. *Where can I do this? There must be an outhouse somewhere. Oh yes. I saw it when I came into the courtyard. But I'm not dressed. I've got to go right now.*

He runs to the manure trough, the place in the stable that the animals use. He straddles the manure trough and scootches. He almost loses his balance but quickly recovers. He doesn't want to fall into the manure trough while urinating so he moves to the end of the trough, near the wall, where he can grab onto a framing timber with both hands. This is better. He urinates, does a bowel movement, then urinates some more.

He walks slowly away from the manure trough to get the rag that he normally uses to wipe his bottom after doing a bowel movement in the bushes. It is in one of his saddlebags. After wiping, he feels a lot better. He slides his hands down the sides of his body from his neck and narrow shoulders to his armpits, past his ribs to his waist and hips, feeling very little pain. *I'm sweating. My flesh feels moist and firm. I'm not as fat as I was before. I can feel each rib under the skin. My waist is really small but my hips seem to spread way out – like Tiarra's. I thought I would be more plump than*

38

this, shaped more like the Dwarven women, but taller, with a belly about the same size as I had. Lots of Human women look like that. I must have lost a lot of weight. Where did it go? Not as much pain is left. My arms and legs hurt the most.

He bends down to massage his thighs and legs with both hands trying to erase the pain, then straightens to rub his arms, first left then right.

My skin is so soft and smooth. It doesn't seem possible. It's as smooth and hairless as it was when I was a small boy. It feels kind of good. I feel really warm. No wonder I'm perspiring. I hope I'm not going to be sick.

His face feels just as smooth and soft as his arms do, maybe softer. Moving his hands back towards his ears he feels the long hair where it fell when he took off the turban. He pulls a snatch of it in front of his face. It is still black.

My neck hurts a little. My neck must have stretched too, or changed somehow.

He looks up and around, flexing his neck muscles to loosen them. He rubs them with his hands. He rubs his shoulders, ribs, and hips as well.

I have really narrow shoulders and my chest has become really small. I don't have much upper body at all – except these bulging breasts. They feel softer than I thought they would, and the nipples are much more prominent than what I had before. I think the breasts look big because there is so little else left of my chest. My hips are fine; just a little soft is all. My waist and tummy are really small. How can there be room for food in there?

The feeling of warmth has gone away and the perspiration is evaporating.

Now I feel a little cold. Sparrow will be coming back soon and I'm naked. I've got to cover myself up. The clothes I was wearing won't fit.

He dumps everything in the pillowcase out onto the floor. Among other things he sees a white cotton nightshirt with long sleeves. He quickly pulls it on over his head. It is fairly open at the neck so it goes over his head very easily. It is quite loose and comes well down below his knees.

This is better. Now I'm covered up. What else is here?

He finds two long wool skirts, three blouses (one with short sleeves), two pairs of white linen pants, and something that looks like a red leather vest. He also sees a towel, some washcloths, and a long strip of cloth rolled up and held together by a large common pin. He doesn't know what that is for. There are no stockings and no shoes.

He drinks some water from his bottle of endless water, then goes to his backpack and takes out the mirror he uses sometimes when he combs his long hair and beard. Most of the pain has gone away. The light is dim but he can see his face and hair. His bulbous nose has become quite small but his lips are quite full. He forces a smile. His teeth are clean, white, and regular. He pulls his hair back to get a good look at his ears. What had been very large ears have become quite small.

I didn't suppose that my face would change so much. My cheeks look so hollow. I've still got brown eyes. My bushy eyebrows are gone. What's left is much thinner and – and – feminine looking. I thought my face would look more like my mother's face, or Rachel's - and my body too. There are lots of stout human women. Why couldn't I be like that? I look more like Tiarra, or Sparrow. I guess it's all right. It's a good disguise. I should have no trouble walking around in The People's Republic. I look like a woman but it's just a disguise. I can change it any time I want to. My thoughts are mine. I'm still Reuben Huskins. Sparrow said that the pain wouldn't last, and it didn't.

He returns the mirror to his backpack, then walks around a little trying to get used to his longer legs. His arms move as needed to maintain body balance without his being conscious of it.

He thinks, It feels strange to be so tall. I can take longer strides, but it feels natural. Maybe most of the pain is over. This will be a good disguise. Maybe I can handle this. It's only for a few days.

CHAPTER FOUR

SPARROW'S ADVICE AND GUIDANCE

Greening Ten – Sparrow's Stable

Reuben hears a knock at the smaller door. He hears a voice.

"It's Sparrow. You did it, didn't you? I heard you scream. Everybody did. I want to come in and see you. Are you ready?"

Reuben had hoped nobody heard him scream. He opens the small side door. He says, "I'm ready. Okay. Come in."

Reuben is surprised at the sound of his own voice. It is high-pitched and somehow soft, much different from his normal voice, A lot like Sparrow's or Johanna's, not as high pitched as Eridana's or Tiarra's. It is not a male voice.

"Was that me?"

Sparrow comes into the stable, shuts the door behind her, puts her hand over her mouth, and sort of laughs. "Hm, hm, hm, hm."

She says, "That was you. You have a very nice voice for a woman. How do you feel?"

Reuben says, "My muscles hurt badly at first, like you said they would, but the pain is a lot less now. I can handle it."

"I'm proud of you. What you did took a lot of courage. Many men wouldn't do it."

Reuben thinks, *It's nice to feel brave, but maybe I shouldn't have done it.*

Sparrow says, "You have a beautiful voice. I like it. You don't sound anything at all like a male Dwarf. You don't look like one either. What a wonderful disguise!"

Reuben asks indignantly, "Why did you laugh?"

Sparrow says, "I'm sorry. You seemed so surprised at the sound of your voice. It just came out. Have you tried on your clothes?"

"Just this shift. I was cold."

Sparrow says, "Take off the shift and let me get a good look at you. Don't be shy. We're both women. I'll help you dress in your daytime clothes."

"No. I'd rather dress myself alone. I can figure it out. Come back in a little while. I'll be dressed."

Sparrow's reply sounds a bit impatient. "All right. If that's the way you want it. You are about the same height as I am, five feet and three inches, and about the same size. The clothes I left in the sack should fit you very well. I'll come back in a few minutes. I do want to see that you get it right. I also have some things to tell you."

"What do you want to tell me?"

"Get dressed first. Then I'll tell you."

Sparrow leaves. When she gets back in the kitchen, Tiarra ask Sparrow, "Did Reuben put on the Amulet?"

Sparrow says, "He did. He looks like a female Human now. He'll be able to go with you."

They all smile. Eridana says, "A female Human. I can't wait to see what he looks like."

Sparrow says, "Give him some time. He's putting on his female clothes now."

Eridana says, "I can't wait."

Sparrow says, "When you see him try not to laugh. This is going to be hard for him. We need to help him get used to his new appearance."

Back in the stable, Reuben pulls the nightshirt he is wearing off over his head. He puts on a pair of white cotton split drawers, using a bowknot to tie the drawstring at the front of his slim waist, just above the small protrusion of his belly. Then he puts on a white linen blouse with long, very full sleeves. It buttons up the front. It has a very open neck but there are white cloth strings that can be tied together to close it up a little more. He leaves it open for now. It is full enough to fit around his breasts, narrows down at the waist, then spreads out to make room for his hips.

Next he takes a brown wool skirt, steps into it and pulls it up past his hips to the smallest part of his waist. The bottom hem is barely off the floor. He pulls the drawstring tight and ties it in front with a bowknot.

He looks at the red leather garment and sees that it is like the bodice that Tiarra wears sometimes, and that Sparrow is wearing. His former Dwarven girlfriend, Rachel, almost always wore one. *I suppose I should put that on too.* He puts it on like a vest, then laces it up the front with leather thongs, pulling it snugly around his waist. It also fits snugly around his breasts pulling them closer together.

He looks in the small mirror. The figurine of the woman hangs on the chain of the amulet precisely in the middle of the area of bare skin.

Like this. I'm dressed. That wasn't hard. I didn't need any help. Sparrow will see that when she comes back. I wonder what it is she has to tell me. I wish I had shoes. My mother almost always wore shoes.

He finds his battleaxe on the floor. He wants to put it right beside his bedroll so that he can get it quickly if he needs it during the night. When he picks it up it seems terribly heavy, much heavier than it was before.

Suddenly he realizes what happened. *It's not the axe that's heavier. I'm weaker. I don't have the strength of a male Dwarf anymore. I've got the strength of a Human female.*

He looks at his arms again. *There isn't much muscle there. I'm probably weaker than Tiarra is. She has thicker arms than I do now. I'm puny.*

He tries to swing the axe horizontally, as he normally would in combat. He can't do it. It hits the floor and bounces up. He has taken a small chip of wood out of the floor.

He tries the Magic Short Sword he has been carrying as an extra weapon; the one taken from the thieves they fought when they were following the trail of Robert Swift's wagon train. *This is much lighter. I think I could use it effectively despite my lack of strength, but I have never practiced with it.*

Hepulls up his sleeve and puts the wristband of strength that he got from the fortune-teller on his right arm. It adjusts to the tiny size of his wrist. It looks different from the way it did before – more like a thin bracelet than a band, fitting his wrist very nicely. He pulls the sleeve back down to his wrist. The wristband is out of sight.

Reuben thinks, *I wonder if that fortune-teller foresaw that I would be using this disguise and might need some extra strength. Maybe I should have paid her to read the fortune cards and tell me what she could see.*

He tries the axe again. He can swing it much better now. It doesn't hit the floor.

He puts the wristband of protection that was given to him by Queen Cassia on his left wrist. It will help him avoid being hit by his foe in hand to hand combat. When he pulls his sleeve back down this wristband is not visible either. He speculates. *It would have been all right to leave the wristbands on when I put on the Amulet. They would have adjusted to the changing dimensions of my arms because they're magic.*

He puts the Ring of Protection from Fear on his middle finger. It adjusts to fit his smaller finger but the stone itself doesn't change. His middle finger is now smaller than his little finger used to be.

He thinks, *This disguise is going to work. I can handle it. I wonder what Sparrow is going to tell me.*

He walks around a little, trying to get used to a slightly different way of walking. In a few moments Sparrow returns, opening the small door of the stable to enter.

Sparrow says, "Stand in the sunlight so that I can get a good look at you."

Reuben does. Sparrow walks to a place between the large window and Reuben to get a good look.

Sparrow smiles. "Good. This disguise is perfect. You can go on your expedition with the others. Just keep wearing the Amulet and you'll be all right. You look about twenty-three years old, and you have a fantastic figure. I would say that you are more beautiful than any of your companions. The women will probably be jealous."

Reuben's face feels hot. *I'm blushing.* He tries not to, but he can't control it.

Sparrow says, "You look great with your blouse open like that but when you leave here you'll need to close it up enough to cover the Magic Amulet and chain. A peasant girl wouldn't have a fancy looking piece of jewelry like this. When you get into The People's Republic, any display of magic can be a problem. If somebody in authority were to cast a Detect Magic spell on you, the amulet would be confiscated. They would then find out that you are really a Dwarf. That would be the end of you. You won't be able to wear that ring or your wristbands either."

Reuben laces the blouse up as tight as he can, putting the Amulet and chain completely out of sight.

"I'll do this then. What is it you want to tell me?"

Sparrow says, "I need to tell you a few things about being a woman. You may know these things already, but I want to tell you now just in case you don't. First of all, you will have to scooch when you urinate. I know men don't have to but women do. Afterward you will need to wipe the place where the urine comes out. If you don't you will get some of your clothes wet. An outhouse won't always be available. You can do it that way when you do it in the bushes outside too."

Reuben feels embarrassed. "I didn't know that. Is there anything else you want to tell me?"

All women have two problems to deal with that men don't have. One is getting pregnant. The other is bleeding. Let's talk first about bleeding. I suppose you know about the female bleeding cycle?"

Reuben says, apprehensively, "No. What's that?"

"Don't Dwarven women tell their men anything? Well, you need to know. About once a month Human women bleed. The blood comes from about the same place that the urine does. A little blood comes out, but it's not a serious problem. It's kind of messy though. You need to know that if you bleed like this you're not going to bleed to death. It's a very slow bleed."

Reuben feels very concerned, a little frightened and embarrassed. He senses that his face is getting red again.

"I know you feel uncomfortable but I need to tell you about this. The bleeding will last a few days, then it will stop. It's a regular cycle. It will happen again and again. I have counted the days. For me, the bleeding almost always starts just twenty-eight days from the last time it started. I wouldn't be surprised if the cycle is twice as long, or maybe three times as long for Dwarven women, but I feel very certain that they have a regular cycle just like I do. Every woman I know has this cycle. It starts when a girl changes into a woman. It starts at about the same time the breasts develop. You are already a mature woman. You will probably have a twenty-eight day cycle like most Human females do, but you probably won't be a woman that long. The point is, it could start anytime. It could easily happen within the next six days or so when you will be in this female body. You need to know what to do if it does. I don't want you to panic."

Reuben asks, "What do I do?"

Sparrow says, "It's really very simple. You have to catch the blood as it comes out so that it doesn't dribble down your legs and stain your clothes. Basically, you put a cloth bandage over it. I use a cloth strap to hold the bandage in place. That is what you will want to do. You need at least two bandages because it sometimes gets so soaked with blood that you have to change it. Don't throw the bloody bandage away. Soak it in cold water and wash it out. Let it dry, so that you can use it again. The bandage is just a folded up piece of cloth, like the one I gave you."

Sparrow picks up one of what Reuben thought was a small washcloth from the pile of clothes and folds it.

"And this is the cloth strap that holds it in place."

She holds up the rolled strip of cotton cloth with the pin in it. "If you start to bleed, use these. If you can't figure out how, ask one of the other women. They will help you. Have you got that?"

Reuben says, "Yes."

"Now let's talk about getting pregnant. Dwarven women don't give birth very often, but I assume that when they do the process is pretty much the same as it is for Human women. How often do Dwarven men normally have sex with Dwarven women?"

Reuben says, "I don't know."

Sparrow says, "I suppose Dwarves are so shy about sex that they don't talk about it. You probably don't do it very often. That would explain why you don't have many children. I expect Humans have a much stronger desire for sex built into them than Dwarves do. I mean, both men and women. We women do have a strong desire for sex, you know, even if some of us try to hide it. Don't be surprised if in a few days you feel a strong desire to have sex with Aaron, Tamaranis, or some other Human male you meet along the way. My advice is don't do it. I don't think you want to get pregnant right now. Do you know how a woman gets pregnant?"

Reuben says, "A man plants a seed in the woman's body. If it falls into a fertile place, the seed grows into a baby. For Dwarves, most of the time it doesn't seem to fall into a fertile place. That's why Dwarven women don't have babies very often. I have been told that Human women give birth much more often. I suppose maybe you are much more fertile."

Sparrow says, "That's probably it. Your description is close enough for now. Actually, women produce seeds called eggs that are fertilized by the male's fluid, which can be compared to the pollen that bees carry from flower to flower as they gather honey. Human women do seem to be more fertile than Dwarves. Human men also seem to want to plant their pollen more frequently than male Dwarves do. I think there's another factor, and that brings us back to the female bleeding cycle. Women usually don't get pregnant when they are bleeding, but are very likely to become pregnant at certain other times. I just thought you ought to know that. Is this conversation making you nervous?"

Reuben's face is again quite red. "A little. But I'm glad you told me."

Sparrow says, "Good. I won't mention the subject of sex again."

Reuben doesn't ask any questions about it either. It is a subject that he finds quite embarrassing. His mother and father never offered information about sex unless he asked. Apparently he didn't know what to ask. When he asked his mother how to make love to a woman she just said, "When the time comes you'll know what to do. It comes naturally." Maybe Sparrow is right. If Dwarves talked about sex more, maybe there would be more Dwarven babies.

Reuben thinks, *Sparrow is enjoying this situation a little too much. I kind of resent that. I know that I look like a Human female, and sound like a Human female, but I still feel like myself, Reuben, the male Dwarf. This is just a disguise. I can change back to a Dwarf any time I want to by taking off the Amulet. I think it will be difficult for me to play the role of a woman, even though I have the body of a woman. I don't know how a woman thinks about some kinds of things.*

Sparrow says, "I gave you a change of clothes so that you'll have something to wear when you want to wash the ones you're wearing. I suppose you'll use the shift for a nightgown. That is what I wear in bed most of the time. It's quite comfortable. On a really cold day you could wear it under your other clothes. Some people do. I see you have a mirror. Do you have a comb?"

"Yes."

"Your hair looks terrible. You need to comb it every morning, and maybe sometimes during the day."

"I always comb my hair in the morning before I wind it into my turban. I comb my beard too."

"You won't be wearing your turban. You should part your hair in the middle and pull it both ways. You know what I mean?"

Reuben says, "I know. That's the way my mother combs her hair."

Sparrow says, "It will be hard for you to see how it looks in the back. I'll help you in the morning. I want it to look good all the way around. Have Tiarra or one of the other women help you each morning on the trail."

Reuben says, "I'll manage."

Sparrow asks, "Do you have any questions for me right now?"

"There are no shoes with the clothes you brought me. Can I wear boots? I have magical boots that will fit me."

"I probably have some shoes in the house that will fit you, but I thought you wouldn't be wearing shoes. Most peasant girls go barefoot. Your feet may be a little tender at first, but they will get toughened up long before you get near Divinity City. Is there anything else?"

Reuben asks, "Is there anything you are not telling me that I should know?"

Sparrow says, "I don't think I should need to tell you that women often react differently to some kinds of situations than men do. Some of this is because we are physically different, with certain limitations and some of it is because we have been taught to behave this way from birth. Most of the teaching comes from practical experience from generations past for what we must do to survive in a male dominated world. For example, Men are almost always stronger than we are. Accordingly, you should try to avoid making a man angry with you. Avoid confrontation. Women have to use their wits to deal with men in ways that will not make them angry. I doubt that you will have this problem with Aaron or Tamaranis; they seem to be quite gentlemanly. In fact, if you get in trouble with some man you meet at an Inn they will probably fight if necessary to defend you. But you should try to avoid putting them in that situation. Unnecessary fights will not be good for your mission."

Reuben says, "I won't be as weak as you think. I have a Wristband of Strength and a Wristband of Protection. I will be able to defend myself quite well."

Sparrow says, "As I said before, you won't be wearing those magic items. I can't emphasize this too much. If anyone in The People's Republic realizes that you have magic they will probably report you to the police and the magic will be taken away from you. Magic items are not allowed in the Alliance territory. It is rumored that Keepers have a way to detect magic. If they see you wearing something that looks like it might be magic you could be in a lot of trouble. It could cause your entire mission to fail. So you won't have those magic things. You will indeed be weaker than most of the men you meet. Tiarra, Eridana, and Johanna will have the same problem. They won't be able to wear any of their magic that helps them fight either. Aaron and Tamaranis won't either, but they will at least have their natural masculine strength. They will have to protect you. Don't go walking around along the streets of Divinity City or any of the towns you may come into alone, especially after dark."

Reuben says, "My wristbands are covered up by the sleeves of my blouse. Nobody will see them"

Sparrow says, "Unless for some reason the sleeve gets pushed far enough for the wristbands to show. That can happen, you know."

Reuben says, "I understand. But I do expect to get involved in combat. Aaron and Tamaranis are not particularly adept at physical combat. I will need to help them. I don't like this at all. I have always fought my own battles. They won't be able to use magic weapons either."

Sparrow says, "I see that Aaron has a staff and Tamaranis has a hammer. They have told me that neither is magic. I presume that they know how to use them. I understand that Tamaranis is a pretty good kick fighter. That's a plus. They may not be as highly proficient at fighting as you were, but they will be the best that you have to protect you. If you don't think it will be enough, don't provoke a confrontation. Try to avoid getting into a fight."

Reuben says, "I'll do the best I can. Is there anything else?"

Sparrow says, "Not that I think of right now. It's time for you to go to bed and get some rest. You want to get a good early start in the morning.

Sparrow leaves.

Reuben nervously walks around in the stable, trying to get used to the feel of the clothes he is wearing. He thinks about going outside, but he is barefoot. He thinks, *It's better walking on the smooth planks of the floor than it would be walking on the gravel courtyard. I wonder what it will feel like to run with these long legs. I should be able to run faster. I can run here in the stable.*

As soon as he starts to run he steps on the hem of the skirt and almost falls down. *This won't do. I have to be able to run. What do women who are wearing long skirts do? Oh yes. Rachel grabbed her skirt with one or both of her hands and held it up out of the way.*

Reuben grabs the skirt with both hands and starts to run. This seems to take care of the problem. As she speeds up, she realizes that her hands, holding the skirt, are swinging back and forth in front of her in rhythm with the movement of her legs.

He thinks, *Rachel did this too. It feels natural. I think it helps me stay in balance. She tries to analyze it, running more slowly for a while. It's a lot like moving my arms forward and back when I'm walking or running. I've always done that without thinking about it. I'm taking longer strides with my longer legs but I wonder if I'm really running any faster than I did as a Dwarf. I don't think so. But maybe I can if I practice.*

Reuben trots a few laps around the inside of the stable trying get used to this kind of running, and loosen up his muscles. As he runs, some of his long black hair sometimes flops into his eyes. He can't brush it out of the way without letting go of his skirt with one hand. *I didn't have this problem when wearing my turban. I've got to comb my hair. But first I've got to try to work out this stiffness in my muscles.*

Reuben is glad that he tried running when nobody else was looking. The bodice does a pretty good job of holding his breasts in place and he soon develops a nice easy rhythm that works.

He runs for at least ten minutes, sprinting a bit at the end. He stands and rests for a while, until he is breathing normally again. Then he finds a place to sit before his mirror and comb his hair, parting it in the middle as Sparrow had suggested, and trying to comb it away from his eyes. He is not satisfied with the results. He thinks, *This is a waste of time. No matter how good I do it, I'll have to do it again in the morning anyway.* He stops combing and stands up.

Reuben thinks, *I don't feel as much pain as I did right after I put the Amulet on, but I still feel it. I wonder if I'll be able to fall asleep. I could take it off now, get a good night's sleep, and put it on again in the morning. But Sparrow said I should keep it on. But I wonder. What if I take off the Amulet at some future time and don't change back into a male Dwarf? I'd like to know for sure what happens. If I don't change back into a Dwarf when I take it off, I'm going to be pretty angry. I'm going to take it off now, and find out. If I don't change back to myself, I'm going to tell Sparrow. She has magic abilities. I don't know what to do.*

Reuben thinks about it some more. After a while he decides, *I'm going to take the Amulet off now. If I don't do it now, I'm going to spend too much time worrying about it. I've got to find out what happens. I know it will be painful, but I've got to know. The Amulet probably works the way Sparrow said it would but if I don't change back into a male Dwarf when I take it off, I've got to do something about it right now. I can't afford to wait until I'm miles and miles away from her. I'm going to be angry, and I'll need her help to fix the problem. Maybe she won't be able to fix it. Whatever happens, I'll use this disguise go to divinity to rescue Robert Swift. But I've got to know what happens when I take it off.*

Reuben removes the wristbands and the ring. Then he removes his clothes, first the red leather bodice, then the skirt, and finally the white linen blouse. He is naked.

He puts his hands on the chain. I know there'll be pain. I've got to keep myself from crying out. I don't want Sparrow or the others to hear. He unhooks the chain. Again he feels intense pain and a flash of intense warmth. As quickly as he can he puts his hand over his mouth. He is unable to muffle his cry of pain entirely, but it is not nearly as loud as it was the first time. Maybe nobody heard it.

The floor gets quickly very much closer to his eyes – the way it is supposed to be. All his muscles hurt. He checks his body. All the parts are the way they should be. He even has the same long black beard he had before and scattered dark hairs cover most of his body. He picks up his Battleaxe with no difficulty, even without his wristband of strength. This is better. I didn't think she was lying. Now I know. The Amulet works the way she said it would. I feel a lot better about that. He has perspiration all over his body. He wipes it off and puts on the nightshirt. His muscles hurt more than ever. He rubs his arms and legs.

After a few minutes Reuben thinks, *I better change back into my disguise right now. The quicker I do it, the less it should hurt. I'll have to put it on and change again in the morning anyway. I don't want to be hurting like this in the morning, and be exhausted when I have to start walking to Divinity City. Sparrow said it will take some time to get used to a different body. That's what I should be doing during the night.*

Reuben takes off the nightshirt and puts the Amulet back on, even though it hurts. It takes both hands to operate the clasp so he clenches his jaws together until he can get his hands over his mouth, keeping his cry of pain to a whimper. He is confident that no one outside the stable heard it. He is again in the same female body that he was in before. He is completely exhausted and warm. He doesn't bother to wipe off the sweat. He puts on the nightshirt, lies on top of his bedroll, and tries to fall asleep. The muscle pain is somewhat intense but doesn't last.

Reuben thinks, *I need a new name that sounds like a woman's name. All the women in my group have last names that end in 'A'. How about Lara? That's a pretty name but it doesn't sound at all like the name I'm used to. I might not respond. How about something that starts with an R – Rowena? Still not enough like what I'm used to. I should just add an 'A' to my name. Reubena. That would work – but I don't like the sound of it. Sparrow's name doesn't end in 'A'. Neither does my mother's. How about Reuby – my mother used to call me that when I was real little. I made her stop when I realized that it sounded like a female name. I would recognize that. I would answer to that. How do they spell it? R-U-B-Y. Yes – Ruby. I like that.*

The town bell in the distance rings seven times. Reuben tries to remember what that means. *In Exodus the bell rings twenty-four times at noon. This means that it is seven hours since noon. I think the sun will set pretty soon. It's too early to go to bed, but I feel exhausted.*

He lies on top of his bedroll. He feels warm enough, but has trouble falling asleep. Eventually he does. He wakes up several times during the night, changes position, and goes back to sleep. When he wakes up cold he crawls under the covers. He gets as much rest as he can.

CHAPTER FIVE

BREAKFAST WITH SPARROW

Greening Eleven – Early morning

Reuben wakes up to the sound of a rooster crowing somewhere nearby. Cock-a-doodle-doo. It is a sound of home and at first he thinks that he is at home in the Dwarven village of Springbrook. Some light is shining on his face. It must be coming through a window. When he looks around he suddenly remembers where he really is – in Sparrow's stable. Then he remembers what happened when he put the Amulet That Disguises on his neck.

He says out loud, "I'm not a Dwarf. I'm a Human female!"

He remembers the pain he felt when it happened. He remembers that his muscles are not nearly as strong as they used to be. He remembers why he did it. *Now I can go with the others to rescue Robert Swift. It's a good disguise. When I go into the People's Republic to find Robert Swift they won't kill me because I am not a Human. My name is now Ruby.*

The feminine sound of Ruby's voice seems very strange. She feels other parts of her body. Her muscles hurt a little when she climbs out of the bedroll. *It's not as bad as it was when I first put on the Amulet but I feel a little stiff.*

When she stands up, she feels quite tall.

My muscles feel odd but not really painful. I can feel every muscle a little each time it moves, whether the movement is voluntary or not. I can feel my rib muscles and abdominal muscles moving each time I breathe in and out. But it's not really painful; it's more like my muscles are sending a message to my mind saying, "I'm moving now. It doesn't feel normal, but it's all right. I just want you to know that I'm trying to adjust to my new configuration. Are you sure that you want me to be this way?"

Ruby fingers the Amulet with her right hand.

Ruby thinks, *Yes. I want to be this way. I'm just wearing a disguise. I can take this Amulet off any time I want to and return to normal, but not now. Right now I need this disguise. My name is Ruby for now. I've got to try to behave like a woman.*

She says aloud, "My name is Ruby." She thinks, My voice sounds strange to me but I know it's the way it has to be. I can't look like a woman and sound like a man.

Ruby feels the urge, so she straddles the manure trough, pulls up her shift, and scooches near the wall, where she can grab onto a framing timber with both hands. She urinates and does a bowel movement. She wipes herself. Then she walks back to the bedroll.

She is thinking, This activity exercises muscles that are a little stiff but they feel much better than they did last night. It actually feels good to use them. This reminds me of the way I felt on that morning after the first day I helped my father load heavy timbers from the sawmill onto wagons to be delivered to the mines.

Ruby washes her body. She has been trying to avoid touching her bulging female breasts but she can't avoid that now.

I think more than anything else, these breasts will announce to everyone who looks at me that I'm a woman. They are right up front and I can't hide them. Except for these I might be able to wear male clothes and pass as a Human male. Sparrow must have some clothes that would fit me well enough. I would like that better, not wearing a skirt. I hate trying to run in a skirt, even if I can run pretty fast. It would feel more like me to be wearing trousers, or even the kinds of leggings that Tiarra wears.

Ruby tries to speak in a deep male tone. "My name is Reuben."

It doesn't sound right. Not very convincing. I guess if I tried to disguise myself as a man, I would have to avoid talking. That doesn't make any sense.

Before putting on the clothes Sparrow has given her she puts on Reuben's Dwarven shirt. She looks in the mirror. It is much too big and loose and the sleeves are far too short. She was hoping that her breasts would not show, but they clearly do. When she pulls on the Dwarven trousers and tightens the belt around her small waist the breasts are even more obvious. It is also obvious that she has the broad hips and small waist of a woman. She can also see that her smooth face and small hands look like those of a woman. No. It will take more than male clothes to make me look like a man. I might as well look like a woman for a while.

Ruby dresses quickly, making sure to lace the front of her blouse all the way to cover up the Amulet. When she puts on the bodice she thinks, *This is good leather; it will give me some protection in combat.*

Ruby sits and combs her hair, using her mirror. It takes her quite a while to get it to look the way she thinks it should be. She thinks, *I look a lot like Sparrow does. I'm the same size. Maybe the clothes I'm wearing are Sparrow's clothes. Could it be that Sparrow is really something else, maybe a male Dwarf, that is using an amulet that is just like the one I am wearing?*

Ruby stands up. *I wonder how tall I am now. I think maybe a foot or so taller than I was as a Dwarf. I think I'll measure.*

She takes a measuring stick, a square, and a pencil from her toolbox. Standing against the wall, she puts the square on top her head and against the wall, marks the wall with her pencil, and steps away. She uses the measuring stick (only two feet long to fit in the box) to measure the distance from the floor to the mark. *Five feet three inches. I was right. I grew a foot and an inch. I used to be four feet two inches tall. Now I'm taller-about the same height as Tamaranis. I guess I'm going to be the shortest female in the group, even shorter than Eridana.*

Ruby returns her tools to the box. Feeling thirsty, she drinks from her bottle of endless pure water. Then she picks up the wooden bucket of water she used for washing, opens the stable door, and walks out into the sunny courtyard. She dumps the wash water on the ground in an out of the way place and walks to the well. Some of the tiny pebbles in the courtyard hurt Ruby's bare feet a little but she can bear it. She draws water from the well, using the bucket attached to a rope and windlass, rinses out the bucket, then gives water and feed to the animals outside.

While doing this she hears Sparrow calling. "It's time for breakfast! Eridana! Reuben! Come into the house now!"

Ruby thinks, *It's about time. Am I ready? I guess I should take off my magic ring and wristbands. Maybe I could put my wristbands on my ankles.*

She goes back into the stable and puts her wristbands onto her legs a little way above her ankles. They are completely covered up by the length of her skirt. She takes off her ring and it into her money pouch.

She detaches her money pouch from her belt, thinking, *My belt is much too long for my slim waist. It wouldn't look right anyway. Farm women who wear skirts and blouses don't wear belts and money pouches. My mother doesn't wear a belt and pouch. I don't have to wait for Sparrow to tell me that. So how am I going to carry my money pouch? I guess I could leave it here in the stable for now, but it doesn't seem right. I guess I'll have to make a strap so I can carry it on my shoulder.*

But for now, Ruby carries it in her left hand.

Walking toward the back door of the house she sees the tent that Aaron and Tanaranis slept in. She also sees the tent that Eridana and Johanna slept in. The flap of that is open but no one is inside. She thinks, *Eridana and Johanna must have gone into the house already. Probably the men did too. Good.*

When Ruby gets to the door of Sparrow's house, she has to climb up a couple of steps to get to the door and finds that to do this she must hold up her skirt to keep from stepping on it. She uses her right hand because her money pouch is in her left hand. She thinks again, *I hate wearing a skirt!*

She knocks on the door. A peasant girl with a face that looks like Tiarra's opens it. It is Tiarra, without makeup on her face, and without the ponytail. Her pointed ears don't show. She looks Human.

Tiarra laughs out loud. "Ha, ha, ha, ha. Reuben! Is it really you? You're beautiful!"

Ruby gives Tiarra a big smile, touches her hair with her right hand, and says, "Yes. I am. Sparrow told me last night. She told you too, didn't she? My name is now Ruby."

Tiarra smiles and says, "Ruby. Of course. Come in, Ruby."

Ruby goes into the hallway, then through the open door on the left into the kitchen. Eridana, Johanna, Tamaranis and Aaron are seated at the kitchen table. Sparrow is bringing a platter of scrambled eggs and bacon to the table.

Tiarra says with a smile, "I want you to meet Ruby! She was previously known to you as Reuben Huskins. Isn't she beautiful?"

Aaron looks at Ruby with a big grin on his face. "Hello beautiful! Want to go with us to Divinity City? You do look much better than you did the last time I saw you. What a perfect disguise!"

Ruby doesn't know what to say.

Eridana smiles and says, "Sparrow told us what kind of disguise she had for you. I think it will work very well. Many men wouldn't have been willing to do what you have done. I admire your commitment to our mission."

Sparrow says, "It wasn't easy for you, was it Reuben? It was painful." Sparrow looks at the others. "See how much taller she is than before. That took a lot of stretching of muscles, especially legs and arms. That hurts."

Johanna is smiling. She says, "I like your disguise, Reuben. I am going to be the mother of our family. I think you may be the most beautiful member of our family. She smiles, "So I'm a proud mother." She laughs a bit.

Tamaranis smiles broadly. He says, "You have a perfect disguise. No one could ever think that you might really be a male Dwarf, or that you ever could have been. What did Tiarra say your name is? Ruby? I want to get to know you better."

Ruby says, "Yes, my name is Ruby." She feels that her face might be blushing a little.

Aaron says, "Good name. It matches your face perfectly. I don't think I will ever forget it."

Sparrow says, "You shouldn't. It's a lot like her real name. Don't forget that name either. This disguise is temporary. When you all go home in a few days, Reuben will be back in his appropriate body. In the meantime, you should all treat Reuben with respect. As Eridana said, it took a strong will and dedication to a promise for Reuben to accept this disguise, even for a little while. Many men would not have done it."

Tamaranis says, "I agree. Three cheers for Ruby! Hurrah! Hurrah! Hurrah!" The others, including Sparrow, join in.

Despite the cheer, Ruby still feels self-conscious and uncomfortable about being with them in her female disguise. She looks at her companions. All are dressed in peasant's clothing except Sparrow, who could pass as a peasant woman herself if she wasn't wearing so much jewelry. Sparrow can, because she isn't going into The People's Republic with them. No one else is wearing any jewelry. Despite their disguises, it is fairly easy for Ruby to recognize the identity of each. Both men are dressed in old-looking, off-white, long-sleeved, wool shirts and dark, wool trousers held up by nearly worn out leather suspenders. Ruby recognizes Aaron by his beard and build. He looks older, like a middle-aged peasant farmer, maybe a woodcutter. A money pouch hangs from his belt. There seem to be lines in that part of his face not covered by his beard, especially around his eyes. Ruby thinks, *Is that makeup? Or did Sparrow use magic to make him look older? He looks like a person who has worked hard all his life out in the sun.*

The other male is the right size and shape to be Tamaranis. He is barefooted, clean-shaven, and looks young enough to be Aaron's son.

The older woman sitting beside Aaron must be Johanna. Her face looks old and creased, seeming to show the strain of a hard life. She might be forty-five years old, about the right age to be Aaron's wife. She is wearing the same kind of clothes that Ruby is wearing. She looks much more feminine than she did in the plain brown robe over chainmail that she had worn until now. Her bodice emphasizes the smallness of her waist. Her breasts and hips seem larger than before. She looks quite motherly. Because of her long skirt, Ruby can't see what Johanna might be wearing on her feet.

Ruby thinks, *Johanna looks better dressed this way. A little like a tall thin Dwarf. The other woman must be Eridana.* Eridana looks very different too. Instead of the single ponytail braid, her long hair is parted in the middle and hangs down to her shoulders, completely covering her pointy ears so that they are completely out of sight. She has laced her blouse up to her neck like I have. She must be trying to cover up the necklace that Cassia gave her. Tiarra has left her blouse open at the throat, showing a lot of bare skin but no jewelry. Ruby thinks, *She looks prettier than I do. Her long, blonde hair, parted in the middle, covers up her pointy ears quite well.*

Ruby and Tiarra take seats at the table. Ruby's money pouch settles naturally into her lap. Because of the skirt she doesn't have to worry about having it fall between her legs. Everyone is looking at Ruby, smiling.

Aaron says, "Is that really you, Reuben? I think I'd like to get to know you much better." He has that glint in his eyes that he often has when talking to Tiarra, Johanna, or Eridana. He chuckles in a friendly way, but his comment makes Ruby feel even more uncomfortable.

She replies in her softer and higher voice, "I told you before. My name is Ruby."

Eridana says, "It's a nice name - and a wonderful disguise. You look perfectly Human. I was afraid you might not be able to come with us. I'm so glad you can."

Johanna says, "I'm glad too. We are going to need you."

Tamaranis doesn't say anything; he just stares at Ruby's breasts the same way he usually stares at Tiarra's, and lately, at Eridana's. Sometimes he switches his gaze to Johanna's upper body.

Ruby feels self-conscious. Even Sparrow is staring at her. Ruby feels as if she should say something. "I'm glad I'm going to be able to go with you. I want to help rescue Robert Swift."

Johanna says, "Ruby. I like that name. How did you come up with it?"

Ruby says, "It sounds a lot like Reuben. If you say Ruby, I'll probably realize that you're talking to me."

Aaron says, "Very practical."

Sparrow says, "Good choice. You'll get used to that name very quickly."

Ruby thinks, *It will be easier to get used to the name than the body.* She asks, "Are we going to use the story Sparrow suggested last night, or have you thought of a new one? Where do I fit in?"

Johanna says, "We are using the same story. You can be my oldest daughter. You look a little older than Tiarra does."

Tiarra says, "Isn't that nice! We're going to be sisters."

Aaron says, "That doesn't make sense. Ruby doesn't look like you, Tiarra. Ruby has black hair, yours is blonde and Johanna is also blonde. I think Ruby must be an indentured servant, like Eridana."

Johanna says to Aaron, "**Your** hair is black. She is **your** daughter."

Sparrow says, "That part of your story is up to you. Work it out. Just make sure you all agree on it, whatever it is."

So far Ruby has not eaten anything at all. Sparrow says, "Eat something, Ruby. We're ahead of you."

Ruby starts picking at her food. She is afraid that if she eats very much she will get nauseas, as she did last night. The bacon and scrambled eggs taste good. She doesn't feel nauseous. She eats some more, but not a lot before her stomach feels full. Then she stops eating.

Ruby says, "The food tastes good but I'm not very hungry."

Sparrow says, "I understand. Your tummy's a lot smaller than it used to be, isn't it? You're still adjusting. Don't worry."

Sparrow says, "Now that you're all together I'm going to ask Aaron a few questions to test his ability to explain who you are and what you are doing. You should all be prepared to answer these questions, but Aaron is your spokesman. Pretend that I am a soldier of The Alliance who has stopped your wagon somewhere on the road to Divinity City. Answer my questions as you would to avoid getting into trouble."

Aaron says, "I'm ready."

"Suppose the soldier says, 'Stop your wagon. We're doing a routine check to see if any non-Humans, spell casters, or fortune tellers are trying to sneak into Divinity City. The first thing I need to know is your names. You, sir, look to be the oldest. Is this your family? What is your name?'"

Aaron says, "My name is Aaron. Yes, this is my family."

"Your last name please. I need to know your last name."

"Er...Smith."

"And the name of your wife? Is this your wife?"

"This is my wife, Johanna Smith."

"Are these your children? What are their names?"

"These are my daughters, Tiarra, and er... Ruby. This other young woman is my indentured servant. She helps my wife. This young man, Tamaranis Jones is also an indentured servant. He helps me."

"And her name is?"

"Her name is Eridana...Wood."

"What town are you from?"

"I...We don't live in a town. We live at the edge of the woods near...er... north of Exodus. I'm a wood cutter."

"What do you have in your wagon?"

"We have some things we hope to sell, some grain, some wine. We have some of our personal belongings, bed rolls and extra clothes, food for the trip, stuff like that."

"Do you have any weapons?"

"I just have this big stick. I can use it like a staff. Tamaranis has a dagger."

"Do you mind if I take a look at the things in the back of your wagon?"

Aaron pauses – then says, "I don't know what to say. If he looks, he will probably find our weapons and we'll be in trouble. If I tell him not to look, he'll probably look anyway."

Sparrow says, "So you might as will tell him to look and hope he doesn't bother. If he does, hopefully, it is just a quick glance at the things on top. That wasn't bad for a first test, but if I were the soldier I might be a little suspicious. Ruby has a good name. It might be better if the rest of you made up names instead of using your own. Tiarra and Eridana don't sound like peasant girls' names. Tiarra sounds like a princess, Eridana sounds like an Elden. More typical Human names like John, Robert, Mary, Bess, and Jane would be better. Johanna is okay. What if the Keepers have found a way to get a list of your names from Sarah? The soldier might have a list that consists of your six names. If he finds them all in one wagon, that may trigger a very thorough inspection. Smith sounds like an acceptable last name. It's very common. It's so common that almost everybody uses it for an alias. A less common last name might work better. This is my advice."

Aaron says, "Too strange or too common, nothing is perfect. I like my name, Aaron. I'm going to use it."

Sparrow says, "You mentioned having grain and wine to sell at the festival. That's good, but grain is bulky and heavy. It's a small wagon. Wine is good. It has a high value as compared to its bulk and weight, and I happen to have some in the stable. I can imagine a woodcutter making kegs during the cold winter months, but less likely wine. You might be taking a neighbor's wine in kegs that you made. Aged wine would be a good thing to sell at the festival, and that is what I have in my stable. I bought it at a good price and it has continued to age since I bought it."

Ruby says, "I know how to make kegs and I have the tools with me to make them."

Sparrow says, "My wine is already in kegs. You should leave your tools here with me. You wouldn't be taking tools to the festival unless you intend to sell them. You would not be a keg maker either. That's man's work. Remember, you are not a man for the time being."

Ruby says, "I could do it though. I'm good with tools." Ruby thinks, *I am a man, I just look like a woman.* But she doesn't say it.

Sparrow says, "But don't use that in your story. If the soldiers get suspicious, they may separate you and ask each of you the same questions.

You won't know how anybody else answers the questions, but you must all be prepared to give the same answers. Most of the time Aaron will do the talking, but sometimes it won't be that way. You all have to be able to answer the questions the same way. Now, again pretend that I'm the soldier."

Sparrow looks directly at Ruby.

"What is your name?"

"Ruby."

"How old are you?"

"Twenty-three."

"Are you the oldest daughter?"

"I think so."

Sparrow says, "You can't say 'I think so' to that kind of a question. If you are the oldest daughter, you know that you are. You don't just think so. What skills do you have?"

"I'm a... I... I... I help with cooking and that kind of thing."

Sparrow says, "That's a good answer. A farm girl might well be quite nervous about being questioned by a soldier. You should be prepared to be more specific if he asks for more information, but he probably wouldn't. You could say that you milk cows, tend the garden, cook, wash dishes, bring in firewood, and wash floors. Peasant girls do those kinds of things. Peasant girls also know how to spin thread and weave cloth."

Ruby says, "I know. My mother does all those things. I just wasn't ready for your question."

Sparrow says, "You need to be ready. So do you, Johanna and Tiarra."

Johanna says, "I know. I have done all of those things."

Sparrow asks, "What about you, Tiarra? Do you know how to milk a cow and weave cloth?"

Tiarra says, "Of course not. I'm a fighter. My family has servants to do those things."

Sparrow says, "Then you should try to avoid talking about it if you are questioned. And you, Eridana?"

Eridana says, "I'm a horse herder, but I know how to milk a cow and weave cloth. I can also sew cloth together to make a dress. I have done these things."

Sparrow says, "Then you and Johanna better try to educate Tiarra before you get to Beastgate. You will be questioned there when you go through the gate. I think you all need to work on this. You need to work on it together. But we don't have time now. You need to pack your wagon and get on the road. Work on it while you are traveling to Beastgate. Try to think of every possible question somebody in authority might ask. Make sure you are prepared for it. It's part of your disguise. Make a game of it. Be prepared to tell the same story to everybody you meet, even the lowliest peasant that you think you should be able to trust. Don't trust anybody."

Aaron says, "I will be the spokesman. I will always tell the same story. And I won't trust anybody – except my family."

Sparrow asks, "What do you have in your pouch, Ruby."

Ruby says, "That's got my magic Ring of Protection from Fear and some money. You said I can't wear any magic except my Amulet That Disguises. That is on my neck, but you can't see it. My blouse covers it. I'm wearing my magic Wristbands just above my ankles. My skirt covers those so nobody can see them. I don't like carrying a pouch, but I want to be able to get my magic ring quickly and I don't have any pockets. The wristband that belongs on my right arm gives me strength. I can't use my Battle axe if I'm not wearing that Wristband. I'm not strong enough anymore. The other wristband provides me with protection. It's like armor. I need that too. I'm going to make a strap for my pouch so that I can carry it on my shoulder. My mother did that sometimes."

Sparrow says, "I don't think you should be seen wearing a pouch on your shoulder or carrying it in your hand either. It would be better to tie your pouch to your Battle Axe. That weapon will be hidden in the secret compartment under the seat of the wagon. They should both be safe there. I did check with Queen Cassia. She said that you should take some of your magic with you into The People's Republic and Divinity City. She wants Eridana, to wear the silver necklace that enables her to know where you are at all times, but keep it out of sight under your blouse. She also wants you to take the silver chalice of resurrection with you, keeping it hidden under the seat of the wagon until you need it. She wants you all to take your magic weapons and defensive devices with you, but keep them hidden in the wagon until you really need them."

Tiarra says, "We should be carrying our weapons. We need to be prepared to defend ourselves if we are attacked."

Sparrow says, "The men can carry weapons but they can't be magical weapons. Peasant women don't carry weapons, but at least one of you will be riding on the seat of the wagon. If you need your weapons they'll be right there under the seat. You'll be able to get at them quickly."

Aaron says, "I'll carry my staff then. It's not magical."

Tamaranis says, "My hammer isn't magical either."

Sparrow says, "When you leave Exodus, I suggest that you use the back roads. Go northeast first, then southeast so that you approach Beastgate from the northwest. That will be consistent with your story, and you won't encounter as many other people along the way. I'll get you started on the right road out of Exodus. Take that road until it comes to another road where you have to turn either left or right. Turn right. That road will take you all the way to Beastgate. You won't get lost."

Tiarra says, "According to the map I saw, the route you are suggesting is longer than the road that goes directly from here to Eastgate. I don't like the idea of going any extra distance. We should go to Eastgate by the shortest route and get to Divinity City as fast as we can."

Sparrow says, "The shortest route between here and Beastgate will be very heavily traveled. That will slow you down. You will have to go a little further on the road I am suggesting, but you will be able to move faster."

Aaron says, "Sparrow knows what she's doing. When we use the route that she suggests, we'll enter Eastgate from the north instead of from the east. That will support our story that our home is in the wooded area northeast of Exodus.

Tiarra glares at Aaron. She resents being overruled by him on this issue, yet she respects Sparrow's advice on matters of deception. She says nothing more about it.

Ruby looks at Sparrow. "You said that you might have some shoes that would fit me. Tiarra, Eridana, and Johanna are not barefoot. I want shoes too."

Sparrow says, "I'll get them for you, but in my opinion none of you women should be wearing shoes. Think about it. How many peasant girls have you seen along the roads wearing shoes? I doubt if it was any. If you take shoes, it might be best if you put them in the wagon to wear when you dress up to enter Divinity City. Peasant women might want to look dressed up for the festival."

Sparrow brings a pair of soft leather shoes from the back room. They are almost sandals, with wide leather strings to tie them securely onto her feet. Ruby tries them on. They fit well enough.

Ruby thinks, *I think my changed appearance has altered my relationship a little with the other members of our group. They think of me as a Human instead of a Dwarf. Nobody paid much attention to me when I looked like a Dwarf. I think Aaron and Tamaranis like me as much as they like the other women. That makes me feel pretty good.*

PART TWO

EXODUS TO EASTGATE

CHAPTER SIX

PACKING THE WAGON

Woden's Day - Greening Eleven – Sparrow's stable

Sparrow says, "Let's go out and get the wagon packed."

They all go outside. The wagon is right beside the stable under a tree. It has a canvas canopy stretched over curved bows, designed to protect the contents of the wagon from rain and sun. It has a pair of shafts so that a single horse can pull it. There is a seat at the front with room for up to three people to sit.

Sparrow says, "You men, bring the wagon inside the stable. It will be easier to load it there. Hitch up Toby, my old workhorse. He's the old gray one in the pen."

Ruby goes with Aaron and Tamaranis to the wagon.

Sparrow says, "Ruby, you are not one of the men. You have to remember that. You need to go into the stable and get your bedroll out of the way."

Ruby feels embarrassed for forgetting. Her face turns a little red. Everybody else laughs. Aaron and Tamaranis laugh loudest. Ruby goes into the stable, puts her money pouch near her backpack, and rolls up her bedroll to get it out of the way of where the wagon will be. Eridana and Johanna take down Eridana's tent.

Tiarra takes Sparrow aside and asks, "I don't suppose you have another magic necklace that would disguise me as a Human male?"

Sparrow says, "If I did I would have given it to Reuben."

Tiarra says, "That's what I figured, but I thought I'd ask, just in case."

When all are in the stable Sparrow says, "See that pile of old empty grain sacks over there? Think of them as clean cloth bags. They are clean. You can put the things you want to take with you in them. Leave your backpacks here. Peasants can't afford nice backpacks like you have. You can take one, Aaron, because you are the head of household, but take the most tattered one any of you have. Don't take anything you don't absolutely need. Everything else you should leave with me. I will save it for you. You can pick it up here on your way back, or even later if you'd rather."

Tamaranis says, "Take my backpack, Aaron. It's pretty old."

Ruby thinks, *I'm glad Tamaranis said that. I don't want Aaron to take my father's backpack, the one he carried during the Nog war. It's a family heirloom. It will be safer left here with Sparrow.*

Ruby starts by sorting everything she has into piles, one for those things she will take with her and another for those that she will leave behind. She puts her chainmail armor, shield, backpack, two boxes of carpenter tools, and the turban with its jeweled pin in the pile to be left with Sparrow. Everything else goes in the other heap, which is actually several piles. She intends to take all of her weapons with her. The battleaxe, Crossbow, quiver of Crossbow Bolts, and Magic Shortsword will be put under the wagon seat. She uses a leather string to attach her money pouch to the battleaxe. It has her money, two magic wristbands, and her magic ring in it. They will go under the wagon seat with her weapons.

The clothes that fit Reuben go into one of the cloth sacks. *I will need them when I take the amulet off and that might well be before I get back here.* The extra female clothes Sparrow gave her are in the pillowcase. She puts the dusty, gray, Cloak of Blending that Ruby bought at Lady Lucy's Magic Emporium at Althen into the sack of Dwarven clothes.

Ruby's shoulder pouch has her comb, mirror, flint and steel, tinderbox, tin cup, handkerchief, leather thongs, Bottle of Endless Pure Water, and Potion of Healing in it. She won't be wearing her sheath knife so she puts that in there too. She will put the pouch under the seat.

She puts the scruffy boots she wore as a Dwarf into another sack. She thinks, *The Boots of Jumping are magic. I think I could wear those under my skirt right now if I wanted to. They would magically adjust to fit my feet.* She goes outside the stable for a moment, where nobody else can see her, and puts them on. She tries them out. They magically adjust to fit her feet very well. She can jump more than twice as far as Reuben could jump, and also twice as high. She wants to try jumping over the fence around the animal pen, but decides not to. The horses might get excited. She takes off the boots, goes back into the stable, and puts the Boots of Jumping into the sack with the other boots.

The others don't have as much sorting to do. They will take with them just about everything they have except their horses, saddles, and backpacks. They have put most of what was in their backpacks into cloth sacks to be put in the back of the wagon.

Sparrow watches everyone, occasionally making suggestions about things they won't need and shouldn't be taking with them. When Ruby puts the packsaddle on Jenny, Sparrow says, "I'm sorry Ruby, but you won't need the mule."

Ruby has a lot of affection for her mule. She says to Sparrow, "I can't leave Jenny here. Jenny has to be with me. I always take good care of Jenny. Peasants have mules. Why wouldn't they bring one? The back of the wagon will be crowded. Whatever is on Jenny's back will make it easier for that poor old horse."

Sparrow can see in Ruby's eyes and expression that she has strong affection for the mule. She says, "I'm sorry. I clearly understand your love for your mule. I agree that peasants might take a mule to sell or carry some things that there is no room for in the wagon. The wagon is pretty full. I guess it would be all right for you to put some of your things on your mule, and also some tents and bedrolls. Three tents will be enough. That would give you all places to sleep if it rains."

Ruby smiles. She is glad that the mule will be going with her. She thinks, *This means that two people will have to sleep in each tent. I guess that means I'll have to sleep with one of the women. I guess that's okay."*

Sparrow says, "Make sure you have a good story to tell about the mule, if somebody asks. You might say that you plan to sell it at the festival."

Ruby says, "I'm not going to sell her."

Sparrow says, "I know. That's just a story."

Ruby says, "I don't want to tell a lie."

Sparrow says, "It would be a good reason in this case."

Ruby loads three tents, her fifty-foot coil of rope, lantern, flasks of oil, camp axe, kettle, frying pan and bedroll onto Jenny.

By now Toby has been hitched to the shafts and whiffletree of the wagon. While somewhat old, he seems to be big enough and strong enough to pull it. Aaron and Tamaranis are loading kegs of wine.

Sparrow says loudly, "Load your weapons into the secret compartment under the seat. Put your magic items there too. The Keepers may use a Perceive Magic spell on you. If they find any magic items they will take them away from you. Worse, they might take you to the tower and later execute you."

Sparrow shows them the hidden latch that has to be released to lift the seat.

When Ruby picks up her Crossbow Sparrow says, "You won't be able to take your Crossbow. It won't fit under the seat."

Ruby says, "It will. I just have to turn this latch. The bow can be removed from the stock like this."

She turns the latch on the bottom of the stock, removes the bow from the slot in its underside, and lays it beside the stock.

Sparrow says, "What an amazing device. You Dwarves are indeed very clever."

Ruby smiles.

Sparrow asks, "By the way, Ruby, do you know how to sew?"

Ruby says, "I've watched my mother sew. I could do it if I had a needle and thread."

Sparrow says, "I'll give you a sewing kit then. Every peasant woman carries a small sewing kit with her. With this you can mend your own clothes. Did you know that Johanna, Eridana, and even Tiarra all brought sewing kits with them from home? It's something women do."

Ruby says, "I won't need it then. They can do the sewing, if needed. I'm surprised that Tiarra brought one."

Sparrow says, "Take it anyway." She tosses her a small cloth bag. "It contains a small scissors; several short, fat, wooden rods wound with thread; three different sized needles and some common pins in a small pincushion."

Ruby puts it in the cloth sack with her female clothes, then puts her weapons and money pouch under the seat. She loads her shoulder pouch and the three sacks with her things in them into the back of the wagon, leaving them in plain sight with the other bedrolls and sacks.

Sparrow makes a last check of the wagon, inside and out. All that she sees inside are kegs of wine, a bag of oats for the horse to eat, bedrolls, sacks of extra clothes, a few extra blankets, some cooking gear, and food.

She takes out two of the bedrolls and gives them to Ruby. "Put these on your mule."

Ruby does, then ties the mule's lead rope to the back of the wagon.

Sparrow says, "I think you're ready to go, but I want to take one more look at your disguises. You really have to look like a woodcutter family you know. Line up."

She looks at the group as a whole first, then at each individual. Aaron is wearing boots. Johanna, Tiarra, Eridana, and Tamaranis are wearing soft leather shoes similar to those that Ruby has. All of the shoes show a lot of wear. She sees no magic, jewelry, or expensive looking clothing. Johanna, Eridana, and Tiarra have bright colored but worn looking shawls over their shoulders.

Sparrow says, "I'm glad you are wearing the sunbonnet I gave you, Johanna. It will protect your makeup if it rains. It will also keep the sun out of your face."

Johanna says, "I like it."

Ruby notices that Aaron is wearing a hat with a very broad brim. She never saw him wear that before. She thinks, *I bet Sparrow gave Aaron that hat to protect his makeup, in case it rains. It should keep some sun away from his face also. I wonder if too much sun would be bad for their makeup. The weather never seemed to bother the makeup that Tiarra has always worn. Maybe hers is a different kind.*

Sparrow says, "Aaron, cast Perceive Magic. I want to make sure there is no visible magic."

Aaron does. No one sees anything glow. Ruby's Amulet might be glowing but it is entirely covered up by her blouse. It doesn't show.

Sparrow looks at Ruby. Did you pack some Dwarven clothes? You will need them if you decide to take off the Amulet before you get back here."

Ruby says, "Yes. They're in a sack in the wagon, but not with my other clothes. She thinks, *I'm glad Sparrow thinks I may be able to change back into a Dwarf before I get back here.*

Sparrow says, "Good. Oh, I almost forgot. Ruby, you should have a shawl. If it's cold you can put it over your shoulders. If it rains you can use it to cover your head." Sparrow puts the brown shawl she is wearing around Ruby's shoulders.

Ruby says, "Maybe I should have a bonnet like the one Johanna is wearing."

Sparrow says, "You are not wearing any makeup. Besides, I don't have any more bonnets. You and Tiarra and Eridana will have to make do without bonnets. None of you had bonnets when you came to my house. You don't need bonnets."

Ruby says, "Okay. I guess I don't need anything on my head. I have been used to wearing a turban, but I know that wouldn't fit my disguise."

Sparrow says, "No. It's better if you look much the same as Eridana and Tiarra look. You are all young women. You all look fine. You should leave now. I'll walk with you to the town gate."

Aaron says, "Johanna, get up on the seat. I want at least one person riding on the seat near the weapons in case we need them. Everybody else should walk. It will be easier on the horse. I'll lead Toby."

Johanna climbs up on the seat. "We can take turns riding. I won't mind walking at all."

Ruby says, "I'm glad to walk. I want to work out the stiffness in my muscles. There's still some left."

Aaron takes a short hold on the lead rope attached to the horse's bridle and they start to move. The wheels creak and the wagon groans. They look like a peasant family starting out on a long trip.

Sparrow opens the courtyard gate. She tells Aaron to turn left. When the wagon is clear, she closes the gate and takes them mostly along crooked side streets to the edge of town.

When they reach the town gate she says, "Follow this road about twenty miles until you come to a place where you have to turn either right or left. Turn right. It's a right angle turn; you can't miss it. I have done what I can for you. Remember—Aaron is the head of the family. He is in charge. Everyone else must respect his authority. Practice your story. Don't get slack about your roles, and keep your magic and weapons out of sight. Good luck. You are on your own now. I'm looking forward to seeing you on your way back."

Tiarra thinks, *I'm still the best qualified to lead this group. I'm going to talk to Aaron about it the first chance we get.*

Chapter Seven

Leaving Exodus

Greening Eleven – About an hour after dawn

The group trudges along the road under a clear blue sky, going northeast. Ruby finds that her long legs enable her to cover a good distance with each stride. Her stomach feels much better.

When they are well away from the city gate Tiarra happens to look back toward Exodus. She says, "Look, there it is again, the Red Mist thing. Damn! I thought we had gotten away from it. I guess our disguises aren't good enough to fool it."

Johanna says, "The fortune teller told us that we weren't rid of it."

Tiarra says, "But we killed it since then. When something is dead, it should stay dead."

Johanna says, "The fortune teller knew. Everything she told us is true. She said she saw me traveling in a wagon, looking much older, and with a man who might be my husband leading the horse. That is how we are now."

Aaron says, "She was correct about the money too. I wish she had told us more. There were four cards left on the table. I think she didn't want to give us bad news. That bothers me. I wanted to have my fortune told but Tiarra said we didn't have time. It wouldn't have taken that long."

Tiarra says, "You could have gone back the next day. I wish we knew what she was going to tell us about you, Ruby. Do you suppose she would have predicted that you were going to change into a woman?"

Ruby doesn't answer.

Aaron says, "Probably. She seemed to be amused by what she saw."

Tiarra says, "Maybe it's something else that hasn't happened yet. I bet you wish you knew, don't you, Ruby?"

Ruby thinks, *She's trying to tease me. I'm not going to let her.* She says, "We are not supposed to know what our future is. If God wanted us to know, he would tell us."

Johanna says, "Don't you think a fortune teller could be one of God's ways to tell us? I do."

Tiarra says, "You had your chance, Ruby, and you didn't take it."

Tamaranis says, "Don't pick on Ruby. You had your chance too, Tiarra, and you didn't take it either. You told Aaron we didn't have time for his fortune to be told. Do you still have the magic beads that the gypsy gave you, the ones that gave you the premonition dream of Robert Swift's wagon train being attacked at Derlenen? It would have been nice if when you woke up this morning you told us something important about our future now. You should do that every morning."

Tiarra says, "Nothing like that has happened since Amrath had to leave us. I don't think the beads work unless the Imp of Wishes is here. I hope you all realize that I'm still the most experienced adventurer here. Aaron is our nominal leader for purposes of deception, but I hope you will continue to listen to me on matters of strategy and tactics."

Aaron says, "I respect your experience and will always consider your advice. But please don't ever blow our cover by giving me orders. I'm playing the role of your father now. Remember? And you are acting in the role of my daughter. You have to show others that you respect me."

Tiarra says, "That's for when we are in the presence of other people. Most of the time we aren't."

Johanna says, "We have to get used to the idea that, for now, Aaron is our leader. We can't always be jumping in and out of our roles. I don't want to hear any more of this discussion. Also, when we speak of Reuben we should always say Ruby."

Tiarra says, "You sound like my mother."

The road is paving stones for only about a mile and then it changes to plain dirt. They are passing the usual rural landscape of scattered farms and farm villages. The sun quickly warms the morning air. Occasionally the road crosses a small stream. Sometimes there are wooden bridges.

Sometimes they simply ford the stream and get their feet wet. Rarely they cross on a stone bridge.

By late morning they begin to see a few people on horseback traveling in the opposite direction. As the sun gets higher, closer to noon, they begin to pass several groups of walkers, riders, and wagons, also going in the opposite direction. A few people on horseback catch up to them, pass, and go out of sight over the next ridge ahead of them. There is no communication with anybody except a few simple hellos.

Tiarra says, "They don't even pay attention to the Red Mist. I think they must be walking in a fog of their own. Oblivious."

Eridana says, "The Red Mist doesn't pay any attention to them either; it just keeps following along behind our wagon. It is our demon, not theirs. I don't think the other people can see it at all."

Aaron says, "Our disguise is working. No one who sees us is suspicious at all. Whoever they think we might look like, we look normal to them."

Tiarra says, "They treated us the same way when we were riding horses. It seems to me that we should have been disguised as people wealthy enough to ride horses, not as farmers. We would get to Divinity City much quicker. We haven't come very far. Let's go back to Sparrow and ask her about it. I want my horse."

Johanna says, "It would be a waste of time. Sparrow knows what she's doing. It's harder to hide wealthy looking people. Everybody notices them."

Eridana says, "I would much rather ride. I like the idea of getting there quicker. You and Aaron wouldn't have to be made up to look old either. We would just look like a group of travelers. Like some of those who have ridden past us this morning."

Johanna says, "Those we have seen riding horses were just one or two at a time. We would be a group of six with pack animals. We would attract much more attention than they do. What would our explanation be if someone asks who we are and where we are going?"

Tiarra says, "We could think of something if we try."

Aaron says, "We should have thought of that last night. It's too late now. We are on our way."

Tiarra says, "Last night I didn't realize how slow we would be moving with this old horse pulling our wagon. This has all happened too fast."

Aaron says, "We are not really going that much slower than the people on horseback. You just think you are. We could save some time, but probably not even a day. But we would lose a lot of time getting different disguises. We chose to be a woodcutter family. Let's live with it. Tiarra, you can be next to ride on the wagon."

Tiarra says, "I don't want to ride on a wagon like a farm woman. I want to ride a horse."

Tamaranis says, "I don't mind walking. In fact, I prefer it. We have good disguises. They will be more important when we are in Alliance territory than now. It is those people who will be more likely to wonder what a group of riders is doing on the road, especially those in authority at the gates. We have made a good plan. We should follow through with it. Don't change horses in the middle of a stream. What do you say, Ruby?"

Ruby says, "Tamaranis, you sound just like my father. He has said, 'Don't change horses in the middle of a stream' more times than I can remember. I think we should follow through with what we are doing."

Tiarra says, "Wouldn't you rather be riding a horse?"

Ruby says, "I guess so, but I have no idea what we would be pretending to be."

Tiarra says, "We could have disguised ourselves as merchants with a couple of wagons pulled by teams of strong, healthy horses."

Johanna says, "Sparrow didn't have two wagons and two teams of horses. We have to be this way. The fortune teller predicted it."

Tiarra says. "The fortune teller's prediction has already come true. If we go back and get our riding horses that doesn't change. We've done that. Now we can do something else."

Aaron says, "Tiarra, you and Eridana have been outvoted. If we go back now, we lose a whole day of travel. We will continue the way we are. Let's practice our story. I've been thinking about it. I'm a woodcutter so my name will be George Wood. How does that sound?"

Tiarra says, "It sounds like George would do it with any of us if we would let him. Nice try, but I'm your daughter. My name is Jessica Wood, but I won't."

Everybody but Ruby laughs. Ruby thinks, *There she goes again, making a sex joke out of something perfectly innocent.*

Johanna says, "I'll be Mary Wood then. No jokes please."

Everybody laughs again. This time even Ruby giggles slightly. It seems funny coming from Johanna and a kind of put-down to what Tiarra said. *God, that was a girlish giggle. Is that me?*

Eridana says, "My name is Emily wouldn't."

Everybody laughs again, including Ruby.

"All right, my substitute name is really Emily Herds," Eridana adds, "I like horses."

Tamaranis says, "My name is Tom Clerkin. In addition to hard labor, I keep track of the money the Wood family has, what comes in from selling anything and goes out for buying things. If my name were Wood, I Would."

Everybody looks expectantly at Ruby. Finally Ruby says, "My name is Ruby. Wood. But I wouldn't."

Everybody laughs, including Ruby.

They continue to walk at a good pace. It is a warm humid day. Everyone except Johanna is getting pretty hot and sweaty. Johanna is perspiring a little.

At noon they stop for lunch. The Red Mist Creature stops and lingers about thirty yards away. Everybody watches, expecting it to attack them at almost any moment. But it doesn't.

After a while Tiarra says, "It won't attack now. Remember - when it followed us from the haunted city to Exodus it never attacked at noontime. It attacked at suppertime. We might as well relax – and enjoy our lunch."

They do. They don't bother to cook. They take some bread and cheese from the basket in the back of the wagon, and Ruby's Bottle of Endless Pure Water, taking it from where it is hidden under the seat. While eating, they practice their story again, talking to each other using their story names according to the roles they are supposed to be playing.

Aaron asks each of them to explain what particular skill they have as a member of the family. When it is Ruby's turn, she says, "I wash dishes, sweep floors, and help keep the house neat and clean. I'm also good with animals. I do what I'm told to do."

Johanna says, "You didn't mention cooking. Can you cook? If you are a female growing up in a peasant woodcutter's household you had to have learned to cook. What can you cook? Really."

Ruby says, "I've watched my mother cook. I don't pretend to be an expert, like my mother is, but I can do all right. I've camped out lots of times with my father and did some of the cooking."

Johanna says, "Next time I cook, I want you to help me. It might freshen your memory, so that you can answer questions about it if you have to."

Ruby drinks some water from her Bottle of Endless Pure Water. She eats, but not as much as she did when she was a male Dwarf. The others drink some of that water too.

Aaron notices that Ruby didn't eat much. He knows that she is adjusting to a different body. He knows that her muscles had to stretch out, and that this has affected her muscle comfort.

Aaron asks, "How does it feel to be a long legged woman, Ruby? Sparrow told us that it would take a while for you to work out the pain from having your muscles stretch out. You seem to be doing pretty well, but maybe you would like to have a turn at riding on the seat of the wagon for a while."

Ruby says, "I'm doing very well thank you. I think my longer legs make it easier for me to walk. Walking seems to ease the pain. Really there's not much pain left."

Aaron says, "All right then. I'm just trying to be considerate. Is there someone else who wants to ride for a while?"

Tiarra says, "I would like to ride. I'm tired of walking."

Johanna says, "All right. I won't mind walking for a while."

Eridana says, "When we had riding horses one of us rode ahead to warn the others of anything dangerous that we might be approaching. Maybe one of us should walk a little way ahead like that now."

Aaron says, "I don't think it would do any good."

Eridana says, "I'll do it. I did it before. I want to."

Johanna says, "No, you should do it, Aaron. You're our leader. You should be out front. It wouldn't look right for a woman to be up front like that, with no weapon."

Aaron says, "All right. I'll do it. Someone else will have to lead the horse."

Tamaranis says, "I'll do that."

So Tiarra climbs up onto the seat of the wagon and they continue along the road. Aaron walks alone about ten feet ahead of Toby, carrying his staff. Tamaranis leads the horse, walking at the left side of its head. Ruby walks to the left of Tamaranis. Eridana and Johanna walk on the other side of the horse's head. There are not as many farms and villages along this road as they expected. Some parts of the roadside are heavily wooded.

They experience a sudden light shower in the middle of the afternoon.

As soon as it starts, Aaron stops, turns to face the others and says, "It's raining."

Tamaranis stops and so do the others.

Aaron says, "It's raining but we don't all have to get wet. Tom and I will continue to walk, but the rest of you can get into the wagon and stay dry. There's room enough."

Ruby says, "I don't want to ride in the wagon. I want to walk. Four people in the wagon would be too many for poor old Toby."

Johanna says, "I can walk too. My bonnet will keep the rain from damaging the makeup on my face. I'll also wear my Brown Cloak that Cannot Be Cut, Stained, or Ripped."

Aaron says. "But that cloak is magic. You shouldn't wear that."

Johanna says, "I know. But it doesn't look magic. It just looks old and scruffy, just right for a woodcutter's wife to wear. No one will think it's magic."

Tiarra says, "But if someone casts a Perceive Magic spell on it that will get us in trouble. There's no need to take that risk. I've got a non-magical cloak that you can wear. I won't need it; it's my turn to ride in the wagon anyway.

Johanna says, "All right. Give me your cloak then."

Eridana says, "I'll ride in the wagon too. Just two of us won't be too much for Toby." Eridana quickly climbs into the wagon.

Tiarra and Eridana go to the back of the wagon and find non-magical cloaks for Ruby, Johanna, Aaron, and Tamaranis to wear. Johanna has her bonnet. The cloak that Ruby is wearing has a hood that keeps her hair dry. Aaron and Tamaranis find straw hats to wear.

So Eridana and Tiarra ride in the wagon, but not sitting on the front seat where they would get some rain on them. They sit on kegs of wine a little way behind the front seat.

The people walking in the light rain get a little wet, but they are not soaked. They dry off quickly when the sun comes out again. There is also a light wind which helps.

Those walking remove the jackets that they were wearing and put them in the wagon. Both Eridana and Tiarra stay on the wagon, sitting on the front seat.

The wind is quite refreshing, but it blows Ruby's hair and it gets across her face. She pulls it away with her hand but it continues to be a problem. She thinks, *I don't like this. I didn't have hair in my face when I was wearing my turban. I want my turban.* Ruby uses one hand, then the other to try to keep her hair out of her face, especially out of her eyes.

Fairly soon Johanna notices how badly the wind is blowing Ruby's hair. She says to Ruby, "I've noticed that you are having some trouble with your hair getting in front of your eyes. You keep pushing it back. Maybe I can help you with that."

Ruby says, "It's a nuisance. How do you keep that from happening?"

Johanna says, "Right now I'm wearing a bonnet. But my hair didn't blow around like yours when I didn't. I normally use hairpins to hold my hair in place. I've got some extras I could lend you. Let me show you how to do it."

Johanna uses two large hairpins, one for each side. They are black, the same color as Ruby's hair. The way Johanna does it, once in place they don't even show.

They continue to walk along the road, Toby patiently pulling the wagon behind him. There is little conversation. Everyone seems to be keeping their thoughts to themselves.

Tiarra thinks, *It's going pretty well. Whether Aaron knows it or not, I've been able to retain most of my role as leader of this group.*

Aaron thinks, *It's going pretty well. I've managed to calm Tiarra down by letting her think she is leading our group most of the time, but I'm really in charge. We didn't go back to Sparrow for riding horses, did we?*

CHAPTER EIGHT

THE RED HAZE CREATURE AGAIN

Greening Eleven – Late Afternoon

It is late afternoon when they come to the place where the road turns both left and right. There is a big river directly ahead of them, and no bridge. It looks like someone, years ago, placed a slab of stone that can be used for a table in a clear area between the road intersection and the river. Other slabs are placed where they can be used for bench seats. Apparently they are often used. Grazing horses and the padding of many feet has prevented the grass from growing very high.

Aaron says, "This seems to be a good place to spend the night."

Tamaranis leads Toby to a place beyond the stone slabs and behind the cover of trees and bushes from the road. It looks as if tents have been erected here many times.

As soon as the wagon stops, Tiarra says, "Get out our weapons. The Red Mist will soon be here to attack us."

She and Eridana open the box under the seat and distribute the weapons and Magic. Ruby takes her Wristbands and Ring out of her money pouch and puts them on. She puts on the Boots of Jumping. She is still wearing a skirt and blouse, and her only armor is the leather bodice and one of the Wristbands. Tiarra puts on her Belt of Strength. Johanna puts on the Brown Cloak That Cannot be Cut, Stained, or Ripped. Tamaranis puts on his Ring of Protection. Eridana puts on Aaron's Red Cloak of Protection from Fire. Aaron puts on his Ring of Spell Storing and his belt with a Silver Buckle of Protection. He has attached that to another belt. During the day he has worn a belt with a non-magical buckle, just as Sparrow had told him to do.

Tiarra says, "Form a fighting line facing in the direction of the Red Mist. We will be ready for it when it comes."

Johanna says, "I want to be in the front line this time, instead of Emily (Eridana). *She is glad that she remembered not to use Eridana's real name.* She can do healing as well as I do and she can use her sling from the second line. I don't have a missile weapon. I fight with a mace."

Eridana says, "I like that idea."

Tiarra says, "All right. It makes good sense to me. You could have suggested it before."

Eridana takes her place beside Aaron in the second line and casts an Empower Companions spell on her whole group.

The Red Haze moves to a place about fifteen feet in front of them where it changes into the Dried Blood Creature with the bleeding eyes. It is now a solid looking thing with two arms, two legs, and a head instead of an amorphous blob of color. It shoots an arrow at Tamaranis and hits him in the chest, but not in the heart. Tamaranis falls down, bleeding badly.

Tiarra shoots back at the Creature with her One-hand Magic Crossbow. She hits it, but the bolt bounces off, seeming to have no effect at all. Eridana casts her Glowing Target spell on the Creature.

Johanna casts a Heal Minor Wounds spell on Tamaranis. He stands up.

Ruby uses her Crossbow. The Crossbow bolt hits the red haze creature, but bounces off, just as Tiarra's did. Ruby remembers that the Crossbow didn't do any damage at all the last time they fought the Creature, near the pool east of Exodus. She wonders, *Why doesn't this weapon work anymore. The first time we fought this creature, it delivered the final killing blow. Clearly something is wrong.* I guess I'll have to use a different weapon. Ruby drops her Crossbow and picks up her axe with both hands. She yells, "Charge!" And runs toward the Creature.

Aaron hits it with a Magic Beam of Energy, but the Creature doesn't seem to react at all. Aaron thinks, *I'm going to have to try a different spell. I'll try Blazing Hands.* But I'll have to get much closer for that. He runs toward the Creature, right behind Ruby. Tamaranis runs up with them.

The blood red Creature shoots an arrow at Johanna, hitting her left arm. Johanna heals herself. Eridana hits the Creature's mouth with a sling stone. It bleeds. Tiarra hits it again with a Crossbow bolt, but again, it does no damage at all.

When Ruby, Tamaranis, and Aaron run toward the Dried Blood Creature it stands its ground. When the three of them get close, the Dried Blood Creature's bow changes into a blood red club. The Creature swings it in a horizontal arc. Ruby dodges, jumping high in the air with the help of her Magic Boots. The club goes under her but it hits Tamaranis on his left hip.

As soon as she lands, Ruby swings her axe at the upper part of the Creature's legs. It dodges and she misses. Tamaranis hits the Creature with his hammer, a direct hit right in the middle of its chest. Blood oozes out of the wound.

When Tiarra saw Ruby, Tamaranis, and Aaron running toward the Creature, she dropped her Crossbow and ran too, drawing her Longsword as she went. Now she hits the Creature on his left shoulder. Johanna runs up with her, gets behind the Creature, and hits it on the hip with her mace. When Eridana heard Ruby yell, "Charge", she realized that it would not be a good idea to use her sling again. She ran up too. Getting behind it, she uses her scimitar to hit the Creature's lower back, making it bleed badly.

Aaron tries to get into a position to use his Blazing Hands spell, but too many of his companions are in the way, so he doesn't cast the spell. He uses his staff instead, trying to hit it on the head. But the Creature dodges and he misses.

Ruby hits the Creature again with her axe; this time in the neck, feeling delighted at her ability to hit it there without jumping. There is lots of blood. Tamaranis hits it on the thigh with his hammer. The wound seems to bleed for about five seconds then closes.

Tiarra tries to hit the Creature in the neck but he dodges and she misses. The Creature swings at Tiarra, but misses.

Johanna tries to hit it again with her mace but fails because the Creature uses his blood red club to parry her blow. This does seem to have damaged his club.

The Red Blood Creature is facing six people in hand-to-hand combat. It uses its free left hand to grab Tamaranis by his right arm, lift him, and throw him down. Tamaranis falls limp and motionless on the ground, dropping his hammer.

Eridana hurries to help Tamaranis. His head must have hit a stone when he was thrown down. She pulls him away and casts her Heal Minor Wounds spell on him to bring him back to consciousness.

Aaron hits the Creature on the back of its head with his staff.

Ruby leaps forward, using her Magic Boots of Jumping. She hits the red monster hard with her axe right at the narrow part of its waist. Then she jumps right back. Somehow her feet get tangled in her skirt and she falls down. The Creature swings its mace at Ruby hitting her leg and ripping her skirt. Ruby is totally frustrated. She tries to roll out of the way before it can hit her again.

Tiarra thrusts at the Creature's chest with her Longsword. The Creature jumps back so that only the tip of the sword penetrates, making a wound, but not deep enough to reach the heart, assuming that this Creature has a heart. The return blow of the flaming mace hits Tiarra on her left shoulder. Tiarra jumps back

The Creature seems to be badly hurt; bleeding in several places, but continues to fight.

Johanna tries to hit it on the side of the head with her mace, but misses.

Tamaranis has regained consciousness, but is till lying on the ground. Eridana uses another healing spell on him.

Aaron hits the Creature with his staff, right on top of its head. It drops to the ground and lies still for about ten seconds. Then it disperses into the atmosphere as it did before.

Eridana casts another Heal Minor Wounds spell on Tamaranis. Johanna casts a Heal Minor Wounds spells on Ruby, Tiarra, and then herself.

Eridana says, "The Creature seems to be getting stronger and harder to kill."

Aaron says, "That's what I think too. I don't think my Magic Beam of Energy spells do any damage to it at all. It may be immune to magical damage. That's why I decided to use my staff."

Eridana says, "I mean that we have to hit it more times before it dies."

Aaron says, "And we have to use different spells."

Tiarra says, "You're right Eridana. It took us longer to kill it this time. So far none of us has been killed, but if it keeps getting stronger like this, one of us is going to die."

Eridana says, "It's a good thing Cassia gave me the Silver Chalice of Resurrection, isn't it?"

Tiarra says, "I don't want us to ever have to use it. We need to figure out a way to get rid of this Creature so that it never comes back."

Ruby says, "The first time we fought it we all damaged it but my Magic Crossbow delivered the wound that finished it off, well – made it disappear. But now I'm convinced that my Crossbow doesn't harm it at all any more.

Tiarra says, "The second time we killed it was my magical Hand Held Crossbow that was the final hit that finished it off. But that didn't work this time either. So I used my Magic Longsword instead"

Aaron says, "This time it was my staff that made the final hit before the creature disappeared. I used the staff the first time I hit it today too. But because it was my staff that hit it the last time before it went away, maybe that weapon will have no effect on it next time either. But my staff is not magic, as your crossbows are, so maybe my staff will work next time it comes back."

Tiarra says, "I don't want the Creature to ever come back. I don't want to have to fight it again. There must be some way to get rid of it – once - and for all time."

Tamaranis says, "We haven't killed it. All we have ever done is cause it to vaporize. It has time to recover. Maybe it develops immunity while it's recovering, immunity to whatever did the most damage to it, or the damage that caused it to vaporize. When it comes back, that weapon will have no effect upon it."

Eridana says, "I don't want it to come back again, but I don't know how to make that happen. I hope it never comes back, but if it does, we need to be prepared to fight it. We need to think about what works on this Creature and what doesn't work. It seems to be immune to magic spells. I hope that my Empower Companions spell worked. I cast it on you, not the Creature. It should have worked."

Tiarra says, "Then we have to use a different weapon each time than one that we have used to turn it into vapor before. We have to remember what we have used to finish it off, that is, make it disappear. So far we have used Reuben's Crossbow, my Crossbow, and Aaron's staff. Next time we fight the red haze creature don't even try to use those weapons. Use something else."

Aaron says, "I never killed it with my Magic Beam of Energy spell, but it doesn't seem to work. I'm not going to use that again.

Tiarra says, "Then try using one of your other spells."

Aaron says, "Maybe it is immune to all my spells."

Tiarra says, "You won't know until you try them, will you?"

Aaron says, "All right. Next time I'll try Blazing Hands. I don't like to because I have to get close to do that. It's a good spell. I can try it, but it probably won't work. So then what do I do? Use my knife? That won't do much damage."

Ruby says, "I'll help you make a new staff. There's lots of wood around. There's a sapling over there, we could cut that the right length and use that. But it would probably be best if the wood has been seasoned, it's harder. Let's see what we can find."

Aaron says, "All right."

They put their magic items back under the seat of the wagon. They don't expect visitors in this out-of-the-way location, but it seems to be the best thing to do.

Tamaranis unhitches Toby from the wagon. He and Ruby take Toby and Jenny down a well-traveled path to the river to drink, leaving them tied to trees where they can eat some of the rich, green grass near the water. They have often cared for the animals together.

Aaron says. "Mary (Johanna), I'm hungry. Prepare us a hot meal."

He thinks, *I'm glad that I remembered to use the name that we agreed upon to fit into our family disguise, even though there is no one else here. But I suppose that there could be someone nearby that we don't see.*

Johanna says, "I always do the cooking. You never had to tell me to before. But right now I think it's more important for me to meditate and restore my spell energy, don't you? Isn't that what you are going to do?"

Tiarra says, "You both should, and Emily (Eridana) also. Don't worry. I'll get a hot meal going – but I could use some help collecting some dry wood and getting a fire started."

Aaron says, "That's right. We need to meditate. Tom (Tamaranis) and Ruby will help you as soon as they get back." He tries to speak loud enough for Tamaranis and Ruby to hear him.

When Tamaranis and Ruby return Tiarra says, "After you get the fire going, Tom (Tamaranis), erect the three tents, one for you and Father, one for Emily and Ruby, and one for Mary and I to sleep in. Ruby, you can help me cook."

Tamaranis takes an axe. He looks for fallen dead branches that would burn well.

Ruby thinks, *This is the first time I have been asked to help with cooking. Why did Tiarra think of that? I suppose it's because I look like a woman. Maybe she heard Johanna suggest that I help with cooking, so that I can better answer questions about cooking if anybody asks. Nobody's going to ask. But I'll help. Tiarra probably needs somebody's help and I've done camp cooking before. I wouldn't be surprised if I have more experience at cooking than she does.*

Ruby says, "While you are looking for firewood, Tamaranis, look for a piece of wood that can be made into another staff for Aaron to use against the Dried Blood Creature, if it comes back. He has to be prepared."

Tamaranis says, "All right. But I want you to help make it into a staff."

Ruby says, "I will."

Then Ruby asks Tiarra, "What kind of meal are we going to make?"

Tiarra says, "Boiled rice and beef stew. We've got the ingredients and I've cooked it many times on an open fire. I have often done most of the cooking when on expedition."

Ruby says, "I guess I misjudged you. I didn't think a woman of noble birth ever did things like this."

Tiarra says, "The world is full of surprises. I thought I might teach you something tonight about camp cooking. As a farm girl, you are supposed to know how to cook."

Ruby says, "I told you I've done camp cooking before with my father. I also watched my mother cook at home a lot, and sometimes helped her, when growing up. There were no girl children in the house to help. So I helped."

Tiarra says, "Good. Then I won't have to tell you everything. Let's get started."

Ruby and Tiarra get out the cooking dishes. The food ingredients they need are in a basket in the covered wagon. They boil rice in one kettle and make a stew from salted dried beef mixed with a few vegetables in another.

It tastes good. Ruby eats her share. She doesn't feel sick to her stomach at all this time. She is glad that problem has ended.

Johanna, Aaron, and Eridana have spent an hour meditating before eating. Afterward, Tiarra and Ruby wash all the dishes and put things away. Tamaranis puts the bedrolls in the tents. Johanna, and Eridana spend another hour meditating. Aaron doesn't need to; he only cast one spell in the fight. Aaron gets some more firewood.

Ruby looks at the long sticks that Tamaranis brought to a place near the fire and selects one that she thinks would make a good staff for Aaron to use against the Dried Blood Creature. She left her toolbox with Sparrow, but she had put a few of her tools in a bag in the back part of the wagon. She uses a small saw to cut off both ends, making the stick the same length as the staff Aaron has carried with him from the beginning. It is almost the same diameter. Ruby uses a small, sharp knife to whittle off some of the places where there had been branches. It is not perfectly straight but she thinks it is good enough. She gives it to Aaron. Aaron takes it.

Ruby says, "This is your new staff. How do you like it?"

Aaron swings the staff in a horizontal arc. He says, "I like it. It's about the same weight as the one I brought with me. But it doesn't have any of those nicely carved decorations. Do you think you could put some symbols on it? I would like it even better."

Ruby says, "If you want decorations, you can do that yourself. I'm going to make another staff. If you kill the Dried Blood Creature with this one, you might need yet another one. Or maybe somebody else will need an extra weapon. If I kill the Creature next time with my battleaxe, I might need a different weapon. I could use a staff. Maybe Tamaranis, Eridana, Johanna, or even Tiarra will need another weapon. Any of us could use a staff. Tamaranis, maybe you could look around and find some more straight sticks that would be good to make into a staff."

Tamaranis searches. Ruby takes the best-looking stick she can see handy and makes a staff for herself, or someone else, to use if they want to. By then it is getting dark and time to get some rest.

Aaron says, "I'll take the first watch with Tamaranis. Tiarra and Johanna can take the second watch, and Ruby and Eridana can do the third watch. People who sleep together might as well be on watch together."

Johanna says, "I want to take the third watch with Ruby. I want to teach her how to make bread using a campfire. Wouldn't you all like to have hot rolls for breakfast?"

Tiarra says, "Sounds good to me."

Aaron says, "And to me."

Ruby isn't sure now if she will be sleeping with Johanna or Eridana.

When Eridana goes to the tents and looks for her bedroll, Ruby goes with her. That is where Tamaranis has put her bedroll.

Apart from the others, Eridana says, "You have a perfect disguise, Ruby. I had no idea that you would look so beautiful. What was it like to undergo such a dramatic transformation? Did you feel anything?"

Ruby says, "It was very painful. My legs and arms had to stretch a lot. There are stories about Odin changing into a woman and back again. I don't think it hurt Odin at all. I had the idea that such changes are painless, but it hurt me. My muscles don't hurt now. At first I didn't feel much like eating. I don't know why. But that seems to have ended."

Eridana says, "Your stomach is ever so much smaller than it was before. I probably had more adjusting to do than your legs did. Then Eridana says in a very low voice, so that others cannot hear. "I'm not sure if I should be sleeping in the same tent with someone of the opposite sex."

Ruby says quietly, "I understand. It's okay. I'll sleep outside under the stars." She picks up her bedroll.

Eridana says, this time in a whisper, "Wait. It may be okay. You shouldn't have to sleep outside. It might rain. Tell me, when you put the Amulet on, was it a complete change? Did your sex…well… between your legs…change?"

Ruby feels her face turn red but she whispers back, "It was very complete. I pee like you do now. You don't have anything to worry about."

Eridana whispers, "Are you going to take the amulet off before you go to sleep and put it on again in the morning."

Ruby whispers, "No. I thought about it, but I don't think it would be worth the pain. It's very exhausting. I was completely worn out last night, and felt kind of sick. I must have sweated a flagon. I don't want to do that every night. I don't want my stomach to give me trouble again."

Eridana whispers, "Then you can sleep with me in the tent but I still think of you as a male so I don't want you to see me naked. Please wait until I put on my shift before you come into the tent."

Ruby is glad to hear Eridana say that she still thinks of him as a male. She whispers, "I don't think I want you to see me naked either. We each ought to have a little private time in the tent."

Eridana says, "Okay. You change first. I'll spend some time communicating with the spirits – meditating and praying - while you change."

Ruby goes into the tent and closes the front flap. When she comes out she is wearing her shift. By firelight, Eridana gets a good look at her slim legs and arms.

She says in subdued tone, "You're not nearly as strong as you were before, are you?"

Ruby frowns and says, "Not even when I'm wearing my Wristband of Strength, but I couldn't swing my axe at all without it. I'm strong enough to do what I have to do. You saw me fight the Dried Blood Creature today. I did okay."

Eridana says, "You fell down."

Ruby says, "But I wasn't hurt. I seem to have tripped on my skirt and ripped it. I'm not used to wearing a skirt."

Eridana says, "Let me see it. I'll mend it for you when I get a chance."

Ruby gets the skirt and shows it to Eridana. "I can do some sewing. I think I can mend it myself, but thanks for the offer."

It is already too dark to sew it back together now.

Eridana goes into the tent and puts on her shift. Ruby can see Aaron and Tamaranis standing watch near the fire. She doesn't go over there to talk to them.

Ruby reflects on her first full day of experience in the body of a Human female. *So far, so good. My muscles are resisting, but walking helps. My biggest problem now is that I don't feel like eating. I hope that ends soon.*

Very soon Eridana whispers, "I've got my shift on. You can come in now and get some rest. I think you did a fantastic job of making those sticks into weapons. I'm going to try one out in the morning."

They are soon both fast asleep. Ruby doesn't even notice when Tamaranis wakes up Eridana for the second watch. It is Eridana who wakes up Ruby for the third watch. She waits outside the tent while Ruby gets dressed. In sleep, Ruby had once again forgotten that she is not in the body of a male Dwarf. It takes a moment after waking to get her head readjusted to that fact. Her muscles need to readjust again also. She had been feeling no pain during the previous afternoon, but now her muscles feel a little stiff again. She feels every movement. It's not real pain, but she rubs her muscles firmly for a while before getting dressed.

When Ruby joins her, Johanna is already getting out the ingredients for making bread or rolls. She has whole-wheat flour, yeast, salt, some tallow, and honey. She tells Ruby what to do, and sometimes demonstrates. The first thing they do is melt tallow in a frying pan. They heat some water. It isn't long before Ruby is kneading dough on a clean smooth board at the back of the wagon. It is close enough to the fire to have some light there. Then Johanna puts a clean cloth over it. "We've got to let it sit and rise for a while."

Ruby says, "I know. I've watched my mother do this many times. But how are we going to bake it? We don't have an oven."

Johanna says, "I'll set up a reflector oven using one of my baking sheets. It's not as good as an oven, but it works."

While the dough sits, they engage in a wide-ranging conversation. At one point Ruby says, "You said you went to a special religious school to learn healing and other things a cleric needs to know. What else did you learn?"

Johanna says, "We learned reading, writing, numbers, combat with a mace, and much more about our religion. We spent a lot of time practicing our prayers. There were a lot of lectures about our faith and we had a chance to have our questions answered by the foremost theologians of our religion, several of whom are on the faculty. We had chapel services every day and we usually had a different distinguished speaker give the sermon on each Sabbath day, sometimes not a member of the faculty. I have had the best education possible for anyone."

Ruby asks, "Did both boys and girls attend this school? Tamaranis says that only boys attended his school."

Johanna says, "You mean young men and young women. Yes and no. My classes were restricted to young women. I was on the healing track. Young men take classes in healing too but they have different classes for the young men. I guess they learn differently. We were told that we could cover more material in a semester if there were no young men in our classes to hold us back. Our philosophy is that it is better for young men and young women to be kept separate from each other for the most part during the teenage years. I mean teen-age years for Humans when we are going through puberty. I know that may be a different time for Dwarves."

Ruby asks, "You mean you went away from home to school when you were only thirteen years old?"

Johanna says, "Yes. That is the usual age for us to leave home for school. When I was younger I lived at home and went to a smaller school that I could easily walk to. Girls and boys were in the same classes then. At twelve or thirteen we go to a bigger school. It was too far from home for me to walk, but even the teachers' children lived in the dormitories instead of at home. It's better that way. Young men and young women live on different campuses but not very far apart so that the lecturers can spend time at both campuses. Most of my lecturers were women who lived at my campus. The lecturers at the other campus are mostly men. Occasionally a man from the other campus would come to ours to give a lecture on a topic he was especially good at. We always looked forward to those lectures. So we didn't see much of the young men except on the Sabbath day at the chapel to hear the sermon. They sat on one side of the aisle and we sat on the other. There were also special social occasions, like dances, when the young men were invited to our campus and sometimes we were invited to theirs. I had chances to dance with several different young men. That was very special."

Ruby says, "I didn't have much chance to get acquainted with other boys my age when I was growing up because there were no other boys my age in my village. I guess my village is a pretty small place. My best friend, when I was growing up, was a girl - Rachel. We were about the same age and we did lots of things together. I don't think that was a problem for us. After puberty, though, we didn't spend as much time together because we were working all day. I worked in my father's carpenter shop and sometimes worked in the saw mill with the other men. Rachel worked with her mother and sometimes at the inn. She liked that. Sometimes I worked at her father's blacksmith shop. We saw each other in the evening though, at village social events or sometimes at her house or my house."

Johanna says, "That sounds like a good way to grow up. I have no idea what it might be like to be one of only two children my age in a village. I have six brothers and sisters but I'm the oldest. They aren't much younger than I am though. There were lots of other girls and boys my age in my village. It's probably a lot bigger than yours is. I was glad to go away to school when I was old enough. All the young men and young women do that, even if they are not going to be clerics or healers. All the young women my age that I grew up with went to my school at the same time I did. This adventure is the longest time in my life that I have been away from them. I miss them."

Ruby says, "This is the first time I have been away from my village for more than a day or two and then I was with my father. I miss home."

Johanna says, "Life for Dwarves must be very different. It must be difficult for you to be away from home and your own kind of people, especially now that you are in the body of a woman, and also of a different race. You seem to be handling it very well. If there is anything I can do to help, please let me know. I'm someone you can talk to. I have had training in counseling you know. That is one of our required classes. I will not be judgmental. I have been taught how to listen. Tell me what it is like to be in the wrong kind of body."

Ruby says, "Thank you. I don't think I need to talk any more about it right now. I know it's just a temporary disguise."

Johanna says, "That's all right. I'm here for you if you ever want to. Remember, God loves you no matter what kind of a body you're in."

When Johanna thinks the time is right she sets up the reflector from thin sheets of metal that take up very little space. She shapes a piece of the dough into a loaf and puts it on another metal sheet. Then she supervises while Ruby makes several more. Some of the dough is shaped into rolls. Johanna places the pan near the reflector.

By now the early morning air is quite cool so they both stay near the fire. The other campers wake up to the smell of fresh bread and rolls. They eat the rolls for breakfast with a little honey for flavoring and save the bread for another meal. Ruby doesn't even think about mending her skirt. When she got up in the dark she put on the one that is not torn.

This morning Ruby has no trouble eating.

CHAPTER NINE

BATS, RATS, AND RED HAZE

Thor's Day - Greening Twelve – Dawn

After eating breakfast Tiarra applies makeup to Johanna and Aaron. She uses a fine-tipped paintbrush to draw the lines on their faces using dark, water-based paint. It takes a lot of time.

Tamaranis gets the two animals, Toby and Jenny. He puts the harness on the horse. Ruby packs the mule. Eridana and Ruby hold up the shafts of the wagon while Tamaranis attaches them to Toby's harness. Tamaranis and Aaron take down the tents and pack everything they can into the wagon. Ruby puts the packsaddle on Jenny and loads it up. Tiarra and Eridana wash the dirty dishes and put them on the wagon.

When the dishes are clean and put away Aaron announces, "The wagon is loaded. We're burning daylight. I want to get in a full day of travel toward Divinity City. The quicker we get there the better chance we are going to have to save Robert Swift."

The toad they traveled along yesterday in an easterly direction has ended at an intersection with a road that goes in a northerly and southerly direction. They know that they must now go in a southerly direction to get to Beastgate. At Beastgate they will cross the Beast River to get into the People's Republic. The river near them now does not go in that direction. So they go along a road that is headed a little bit east of south and not near a river.

This time, Ruby leads the horse. Johanna and Tiarra walk on the other side of Toby. Aaron walks a little way in front. The regular tapping of the end of his staff against the packed earth of the road happens each time his left foot hits the road. Tamaranis walks beside Aaron. Eridana has managed to arrange a place in the back of the wagon where she can stretch out and rest, maybe even sleep. It is hard to tell if the water in the air is very light rain or very heavy dew, but it is not pleasant. They go through woods and farmland, occasionally passing through a very small village. Sometimes they encounter other travelers going both ways. No one challenges them. Johanna changes places with Eridana after a morning break. They are still in the territory of Ezrada. It is nearly noon when the sun finally breaks through and reveals that the Red Mist is continuing to follow them.

At noon they stop for lunch. Another family stops at the same place. The oldest man is unusually gregarious and socially inclined. Ruby thinks, *This may be the first real test of our story.* But despite his many questions, there is no expression of disbelief.

A younger man flirts with Eridana, Tiarra, and Ruby. This makes Ruby feel very uncomfortable. She walks away.

The young man says, "Where are you going? Don't you want to hear the rest of my story?"

Ruby thinks fast. She says, "Our horse has been limping. I think he has a stone caught in the frog of his front left foot. I'm going to check it."

The young man says, "Yeah, sure. Well, do what you want to do."

The young man continues with his story. Eridana and Tiarra seem very interested.

Tamaranis has detached Toby and Jenny from the wagon and taken the animals some distance away, where they can get water and grass. He is holding the lead ropes while they graze. Ruby lifts Toby's left front foot. There is no stone, but Ruby fusses with it anyway, just in case the young man is watching.

Tamaranis asks, "What are you doing?"

Ruby whispers, "I wanted to get away from that young man. I don't like the kind of story he is telling. I told him I needed to check to see if there is a stone caught here in Toby's shoe, but there isn't."

Tamaranis asks, "Would you like to be on watch with me tonight?"

This question is a surprise to Ruby. She says, "Maybe. I was thinking that I might do some more cooking with Johanna."

"I want you to. We would have a chance to talk and get to know each other better."

Ruby says, "All right." She thinks, *Tamaranis and I already know each other pretty well. We have talked a lot. We like each other. I guess we could talk some more.*

They are soon on the road again; glad to be away from the other family. Everyone was afraid that someone would make a slip that would cause suspicion that they weren't really what they appeared to be. Now Johanna is riding in the wagon and Eridana is walking with Tiarra.

Soon after noon they notice that there is a small river fairly close to the west side of the road, the water flowing in the same direction that they are going. Many tributaries cross the road; most of them have bridges. The Red Haze is still following them. The sun has become quite hot. The walkers are perspiring freely.

At mid-afternoon they notice that a second dark haze is also following them. It is moving faster than the Red Haze, passing right through it and apparently causing a dark shadow to appear on the ground under it. It is catching up to them. When it gets closer, they see that it is actually a cloud of flying bats and the shadow on the ground is really hundreds of rats running along underneath it.

Ruby coaxes Toby into a slow trot. Johanna jumps out from the back of the wagon to lighten the load. Everybody trots along beside the horse. Ruby urges Toby to go faster, but not fast enough. The bats and rats are going to catch up to them anyway.

Aaron turns and stands to face the pursuers. He says, "The rest of you keep on going as fast as you can. I'll catch up in a minute."

At a distance of about fifty feet he casts the Fiery Orb spell from his Ring of Spell Storing, saying, "Zed, Fiery Orb at the center of the horde of flying bats, forty-five feet to my front!"

Instantly, a ball of flame twenty feet in diameter appears at that location. The sound is a low roar. It only lasts for about five seconds, but all of the bats and rats within that inferno are instantly burned, most of them into tiny ashes. The only ones surviving are those well outside its area of effect, either beyond the fireball or at its outer edges, but those that are left keep on coming.

Aaron turns and runs at top speed, quickly catching up with the others. The remaining rats and bats are right behind him.

The rats catch up to Tamaranis first. He can't run as fast as the others. He is bitten on the leg while trying to kick and stamp them to death with his bare feet. Eridana is bitten by a bat.

Eridana says, "I think I've been poisoned!"

Ruby urges Toby to trot even faster. They are all trying to swat and brush off the bats and rats that are trying to bite them. The creatures are pretty easy to kill, but there are too many of them. Soon, they have all been bitten, some of them several times.

There is a tributary ahead. The crossing is a ford instead of a bridge. They run through the water, which is at least a foot deep in the middle. It slows the horse down, but it stops the rats. They will not cross it. The bats keep coming.

Aaron is first to get to the other side. He turns at the edge of the water and casts another spell, this time from his own spell energy. He jams his staff upright into the mud so that it will stand by itself. He stretches out his arms and spreads his fingers, thumbs barely touching each other.

He yells, "Blazing Hands!"

Jets of searing flame shoot from his fingertips forming a fan shaped sheet of flame three feet long. The flame intercepts several of the remaining bats. Their wings are immediately burned to a crisp, causing their bodies to fall helplessly into the running water at Aaron's feet. This spell lasts for about a minute. Some of the bats try to get around the blazing fan but when they try Aaron manages to reorient his fan of flame to catch each of them, sometimes one by one, until they are all burned to death.

Realizing that the rats will not cross the stream, Aaron's companions stopped on land about twenty feet from its edge. They watch Aaron battle the bats with his magic flames. Everyone collapses with a sigh of relief when the last bat falls. Aaron and his companions are exhausted and drenched with river water and sweat, including the two animals.

Tiarra exclaims, "Aaron. You saved us! I didn't think there was anything we could do! You destroyed them all by yourself! You are my hero! Thank you!"

Aaron says, "I'm thankful Cassia gave me that ring with a Fiery Orb spell in it. That is what saved us. It's also good that the rats won't cross the ford."

Tiarra yells, "Three cheers for Aaron!"

The others join in with enthusiasm.

"Hip hip hooray! Hip hip hooray! Hip hip hooray!"

Aaron says, "Before we get too excited, let's find out how badly we've been hurt. I feel as if I've been bitten in about fifty places. I think I need healing."

They examine their wounds. They all have multiple bites. Some of the bites are bleeding a little, but that is not the worst of it. Many bites are surrounded by bumps of swollen flesh. They seem to have been infected with poison, or perhaps a disease. Their bodies are very wet with perspiration.

Eridana has some cold milfoil tea in a bottle. She drinks half of it, thinking that it will counteract the poison. It doesn't help at all. She saves the second half.

They are all sick. Even Toby and Jenny have been bitten. They look very distressed and are obviously very tired. Johanna and Eridana use their healing spells and potions but no kind of healing that they have does any good. They all notice that Red Haze is getting closer. They are getting weaker. Their situation is desperate. No one knows what to do.

First Tamaranis, then Eridana lose consciousness. Johanna feels their pulse. It is not strong. Their breathing has become difficult and weak.

Johanna says, to whoever might be able to hear her, "They're dying. I'm going to ring the Crystal Bell. We can only use it once, but I'm going to use it now, before we're all dead and it's too late."

Joanna gets the Crystal Bell out of the secret compartment under the seat of the wagon. She rings it loudly until it breaks into hundreds of pieces.

Johanna looks around and thinks, *Where is Quicksilver?*

Suddenly a very large housecat appears out of nowhere. It seems to be smiling – if a cat can smile. Everyone is being healed. The bleeding stops and the swollen places disappear. Tamaranis and Eridana regain consciousness. It becomes again easy to breathe. Their pulse is again normal. Even the horse and the mule are being helped. The rats recede from the proximity of the stream and slowly go away.

Johanna says, "Thank you Quicksilver. I've never met you, but I know who you are. If you didn't heal us, we would certainly have died."

The cat speaks. "You don't need to thank me. I have just done my duty. I kept my promise to Cassia. No, we have never met, but I have observed you, even though you couldn't see me."

Johanna says, "We thank you anyway."

Eridana thinks, *Quicksilver is a talking cat.*

Quicksilver says, "I smell a strange offensive odor about you. I wish you'd get rid of it."

Johanna says, "I don't notice it."

Quicksilver says, "You probably wouldn't. It's coming from you. But it's recent. You all smell different than you did the day you left Ereba."

Johanna says, "We are wearing different clothes. These were not new when they were given to us. Maybe that is what you are noticing."

Quicksilver says, "No. It's not your clothes. It's you."

Johanna asks, "Do you think the bats and rats that bit us caused the odor?"

Quicksilver says, "I don't know. The thought crosses my mind."

Johanna says, "This morning, Ruby and I did some cooking. We made bread and rolls. Maybe that's what you smell. I don't smell it now, but I like that smell. Maybe you don't."

Quicksilver says, "You smell bad. It's not just you and Ruby. You all smell bad."

Johanna asks, "Are we all cursed then? Can you remove it?"

Quicksilver says, "I have already saved you once today."

Eridana says, "Maybe it's the herbs I've been carrying. I'll get rid of them. I'll bury them."

Eridana takes a shovel from the wagon and looks for a place to dig.

Tiarra says, "Quicksilver. Do you see that Red Mist over there? It follows us every day that we travel. Sometimes when we stop for very long, it changes into a Creature in the shape of a Human, made of Dried Blood. It attacks us. When we do enough damage to it, it scatters into fragments. Almost immediately the pieces seem to melt into the atmosphere. There is nothing left. The next morning the Red Mist follows us again. When we stop for the night it attacks us again. We've learned that the weapon we've used to destroy it has no effect on it the next time we fight it. We've used

Ruby's Crossbow, my Crossbow, and Aaron's staff to destroy it. What will we do when only a few of us have a weapon left that can have any effect upon it? Will it kill us? What is it? Why does it attack us? Look. The Red Mist is just hovering there. I think it's waiting for you to leave. Maybe it won't attack us while you are here. It usually attacks soon after we stop. Can you destroy it?"

Quicksilver says, "I have already saved you once today."

Johanna feels exasperated. "You could save us again! Destroy the Red Mist! Don't you know that Cassia wants us to succeed in our mission? We can't do that if the Red Mist Creature kills us before we get to our destination. You should help us! Can't you at least tell us what it is?"

Quicksilver says, "Losing your temper won't do any good."

This answer makes Johanna even more exasperated. She says, "I'm not losing my temper!"

Quicksilver asks, "By the way, whatever happened to that little Dwarf that was with you? Did he chicken out? Did he abandon the mission?"

Johanna says, "I'm not going to answer your question until you answer mine."

Quicksilver says, "So now you are being stubborn."

Johanna says, "I was never stubborn before! I'm learning it from you!"

Quicksilver laughs. "If you survive you should come back to see the Queen. I know she would like to talk with you."

The cat disappears into nothingness just as quickly as it appeared.

Johanna tries to calm down.

Eridana and Aaron are digging a hole near the base of a distinctive pine tree about twenty-five feet away from the wagon. Johanna and Tiarra go to where they are digging.

Johanna asks, "What are you doing?"

Eridana says, "We are going to bury all the herbs that any of us have. That should get rid of the stink."

Johanna says, "That won't do any good. We don't smell any different than we did before. Quicksilver just told us that to get us worked up. Remember how Michael Abner's book said that Quicksilver loves to make other people feel uncomfortable? I don't trust her. I don't trust her at all! Ruby, you did well not to rise to her bait when she insulted you. She was just trying to prod you into anger when she suggested that you might have chickened out and abandoned the mission. She was trying to make you feel uncomfortable."

Ruby says, "She did! I don't like her! I don't trust her! If she didn't know I was here I wasn't going to tell her. If she did know, I didn't need to tell her. I would like it better if she doesn't know. If I had told her that I'm Reuben, she would have laughed at me. I know she would have! I wasn't going to give her the chance! I'm glad you didn't tell her!"

Eridana asks, "How can you be sure that we don't stink?"

Johanna says, "I'm not fully sure. But Quicksilver never said the herbs caused it. It seems very unlikely that they would. Some of these herbs may be very helpful to us. We should take them with us."

Tamaranis says, "Johanna is right. Aaron and I didn't carry any herbs. Yet Quicksilver claimed that we had a bad odor. I doubt if we really do. Why give up good herbs for no good reason?"

Eridana and Aaron fill in the hole and return the pouches of herbs to the wagon.

Tamaranis says calmly, "I think we should get moving. The Red Mist Creature is coming toward us again. I think if we keep moving it won't attack us."

Aaron says, "Tamaranis is right. We've had a rest. Let's get moving again."

He takes the lead rope of the horse and leads it along the narrow dirt road toward Beastgate. Tamaranis gets out front. Ruby takes a turn riding in the wagon. They can still see the river most of the time. It is close to the right hand side of the road. It is late afternoon when they come to a bridge that takes them across the river. They go another five miles before making camp for the night, pulling off the road to the left into a secluded grove. Tamaranis finds some dry wood and immediately builds a fire. The others get their weapons and magic items out of the hidden compartment under the seat of the wagon, anticipating an attack from the Red Haze Creature. The smoky Red Haze has been following them all day, and they know that it will attack them again.

The campfire has barely begun to flame when the Dried Blood Creature comes out of the Red Mist. It stands about fifteen feet away from where Tiarra and most of the others are standing and shoots a blood red arrow at Aaron, hitting him in the chest. Johanna casts a Heal Minor

Wounds spell. It stops the bleeding, but does not entirely heal him. Eridana uses her sling. She hits it in the head with a sling stone. She sees blood. The others run up to it. Nobody even tries to use a weapon that has destroyed it before. Aaron gets close enough to use his Blazing Hands spell, as he did to burn the bats. It takes both hands to do this, so he first lays the staff that Ruby made for him on the ground nearby. The spell has no apparent effect on the Red Blood Creature, but he continues to direct the fire onto it anyway.

The others do not try to use their hand weapons to fight the creature for fear of being hurt by the fire of Aaron's blazing hands spell.

Aaron soon realizes that his Blazing Hands spell is doing no damage to the Creature and that the flames are interfering with the ability of his friends using hand weapons to get close enough to strike the Creature without being burned. So he turns, directing the flame in a different direction, and steps away, waiting for the one-minute duration of the spell to pass by.

Ruby then steps forward and uses her two handed axe. She hits the Creature on its right arm, near the elbow. It bleeds.

Tiarra uses her Longsword. She hits the Creature in the neck. It bleeds a lot.

Tamaranis hits the Creature on its right thigh with his hammer. This does damage.

The Dried Blood Creature looks angry. His blood colored bow changes into a blood colored staff, much thicker than any of the staffs that Ruby made the night before. He swings it at Tamaranis and hits him hard right in the middle of his left side, knocking him off his feet. Tamaranis lands a few feet away. He is bleeding. It looks as if some of his ribs have been broken.

Johanna runs up and uses her mace. The Creature dodges and she misses.

Eridana uses her sling again, aiming again at the Creature's head, but she misses because the Creature's head suddenly bobs away.

Ruby uses her axe again. This time she misses.

Tiarra hits it again in the neck with her sword.

Tamaranis tries to stand up, but he can't.

The Dried Blood Creature swings his staff at Tiarra. She dodges, but not enough. She is hit on the wrist of her weapon hand. She drops her sword.

Johanna goes to assist Tamaranis. She casts a Heal Minor Wounds spell on him.

Aaron has picked up the staff that Ruby made for him. He brings it down hard on the right side of the Creature's head. Aaron thinks it would have made a normal Creature unconscious, but the thing looks directly at Aaron and glares.

Eridana hits the Creature in the head with her sling. The creature is so tall that she thinks that she can hit its head with a sling stone with very little chance of hitting one of her comrades who are next to it instead. The Creature glares at Eridana.

Eridana thinks, *I must be doing a lot of damage to it when I hit it in the head. The Bloody Creature resents it. Good for me.*

Ruby has a chance to get right behind it so she hits him hard right between his shoulder blades. This opens up a large bloody wound.

Tiarra picks up her sword with her left hand and steps back. Her wrist hurts.

Tamaranis is standing. He picks up his hammer. Having seen what Ruby did, he tries to get behind the monster, hoping that it will be safer than trying to hit it from the front.

The Creature's weapon changes back to a bow. He aims at Eridana and hits her in the neck with an arrow. Eridana bleeds. Johanna hits the Creature with her mace. She hits it on the right forearm, the one holding the bow, hoping to knock it out of its hand. But the Creature does not drop it. Suddenly it has a blood arrow in its left hand. It just appears there. The Creature doesn't have to take it from a quiver.

Aaron hits the Creature again on the head with his staff. This seems to bother the Creature a lot. It looks at Aaron.

Eridana sees another opportunity to hit the Creature with a sling stone while its head is not moving. She quickly launches a good-sized stone at it and hits its head.

The Dried Blood Creature suddenly disintegrates, falling into many pieces.

Ruby picks up a four inch sized piece of the creature and runs toward the campfire. She wants to burn it up. Johanna does the same. But the pieces dissolve before they can get them to the fire. The other pieces of the Creature dissolve at the same time, changing into reddish smoke, which quickly drifts out of sight.

Eridana says proudly. "I finished it off this time! I killed it with my sling!" Then she says in a more subdued tone. "Because my sling stone was the last thing that damaged it this time, I suppose it won't do any damage at all to it next time we fight it. I will probably have to use my scimitar if we have to fight it again. "We won't have any more missile weapons to use against it. Reuben's crossbow doesn't damage it any more, and neither does Tiarra's."

Aaron says, "Thank you, Eridana. But you are right. Some of our best weapons won't work on it any more. I tried Blazing Hands this time. But it had no effect. Did you see? Blazing Hands worked very well against the bats, but not at this crazy thing. I don't think any of my magic spells will work against it. But the staff you made for me, Ruby, worked well. It is an excellent weapon. Each time I hit the Creature on the head with it, the thing turned and glared at me."

Eridana says, "That made it much easier for me to hit his head with my sling stone. He was holding his head still. It's hard to hit when it's bobbing around the way it usually does."

Ruby says, "We still have some good weapons that work. Tiarra's Longsword did a lot of damage. My battleaxe does a lot of damage. It worked well for me to hit it from behind."

Tamaranis says, "I think it is getting more powerful each time it comes back than it was the time before. We hit it a lot of times, and did damage, but it still kept fighting. We need to keep trying to destroy it so it doesn't come back. There has to be a way."

Johanna says, "Yes, I thought we were going to actually destroy it this time, by burning those pieces in our fire. But they vaporized before we could get them into the fire."

Aaron says, "Blazing Hands didn't work. I don't think fire will damage it either. I don't think any of my magic will work on it, ever."

Eridana says, "Maybe we'll have to drown it then. Something has to work."

Aaron says, "You can try drowning it, but you'll need lots of water. How are you going to get it close to water?"

Johanna says, "Tomorrow night we should be in The People's Republic. It's a magic Creature. Maybe it won't be able to follow us there."

Tiarra says, "That would be a blessing. I hope you're right."

Eridana and Johanna provide healing to those that were hurt. Eridana heals herself first, then Tiarra. Johanna heals Aaron, then Tamaranis. Aaron, Eridana, and Johanna meditate for an hour while Tiarra and Ruby prepare the night meal. Tamaranis takes care of the animals.

CHAPTER TEN

OTHER PROBLEMS

Greening Twelve – Suppertime

While eating they discuss other problems.

Tiarra says, "Someone is trying to stop us. We haven't even entered The People's Republic yet and a magical Creature made of Dried Blood has attacked us four times. Today we were attacked by a horde of diseased bats and rats. Someone must have sent them to attack us. Who could it be?"

Aaron says, "The creature attacked us soon after we left the haunted city that Queen Cassia teleported us to. Who else knew we were there? It must be one of them.

Eridana says, "That would be Queen Cassia, Ander, Quicksilver, and maybe Sparrow. Nobody else knew that we were there. It has to be one of them."

Tiarra says, "It wouldn't be Queen Cassia. She wants us to save Robert Swift. She wouldn't want that nasty creature to interfere."

Johanna says, "It's Quicksilver then. I hate her!"

Tamaranis says, "Just because you hate her doesn't mean that she's trying to stop us. Queen Cassia said that Quicksilver is her most loyal and trusted friend. Cassia wouldn't want Qutcksilver to interfere with our mission."

Ruby says, "It wouldn't be Sparrow either. She is helping us."

Eridana asks, "Are you sure we can trust her?"

Ruby says, "Queen Cassia told us to go to her. She helped us find the place where Robert Swift was being kept in Exodus. She gave us disguises. If Queen Cassia trusts her, so should we."

Tiarra says, "That leaves Ander then, doesn't it? He is probably jealous of Queen Cassia and wants to be King. He may be expecting help from The Keepers to make that happen. He might have used magical means to let The Keepers know that we are coming, and in exchange they will assassinate Queen Cassia and he will be King."

Eridana says, "That wouldn't happen. Queen Cassia's sister would become Queen."

Tiarra says, "The Keepers would assassinate her too."

Ruby says, "Maybe it's Nick Blackwood."

Aaron says, "He doesn't know about our disguises."

Ruby says, "The Red Mist started attacking us before we had disguises. It's magic. Maybe it follows the odor Quicksilver says that we have. Disguises don't mean a thing to it."

Eridana says, "That's right. Maybe Nick put an odor on us way back when we saw him in Gambit. I don't think he's a Magic User, but he could have hired a Magic User to send the Red Mist Creature after that odor, and the bats and rats as well."

Aaron says, "Nick would not have known that we were near the haunted city when the dried blood thing first attacked us."

Johanna says, "I don't think we have an odor. That was just Quicksilver trying to tease us."

Tamaranis says, "Maybe it's that woman we saw just off the ancient trail the same day we left Gambit. I don't think we killed her."

Ruby says, "That, woman - or whatever it was, would not have any way to know that we were near the haunted city."

Tamaranis says, "I don't think we know. I don't think we have enough information to figure it out. All we can do is keep going and hope for the best. Everything that happens to us doesn't have to be part of a nasty plot. Some things just happen. Nobody mentioned that the two giant reptiles were sent to kill us by anybody. They just noticed that we were there."

Johanna says, "They were just wild beasts that wanted something to eat."

Tamaranis says, "That's what I mean. Some things just happen. Maybe the Creature from the Red Mist and the bats and rats just happened. Maybe they want to eat us."

Tiarra says, "Maybe you're right. Maybe not. I don't know. I just know that we have to continue on and complete our mission. We have to go to Divinity City and find Robert Swift."

Tamaranis says, "That's right, my friends. I'm going to believe that our disguises are working and The Keepers don't know anything about us until I have more convincing evidence that I'm wrong. Let's rehearse our story. Tomorrow we should be going through Beastgate into The People's Republic. I'm sure that we'll be questioned there."

Tiarra says, "You're right, Tamaranis, as usual."

So they review their roles. When it is Ruby's turn Tiarra says, "I don't think we have to worry about Ruby's cooking skill. We made two supper meals together. She knows what she's doing"

Johanna says, "I agree. Next time we want bread I think she could make it alone."

During this conversation Ruby gets out her torn skirt and her sewing kit and starts to mend the tear. Eridana moves to where she can watch closely. Ruby doesn't get much done before Eridana says, "You need help. Your sewing is sloppy. Let me do it for you."

Ruby doesn't protest. Eridana takes out the stitches Ruby has made on her damaged skirt and does a much neater job than Ruby had been doing. It is almost impossible to see that the skirt had been torn. Ruby is pleased for the help.

When they think they have reviewed their story enough they prepare for sleep.

Tamaranis says, "Tonight I want to be on watch with Ruby. We'll do the last watch."

Nobody objects. Johanna and Aaron take the first watch; Eridana and Tiarra will take the second.

In their tent, Ruby asks Eridana, "Why did you think we might not be able to trust Sparrow?"

Eridana says, "We were thinking about each of the people who knows where we are and whether we can trust them or not. Sparrow might have known about when Queen Cassia magically transferred us to Ashua. If so, she could have arranged for the Red Haze Creature to follow us and fight us. She knew that we were on this road today. She could have arranged for the bats and rats to attack us. She might have known when we arrived in

Exodus. She convinced us to go forward with a one-horse wagon instead of our riding horses. She has weakened your fighting ability by changing you into a woman. She may have already told The Keepers what our disguises are so that they can arrest us as soon as we cross the border into The People's Republic. All we know about her is that Queen Cassia told us that she would help us find Robert Swift in Exodus. We don't really know if we can trust Sparrow."

Ruby says, "Everything you have told me is speculation. I think Sparrow can be trusted. When I put on the Amulet, everything that happened was just as she said it would be."

Eridana says, "She was trying to gain your trust. What if when you remove the Amulet, you don't change back into a Dwarf? Have you thought about that?"

Ruby says, "I thought about it and I tried it out right there in her stable. I did change back just as she said I would."

Eridana says, "You took a big risk on her word. What if you hadn't?"

Ruby says, "I've thought about that. I'm not as stupid as you think I am. Amrath would be able to change me back into a Dwarf using his Imp of Wishes. He lives in Tarek, which is right near my village. It wouldn't be too hard for me to find him. If he isn't there when we get back, I'll ask his uncle to do it. Ephraim is one of the most powerful wizards there is. I'm sure he can do it. If we succeed in rescuing Robert Swift, I'll have plenty of money to pay him with. I'll be fine."

Eridana says, "I hope you're right. Now let's get some sleep. I have to get up for the second watch."

Despite her backup plan Ruby is still worried about the possibility that the next time she takes off the Amulet she may not change back into a Dwarf. Maybe Sparrow is not trustworthy after all, and maybe Amrath and Ephraim do not have the right kind of magic. Ruby does not fall asleep right away. She tries to think about what it might be like to live the rest of her life as a woman, not a Dwarven woman but a Human woman. *I don't know what it would be like. Human women seem to be quite different from Dwarven women.*

About two hours into the second watch a big rainstorm descends upon them, quickly extinguishing the campfire. Thunder and lightning wake everybody, but they stay in their tents, which keep them fairly dry. The canopy over the wagon keeps the things in it dry. The two people that are on watch sit in the wagon, looking out through both ends. They don't see anything but lightning and rain. The people in the tents have trouble sleeping through the storm, but when the thunder and lightning stop they fall asleep.

It is still raining a steady less intensive rain when Eridana wakes up Ruby and Tamaranis for the third watch. The two guards settle into the wagon for dry cover.

Ruby says, "If this rain keeps up it is going to be a long watch. We're going to have to talk to stay awake."

Tamaranis says, "All right. Tell me a story."

Ruby starts out by telling stories about the Dwarves, which she loves to do. Tamaranis does more listening than talking. When he talks it is more likely to be a discussion of a great truth or social issue, which happens to come into his mind because of Ruby's story. He also recites a few poems that he has memorized - poems that Ruby doesn't understand very well.

Ruby says, "Please change the subject. Tell me all about yourself. Start from the beginning. What did your father do for a living?"

"My father was a librarian, but he died before I was born. My mother died when I was five years old. That is when the monks at the monastery took me in. It is a monastery of scholars. It is they who taught me what I know. They taught me how to read and write. They said I have a natural aptitude for it. They also gave me jobs to do that kept me quite busy. They taught me and the other boys some fighting and survival skills but most of what they taught us was about how to think logically and deeply about the great mysteries of the universe."

Ruby says, "I would like to know more about that. What are the great mysteries?"

Tamaranis says, "You know. What happens to us after we die? Where were we before we were born? What is God really like? Why are we here on this island instead of somewhere else? Is there any purpose to life, or is it simply about survival?"

Ruby says, "My religion says that if I have lived a good life my spirit will go to a very good place and I'll live there forever. My mother and father will probably already be there. Someday my children will join me. What do you think happens to us after we die?"

Tamaranis says, "I don't know."

Ruby asks, "What good was all that education if you don't know?"

Tamaranis says, "Maybe nobody really knows. One of the things I learned from the scholars is that there is value in knowing whether you really know something or not. If you think you know something when you really don't, you may close your mind to other possibilities and never discover the real truth."

Ruby says, "That is very interesting. I agree that it is hard to find the answers to some of my questions. I have noticed that different people sometimes have different answers to the same questions. But as far as I know, all the Dwarves who live in my village believe the same that I do about what will happen to us after we die."

Tamaranis says, "My teachers have told me that there are different groups of people who have different beliefs about that. Maybe it isn't the same for everybody. I don't know. Maybe it is different for different people, depending in part on what they believe."

Ruby says, "This is kind of confusing to me. Let's talk about something else. A lot of what I learned while growing up was what my father taught me about how to saw logs and make furniture, and other things. Did you learn how to make things? Do you know how to make a table out of wood? Do you know how to grow tomatoes? Do you even know how to milk a cow?"

Tamaranis says, "I learned a lot at the monastery about how to plant, grow, and harvest food. We produce almost all of the food we eat at our monastery. We even produce our own wine from grapes that we grow. I know how to maintain and harvest a vineyard. But that is not what I expect to spend most of my life doing. I can do important things that many farmers cannot do. I can do numbers, speak, read, and write several different languages. I know the customs of the different kinds of people who live on the Island of Morgana. I know the history of this island about as well as anybody does. I think that's more important."

Ruby says, "That sounds good. I can do numbers, speak, read, and write my own language, which is the same as just about everybody else who lives on this island uses. I don't see how learning other languages can be useful. Learning a trade, like I did, is useful."

Tamaranis says, "I admit that most of my life has been spent in a monastery, and I need to learn more about how most other people live. That is one of the reasons why I was asked to leave the monastery for a while - so that I could learn by experience. And I'm learning. I like it."

Ruby says, "Well, that makes sense to me. I have noticed that you know how to set up a tent. You didn't seem to know how to ride a horse at first, but you do quite well now. You seem to know about taking care of animals. Do you know how to shoe a horse?"

Tamaranis says, "I've seen it done. I could do it if I had to."

Ruby asks, "Were there any girls at the monastery?"

Tamaranis says, "No. The monastery is for men only. Women don't need to know the kind of things we learn there."

Ruby says, "Maybe men don't either. What did you learn there that wouldn't be just as helpful for women to know as for men? Look at Tiarra. Why shouldn't women have a chance to know the history of the island? Why wouldn't women want to know the answers to life's great questions? What's the big deal about knowing that we don't know the answers to some of them?"

Tamaranis says, "We young men at the monastery are learning things that will enable us to be teachers and advisors to kings. That is a man's role."

Ruby says, "My mother is my father's most important advisor. Don't kings have wives?"

"Of course, but their role is to supervise the domestic affairs of the castle and make sure that the king's children are given a good upbringing. The king will often be away from home. His advisor can go with him. His Queen, most often, cannot."

Ruby says, "It seems to me that the Queen would need a good education for that."

Tamaranis says, "Princesses and other high born women do get a good education, but not at my school."

Ruby says, "In my village children learn the things they need to know from their parents and other villagers. We don't have to leave home to learn what we need to know. Boys and girls learn a lot of the same things and some things are different. Men and women don't have the same responsibilities. I think its better that way."

Tamaranis says, "Education is never wasted. It brings a richer life, no matter what you do with it. The scholars have taught me a lot, but I want to learn things that they can't teach me. I might eventually become a librarian like my father was, or an advisor to kings. Look at you. You are learning. You are now experiencing what it is like to be a woman. When you go back to being a man, you will be a better man because of this experience."

Ruby says, "It's an experience all right, but I'm not doing this for the experience. It's a disguise. If you want this kind of experience, you can use my Amulet when I don't need it any more. Do you want it?"

Tamaranis says, "Maybe. I'll have to think about that."

It is quiet for a while. Then Tamaranis says, "You know I wanted to be on watch with you tonight. I'm glad it worked out this way. I had a reason."

Ruby says, "Of course. You always do. Are you going to tell me what it is?

Tamaranis says, "I'm getting to that. I have told you a lot about life in the monastery. You realize that I have had little opportunity to learn about women except what I have read in books, and that is not enough. I didn't realize it at first, but this adventure is giving me a chance for first hand communication with women. I am learning, but I still have a lot to learn."

Ruby says, "You are talking to the wrong person. You should have asked to be on watch with Tiarra, Eridana, or Johanna."

Tamaranis says, "I have recently been on watch with both Tiarra and Eridana. I learned something from them, but I want to know more. Since you put on your disguise I have had a feeling that I want to kiss you and hug you. Would you mind if I did that?"

"I definitely would mind. Have you gone crazy? Don't do it."

"Then let me ask you a question. Have you, in your female body, ever been kissed by a man? You might like it."

Ruby says, "As a male Dwarf I kissed and hugged the girl I grew up with. I know what it's like."

"It might feel different for females than for a man. This is your chance to find out. Think about it."

Ruby thinks about it. *Tamaranis might be right. It also might be different for Humans than it is for Dwarves. I was thinking about that before my body changed. But I don't want to do this kind of experiment. It doesn't feel right. It's scary.*

Ruby says, "I don't have any desire to do that. Let's talk about something else."

Tamaranis says, "You might like it. Men and women were made for each other physically. We have instincts that allow us to maintain the population of this island. We can..."

Ruby interrupts. "End of conversation. I think I know where you are headed and I am not going there. Don't say another word." She feels terrified at his suggestion. She feels tears welling up in her eyes. *Sparrow warned me about this.*

Tamaranis says, "But..."

"Give me no buts. This is the end of your story. Now you can listen to one of mine."

Ruby starts a story about how to build a bookcase and ignores all attempts Tamaranis makes to interrupt her. She keeps talking until the rain stops. Then she goes outside, takes some dry wood from inside the wagon, and builds a fire.

Tamaranis tries to help by gathering more relatively dry wood from under the wagon.

Ruby says abruptly, "Go away. Leave me alone."

"I only want to help. We are going to need more wood."

"Just pile it over there then. Don't get close to me."

Ruby feels quite agitated. The more she thinks about what Tamaranis was saying, the more agitated she feels. She doesn't often lose her temper, but she is getting more and more upset. *Tamaranis should not be thinking of me as being a woman!*

Tamaranis puts wood where she told him to put it.

Then he says, "I'm cold and hungry. I want to be near the fire. Are you going to make a hot breakfast?"

She finally says, "Stop it!"

Tamaranis asks, "Stop what?"

"Stop what you're doing. It's inappropriate."

Tamaranis says, "I'm not doing anything inappropriate."

Ruby says, "You're treating me like a woman. I feel like you want to... to... Stop. You know what I mean... kiss me. Ooh! You make me feel strange. Again, she feels tears welling up in her eyes."

Tamaranis says, "I haven't tried to kiss you, but yes. I would like to. You are very attractive. And you have been leading me on for the past two days. How do you expect me to feel? I'm only a man."

Ruby says, "But I am not a woman! I may look like a woman, but I'm a male Dwarf. I know it and you know it! We all know it. I don't want you to court me as if I were a woman! I don't want you to kiss me or hug me. Please don't bother me any more!"

Ruby's face is flushed with anger. She can feel tears on her cheeks.

Tamaranis says, "I'm sorry. I thought...well...You're so attractive. I thought you liked me. I think it would be fun for both of us. I don't want to make you angry. I just want to be your friend. I know you were a male Dwarf, but now you are a woman. You should be enjoying the experience. I know you like me. I thought you were coming on to me. What do you expect me to do?"

"Don't treat me like a woman. Let me alone. I'm not coming on to you."

Tamaranis says, "I'm sorry. I won't do it any more."

Ruby gets some oatmeal, a pot, and some water and makes breakfast. Tamaranis doesn't say anything. He wanders around the campsite, keeping his thoughts to himself.

PART THREE
FOLLOWING A COLD TRAIL

Chapter Eleven

In Pursuit of Friends

Tyr's Day - Greening Eleven – Morning

Amrath, Leander, Nick, and Helena wake up in tents and emerge fully dressed to greet the rising morning sun. They are camped beside a very old and seldom-used stone paved road. It is so little used that tall grass is growing up in the cracks between stones and some grass is growing in dirt that covers some of the stones.

Yesterday, on Greening ten, Amrath used his Imp of Wishes to magically transfer himself and his three companions from Sarah Swift's home courtyard in Althen to a place on the heavily used road between Vert and Chama that intersects with an almost never used ancient stone paved road. They followed this old road to the "dead" city called Ashua and beyond to where they are now. Ashua is an old city that was occupied by people of the Ereban race. Humans who invaded the Island of Morgana and now live along the east coast of the island destroyed Ashua a few hundred years ago. The Humans killed all of the Erebans who lived there but were unable to occupy the city because the ghosts of the Erebans who were killed haunt it. When Amrath and his three friends entered Ashua, they were almost immediately driven out by the ghosts. They went east from Ashua along the old stone road and set up their tents before it got dark.

Today they plan to go eastward along this road to the city of Exodus, as they seek to carry out their mission to find Sarah Swift's father, Robert Swift.

Amrath is a Spellcaster of the Elden race. He emerges from his tent wearing a long yellow ochre robe, yellow shirt, green trousers, and a dark green hat. He has no armor. His right hand is clutching a staff. It appears that he has a sheath knife on a belt, mostly hidden under his long robe. He looks like a Spellcaster. He is just under six feet tall, quite slender, and has the pointed ears of an Elden. He has green eyes, shoulder length blonde hair, and a dimpled chin. He is about twenty-five years old.

His father, Leander is also a Spellcaster, very well known as an experienced user of magic who has been on many successful missions. He is wearing a long, light gray robe, gray shirt, light brown trousers, and a gray, conical shaped hat. He also carries a staff. He is about the same height and build as Amrath, and has the same pointed ears. He has shoulder length, light colored hair. He has green eyes. He is about eighty years old, which is fairly young for an Elden. Eldens often live to be more than five hundred years old as compared to about seventy years for most Humans.

Nick is a Human fighter who is very good at sneaking around in the dark, especially in urban areas. He wears a black leather jacket, black leather trousers, a black belt, and black boots that come almost up to his knees. He has a Magic Longsword, a Magic Longbow, and a sheaf of arrows. He looks very fit and agile, probably about thirty-five years old.

Helena is a Human woman about five-feet-six-inches tall, perhaps a little overweight in a very attractive way. She has reddish-blonde hair, gray-blue eyes, freckles, and a friendly smile. She wears a brown leather skirt that comes down a little lower than her knees, a hard leather, magic corset with metal armor placed strategically to provide extra protection for her breasts, and hard leather boots that come up to the bottom of her leather skirt. She has wide, polished-steel bracelets on each wrist and a coil of thin rope is attached to her belt beside her money pouch. She has a Magic Hammer and a Magic Sling. She looks fit and agile. She is about thirty-five years old.

Amrath is carrying a very special magic item called The Imp of Wishes. It is in a bottle in a pocket of his robe. The slight bulge is barely noticeable. The Imp looks like a light brown salamander about six inches long that lives in a glass bottle. It has four legs and a long tail. It has soft moist skin with no scales. It has white eyes with dark pupils and a fairly large mouth. When its owner makes a wish The Imp can do amazing things, but one owner can only keep it for twenty-four days. Then it must be passed on to a new owner. Amrath bought it at Lady Lucy's Magic Emporium for only ten pieces of gold on Greening one. He plans to sell it to his father for ten pieces of gold just before the date of Greening twenty-four, a little less than two weeks from now.

Mostly, Amrath has used the Imp of Wishes to instantly transport himself, others, and objects to places where he has previously been. He has tried to transport people from where they are to where he is, but that has never worked. He does not believe that he should ask the Imp for things that he would like to have because his father has told him that this would be stealing the object from the person who possesses it. Stealing is wrong. He would also be in trouble if the person that it was taken from finds that he has it. This has happened sometimes to Spellcasters who did this. Using magic to move someone to another location is called Transference. It is a magic spell that Amrath has not yet learned, but Leander knows how to cast it. However the Imp of Wishes Transference Spell is stronger. It can Transfer more people or creatures at one time than can the usual spell. Amrath has used the Imp of Wishes to copy pages of written words from a book onto blank pages. He has also used it to open a lock. It can probably do many other things that Amrath has not yet tried to do.

Amrath, Leander, Nick, and Helena have been asked by Sarah Swift to try to find her father, Robert Swift, a traveling merchant, who is missing. They don't know where he is but they strongly suspect that he was captured by the Keepers, secret police of The People's Republic, near the village of Derlenen (near the forest of Ereba) and taken to Divinity City, the capitol city of The People's Republic. The People's Republic, is on the east coast of the Island of Morgana. According to their map, the road they are following heads in that direction, but it will take about four days to travel from where they are to Divinity City.

In addition to finding Robert Swift, Amrath wants to find his friends, Tiarra, Eridana, Johanna, Aaron, Tamaranis, and Reuben. He was with that group of people for a while, when they found Robert Swift's wagon train in the village of Derlenen. Amrath left the group when they went into the Forest of Ereba, because Queen Cassia wouldn't let Amrath continue. He thinks these friends are looking for Robert Swift too. That is what Sarah Swift asked them to do. They may have more information about where Robert Swift might be that he does. He is concerned for their safety, especially if they have to go into The People's Republic. He and his present companions are well aware of the lethal punishment The Keepers will give to people not of the Human race, such as Eldens, Half Eldens, Dwarves, and Erebans, who are found within the borders of their nation. Spellcasters and people caught carrying magic items will be given the same punishment, a painful death.

Amrath and the others are aware that Queen Cassia sent Tiarra, Eridana, Johanna, Aaron, Tamaranis, and Reuben to the dead city of Ashua. They think that these people might have made the trail of horse tracks they have been following since they left Ashua. They hope to catch up to them.

The horse tracks they are following have been going easterly along a very little used road. According to the map, they seem to be headed for a city of some size called Exodus. Only Nick has ever been there before and he used a different route to get there when he did.

The four travelers don't bother with a hot breakfast. They are anxious to get moving. They follow the road and fresh tracks of horses eastward toward Exodus. Amrath, the youngest, leads the packhorse that is carrying their four tents, bedding, cooking equipment, and food. They are making good time, spending as much time trotting as walking. They stop once in a while to let Leander, Amrath's father and by far the oldest of the group, stretch his muscles. He is not accustomed to riding a horse very much. It is a very warm day, and they feel the heat.

At mid-morning they come to a place beside a small stream where the people they are following made camp. Spots where stakes held several tents in place are obvious. They can also see the remains of a campfire, and where horses ate some grass. The rain has obliterated any other sign.

About an hour later they begin to see freshly planted fields; then some farmhouses. Later yet they see a small village that has some commercial buildings, houses, and sheds. The people who live there seem surprised to see strangers passing through.

Nick, using his charming manner and silky voice, stops and talks with one of them, a middle-aged woman.

"Good day. What a fine village you have here. We are just passing through. I was wondering if you happened to see another group of strangers passing this way through your village during the last day or two?"

The woman seems a little tense when she says, "I saw six people on horses the day before yesterday, in the morning. They were going the same way you're going: toward Exodus."

Nick asks, "Was one of them a Dwarf?"

She says, "Yes, and they had three pack animals with them. Are you looking for them? Is that why you're here?"

Nick says, "That's right. They are our friends. We're trying to catch up with them."

She says, "You won't unless they stop and wait for you. They should have arrived in Exodus that night."

Nick says, "Maybe they'll still be in Exodus when we get there. We hope to be there by noon."

She says, "You should have no trouble doing that. When we go to Exodus, we start early in the morning, do all our business, and start back a little after noon. We get home well before dark."

Nick asks, "By the way, did any of them say anything to you that would indicate where they might be going?"

She says, "Not a word. They looked at us, but they didn't talk to us - not very polite, like you are. I don't know where they came from, but they were headed toward Exodus. That's where the road goes. We don't see many strangers here."

Nick says, "Thank you for your help. It has been a pleasure to have these few words with you, but we should be moving on."

The woman asks, "Where did you come from? There's nothing west of here within a day's travel."

Nick says, "We camped out last night."

She says, "I hope you stayed clear of the old ruins. It's called Ashua. Ghosts live there. You didn't spend the night there, did you?"

Nick says, "No. We saw it, but we camped several miles to the east. We know better than to go into that place."

The woman says, "Well, I'm glad to know that. The ruins of the old city are a bad place. We stay clear of it. They say that people who go in there never come out."

Nick says, "Thanks for the warning. Good-bye now. We really must be going."

Nick and the others move on.

Amrath says, "We are on the right trail. She saw six people including a Dwarf go through here toward Exodus. They have to be my friends."

Nick says, "I agree."

Helena says, "I can no longer identify the tracks of the group we are following. This part of the road is more heavily traveled than before."

Nick says, "Probably farmers use this road often, going to their fields and coming back."

The four travelers come to small farm villages at intervals of about three miles. Each has a crossroad. The side roads might lead to yet other villages. It seems that the farmers in this area live in the villages and work on fields that are within easy walking distance. They have seen no farm buildings scattered at intervals along the poorly maintained road.

Helena says, "If the people we are following went down one of these side roads instead of to Exodus we won't know it."

Leander says, "I doubt if they did. Keep going east."

The four travelers urge their mounts into a slow trot. They enter Exodus a little before noon. It is a walled city. There are two guards at the gate.

Amrath asks one of the guards, "We are looking for some friends. Have you seen a group of six people, riding horses as we are, enter this gate during the last couple of days?"

The guard says, "Yes, I have. Five people and a Dwarf come in on the afternoon of Greening nine. I remember it well. We almost never see a Dwarf here in Exodus. That was two days ago. They had two pack horses and a Donkey with them. Is that who you are looking for?"

Amrath says, "Yes. I hope they are still here."

Amrath, Leander, Helena, and Nick move on down a fairly wide street. A sign indicates that it is called "Street of Guilds". There are many people walking around and many shops. Anything and everything seems to be for sale. As they move along they see a shop named Newton's Enchanted Weaponry.

Amrath says, "This looks like place where we could buy some magical items. Let's go in and look around."

Leander says, "Not now. Let's first find a place to eat some lunch. I'm hungry."

They keep moving. They see shops that sell clothing, boots and shoes, non-magical weapons and, armor, food, agricultural tools, logging tools, cooking tools, furniture, bedding, and just about anything you might think of. They even see a sign that says "FORTUNES TOLD".

Helena seems to be interested in a place called 'Baubles, Bangles, and Beads.

Helena says, "Maybe we could come back and look around in several of these shops after we eat."

So far they haven't seen any inns. When they get to the center of the city they see that it is a large round courtyard. Seven principal streets intersect here. One of these streets, ahead of them and a little to the right, seems to have mostly inns and pubs. The other two seem to be lined mostly with houses and shops. A sign indicates that the street that has inns and pubs is called the 'Street of Lights'. They see lanterns hanging in front of each inn but they are not lighted at this time. The lanterns are of different colors, such as rose, amber, blue, and green. They walk along this street. When they see an inn that seems to be serving good smelling food they stop, tie their horse's reins to a railing that has other horses tied to it, and go in. They sit at a table. When a waitress comes by, they order some food.

While eating, Nick says, "As soon as we finish eating we should go up and down this street and ask if anyone has seen a group of six people come by, looking for food or a place to stay overnight.

Leander says, "That sounds like a good idea."

As soon as they have finished eating, Nick goes to the man behind the bar. He says, "I'm looking for some friends. I'm supposed to meet them here in Exodus, but I don't know where. Maybe you have seen them. They are six people traveling together. They probably got here two days ago. One of them is a Dwarf. Have you seen a group like that?"

The man behind the bar says, "I don't remember seeing a group like that in the last two days. Sorry."

They pay for their meal. Then Nick and his friends go from inn to inn asking the person behind the bar if they have seen such a group traveling together. They get negative answers. Sometimes the person they ask says something like "I may have seen a group like that but they didn't stay here. I don't know what may have happened to them.

The large, rough-looking man at the door of the Black Unicorn won't let them in. He says, "We don't allow Eldens in the Black Unicorn." Leander and Amrath turn and go back out into the street. Nick and Helena stay at the door.

Nick says, "We are looking for a group of six people who might have come in here during the last couple of days? Have you seen such a group?"

The man says, "We don't give out that kind of information."

Nick and Helena rejoin Leander and Amrath. They go to other inns. They finally come to the Traveler's Rest. The proprietor there says, "People come and go, but it is my policy not to pass on such information to people that I don't know anything about. It's not the right thing to do."

Leander says, "We understand."

Nick, Helena, Leander and Amrath go back outside. Leander says, "We're not going to learn anything from the innkeepers about your friends, Amrath. This is a waste of time. Let's move on to Eastgate. Your friends have probably gone on to there by now anyway. They would stay here no longer than one night. The quicker we leave, the better chance we will have to catch up to them."

They get on their horses and proceed along the Street of Lights toward the east gate. When they get there they see two guards, just as they did at the west gate.

Nick asks, "Did either of you see a group of six people leaving Exodus through this gate during the last two days? They were riding on horses. They had three pack animals."

One of the guards says, "I saw them. One of them was very short. Maybe he was a Dwarf. It was the morning of Greening ten. They asked me for directions to the Pool of Golden Dawn. I had never heard of it before. I told them that there is a pool about a mile east of town and they went out to look for it. They came back a little while later. I think they may have found it."

Helena asks, "Did they go back out through the gate later?"

The soldier says, "No. I was on duty until fourteen hours after dawn. It was fully dark when I was relieved. I didn't see them again. If they went through this gate before dark I would have seen them. I didn't see them today either."

Nick says, "Thank you for the information."

Amrath, Leander, Helena and Nick talk it over and decide to go out to look for the pool. They find it.

Helena says, "This pool doesn't look that special. I wonder why they were looking for it."

Nick says, "It's a mystery to me. I wonder why they went back into Exodus. I would have thought that they would have just kept going to Eastgate."

Amrath says, "They might still be in Exodus."

Leander says, "Or they might have left through a different gate. The guards seem to be very competent here. Let's check all the gates. According to the map, there should be at least three others."

They go back toward the center of the city. A light shower is falling so they go into an inn. They wait there for a little while for the rain to stop before going out to talk with the guards at the other gates. They go to the gate that heads northeast first because it seems that it could be an alternate way to get to Eastgate. But when they ask the guards at the gate they are told that they did not see a group of six people on horses leaving Exodus during the last two days.

They get the same result when they talk to the guards at the gate at the road that would lead north to Ezrada, the one that would lead northwest to Chama, the one that would lead southwest to Jen, and a road that goes south toward Domas. None of the guards at these gates have seen a group of six people riding horses going either in or out.

They even go back to the gate that leads to Ashua to make sure that Amrath's friends didn't leave the city going in that direction since they entered the city of Exodus.

But they find no evidence that Tiarra, Johanna, Eridana, Aaron, Tamaranis, and Reuben have left the city. They ride back toward the Street of Lights.

Helena says, "If they haven't left Exodus, they must still be here. Where could they be?"

Nick says, "They could be staying at almost any of the inns, but if they are, nobody will tell us."

Amrath says, "Why would they stay here? They should be looking for Robert Swift. Could it be that they expect to find him here, in Exodus? Could it be that they have already found him?"

Leander says, "I don't know."

Nick says, "I don't know what could have happened to your friends, Amrath, but maybe they got into a fight with some Keepers – here in Exodus. Maybe they were killed. Maybe some of them were captured. We may never know."

It is now late afternoon. They find an inn where they will eat supper and spend the night. While eating they talk. They consider that it might have been possible for Tiarra and her five companions to leave Exodus using some exit other than the gates that they have investigated.

After some discussion Nick says, "In the morning we should go to Beastgate City. I should say Eastgate City which is on the west side of the river. There is a bridge there that goes across the Beast River, the border between Ezrada and The People's Republic. Beastgate is on the east side, in The People's Republic. As Eldens, you can't go there. If Tiarra's group is headed for Divinity City, they should be going through Eastgate City. The guards there would probably see them enter through one of the gates if they did."

Leander says, "There is another possibility. Maybe they found a Spellcaster here in Exodus who has the ability to magically Transfer them to Divinity City, and did it for them. If that is so, they are already there. I have never been to Divinity City. If I had, I could use my Transference Spell to get us there. I don't think you should try to use your Imp of Wishes to Transfer us there, Amrath. You haven't been there either."

Nick says, "Using a Transference Spell to get to Divinity City would be very dangerous for Spellcasters with pointed ears like you two have. It would be safer for Helena and me. I've been there before. What about you, Helena? Have you ever been to Divinity City?"

Helena says, "Only once. I didn't like it. They don't like female adventurers there very much. They think a woman's place is in the home - having babies."

Nick says, "There must be something we can do with that Imp of Wishes to find Robert Swift. Can't you just tell the Imp to wish that he was right here with us?"

Amrath says, "I have already asked it to bring Robert Swift to me. That didn't happen. I also wished that the Imp would tell me where Robert Swift is but I didn't get an answer. I guess the Imp can't talk. I don't even know if he would know something like that."

Nick asks, "Have you asked the Imp to bring you some money?"

Amrath says, "No. That is stealing. It's against the rules of wishes to do something like that."

Nick says, "So you haven't wished for a magic item or anything like that?"

Amrath says, "Not exactly."

Nick says, "Well, why don't you try something? Wish for Tiarra or Johanna to be right here with us. Let's find out what happens."

Amrath says, "I have already tried to do that. It didn't work."

Nick says, "Show me the Imp. I want to get a good look at it."

Amrath lets Nick and Helena examine the Imp of Wishes, which they do with great interest. It looks directly at Nick and sticks out its tongue.

Leander says, "You could try again. What have we got to lose? If you can get Tiarra here, she can tell us where they went, and also about their plan for rescuing Robert Swift."

Amrath says, "All right." He holds the bottle in his hand and says, "I wish that Tiarra Galadrin was right here in this room with us."

The Imp looks directly at Amrath. It slides its forked tongue out of its mouth and then back in again. Twice. Nothing else happens.

Leander says, "I guess it's not going to work. I'm not surprised. It was too good an idea to be true."

Nick says, "It should have worked. Even if Tiarra is dead, her body should be here. Try it again."

Leander says, "Don't try it again, not right now anyway. Wishes can be tricky and we don't know very much about this Imp."

Amrath says, "One time Tiarra wanted information about Robert Swift. I didn't ask out loud, but in my head I wished that would happen. We were on watch. In a little while a gypsy wagon showed up in the dark. An old gypsy woman gave Tiarra a magic necklace. She said that it allows the person wearing it to sometimes see into the future and into the past. Tiarra put it on. When she woke up that morning she told us that she had a dream about Robert Swift's wagon train being attacked. The next day we came to the wagon train. It had been attacked in very much in the way

Tiarra had seen it in her dream. Maybe it will take a little while for the Imp to execute this kind of wish."

Nick says, "I hope it doesn't take too long. We might not be here when Tiarra arrives."

Helena says, "Maybe she'll arrive during the night."

Nick says, "Then, maybe you should wish for information about where Tiarra is. Maybe a gypsy will bring me a necklace that will help me dream about where she is and we will find her tomorrow."

Leander says, "Enough. Wishes are nothing to joke about."

Helena says, "I'm not joking. I'd like to have such a necklace. Did Tiarra have any more dreams about Robert Swift?"

Amrath says, "I don't know. We only spent one more night together. She didn't mention any dreams in the morning. That is the last time I saw her."

Helena looks at Amrath, as if she expects him to do something.

Amrath says, "All right. I'll give it a try. I wish that Helena would have a dream that tells her where Tiarra Galadrin is and what she is doing."

Helena says, "Thanks, but you didn't mention a necklace. I want a necklace."

Amrath says, "I'm leaving that up to the Imp. You might get the same necklace that Tiarra was given, but you might get something else – something even better."

Helena says, "You could have mentioned it."

Amrath says, "Now I'm going to use the Imp to Transfer me back to Althen so that I can give Sarah a progress report."

It isn't a pleasant thing for Amrath to do, because Sarah Swift is unhappy at what she considers to be very little progress. She takes out her frustration on the messenger. Amrath uses the Imp again to get back with Leander, Helena, and Nick. They spend the night in Exodus.

CHAPTER TWELVE

ON TO EASTGATE

Thor's Day - Greening Twelve – Morning

The four travelers get together to eat breakfast. As soon as they are seated Helena looks at Amrath and says, "I didn't get a necklace or any other piece of jewelry during the night like Tiarra did. I didn't dream about Robert Swift, Tiarra, or any of the other members of her group. I guess your Imp of Wishes didn't want to help me."

Amrath says, "Don't blame me. I tried. You heard me make the wish."

The morning is cold, foggy, and wet with a very light rain falling. This gives Amrath, Leander, Nick, and Helena a late start, but they refuse to wait all morning. They leave Exodus for Eastgate about two hours after daylight, using the east gate. It is an uneventful journey. They pass many farm villages and also farm families and other types going in the same direction. They also pass some people going from Eastgate toward Exodus. It is bad weather until almost noon. Then the sun comes out. They arrive at Eastgate about an hour before dark. When they go in through the outer gate a soldier asks for their names and residences.

"Leander Darkriver from Tarek."

"Amrath Darkriver from Tarek."

"Nick from Doomgate."

"Helena from Jen."

The soldier asks, "And where are you going?"

Leander says, "We are going into Eastgate. We will spend the night at an inn. I'm not sure how long we will stay."

Nick asks, "Have you seen a group of six people on horseback, one of them a Dwarf, entering the city today or yesterday?"

The soldier says, "I haven't seen a Dwarf go through this gate for at least a month. We don't see many of them and I would remember it. But I'm not the only person who does this job. I've only been on duty since noon today. That's when my shift usually starts. They could have come through this morning or yesterday. Yesterday was my day off. Why do you want to know?"

Nick says, "You keep a record of everybody who goes through here. Couldn't you check the record?"

The soldier says, "I only have a record of what I have seen during this shift.

If you want more information you can ask the Captain of the Guard tomorrow. He may be willing to have someone look it up for you. It would help if you had the names of the people you are looking for. Please move along now. We're awfully busy. People are waiting. Lots of people want to attend the execution ceremonies at Divinity City."

Leander says, "Tell me more about the execution ceremonies at Divinity City. Who is going to be executed?"

The guard says, "Lots of people. It happens once a year. The government of the Alliance executes criminals. For them, that includes people like you and your son. They don't like Eldens. I suppose you know that."

Leander asks, "What day do they do this?"

The guard says, "They start doing it on Greening sixteen. It is a ceremony that lasts several days. Many will be executed. Lots of other things will be happening because so many people gather to see it. I didn't think that you would be going there."

Leander says, "Thank you for the information."

Leander, Amrath, Nick, and Helena move on. They find a place to get a meal and sleep for the night.

While they are eating, Nick says, "I don't think we're going to meet up with the other group. We should plan on going right on to Divinity City. That is where we'll find Robert Swift, if he's alive."

Amrath says, "That's still just speculation. I want to find Tiarra and the others I started out with. They may know where Robert Swift really is."

Leander says, "The guard at the gate referred to execution ceremonies at Divinity City. I've heard about that, but I don't know much about it. We need to know more. It seems like this is just about to happen."

Helena says, "I know about that. As the guard said, The Festival of Light begins on Greening sixteen. It lasts six days. That is when the executions take place. This festival is the only time of year that common people can freely enter Divinity City. At other times, no one enters or leaves without showing proper identification. Many people converge on the city during this festival to see the executions, celebrate, and trade. Shops are open. Many goods are bought and sold. The people who will be killed are kept prisoner in the large tower at the center of the city. As you have seen, it attracts people from a very wide area including the eastern part of the Kingdom of Ezrada."

Nick says, "Then it starts only four days from now. It will probably be underway when we get there. You should have told us about this before."

Helena says, "I assumed that you knew."

Leander says, "If we go there. I would rather intercept Tiarra's group here and find out what they know. We may not all need to go there. It is my understanding that Aaron, Johanna, and Tamaranis are Humans. So are you and Nick. The five of you should be enough to go to Divinity City and find out if Robert Swift is there. Eldens and Dwarves should stay here until you get back."

Nick says, "That might work if we are able to link up with them. Right now that seems unlikely. They must have gone somewhere else. The others could disguise themselves but certainly a Dwarf wouldn't be going into The People's Republic."

Leander says, "I'll think about that. We'll know more after we see the Captain of the Guard in the morning. Amrath, I want you and Nick to stand near the gate tonight. Stay as long as there are people coming through. You have both seen the members of Tiarra's group and should recognize them. If you see them, bring them here."

Amrath says, "I can also recognize their horses. But first I have to go to Althen and tell Sarah what happened today."

Leander says, "I'll take care of that. Eat quickly now, they may be coming through the gate this very minute."

Nick and Amrath do eat quickly, taking some of their food with them.

Amrath says to Nick, "My father should have told us to stay near the gate right after we came through. He could have brought us something to eat. We may have missed them."

Nick says, "I don't think they'll be coming through here."

The guard on duty tells them, "You can't stay here. It is against the rules to loiter near the gate."

Nick says, "We are looking for someone to come in that we want to meet here. Remember us? We just came through the gate a little while ago. Have you seen a Dwarf come through hear since then?"

The guard says, "No, I didn't. But you can't stay here. If you want to look for the Dwarf you'll have to be somewhere else. You are not allowed to linger here."

Nick and Amrath stand in an alley a short distance from the gate where they think that their presence will not bother anybody. They can hardly be seen but they have a good view of anyone who is coming through the gate. The guards don't even seem to know that they are there.

Meanwhile Leander composes a progress report message and magically Transfers it to Sarah's dining room. Well after dark, when travelers seem to have stopped coming through the gate, Amrath and Nick go to the inn. Leander and Helena are waiting in the dining room. There is little to discuss. They all go to bed and get some sleep.

Chapter Thirteen

The Magic Eye

Freya's Day - Greening Thirteen – at Eastgate

In the morning Nick and Amrath go back to their place just inside the gate where they can watch for Aaron, Tiarra, Eridana, Johanna, Tamaranis, and Reuben to come into the city. Leander and Helena find the office of the Captain of the Guard. It takes two and a half hours of waiting, but they finally get an answer. "No Dwarf named Reuben has entered the city in the last three days. In fact, no Dwarf at all has entered the city for several weeks, and probably even longer."

Leander pays three gold pieces for this information.

"I should also tell you that Eldens and Spellcasters are not allowed to enter Beastgate. You, sir, look like you could be both. I hope you are not planning to go there. Also, for you lady, any magic you might want to carry to Beastgate will be confiscated at the entry gate. If you plan to go there, you better leave any magic that you have with your Elden friend and he should wait for you here."

Leander says, "We are not headed for The People's Republic. But thank you for explaining this to us."

The Captain says, "What if the people you are looking for went there?"

Leander says, "It is our intent to meet them here. Apparently we arrived in Eastgate ahead of them. We'll spend a few days here. They'll probably get here today or tomorrow."

Leander and Helena find Nick and Amrath in the alley near the gate and let them know what they have learned.

Nick reports, "We haven't seen any of the people we are looking for enter the city this morning. Of course it's early. Almost everybody we've seen are leaving, not entering. No six people rode through on horseback with three pack animals. We're wasting our time here now. Most of the people heading east will be arriving at the gate in the afternoon, probably late afternoon."

Helena says, "According to the Captain's records no Dwarf has entered Eastgate for weeks. Maybe they're not going this way. They started before we did. They should be ahead of us, not behind us."

Leander says, "We need to make a new plan. Let's go back to our rooms where we can talk freely."

Helena says, "And more comfortably."

They have noticed that there are several shops on the main street that sell magic. Amrath wants to go back and see what is for sale. It occurs to him that the price of magic might be lower here than in most places he has been. But first they go to their inn.

When they are in Leander's room at the inn, Amrath says, "We must have lost them. Where else could they have gone?"

Helena says, "It doesn't really matter. Our true objective is Robert Swift. That's who Sarah Swift hired me to bring back. If the Keepers have Robert Swift they may have taken him to Divinity City for execution during the festival, which will be starting in just three days. We should go there. If Robert Swift is brought out for execution we can try to save him. One of you Spellcasters can magically Transfer him back to Althen."

Leander says, "Ahh, but it would be very risky for Amrath and I to go there. We are both Eldens and Spellcasters. It is likely that the Keepers would notice us long before we got to Divinity City. We would never make it."

Nick says, "You could wear disguises."

Helena says, "Yes. We can all go. Nick and I are Humans. All you Eldens have to do is cover up your ears and wear different clothes. You don't have to look like Spellcasters. Maybe Amrath's Imp of Wishes could transform you into something that doesn't look like a Spellcaster and doesn't have pointy ears. Then you could come with us."

Amrath says, "You mean make myself look a Human. That's a good idea."

Leander says, "Stop! Wishes are tricky. I have a spell that could transform me to look like a Human fighter and go along for a while, but that spell doesn't last more than four hours. That's out. Of course if you use your Imp to wish yourself to look Human, it might last forever. Is that what you want? I'm not going to let you do it to me."

Amrath says, "All I would have to do is wish myself back into my present Elden form when I want to."

Leander says, "Assuming that you still have your Imp of Wishes and it recognizes you as still being its owner."

Amrath says, "Why wouldn't it?"

Leander says, "It probably would if you stated your wish correctly, including all the necessary caveats. The source of wishes usually takes things very literally, and will sometimes interpret your wish in a different way than intended. You can try it if you want to but know that you are taking a big risk. You might not get it right."

Amrath remembers the time he used the Imp of Wishes and found himself standing on the limb of a tree, and had to quickly grab the trunk to avoid falling off. He says, "I'd get it right if you helped me."

Leander says, "It's too risky. You better stay here with me."

Nick asks, "Couldn't you cast your Transform spell and then magically Transfer yourselves there?"

Leander says, "The rule of Transference Spells is that a Spellcaster can't Transfer anybody, not even himself, to a place he has never been, but I have a way around that. I have a Magic Eye that allows me to see places that I have never been. The problem is that someone must carry it there. It doesn't go there by itself. I can't magically Transfer it there. Someone must carry it there, set it up, and actuate it. Once activated, I can see what it sees and I can magically Transfer myself to a location that is seen by the Magic Eye."

Nick says, "I suppose you want me to carry your Magic Eye to Divinity City and activate it in some location that you can Transfer yourself to."

Leander says, "Something like that. You and Helena should be able to move about in The People's Republic with little difficulty. If you can find Robert Swift I could magically Transfer Amrath and myself there and then Transfer him back to Althen. Then Amrath could use his Imp of Wishes to get us all out of there, probably to Althen as well."

Nick says, "So Helena and I take most of the risk while you and Amrath get most of the glory."

Leander says, "I'm not doing this for glory. You can have that as far as I'm concerned. I want to save Robert Swift if I can. You have abilities I don't have. I have abilities you don't have. We have to work cooperatively to a common purpose if we are going to succeed. Of course you could go to Divinity City without us and do the best you can if you want to, but this Magic Eye will, in effect, bring us to where you are–to help you when you need our help, if you don't need our help, so much the better for me. When the Magic Eye has been activated I will know it. Unless deactivated sooner it will stay activated for one hour; then it will stop. It is possible that someone might discover it. That could cause problems. I would hate to lose it. If you activate it, you must defend it and, if necessary, deactivate it to prevent it from being noticed by anybody else. I will try to get us there as soon as I can after you activate it."

Helena asks, "What does it look like?"

Leander takes what looks like an egg out of his pouch. He divides the eggshell into two parts without smashing it at all. Within is a device that looks like a slightly elongated eyeball about an inch in diameter. The pupil seems to be at one end of it. When he puts it on the table it pivots slowly in a clockwise direction, all by itself.

Leander says, "It was activated when I took it out of its case. If I close my eyes I can see what it sees."

Leander closes his eyes for about thirty seconds.

"I know it is activated because I hear a slight buzz in my head. The buzz is a kind of a nuisance, which gives me an extra incentive to go where it is and turn it off. I don't understand what makes it work, but that is how it is meant to be used."

Helena asks, "How does it make a buzz in your head and no one else's?"

Leander says, "I guess that's because I own it. I found it among other treasures of an evil Spellcaster that a group of us destroyed. I didn't know what it was. When I opened the case I heard the buzz and realized that the eyeball was doing it. My Analyze Magic spell gave me the details but didn't tell me any more than what I have told you. I expect that it will work for me and only for me as long as I live."

Amrath says, "I didn't know you had a Magic Eye."

Leander says, "Not many people do. It is best to keep it that way. There are some who would kill me to get it, but that's not what I did. I didn't know the evil Spellcaster had this before we killed him."

Nick says, "Well, all right then. Helena, are you willing to go with me to try to find Robert Swift in Divinity City?"

Helena says, "I'll go. That is what I hired on to do. I think we have a better chance of getting Swift out with magic help. I'll carry the Magic Eye."

Nick looks at her as if he had expected to carry it.

He says, "All right if you want to."

Leander says, "It's best if you can put it on a level place like a table or a flat rock so that it can pivot and I can get a full view of where I will be magically transferring myself to."

Helena says, "I understand. Give me the case."

Leander hands the case to Helena. She puts the Magic Eye into the case and the case into her shoulder pouch.

Leander says, "Thank you. That stopped the buzzing."

Nick says, "By the way, who was the Spellcaster you killed to get this Magic Eye?"

Leander says, "I'd rather not say."

Helena says, "Let's get going, Nick. The sooner we start the sooner we get Robert Swift safely home. I presume you know what he looks like."

Nick says, "I presume he still looks like the picture Sarah showed us in her dining room."

Leander says, "Then you will be able to recognize him."

Nick says, "I think so. But there is one more small problem. Maybe you can use your magic to deal with it. Helena and I both have some magic weapons to take with us into The People's Republic. I've been there once before but not with anything magic. They check you for magic at the gate. This time I would like to have my magic with me. I have an idea how to do it. It would also be a good chance to test out your Magic Eye, to make sure it works the way it's supposed to."

Leander says, "I know how it works. I've used it before."

Nick says, "Okay. Anyway – let's try this. Helena and I will leave our magic weapons with you. Then the only magic thing we'll need to sneak past the guards with is the Magic Eye. Once we get there, we find a secluded place, set it up, and you bring our magic weapons to us. Then you Transfer yourselves back to Eastgate."

Leander says, "We can do that. Give me your magic weapons. What do you have?"

Helena says, "I have a Magic Hammer, a Magic Sling, a Ring of Protection, and Magic Leather Armor. It would be less risky for me if you brought all that over the river by using your Transference Spell."

Nick says, "I have a Cloak of Blending, Boots of Silence, a Magic Bow, a Magic Longsword, Magic Lock-picks, and a Magic Belt that does the same thing that Helena's Magic Leather Armor does, keeps me from being hit so often."

Leander says, "All right. That's a lot of stuff. I suppose you'll want to buy some non-magical weapons and clothes to take with you when you cross the border."

Nick says, "Just boots and a sword of some kind. What do you need Helena?"

"Some kind of a weapon I guess. A staff will do. I don't really need that. A woman doesn't always carry a weapon. I'll have my knife, that's not magic."

Nick says, "You would look more like a woman if you wore a dress."

Helena says, "I could, but it's not necessary. I don't really care if I look like a woman right now. Female adventurers usually don't wear dresses for practical reasons. There's nothing wrong with that."

Nick says, "But we are going into The People's Republic. Female adventurers are very uncommon there."

Helena says, "I'm not going very far without my Magic Hammer. A woman carrying a hammer looks like an adventuress no matter what kind of clothes she is wearing. If you want me to go with you, this is what I'm going to look like. Can you live with that?"

"Yes, for now, but it would be less risk for both of us if you wore an ordinary dress and I carried your hammer for you when we are in The People's Republic. Think about it. We would attract a lot less attention."

Helena says, "You would attract less attention if you wore something different from that totally black outfit you like so well. That outfit exclaims 'Thief! Thief!' Just as if you were a bluejay. I'll wear a common dress if you'll wear something a lot more common yourself."

Nick says, "Point taken. These black clothes make it very hard for anyone to see me at night. That's why I wear them. Besides, I look good in black."

Helena says, "And I think I look good in the clothes I'm wearing. My offer stands. You change your clothes and I'll change mine."

Nick says, "All right. Let's go shopping then and buy some clothes."

Amrath says, "Good. I want to visit the Magic shops."

Leander says, "No, Amrath, you need to go at once to the alley near the gate to look for Aaron, Tiarra, and your other friends. They might still be coming through here. I'll go to the magic shops. I'll tell you what I see."

Amrath groans. "But I want to visit the magic shops too."

Leander says, "You know what your friends look like. I don't. Go to the same place where you were earlier this morning and stay there."

Amrath goes to the same place near the bridge where he and Nick were earlier and keeps an eye on the people coming through the gate. Leander, Nick, and Helena go to a pawnshop to buy some used boots, a mundane looking longsword for Nick, a cheap pair of boots for Helena, and a canvas bag big enough to hold all the magic that will be left behind, temporarily. Helena decides she doesn't need to carry a staff across the bridge.

Then at the inn Nick and Helena change into clothes that are somewhat more ordinary looking. It turns out they both had some other clothes in their backpacks anyway. Helena's dress is not the usual apparel for women that Nick expected. It is a split skirt that comes down to her knees over tight hose, decent for riding horseback, but she still looks like an adventuress. Nick looks much more ordinary with a gray shirt and brown trousers.

They put most of their magic in Helena's backpack and give it to Leander. The Magic Bow, Magic Longsword, and Magic Hammer go into the canvas bag.

As they leave, Helena says, "I was planning to wear this dress anyway. I have to wear something else while Leander has my Magic Armor."

Nick says, "Why did you make such a fuss about it then?"

Helena says, "It was fun. Besides, I wanted to make a point."

Nick says, "You still look like an adventurer."

Helena says, "I look like a woman ready to ride in the hunt."

Leander asks, "How are you going to get the magic eye past the guards at the gate?"

Helena says, "It's not very big. I'll find a place to put it, maybe under my left armpit. I'll put it in a little bag with a string to go over my shoulder under my dress.

Nick says, "Good idea. That should work. The guards won't make you take your dress off.

Nick and Helena decide not to take the packhorse with them. They each tie their bedrolls and tents to their horses, right behind their saddles. They put a little food in their saddlebags. They don't take any cooking dishes. Within twenty minutes Nick and Helena are on their way across the bridge over the Beast River. They have no trouble at the gates. They have started out well behind most of the travelers who left Beastgate that morning, so they pass only a few other travelers, going in either direction, most of them riders coming toward them. The road beyond Beastgate is bordered by well-kept farmland. They are looking for an open area in a secluded grove where they can set up the Magic Eye.

They find such a place after about an hour of travel. It is a very small clearing at the top of a small steep hill surrounded by bushes and trees that grow on the slopes. Helen puts the magic eye on a tall level rock where it turns with no chance of falling off. Leander and Amrath appear within five minutes with Helena's backpack and the canvas bag of magic weapons. Five minutes after that, Leander and Amrath are back in Eastgate.

Nick and Helena put most of their magic items into the saddlebags of their horses. Then they mount and ride their horses toward Divinity City, trotting about half the time and walking the other half. They are making good time without tiring their horses. They have no difficulty fording the several small streams that cross the road. At about noon they meet several wagons coming from the direction of Divinity City, a large group that would have left early that morning from perhaps the town of Tyman, which, according to their map, is halfway between Beastgate and Divinity City. They are now beyond the farmland, so trees border the road. They pull off for a few minutes to eat a quick cold lunch.

A heavy thunderstorm breaks about a half-hour later while they are crossing a somewhat larger than usual stream using an old stone bridge. The storm slows them down because they don't like to trot in heavy rain. They stop to put their canvas ground cloths over their shoulders; which shed much of the rain. It is a really heavy deluge that lasts for more than an hour. The road becomes very muddy so they leave it for the cover of nearby trees. They will continue after it stops raining.

Standing on the ground Helena feels the earth vibrate. She says, "Nick, did you feel that? The ground moved."

Nick says, "I felt it. I've felt it before, years ago. I don't like it. It's a bad omen. The gods are angry."

Helena says, "It happened in The People's Republic. Do you think it happened because the Gods are angry with how they persecute other races and people who use magic?"

Nick says, "Maybe. It's right before the festival when they do the executions. I've heard that sometimes these vibrations are so strong that buildings fall down. Maybe the tower in Divinity City has cracked open and the prisoners are free to escape."

Helena says, "If the tower falls, most of the people in it will be killed."

Nick says, "Sometimes no buildings are damaged."

Helena says, "So we continue on. If the tower still stands, we have to find Robert Swift and get him out."

Nick says, "That's right."

When it stops raining they check the condition of the road. It is still very bad so they walk their horses beside it on better-drained rocky higher ground.

Night falls well before they get to Tyman. They camp at a grove of trees near a small pond, make a fire, erect their tents, and try to dry out their ground cloths, blankets, and clothes.

Helena says, "I'm a light sleeper. I think we can both sleep through the night. If anything strange happens, I'll notice it."

Nick says, "I'm a light sleeper too. I agree. I usually wake up at the slightest unusual sound. It's a special ability I seem to have been born with."

They each wake up several times during the night to add wood to the fire and make sure that the horses are all right.

Amrath spends the day near the gate watching for the people he traveled with from Althen into the Forest of Ereba. Leander stays with him most of the time, although he does take a break to visit the magic shops. He buys another book of Endless Pages for Amrath and makes a list of other things he thinks Amrath might like to have.

Amrath is delighted with the magic book. He looks at the list. "Go back and buy the Ring of Transference. I don't need it now, but I will when I have to give up my Imp of Wishes."

Leander goes back, but by then the ring has been sold. He does stay with Amrath near the gate as long as people are coming through. They don't see a Dwarf. They don't see anybody who looks like Tiarra, Eridana, Johanna, Aaron, or Tamaranis either.

Amrath says, "The others might be hard to recognize if they are wearing different clothes, but I can't imagine that I would not recognize Tamaranis. He's quite unusual looking. I almost never see an Elden either, certainly none that look anything like Tiarra or Eridana."

Leander tells Amrath, "I don't think we will need the packhorse and what it is carrying anymore. We will use Transfer spells to get from here to Divinity city. We won't be sleeping outdoors and we won't need to cook. Let's transfer the packhorse and extra gear back to Sarah Swift.

Before going to bed, Amrath uses a Transfer Spell to send another progress report to Sarah Swift. Then he uses another Transfer Spell to send the lightly loaded packhorse.

Dear Sarah,

> *Leander and I are still at Eastgate. We spent the day watching for Tiarra, Eridana, Johanna, Reuben, and Aaron to enter Eastgate. We didn't see them. This morning Helena and Nick went on across the river into The People's Republic, headed for Divinity City. We think that your father, Robert Swift, may be being held in the dungeon there, but we don't know for certain. We hope that Nick can use his sneaking and detecting abilities to find out. If he needs our help, Leander and I will find a way to get there and help get your*

father free and back home again. We have to be careful because Eldens and Spellcasters are arrested and put in prison for execution when found in The People's Republic. But we are willing to take the risk. We will probably have to use disguises of some kind. We won't need the packhorse anymore so I am transferring it back to you.

Your eager servant,
Amrath Darkriver
Greening 13

PART FOUR
IN THE PEOPLE'S REPUBLIC

CHAPTER FOURTEEN

EASTGATE

Freya's Day - Greening Thirteen – Early Morning

Aaron, Tiarra, Eridana, Johanna, Tamaranis, and Ruby have not slept well, but the rain finally ended during the last watch. The morning starts out clear, calm, fresh, and beautiful, but there are some puddles and the grass is wet. Ruby and Tamaranis, who have been on watch, are looking at the campfire but not talking to each other very much. There is a pot of hot cereal hanging over the flames. It appears that Ruby and Tamaranis have already eaten breakfast. The others help themselves.

Tiarra and Eridana try to do an especially good job at helping Johanna and Aaron put on their makeup. They expect to be passing through Eastgate and Beastgate today. The guards must believe that Aaron and Johanna look old enough to have adult children. As soon as the canvas is dry they pack up their tents, bedrolls, and cooking gear, then move on. The Red Haze follows. Johanna rides in the wagon, while all the others walk.

Ruby can't keep from thinking about Tamaranis's suggestion that she let him kiss her. He should never have suggested such a thing. He, of all people should know better. *I can't do that. Yes, I might like it. I might like it too much. But I can't do it. It would be wrong. I'm a man. I'm not supposed to kiss a man on the lips. It is not done. I don't even want to think about it.*

But she does keep thinking about it. She feels angry with Tamaranis for suggesting it. *If he hadn't asked me to do it I wouldn't even be thinking about this. It's his fault.*

They soon see a green and yellow flag flying just above the horizon. As they get closer they also see a stone tower and red tile rooftops of a city ahead of them.

Tamaranis says, "My friends, that is the flag of Ezrada. We must be approaching Beastgate. We are about to cross into Alliance territory."

Eridana says, "I thought Beastgate was in The People's Republic. That should be a blue and gold flag."

Tamaranis says, "There are two cities here, my friends, although at one time many years ago there was only one - sitting on an Island in the Beast River. The green and yellow flag that you see flies from the City of Eastgate on the west side of the river in Ezrada. Beastgate is on the east side of the river in The People's Republic. We should see their blue and gold flag when we are crossing the river. The Island itself is neutral territory. The city that was once there was demolished several hundred years ago. You'll see. We'll soon be crossing the bridge from Eastgate to the Island and then from the Island into Beastgate. Beastgate is by far the larger city."

Eridana asks, "Have you been here before?"

Tamaranis says, "No, but I've read about it."

When they get closer, they see the walls of the City of Eastgate, twenty feet high. They see a single gate flanked by two taller towers. Other towers rise above the walls at intervals of about one-hundred-and-fifty feet. This is simply the outer defense. The much larger tower and the flag they had seen from a distance are on the east side of the city near the river. Some of the other towers also have green and yellow flags flying above them. They are approaching from the north. It looks as if there is another gate for the road that approaches from the west.

Tiarra says, "There will probably be another gate near the middle of the south wall, and a fourth gate on the east edge of the city that will lead to the Island and The People's Republic. This is the most heavily fortified city I have ever seen."

Aaron says, "It is certainly more strongly built than either Exodus or Ashua."

There are no buildings outside the wall, just farmland. Apparently the farmers who use it live in the city of Eastgate. Several soldiers with green and yellow tabards are standing just outside the gate.

Tiarra says, "When we are inside the city we must do our very best at pretending to be a woodcutter family. The streets will probably be full of people who might overhear anything we say. We can't take a chance that someone who thinks we are not who we are pretending to be will report us to the guards or to the secret police of the Alliance. Before you make any conversation think about whether or not it is consistent with the role you are playing. If it isn't, don't say it. It will be better to say too little than to spill the beans."

Aaron says, "Tiarra is right. I'm playing the role of the father. I'll do most of the talking."

They are approaching the north gate, which is different from the west gate that Amrath, Leander, Nick, and Helena used to enter the city.

There are no travelers in sight on the road ahead of them or behind them. When they reach the gate, one of the soldiers asks them to stop.

Aaron asks, "What's the problem?"

The soldier says, "No problem. I'm just writing down the names of people entering Eastgate today. Your name, please."

"My name is George Wood. This is my family."

The soldier says, "I don't recognize you. Do you live around here?"

"It has taken me two days to get here. We live at the edge of the forest northeast of Exodus."

The soldier says, "Most of the people from that far away spend the night in town."

"We didn't make it last night. We didn't want to spend money for an inn anyway. We brought tents to sleep under."

The soldier says, "Where are you going?"

"We are headed for the festival at Divinity City."

The soldier says, "One of those groups. A lot of people are headed for the festival. We had a crowd of them last night, some of them after dark - just the six of you, right? I'll need each person's name."

Aaron says, "My wife's name is Johanna. My children are Ruby, and Jessica. My male servant's name is Thomas Clerkin. My female servant's name is Emily Herds."

The soldier is writing. When finished he says, "All right. Be on your way, then. I've got all the information I need."

Aaron leads the horse and wagon through the gate onto the paved street. The woodcutter family looks in awe at the two-story and three-story buildings that line both sides of the street. Some are four stories high. While such buildings are common for any large city, only Tiarra and Aaron have ever been in a city this large before. Shopkeepers display much of their merchandise at the edge of the street, which is already crowded with walking and standing people. Everybody seems to be talking. It is a noisy place.

Tiarra notices that the Red Haze does not follow them into the city, but she doesn't tell the others. She thinks, *I know that people other than our group don't see it. If other people hear me say something about it, they might think I'm crazy.*

As soon as they are out of hearing of the soldiers Johanna says, "George, stop. I've got to tell you something."

Aaron says, "Tell me."

Johanna says, "It's private."

Aaron stops and walks back to Johanna. Johanna gets off the wagon. Tiarra, Tamaranis, Ruby, and Eridana circle around.

Johanna says in a subdued tone, "You told the soldier that my name is Johanna. It's supposed to be Mary."

Aaron grimaces. "I'm sorry. It should be okay though. It's a reasonable name."

Johanna whispers, "I know, but now you have to be consistent. You have to tell each soldier who asks that my name is Johanna."

Aaron whispers, "I know, but this isn't a good place to talk about it. We're on a busy street. We all know about it. If you want to talk about it more we can do that later, in a more quiet place."

Tiarra says firmly, "I want to talk about it more as soon as we can."

Aaron says. "All right. Let's get going."

Johanna climbs back on the wagon and they continue on, looking like country hicks - whether they realize it or not. They are all feeling anxious and uncomfortable, not just because they don't like the city, they are afraid that their true identities may be discovered.

Eridana says, "I don't like it here. It's too closed in and crowded with people." She thinks, *What I just said is alright. It's consistent with my role.*

Ruby says, "I don't like it either."

Tamaranis says, "None of us like it, but we won't be in the city very long. We should be back on the open road long before noon."

While there are many pedestrians, there don't seem to be many travelers on the street. They notice several shops advertising the buying and selling of magic. They make their way through light traffic to a four-way intersection. A sign indicates that they must turn left to go to Beastgate and turn right to go to Exodus. Going straight ahead would take them to the City of Jen.

Tiarra says, "Turn left."

Aaron says, "I know."

They turn left. They are soon going in the direction of the larger tower on the east side of the city. They pass many other multi-story buildings. After a time Johanna sees another gate ahead with soldiers dressed in green and yellow. Aaron stops when he gets to them, expecting questions.

A man dressed in the fine clothes of a merchant is with the soldiers. He says, "I suppose you are going to the festival at Divinity City."

Aaron says, "That's right."

The man says, "I suppose you know that no magic is allowed in The People's Republic. If you have any magic you should not take it with you. I'll be glad to buy it from you. If you don't want to sell it, I'll keep it safe for you for a small fee. You can pick it up on your way back to your home. Do you have any magic with you?"

Aaron says, "Magic is expensive. Do we look like we could afford to own magic?"

The man says, "I'm only trying to help. I hate to see nice magical items taken into The People's Republic, confiscated, and destroyed, when good people here in Ezrada would love to have them, and be glad to buy them."

Aaron says, "We don't have any magic."

One of the soldiers motions them to move on through, saying, "You are free to move on."

So they move on.

They have left the shops, residences, and crowds of people and their noise behind them. Now on the north side of the paved road is a large fort with very high towers. Tiarra thinks that it could be a Thane's castle. On the south side is an empty, rectangular parade ground. It's borders include the big fortress at the north edge, smaller walls on its western and southern borders, and the east wall ahead of them which is somewhat more substantial than the other walls. The road leads to a gate in the east wall. This gate is much more substantial than the one through which they entered the city from the north. There are no other travelers near them, but they see a canvas covered wagon about one hundred feet ahead.

Aaron stops. He says, "There are no wagons or people near us now to hear us. We can talk freely. Gather around."

Johanna gets down from the wagon to join the group on the ground.

Aaron says, "I want to apologize to all of you now. I gave the guard at the gate the wrong name for Johanna. I'm sorry. I won't make that kind of mistake again. When we go through the next gate I will use the same name for her, Johanna. Don't be surprised or worry about it if you notice."

Tiarra says, "I told you to be careful, Aaron. That was a dumb mistake. This isn't going to work if you can't get our names right every time."

Aaron says, "I know. I apologized. It won't happen again."

Eridana says, "It was an easy slip of the tongue. It won't do any harm. Any one of us could have made a mistake like that."

Tiarra says, "I wouldn't have."

Tamaranis says, "Enough! It happened. It's not a problem. Let's forget about it."

Tiarra says, "I'm afraid Aaron is going to make a slip again. Maybe the next time it will be more serious. I wish someone else could be our spokesman."

Tamaranis says, "I would have done it right if I had been allowed to pose as the father, but it's too late for that now. Aaron is our spokesman. I'm comfortable with that. Having made one little mistake, I'm sure Aaron will be extra careful from now on."

Eridana says, "This castle is intimidating. I don't like it."

Johanna says, "I bet there are soldiers with crossbows right on the other side of its walls. If the word was given, we could all be killed in less than a minute."

Tamaranis says, "Of course. This is a killing ground. If soldiers of the Alliance were to use this bridge to attack Ezrada they would first have to get through the gate just ahead of us. Then they would have to pass within fifty yards of this castle before they could try to force their way through the next gate. Missiles from here and also from the opposite wall would descend upon them. These are very strong defenses. It shows the extreme animosity between the people of Ezrada and of The People's Republic. This hostile relationship has existed for a very long time. The gate behind us, and especially the gate just ahead of us, is designed to keep people of the Alliance out of Ezrada, especially the Keepers. There is very little trust between Ezrada and The People's Republic. The history books tell of several battles fought at this location. When the Keepers want to enter Ezrada, they don't do it here. They find some other place to sneak across the river, which is quite swift and dangerous to cross without a bridge. Ezrada has guard posts at intervals along the river, and so does the People's Alliance on the other side. There is only one other bridge between Ezrada and The People's Republic, the one much further north between Doomgate and Todd. That one is fortified too."

Eridana says, "Then we will have to answer questions at this gate when we return so that they can make sure we are not Keepers."

Tamaranis says, "Yes, but they won't care if we have magic and Eldens will be welcome."

Ruby asks, "What about Dwarves?"

Tamaranis says, "Dwarves, Eldens, Half-Eldens, Magic Users, and Healers will be welcome at the gate on this side of the river but should not be seen at the gate on the other side. That is where the problem is."

They move ahead. The canvas covered wagon is about two hundred feet ahead of them now. It stops at the east gate briefly, and then moves onto the wooden bridge just beyond. Another wagon is fairly close behind them. They also see a few riders on horseback. Apparently they are joining into a procession of travelers that started this morning from Eastgate and are headed for Beastgate or beyond.

When the wagon Johanna is riding on gets to the gate, one of the soldiers asks Aaron to stop.

The soldier says, "You are about to leave Ezrada and go into The People's Republic. We have no restrictions regarding that, but I am required to warn you that if you intend to return to Ezrada through this gate you will need proper identification."

Aaron asks, "What will I need?"

The soldier says, "You will need a brass pass. I can sell you one. The fee is one piece of silver."

Aaron asks, "One piece of silver for each one of us? That is very expensive."

The soldier says, "No. One brass pass will allow all of you to return, as long as you stay together."

Aaron says, "That is our intention. He takes a silver coin from his money pouch and gives it to the soldier.

The soldier says, "Your name, please."

"George Wood."

The soldier says to a clerk sitting at a small desk nearby, "George Wood, total of six people with a horse, wagon, and a pack mule. Identification pass number three hundred and sixty-six, series GW."

He gives Aaron a square slab of brass about a sixteenth of an inch thick and one-and-a-half inches across. The number three hundred sixty-six is stamped on one side. The letters GW and an ornate symbol are stamped on the other. It looks like a picture of a square knot. The slab has a hole in one corner with a loop of leather cord long enough to go around Aaron's neck.

"Make sure you don't lose this. It will save you a lot of time when you come back through. You will have to return the medallion and you won't get your silver piece back when you come back through, but the cost is well worth it. Consider it a toll for using the bridge. I will need the names of the other members of your party."

Aaron says, "This is my wife, Johanna; my daughters, Ruby and Jessica; my servant, Thomas Clerkin, and my other servant, Emily Herds."

The clerk reads the names back. "George, Johanna, Ruby, and Jessica Wood. Also Thomas Clerkin and Emily Herds."

Aaron says, "That's right".

The soldier who asked the questions says, "You may go now."

Aaron puts the leather string of the medallion around his neck.

CHAPTER FIFTEEN

ARRIVING AT BEASTGATE

Freya's Day - Greening Thirteen – Morning

Aaron leads the horse and wagon through the gate and onto the bridge. It is a high wooden bridge at least one hundred feet above the water and more than one hundred feet long. The guardrails consist of thin poles supported by posts about eight feet apart. It looks as if a person could easily fall under the pole into the water below. Everyone feels apprehensive about the possibility of falling off the bridge.

Aaron guides Toby, the horse pulling the wagon, to walk in the middle of the bridge except when another wagon passes them going in the other direction. Then he has to move the wagon to the right side of the travel way. Thankfully, they only have to pass two wagons. When they do Aaron glances back at Johanna. She is sitting on the left side of the seat and holding very tightly to it with both hands. Tiarra and Tamaranis feel fairly safe walking on the left side of Toby, but Ruby and Eridana, who have been walking on the right side of Toby fall back and walk behind the wagon rather than next to the outer edge of the bridge.

Johanna says, "There must be a better way than this to get to Divinity City. What if the right side wheel fell off the wagon? What would happen to me?"

Aaron asks, "Would you like to walk for a while?"

Johanna says, "Yes. Stop the wagon."

Johanna walks with Ruby and Eridana behind the wagon.

Beyond the bridge is a tall stone viaduct built upon an island in the river. The guardrails beside the road are solid stone walls about four feet high. Everyone feels much safer. There are no buildings on the island, just some rubble remaining from buildings that were there at one time. Most of the stone from those buildings was probably used in construction of the walls and buildings on both sides of the river.

The canvas-covered wagon is now about one hundred and fifty feet ahead of them, and another wagon is even further ahead.

Beyond the island, on the mainland, is another large gate that must be the entrance to Beastgate. The gates on each side of the river are about five hundred feet apart. Aaron and the others can see the blue and gold flags flying from most of the many towers ahead of them. There is another wooden bridge about one hundred feet long just before the gate, which is high above the river. They see no other bridges. It looks as if heavy chains can be used to tilt a short section of this bridge platform upward toward the other side, but now it is down. A twenty-foot high stone wall borders the east side of the river for several hundred feet in both directions.

The canvas-covered wagon ahead of them stops at the other side of the second wooden bridge, fully within the east side tower. A movable wooden bar prevents it from moving further. Several soldiers wearing blue and gold tabards over their chainmail are standing near the bar.

Tiarra says, "Be careful what you say, George. If we are going to have any trouble, this is where it will be."

Aaron says, "I know you would rather be our spokesman, Jessica, but I can handle this. Just make sure you give the right answer if they ask you a question. Be humble if you can."

Tiarra says, "I can play my role."

Only Aaron and Tamaranis have weapons at hand. Aaron has his staff and a sheath knife. Tamaranis has only the knife at his belt. Aaron brings Toby to a halt right behind the covered wagon ahead of them. Johanna climbs back onto the wagon.

From here they can all hear what the soldier is saying as he communicates with the five people, three men and two women, now standing beside the wagon in front of them. This soldier has a more ornate helmet than the others, which probably means that he is of higher rank.

One of the men with the wagon is saying, "We only intend to be in Divinity City for the festival. When it's over, we will be returning home this same way."

The soldier asks, "What are you bringing with you in the wagon?"

The same man says, "Mostly personal belongings. Those bundles are tanned hides we hope to sell. We have bedrolls. Some of us sleep in the wagon; some of us sleep in a tent. We were afraid the inns would be crowded."

The soldier says, "You're probably right."

A different soldier climbs up onto the wagon just enough to get a good look inside under the canvas cover through the front opening where the seat should be. He doesn't go inside. He steps back down. He says, "I don't see any problem here."

The lead soldier says, "All right. Everything seems to be okay. You can move along now. Go straight ahead until you come to a fork. You will see the sign. Bear left. That road will take you to Divinity City."

Another of the soldiers moves the wooden bar aside so that the wagon can pass. The team of horses pulls the wagon forward, led by the man who did the talking. The others walk alongside, rubbernecking at the sights of the city. They enter what appears to be the main street of the city. Two-story buildings line both sides of the street. Johanna notices that there are other soldiers in the towers, also wearing blue and gold. They are armed with crossbows.

The soldier with the fancy helmet waves for Aaron to bring his wagon ahead. Aaron leads Toby up to the bar, which has been brought back to its usual place.

The soldier says, "All right! Everybody out! I want to get a good look at you."

Johanna steps down.

"Is there anybody else in there?"

Aaron says, "No, there are just the six of us."

"And just who are you?" The soldier seems more than a little overbearing.

Aaron says, "I'm George Wood. This is my wife, Johanna, and my two daughters, Ruby and Jessica. The other woman is my servant, Emily Herds. The other man is another servant, Thomas Clerkin."

"Where are you going?"

Aaron says, "We are going to the festival at Divinity City."

"Do you have any magic with you?"

"No."

"What do you have in the wagon?"

Aaron says, "Personal belongings. We have some wine to sell. We have bedrolls and tents. We sleep in tents. We can't afford to stay at an inn"

"Mind if we take a look?"

Aaron says, "Of course not."

The soldier says, "Climb up in there, Harry. Take a good look around."

One of the other soldiers climbs up onto the front seat of the wagon and goes right into the back.

"There are kegs like he said, prob'ly wine. There are tents and bedrolls and several other sacks. I don't know what's in them."

Aaron says, "That's our food, cooking dishes, and extra clothing."

The soldier with the fancy helmet says, "Look inside one of them."

After a pause: "Women's clothes in this one."

The soldier on the ground says, "How about letting us have one of those kegs of wine, George? We get thirsty."

Aaron says, "I mean to sell that in Divinity City"

The soldier says, "Sell it here. Make it easier on your poor one horse. How much do you want for one?"

Aaron says, "Well – five pieces of silver will do it."

The soldier says, "It's not worth half that. I'll give you one piece of silver."

Aaron says, "Not enough. It's very good wine. How about three silver?"

The soldier says, "Put one of those kegs out here, Harry. Open it up. I want to get a taste of it. Willie and Hank, give him some help. Get around to the back."

Two other soldiers go to the back of the wagon. They take off the plank that serves as a back gate of the wagon. They lift down one of the kegs. Harry jumps out of the wagon. The soldier with the fancy helmet has taken a bung starter and a mug from a backpack near the inside wall of the tower. He tosses the bung starter to Harry, who uses it to drive the bung plug into the keg. Then he and Willie pour some wine from the keg into the cup. The soldier with the fancy helmet tastes it.

"Not bad at all. I'll give you two pieces of silver for this keg and you can be on your way. If not, maybe there is something else in the wagon I can buy."

Aaron thinks, *This is a very low price for a keg of fine wine, but I want to get away from this gate. This is taking too much time and I feel uneasy. I don't want the soldiers to do any more rummaging around in the wagon.* He says, "All right. But I'm giving you a bargain and you know it."

The soldier smiles broadly and gives Aaron two pieces of silver. "I seem to get bargains like this all the time. But don't think I don't appreciate it."

Then, louder, "Everything seems to be okay. Put the plank back on the wagon, Willie."

When Willie and Hank have put the plank back in its place, the boss soldier says, "All right. You can move along now. Go straight ahead until you come to a fork. You will see the sign. Bear left. That road will take you to Divinity City."

Harry moves the wooden bar aside so that the wagon can pass. Johanna climbs back on the seat. Aaron leads Toby forward. The others walk along beside the horse. They are all very glad to be getting past the soldiers at the gate. They enter the main street of the city. Two-story buildings and some three-story buildings line both sides. The street is noisy with walkers and talkers. None of the signs on the shops mention buying or selling magic.

Aaron says, "Don't bother to look at the shops. We're not going to buy anything here."

He doesn't stop anywhere. Nobody says anything. They want to, but they don't want any of the city people to hear what they want to say. They don't talk to anybody.

The covered wagon that went through the gate just before them is about two hundred feet ahead. Another wagon is some distance behind, and there are others behind that. Nobody is coming from the other direction.

When they are a little beyond Beastgate, Tiarra asks, "Why, Aaron, did you spend so much time haggling over the price of a keg of wine? That wine means nothing to us. You should have given it to him."

Aaron says, in an undertone, "Don't talk so loud. My name is George."

Tiarra tries to hide her embarrassment at making such a mistake.

Aaron continues. "If I didn't haggle he would have sensed that something was wrong. He might have made a more thorough search and found something that would have been hard to explain. This way he doesn't suspect anything."

Eridana says, "I knew that, but every minute that he made us wait made me more tense. I was ready to scream."

Aaron says, "I'm glad you didn't."

Johanna says, "You handled it superbly, but I was really worried that something would go wrong."

Tamaranis says, "It seems to have worked out all right. Why fuss about it?"

Tiarra says, "First he uses the wrong name for Johanna. I knew that as soon as he said it but I couldn't say anything to correct it. Then he haggles over the price of wine. It's getting pretty hard for me to keep my temper. That's why I called you Aaron – on purpose. No one was close enough to hear me say it. I'm angry. I wanted to tell that soldier that we would give him the keg of wine as a gift. That's what he expected us to do. We didn't need the two silver coins. What if he had decided to look under the seat to see if we had something even more valuable hidden there that he might want? We could have been in deep, deep trouble."

Aaron is getting angry now. "But that didn't happen! What I did worked out just fine! Just because I didn't do it the way you would have done it doesn't make it wrong. There's more than one way to skin a cat."

Eridana says, "Calm down! Both of you! There **is** more than one way to skin a cat. I think I would have done it different, but it wasn't my call. We got through it okay. Let's forget about it."

Johanna says, "That's right. We've got to stop picking and criticizing or I'm going to go out of my mind. I don't want to hear about this any more."

CHAPTER SIXTEEN

DANGEROUS TERRITORY

Freya's Day - Greening Thirteen – Still Morning

They walk in silence for a while. The tension between Aaron and Tiarra seems to go away, much to the relief of everybody else as well. Tamaranis has chosen to walk beside Ruby, which makes her feel a little uncomfortable. Every time she looks at him she remembers his desire to kiss her and hug her last night. She didn't think about it much during the tension of passing through Eastgate and Beastgate but now she can think of nothing else. It upsets her. She tries to avoid looking at him. She thinks, *I should not keep thinking about this. Why do I feel this way? I hate it. I wish I could be in my own body again. But I know I can't right now. I need to look like a Human.*

Eridana breaks the silence, making an observation about the beauty of the landscape. Johanna agrees. The tension between members of the group seems to have eased.

Tamaranis looks at Ruby and says, "I don't think the people here in The People's Republic look any different than the people we saw in Eastgate, do you?'

Ruby thinks, *This seems like a harmless topic.* She says, "Why would they? They're Humans. Humans should look pretty much the same no matter which part of the island they live at."

Aaron hears. He says, "I agree. They wear the same kind of clothes, carry the same kinds of weapons, and use the same language. It's too bad they hate spellcasters and magic the way they do here. We shouldn't have to wear these disguises."

Tamaranis says, "That's their religion. You know that. They're uncomfortable with magic." He looks toward Ruby. "Most Dwarves are kind of uncomfortable with magic too, but they don't kill people just because they use it."

Ruby doesn't respond. She doesn't want Dwarves to be a topic of discussion.

Tamaranis looks directly at Ruby, "But you don't seem to mind magic at all. Why are you different?"

Ruby says, "I accept it because I'm used to my father's Crossbow. He bought it from Robert Swift to use in the Nog war. My mother told me he was very wary of it at first, but he got used to it. Most Dwarves don't own any magic but some do. It's not against our religion."

Tamaranis says, "People often fear what they don't understand."

Ruby doesn't say anything. They walk in silence for a while.

Then Tamaranis speaks again, trying to keep his voice down this time so that only Ruby will hear him. "It's too bad that Tiarra and Aaron don't get along with each other better. It's because Tiarra wants to be the leader and she can't be right now. I can understand her frustration. I think I should have been the father woodcutter in this group. I'm older than Aaron is. I'm a male. I suggested it. Sparrow didn't seem to think I looked right for the part and nobody else supported me. The decision was made. I accepted that. Tiarra has to learn to accept it too. I think Aaron is doing a fine job. You haven't said anything about it. What do you think?"

Ruby says, also in a low tone, "I think Aaron is doing as well as anybody else would. Here we are in The People's Republic. We got past the guards. Our disguises seem to be working. That's what's important."

Tamaranis says, in quiet conversation, "That's one of the things I admire about you, Ruby. You seem to be able to understand what's really important without making a fuss about it. You cooperate without arguing about it. We would be better off if Tiarra were more like you."

Ruby thinks, *Tamaranis is getting too personal. I don't want to be compared to Tiarra. None of them has ever looked to me for leadership. I guess I don't expect them to. They would never have put a Dwarf in a leadership role. I don't want to be the leader anyway.* She replies, "I think everybody should contribute what they can to finding Robert Swift and bringing him home. We don't really need a leader. Tiarra knows a lot about fighting.

You know how to think things through. Aaron's magic saved us from the bats. He knew what to do in that situation. Johanna brought that hateful Quicksilver to heal us. Eridana took the lead in talking with Queen Cassia when we entered the Forest of Ereba. I have done the best I can to fight the Red Haze Creature. I killed it the first time. We don't need a designated leader. We need to respect each other for what we can do."

Tamaranis says, "That's right. I admire you for what you have done. You are one of the bravest people I know."

Ruby thinks, *Once again, he's getting too personal. He's praising me more than I deserve. He must want something. What could it be? Oh no. He wants a kiss, not now but later, and probably a hug. He's trying to convince me that I'm brave enough to do it. But I won't do it. I hope he doesn't tell me that I'm beautiful. If he does, I'm going to hit him. I'm not going to stand watch with him again.*

Ruby feels that she is getting angry again, as she did last night. She says, "I don't want to talk with you. Leave me alone." She goes to the other side of the horse, leaving Tamaranis to walk alone. He doesn't say anything.

It is almost midday and quite warm. By now the people walking are covered with perspiration. They have been following the road near a small stream for some time; now the road crosses over the stream at a small stone bridge. To the left is a nice shady grove of trees.

Aaron notices that they have gained some distance on the wagon ahead of them, which is moving slowly, and that the one behind is catching up. He thinks, It looks to me that we are about to be traveling with these other wagons as if we are a caravan. In some ways it would be safer, but tomorrow morning Tiarra will be putting makeup on my face and I don't want these people to see that. We can't become part of a caravan.

He leads Toby off the road into the grove of maple trees, saying to the others, "Let's take a break."

The other wagons continue on. Aaron stops at a pleasant spot in the grove where the nearby stream has widened into a small pond. They are about two hundred feet away from the road. Aaron and Tamaranis unhitch Toby from the wagon. Ruby unties Jenny. Aaron and Ruby take the animals to a place where they can get some water and graze. They put stakes in the ground and use fairly long ropes to hitch the animals to the stakes.

Johanna says to Tamaranis, "If you make a fire, I'll cook us a hot meal. If someone can catch a rabbit, it could be rabbit stew. We've got some vegetables, and salted meat, but fresh meat would be nice. We haven't had that for a while."

Eridana says, "Come with me Tiarra. I think I can find a rabbit. You can kill it with your one hand crossbow. A rabbit is a small target, but you are very good with your crossbow."

Tiarra says, "I'd be delighted. I love to hunt."

They leave, soon coming into an area of low bushes, stumps, grass and weeds. The area looks as if it was cut over by loggers just a few years ago.

Eridana says, "This looks like a good place for rabbits."

Tiarra says, "It doesn't look like a good place for Eldens. There are too many treetops and limbs lying around, and too many brambles. It's going to be hard walking."

Eridana says, "That's what rabbits like."

Before long Eridana spots a rabbit trail, a well-worn path about four inches wide in meadow grass, weeds, and brambles. It looks like many rabbits have used it.

She says, "Wait here, Tiarra. Rabbits usually run in circles. I'll follow the path to keep any rabbits moving. Pretty soon you should see a rabbit running along this path here. Rabbits usually run a few hops, then stop, look, listen, and sniff. Then they move on. The time for you to kill it will be when it is stopped. Stand off the trail where you can see it well and don't move. Then, when a rabbit stops, be quick with your crossbow."

Tamaranis collects dry wood and builds a fire. Johanna gets out a kettle and starts peeling potatoes, beets, carrots and turnips, cutting them into chunks, and letting them fall into it. That is what they are doing when Aaron and Ruby return.

Ruby says to Aaron, "It looks like it's going to be a while before its time to eat. I think I'll take a short walk. I would like to be alone for a while."

Aaron says, "I understand. Go ahead, but don't get lost, and be careful. Don't be gone too long. I have no idea what kind of beasts might live in this area."

Ruby says, "I'll take care."

She walks away, soon disappearing behind a clump of trees, then into a pine grove. She enjoys the feel of the soft warm blanket of brown pine needles under her feet. She is now in shade. The branches are well above her head, making it easy to walk. It almost feels as if she is in a cathedral.

She says softly, "Alone at last!"

She walks more slowly. *What a bouncy ride this has been. I never expected to be walking around in the body of a woman – a Human woman at that. Look at me.*

She stretches out her arms. *Small hands and thin fingers, tiny wrists, and slim arms with almost no muscles at all. I'm puny! I'm not even allowed to wear my Wristband of Strength. Without a weapon, I'm defenseless! And I don't have a good weapon with me now. I only have the knife and garrote in my pouch.*

She picks up a fallen branch – dead dry wood, not rotten. She tries to break it into a shorter piece, about the right size to use for a club, putting her desired break point against one knee and pulling hard with both hands.

"I can't do it." Tears well up in her eyes and stream down her cheeks. In frustration, she holds one end of the branch with both hands and swings it as hard as she can against the trunk of the nearest tree. It breaks, but not where she wanted it to break. The piece in her hands is too short to be effective as a club. She throws it away in disgust.

I'm crying like a woman. I almost never cry. But since I put on this Amulet it seems that I cry at the smallest little thing. I never would have thought this would happen to me.

She takes a handkerchief from her pouch and wipes her face dry, sopping up both tears and perspiration. Putting it back, she starts walking among the black trunks of the tall trees, not making a sound but listening to the continuing slight swishing of the breeze brushing against pine needles far above. She can barely notice it. There is no breeze at ground level.

That Tamaranis! I can't believe it. Trying to treat me like a woman! Wanting to kiss me, and probably more! I know I must look attractive to him but he knows that I'm not a woman. It's something I thought Aaron might do, but Tamaranis? I wouldn't take Aaron seriously, but Tamaranis is always serious. He, of any of us, should be able to see more than skin deep. I don't think I should have another conversation with him until we have left The People's Republic and I can remove the Amulet. I'll stay as far away from him as I can.

Aaron seems to understand. I can't imagine that Tamaranis wouldn't. Now, whenever he looks at me I'm going to know what he's thinking. It makes me feel... I don't know.... funny... uncomfortable... I don't like it.

She emerges from the grove of pine trees into a cleared area, apparently cut over by loggers a few years ago. She sees no sign of any beasts, nor has she seen any tracks. In the middle of the clearing she sees a lone dead tree with no leaves that looks as lonely as she feels. But the tree is not alone. A crow that is perched on one of its dead and broken branches makes the signal for danger, "Caw...caw...caw...!" Then it flies away. Two other crows on the ground rise up into the air to join it. They all fly to the other edge of the clearing and light near each other at the top of other tall trees, where they can look back at her to see what she is doing.

Ruby looks all around. No one else is in sight. *How could those crows think that I'm dangerous? But it is me that they are flying away from. There's nothing else.*

Ruby walks in that direction, finding that walking in the cleared area is difficult, especially with a long skirt that keeps catching on something. One of the crows flies toward her. It gives the danger signal again, "Caw...caw...caw...!" Then it swoops around and flies back to another tall tree.

Ruby thinks, *The crows are only a little afraid. They're also curious. They probably wonder what I am and if I'm dangerous or not. I wonder that too. Who am I? What is going to happen to me? What will we encounter when we reach Divinity City? Will we be able to find Robert Swift? Will we be able to get him out of captivity – if that is his situation? Will we have to kill him? I don't think I could do that. Oh, I can fight effectively enough when I have my Magic Crossbow. I used it to help kill those huge lizards and the Red Haze. But I don't like killing people.*

She looks around. *I wonder where that Red Haze is. I don't remember seeing it since we entered Eastgate, but it must be following us. Is it waiting for us back near the wagon or is it watching me? I don't think I could fight it alone. I better get back to the wagon. It could be attacking my friends right now. I shouldn't have left them.*

She takes another look at the crows. One of them is flying toward her - again. Ruby caws at it, trying to imitate the voice of the crow as best as she can. "Caw...caw...caw...!" It echoes her call as it turns and flies back to the lonely tree in the middle of the clearing.

There - I warned it away from me, and it went. But what is it really saying to me? Is it trying to warn me? Does it see something I don't see? Does it see the cloud of Red Mist lurking about? These crows aren't going to hurt me. Do they see something else that might?

She walks quickly back to the grove of tall pine trees, thinking that it should be safer there.

But when she gets there she doesn't feel safer. She thinks, I can't see very far. I'm afraid! I shouldn't be, but I am. I wish that I had my Ring of Protection from Fear but it's in the wagon, under the seat. I've got to get back to the others. There's safety in numbers. Maybe that's what the crows are trying to tell me.

She quickens her pace. *Me, afraid to be alone in the woods? I shouldn't be. I've been alone in the woods many times before. I wasn't afraid.*

But I'm far from home now. I don't have a good weapon. I'm in a woman's body. I'm in The People's Republic. I've heard that Human men sometimes force women to have sex with them. I think its called rape. What if some hunter should see me here and decide to rape me? Could I fight him off?

She walks even faster toward where her friends are. She takes her knife out of her pouch and holds it carefully, hoping that if she falls she won't cut herself.

Suddenly she stops. *I'm ashamed of myself. I shouldn't be scared like this. I'm a male Dwarf, a good fighter, brave and courageous.*

But she doesn't put her knife back into the pouch. She looks around to see what or who might be watching her. She sees no one. She hears a chattering sound.

I recognize that sound. It's a squirrel. It's nothing to be afraid of.

She looks in the direction of the sound. *Maybe I made it get excited. Maybe somebody else did.*

She starts walking again, back toward the wagon. *I need my Crossbow. I should have brought it with me.*

When she nears the edge of the pine grove she first sees the yellowish-white canvas of the wagon and the smoke of a fire. As she gets closer she can see that Aaron and Tamaranis are at the fire, watching a pot boil. She cannot see Tiarra, Johanna, or Eridana anywhere.

She thinks, I wonder what they're talking about. Probably about me. Maybe Tamaranis is telling Aaron about what he tried to do last night, laughing about it. But it's not funny. I wouldn't be surprised if Aaron wants to do the same. Aaron is always telling that kind of joke. If any of us is obsessed with sex it would be him. I can't join them now. I wonder where the women are. I feel pretty safe right here. I'll wait a while.

She moves to a place where she can watch without being seen and waits in silence, breathing easily. She tries to think about something else.

Ruby thinks, It should only take us a couple of days for us to get to Divinity City, then a couple of days to get back to Eastgate. Then I can take off this cursing Amulet and be myself again. Can I stand it for that long? I have to. If I decide to give up our mission and take it off now I will have to walk back to Eastgate alone. I wouldn't make it more than a hundred feet into Beastgate before I would be surrounded by soldiers. I don't dare to walk back to Eastgate alone looking like a woman, either. I have no choice but to go on. Tiarra, Eridana, and Johanna won't let Aaron and Tamaranis do anything bad to me. I can count on them. Yes. It will be safer to go on, and I'll be keeping my promise to Sarah Swift. I don't want my father and mother to be ashamed of me. What would they think of me if they saw me now? They wouldn't believe it. But they would understand how important it is to carry through with this mission. They would know I'm doing the right thing. Rachel would understand also. I wonder what Odin thinks. He himself used magic to change himself into Human form - Lots of times. He seemed to like it. He even changed himself into a Human woman at least once, probably more than once. He seemed to like that too. It's all right. If he could do it, I can. Well, he is much more powerful and wiser than I am. But with his help, I can do it. It's the right thing, and he will help me.

Ruby says aloud, "Oh, Odin, greatest of the Gods. Thank you for helping me. Thank you for helping me to find my way to do my duty to you, my mother and father, Sarah Swift, and my companions on this mission. Please continue to help me. Give me the courage, the wisdom, patience, and strength, to endure this hardship, and this Amulet. Help us find Robert Swift, and bring him safely home. Bring me and my companions safely home as well. I ask in the name of Fror Ingren. Bless us all.

Ruby feels better, safer, and more confident than at any time since she put on the Amulet. She just stands calmly, continuing to breathe easily and evenly, and watches Aaron and Tamaranis at the fire. In less than five minutes she sees Tiarra, Eridana, and Johanna walking toward the fire from the direction of the pond, each carrying one of the grain sacks provided by Sparrow, with something in it, in one hand. They carry what looks like wet cloth in one hand and clothes in the other.

Ruby walks toward the fire. She should arrive at about the same time that the other women will. Aaron and Tamaranis are wearing different, cleaner looking clothes than they were before and their hair looks wet.

Aaron says, "Welcome back Ruby. I'm glad to see that you're all right. You were gone a pretty long time. I was getting worried."

Ruby says, "You didn't need to. I was safe enough."

The women also have wet hair and are wearing different clothes.

Eridana says, "We just took a swim and washed our clothes. Got rid of the sweat and grime we accumulated the last couple of days. Then we put on clean clothes. You ought to do the same."

The wet and twisted cloth in their hands is evidence that they washed the clothes they had been wearing, and wrung them out by hand.

Johanna says, "But first let's eat. Our food should be ready by now. It's a rabbit stew. Tiarra and Eridana hunted down the rabbit. Grab a bowl and help yourselves while we hang out our clothes to dry in the sun."

The three women quickly spread their wet clothes over low bushes. Then they eat. Ruby tries to avoid any eye contact with Tamaranis. The stew is delicious.

Aaron says, "Best meal we've had so far."

Johanna finishes eating first and takes charge of washing dishes. A second kettle hanging over the fire is full of boiling water. She turns some of it into a third kettle of cold water and sets the steaming kettle on the ground. She adds soap to the slightly cooler kettle, washes her bowl and spoon in it, and then rinses them carefully in the boiling water. To avoid burning her fingers she has tied a string to the handle of the bowl and to the spoon. They dry quickly without wiping and she puts them away.

Eridana says, "All right, Ruby, go take a dip in the pond. We'll wash dishes and pack the wagon. Don't forget to take soap."

Ruby takes her bag of women's clothes, a towel, and a bar of soap to the pond. Aaron and Tamaranis go to get the animals ready for travel.

The women wash dishes and talk about recent events. Eridana mentions Quicksilver.

Johanna responds, "That Quicksilver! I can't get over her attitude. I asked her to get rid of that Dried Blood monster but she wouldn't do it. She said, 'I saved you once and that is all I'm obligated to do.' Do you remember what the fortuneteller said? She said, 'The Red Haze can be controlled by a cat. The cat is a woman, but is not a woman.' I think she was referring to Quicksilver. Quicksilver is a cat and a woman. Do you think the Red Haze monster was created by Quicksilver to make us feel uncomfortable? Does she send it to follow us every day? Does she tell it when to attack us? Is she secretly watching when we fight it?"

Eridana says, "Maybe, I guess. It's too bad you had to break your crystal bell. I have a feeling we may need Quicksilver's help when we get to Divinity City."

Tiarra says, "I don't like Quicksilver. I kind of like fighting the Red Haze Creature though. We always manage to kill it somehow."

Johanna says, "I don't think we really kill it. We weaken it. Then it recuperates. It's getting stronger. I fear that one time it will kill one of us."

Tiarra says, "If it kills me, then Eridana will have to resurrect me with her silver chalice. We can recuperate too. This is a grand adventure, and we will succeed."

Eridana says, "We must. The very survival of our people depends upon it. You heard what Queen Cassia said. The People's Alliance will destroy everyone who is not Human. That includes your people, Tiarra, as well as mine."

Tiarra says, "And Reuben's"

Johanna says, "Queen Cassia could be wrong. It's hard to believe that very many people could be so bigoted and vicious as she says they are. My religion teaches that we are all of equal value in the eyes of God. My God watches over all of us, whether we believe in Him or not. God will not allow that to happen. There are places for all kinds of people on this island. I will help show the way. The people of the Alliance will learn, and they will not allow the Keepers to destroy your people."

Eridana says, "I worry that the Humans of the People's Alliance do not respect the wild areas as they should. I was impressed with the varieties of wildlife described in Michael Abner's book. Many of those creatures are unknown outside the Forest of Ereba. We must learn to nurture and protect the wild creatures that are left in the places where we live. We should not make the entire island into farms. We need to leave good places for wild animals and birds to live."

Johanna says, "Look. I see dark clouds in the west. We may have rain. Let's finish quickly and put everything in the wagon"

Meanwhile, at the pond, Ruby takes off her clothes and washes herself. While scrubbing herself with soap and a small wet cloth she is again amazed at the strange kind of body she now has. She thinks; *By human standards, I suppose I would be considered to be quite beautiful. But I look so puny. Most of my muscle is below my waist. My upper body is so small. How do women manage to do so much hard work?*

She rinses herself by wading into deeper water, ducking under, and swimming a few strokes. Her body seems quite buoyant. While on her back she notices dark clouds coming in from the west.

She thinks, *It looks like rain. I better wash my dirty clothes and get back to the wagon.*

Aaron and Tamaranis go to where Toby and Jenny are eating grass, bring them back, and attach them to the wagon. They are ready to go by the time Ruby gets back – fresh, clean, and dressed in clean clothes. Johanna hangs Ruby's wet clothes inside the wagon off the hoops that support the canvas. They get moving.

Aaron leads Toby. Ruby walks behind Aaron. Johanna rides the wagon. Tiarra and Tamaranis walk together on the other side of Toby. Eridana walks up front as scout.

There are no other travelers on the road near them. The people who started out for Divinity City from Beastgate this morning must all be well ahead of them. A cool breeze is coming from the west. They are making good time.

Ruby thinks, *I feel a lot better than I did before the break. The chance to be alone for a little while helped. And it's good to feel clean.*

I don't feel that I can trust Tamaranis and Aaron as much as I should, but I can trust the women. From now on when I'm on watch at night I want to be with one of them. Aaron and Tamaranis can be on watch together, not with one of us.

CHAPTER SEVENTEEN

A NATURAL DISASTER

Freya's Day - Greening Thirteen – A Little After Noon

The travelers soon hear low rumbling sounds. It must be thunder. The dark clouds are much closer. There are flashes of lightning. The thunder gets louder and closer. It starts to rain.

Johanna says, "Let's put up a tent so that we can get out of the rain."

Tiarra says, "We need to keep going or we may get to Divinity City too late. We spent too much time eating lunch. We haven't gone far enough yet today. We can stop here for a minute or so to put on rain gear, but then we need to keep moving."

Aaron says, "Yes, we need to keep moving. He takes his cloak from his sack of personal belongings and puts it on. He is already wearing his broad brimmed hat. Ruby puts on her yellow cloak. She puts the brown shawl over her head. She takes her old pouch with her magic bracelets, ring, and a dagger out from under the seat of the wagon. It is attached to her belt and she puts that over her shoulder. Tamaranis and Eridana, who have also put on their cloaks, get on the seat of the wagon. They are partly protected from the rain by the canopy. Johanna and Tiarra are in the back of the wagon where they are totally protected. They have not put on their cloaks, but Johanna is wearing her bonnet, as usual.

Aaron leads Toby, and Ruby walks with him. It isn't long before they are walking in mud. They are getting soaked, but there is no room for anybody else in the wagon and somebody has to lead the horse. They keep slogging on. Ruby notices that her skirt is dragging in the mud. The thunder and lightning continue. Suddenly there is a huge crack of thunder concurrent with a flash of lightning. It seems to be right where they are. The earth shakes. Leaves and even the trunks of trees beside the road vibrate. Suddenly a huge crack opens up in the road right in front of them. It is a deep chasm several feet wide completely crossing the road.

Aaron leads Toby, the horse, to the left to avoid the big opening in the road but before he can get very far, it opens wider and longer into a huge crevasse. The surface of the earth itself seems to be tilting. Large chunks of wet dirt and bushes are sliding and falling into the big hole. The ground near it is becoming very soft and mushy. The horse's hooves and legs are sinking deep into the soft ground. The wagon's wheels are sinking too. Toby is trying to back up but instead the horse is sliding toward the chasm pulling the wagon along with him.

A feeling of panic strikes everyone. Ruby wishes she were wearing her Ring of Protection From Fear. She runs from the rift in panic, skirt dragging in the mud. Her path takes her to the back of the wagon where Jenny is tied. Jenny is braying and straining to get loose. Ruby tries to untie Jenny's lead rope from the wagon.

Aaron drops Toby's lead rope and runs away from the chasm too. At the front of the wagon, he quickly cuts the traces with his knife, giving Toby a chance to look out for himself. He hopes that neither the horse nor the wagon will be drawn into the chasm. He slogs through the mud to the rear. He can't run in the deep mud. By now the wagon is up to its wheel hubs in mud. Ominously, it is sliding in the direction of the deep pit. There is no apparent way to stop it.

The mud is not as deep at the tailgate. Ruby and Jenny have sunk less than knee deep. Johanna jumps out of the back of the wagon carrying as many sacks as she can manage, and a long piece of rope. Ruby grabs the rope and ties one end to Jenny's halter. Aaron slashes Jenny's lead rope with his knife. Ruby gives Jenny a slap on the rump. The panicked animal runs and scrambles for higher ground. Ruby lets the long rope slide through her hands.

Eridana jumps out of the wagon with several sacks. Tiarra pushes everything in the wagon toward the rear. Tamaranis opens up the secret compartment under the seat.

Toby is squealing in fear, desperately struggling to fight the gravity that is pulling him toward the chasm. He isn't doing very well because the ground itself is sliding downwards toward the giant fissure in the earth.

Johanna, loaded with as many sacks as she can carry in one hand, holds tightly onto the rope tied to Jenny with the other. She pumps her feet in the slippery mud as fast as she can, but it is Jenny that is pulling her to higher ground. Jenny pulls Johanna to a large outcropping of rock ledge that is not moving. Johanna drops the sacks she is carrying on the ledge and stands there with Jenny. The mule is frantically trying to find secure footing, still squealing excitedly. Johanna, wearing no cloak, is now thoroughly soaked by the rain. Her clothes cling to her body almost like another layer of skin.

The rope attached to Jenny reaches all the way back to Ruby at the tailgate of the wagon. Ruby wraps the rope once around her waist, securing it with one hand while the free end dangles where it will, mostly on the mud.

Toby falls into the chasm, squealing with terror as he goes.

Tiarra and Tamaranis are still in the wagon. Tamaranis takes magic items and weapons out of the place under the seat, two or three at a time, passing them to Tiarra. Tiarra passes them outside to Ruby. Ruby passes them to Aaron. Aaron passes them to Eridana. Eridana puts them on the ledge near Johanna, who moves them yet further up the slope of the ledge. Johanna is chanting loudly. It must be some kind of prayer, but the continuing sound of thunder makes it impossible for any of the others to really know.

Aaron and Eridana are now holding the rope in one hand and climbing with their feet just to stay in the same place while they pass things along with the other hand. Ruby is holding the rope around her waist with one hand, letting it slip a little so that she can stay near the tailgate, and passing things with the other. Jenny has found good footing on the ledge and is standing there, stubbornly refusing to let the rope pull her toward the wagon and the chasm.

The wagon is sliding toward the abyss. The bucket brigade is getting longer. Johanna now has her feet in mud, holding on to the rope for support like the others.

All of the weapons are out. All of the sacks of personal belongings are out. The wagon is at the rim of the chasm. It is about to fall in.

"Tiarra, jump!" yells Tamaranis.

Tiarra jumps out the back of the wagon. Tamaranis grabs a last couple of things and jumps out too.

Ruby grabs Tiarra and pulls her to the rope. Tiarra grabs it and works her way up toward the ledge, pumping her feet in the mud and pulling with her arms. Ruby tries to grab Tamaranis but he's too far away. Johanna is back on the ledge, leading Jenny further up the slope, pulling the rope as they go. Eridana is helping Jenny pull on the rope. Aaron drops what he has on the ledge and helps pull too. Tiarra reaches the ledge.

Where are Tamaranis and Ruby? Everybody looks down the slope. Tamaranis did not manage to get a hold on the rope when he jumped. He is struggling to climb the steep slope of sliding earth without anything to hang on to.

Ruby is trying to get to him with the end of the rope. She lets the rope slip around her waist getting further and further from Jenny, but the distance between her and Tamaranis is also getting bigger.

It is a losing endeavor. The ground is sliding toward the chasm faster than Tamaranis can move against it. He is up to his armpits in slimy earth.

Everyone on the ledge watches the wagon slide into the chasm. Then they watch helplessly, as Tamaranis follows the wagon. They hear his scream of despair. Then all that they hear is the continued rumbling and sliding of unstable earth as it continues to slide into the chasm.

Johanna yells, "Oh no!"

The others express the intensity of their shock with unintelligible shrieks of despair.

Ruby is screaming too. She is sliding toward the chasm. She can't hold the rope around her waist from slipping.

Tiarra yells, "Quick Ruby! Tie the rope around your waist! We'll pull you up here!"

Somehow Ruby manages to get a knot in the rope that keeps it from slipping, but by the time she does she is much closer to the chasm. The others pull as hard as they can. With Jenny's help they manage to pull her out of the muck and finally onto the ledge.

Johanna says, "Thank God we were able to save you."

Ruby's tears don't show because of the rain. Her clothes are covered with mud.

Eridana says, "We weren't able to save Tamaranis though. He's gone."

Johanna says, "This can't be happening. I prayed that we would all be saved."

Ruby says, "I tried. I tried. I couldn't reach him."

Tiarra says, "I know. You did the best anyone could have done. I'm glad you didn't slide into the hole with him."

Aaron says, "He could have saved himself if he hadn't spent so much time trying to save all our weapons and magic. I've got his hammer here, and his sack of clothes. I would much rather have him."

Johanna says, "It must have been the will of God, but I don't understand why."

Aaron says, "Sometimes the wishes of the Gods are hard to understand. We can't see things from their perspective."

Eridana says, "But we need God. He is our voice of reason, who helps us maintain our perspective when we are confused."

Tiarra says, "I don't think this was an act of God. It was an act of evil, probably caused by the same magical force that brought the bats and rats and the Red Mist."

Johanna says, "Quicksilver!"

Tiarra says, "Maybe."

Eridana says, "Poor Tamaranis. Pray for his soul, Johanna. He's already buried. You are the one who can do that best."

Johanna offers up a special prayer for Tamaranis. In her prayer she mentions all the good things about Tamaranis that she can remember, ending with, "He was the bravest of us all."

Eridana says, "Let's have a moment of silence while we each offer our own silent prayer."

The rain obscures the tears on everyone's cheeks. Ruby is sobbing. Her body is shaking. Ruby had shed tears before, but never anything like this and she can't seem to stop. In a way it feels good. She can't tell if anyone else is crying or not. In fact they all are, even Aaron. They stand there on the ledge for a long time, in the rain, without talking, watching the earth slide into the chasm. Ruby's thoughts about Tamaranis are jumbled. She feels guilty for not having saved him, angry for what he wanted to do with her while on watch, good about the good times they had shared, and respect for his wisdom.

Everyone is soaked to the skin, whether wearing a cloak or not. Eventually they stop crying. The thunder and lightning slowly diminish into the distance but the rain continues. The earth finally stabilizes somewhat. There is only an occasional shifting and sliding in a few scattered places. There is a steep slope from where they are standing on ledge toward the still open chasm, much of it now bare ledge. The area of ledge is slippery and has grown bigger because so much of the earth over and around it has slid down the hillside into the chasm. There are other outcroppings of ledge all around that weren't there before. The soil that had covered them is gone.

Eridana says, "I can't believe we've lost Tamaranis."

Johanna says, "We have paid our proper respects. We must look out for ourselves now."

CHAPTER EIGHTEEN

FOOT TRAVELERS

Freya's Day - Greening Thirteen – Afternoon

Tiarra says, "We can't stay here. Gather up your gear and let's get going. We've got to find a place to spend the night. Bring your weapons and magic. Don't worry about trying to hide them. We can't. We must put what we can on the mule and carry the rest. We just have to hope nobody sees us."

They gather up all their valuable things, all of their weapons, magic, and sacks of personal belongings that are on the ledge. Everything is soaked from the rain. They repack the mule with some of their gear, including cooking dishes, what little they have been able to salvage of the food, the three tents, and other items that Jenny was already carrying.

Aaron finds Tamaranis's hammer and sack of clothes. He puts those on the mule too. He says, "That's all we can put on Jenny. We'll have to carry everything else ourselves. Each of you will have to carry your own things."

They sort out the sacks of belongings, bedrolls, and weapons. Only Aaron has a backpack. The rest will have to carry what they have in sacks.

Ruby discovers that somebody had put her change of clothes that had been hanging inside the wagon into one of the sacks that were salvaged. She puts on the Ring of Protection from Fear and the two Wristbands. She feels better already. She puts the Magic Boots of Jumping on her feet. The quiver of crossbow bolts and the shoulder pouch go on her left shoulder, hanging across her body to rest against her right hip. The Magic Shortsword they took from the thieves has a scabbard and belt. She tries to wrap the belt around her waist but it is too long so she drapes it over her right shoulder and the sword hangs at her left hip. She puts her Magic

Cloak of Blending over these, so they can't be seen very well. She ties her two sacks together at the top so that she can throw them both over her right shoulder. With her hands now free, she is able to take her Crossbow in her right hand and her battleaxe in the other. She is heavily encumbered, but with her Wristband of Strength she can carry all these things.

Her bedroll is still on the ledge. She can think of no way to carry it until she sees what Johanna is doing. Johanna is putting her bedroll between her left arm and her waist so Ruby tries that. The bedroll nestles nicely into the narrow part of her waist, partly supported by her hip and the hilt of the Magic Shortsword. She can still carry her axe in her left hand. She thinks, *I don't think I could have done this as a Dwarf because my arms were too short then and my waist was too broad.*

Johanna is wearing the Cloak That Cannot Be Torn or Ripped to shed most of the rain. She thinks, *It's magic, but I don't care. It doesn't look magic.* She carries her mace in her right hand, her sack of clothes in her left, and her bedroll under her left arm. The strap attached to her pouch is on her left shoulder under the cloak.

Eridana's scimitar dangles from the belt with the Magic Silver Buckle of Protection, which hangs from her shoulder. Her sling and small magic items are in her pouch attached to a strap that is over her other shoulder. Her hooded cloak covers them up. She carries her clothing sack in her right hand and her bedroll on her hip under her left arm.

Tiarra has slung her Longsword from her shoulder also, hoping that the tip will not be seen below the hem of her cloak. The hilt is right under her left armpit. The strap attached to her pouch is on the other side. The hooded cloak that she brought from home sheds the rain and hides the Longsword. She carries her small Crossbow in her right hand. Having left her shield with Sparrow, she can carry her clothing sack in her left hand while holding her bedroll on her hip with her left arm.

Aaron is also wearing the cloak he brought from home, his pouch under it. He is holding his staff in his right hand but his other hand is free because his clothes and other equipment are in his backpack, which is on his back over his cloak. His bedroll is tied to the top of his backpack. He will lead the mule.

The kegs of wine that were in the wagon went down into the deep crevasse with the wagon.

Tiarra says, "Let's go."

Johanna asks, "Which way?"

Tiarra says, "The only way we can go; up the hill. Follow me."

Aaron says, "She's right. We have to get away from the chasm. Going in any other direction would put us on ground that looks unstable. We could easily find ourselves sliding into that big hole in the ground."

He follows Tiarra up the slope.

Tiarra says, "Up there on top of the ridge we should find stable ground or other ledges that will take us in the direction the road was going."

Before they go very far they stop to tie themselves together with the long piece of rope so that if one of them starts to slide, the others will be able to keep that person from sliding too far.

From the top of the ridge they plot a new course, roughly parallel to the road they were following, generally northeast. Sometimes they have to leave the ledge they are on to walk across a patch of bare ground that is not entirely stable. When they do their feet sink several inches, so if they can, they leap from one piece of solid ledge to another. When they do, they usually toss most of their baggage to the next ledge before leaping. They try to be careful because the rocks are wet and slippery. It is slow going. From time to time someone says something about Tamaranis - or how much better it would be if they still had Toby and the wagon. Of course Toby and the wagon could not possibly travel on the uneven ground they are on.

Everyone is soaked to the skin. The rain diminishes and finally stops. Soon after that they see a large stream ahead of them. They are now having less trouble. They still follow high ground as much as possible, mostly ledge. When they get close to the stream they see that it is flowing swiftly because of the recent extremely heavy rain. The ledge they are walking on goes part way across the stream. When they reach the edge of the water they find that the ledge continues under the water making good solid footing to reach the other side. The water is not very deep, only coming up to their knees. The ground on the other side is much more stable. There is a small pond at the upstream side of the ledge, perhaps formed in part by the heavy rain.

It is late in the day so they set up camp on high ground right near the river. They are well away from the road they were following when the rain came and the wagon fell into the chasm. It seems unlikely that they will encounter other travelers here.

They make a more careful inventory of what they have been able to salvage. Other than Tamaranis himself, they haven't lost much that was really important to them. They are still wet, but so is almost everything else. They wish they still had Toby and the wagon.

Aaron unpacks what Jenny is carrying. Tiarra inspects Tamaranis's sack of clothes. Johanna looks in the small pouch tied to his hammer. That is where his magic would be. There isn't much. Tamaranis didn't seem to care much for magic.

Johanna asks, "Is it all right if I wear Tamaranis's Ring of Protection? I want something to remember him by."

It is the one that was taken from one of the four thieves.

Tiarra says, "Good. You should have some additional magical protection. We may have to fight the Red Mist soon."

Johanna puts it on.

Aaron says, "I want the scarf then. I need additional magical protection too."

Tiarra says, "Of course. I want you to have it."

Aaron takes the Black Scarf of Protection that was given to Tamaranis by Queen Cassia, putting it around his own neck for now.

Tiarra says, "Make a fire. We need to dry out. Try to find some dry wood."

Ruby remembers that Tamaranis usually gathered wood and started the fire when they stopped for the evening. It doesn't seem to be a good time to talk about Tamaranis.

She says, "I'll do it."

Tiarra says, "Everybody should look for wood. It's a priority. Look for tent poles too."

There is no dry wood but they manage to make a fire using driftwood. Ruby uses her camp axe to cut it open, exposing the dry inner parts to get it to start burning. The fire makes a lot of smoke. Eridana helps her, using her scimitar to cut into the wood. Aaron and Tiarra cut saplings to make poles for the three tents. Johanna examines the condition of the food they were able to salvage, trying to plan a meal.

Tiarra thinks about the Red Mist. *Maybe it has followed our path along the ridge toward the river. We couldn't see it in the rain, but I see it now. It is crossing the river, coming toward us.*

Tiarra alerts the others. "Look! There it is, the Red Mist. Get ready to fight it."

The others all turn to look. As soon as the Red Mist crosses the river it turns into the eight foot tall Dried Blood fighter that always attacks them. They know that any weapon that has been used to finish it off will no longer be effective against it. So far they have killed it with Reuben's Crossbow, Tiarra's Crossbow, Aaron's staff, and Eridana's sling. What can they fight it with?

Ruby thinks, *I'm going to use a piece of firewood this time, holding my battleaxe in reserve just in case the firewood doesn't do much.*

They form a line right next to the river. Ruby has her battleaxe in one hand and a long stick of firewood in the other, Eridana has her scimitar, Johanna has her mace, and Tiarra has her Longsword. Aaron gets in line with Tamaranis's hammer in his hands.

But as usual, the Creature does not advance into close combat. It stands at the edge of the river and shoots at them with its bow. The bloody arrow hits Aaron in the chest. He falls down, bleeding badly.

Johanna rushes to Aaron and uses a Heal Minor Wounds spell to stop the bleeding.

Tiarra knows that her group has already used their best missile weapons to disable the creature, so they will have to use their hand weapons. She yells, "Charge!" She runs toward it, Longsword ready to strike. Ruby, and Eridana also charge. Tiarra gets to it first. She hits the Creature in the neck with her Magic Longsword.

Eridana is next. She drives her shoulder right into the Dried Blood Creature, knocking the hateful thing into the water. She grapples with it, trying to put its head under water. She yells' "Maybe I can drown him!"

She sits right on top of his chest, using both hands to hold its head under water. Her own legs are under water as well.

Ruby has noticed that while the Creature seems to be made of Dried Blood, it has the configuration of a man, not a woman. Now that it is prone, partly underwater, she sees the opportunity to hit him in the crotch with the firewood. She thinks that this will cause great pain by bruising his genitals. She hits him in the right place but her plan doesn't work because the Creature has no genitals. *What is it?*

Ruby drops the piece of firewood. She takes her long knife out of its sheath and tries to cut off the Creature's right leg. "I want to burn its leg in the campfire. If we can do that, the next time it comes back to fight, it will have to fight on one leg."

The Creature now has its bloody looking club in its right hand. He swings at Ruby, hitting her upper back. This hurts a lot, but Ruby keeps slicing away at the Creature's leg.

Tiarra hits the Creature again with her Longsword, this time on its right arm, trying to make it let go of its club and avoiding the possibility of hitting Eridana or Ruby.

Aaron wallops at it with Tamaranis's hammer, hitting its left leg.

Johanna is there, trying to find a good place to hit it with her mace. She hits it on the right arm, hoping to make it drop the club. Eridana continues to sit on its chest and hold its head under water. But Eridana wonders if it even has to breath. *Maybe this wasn't such a good idea after all.*

Ruby manages to cut the bloody thing's leg off. There doesn't seem to be any bone in it. Ruby grabs the leg, runs to the fire, and puts it in the fire to burn.

In time, the Dried Blood thing seems to be subdued. It has stopped flailing its arms, but it has not been destroyed. It has not drowned. It doesn't seem to need to breathe air through any part of its head, maybe not at all. The leg on the fire is burning up quickly. Very little is left.

Ruby yells, "Put the rest of him on the fire!"

Ruby grabs its other leg. Tiarra and Aaron each grab an arm. Eridana grabs its head. But as soon as they pick him up the Dried Blood Creature explodes into nothingness.

Tiarra says, "We should have continued to burn it piece by piece instead of trying to burn it all at once."

Aaron says, "At least it's gone."

They are all exhausted. Eridana uses her Heal Minor Wounds spell to help the pain in Ruby's back. Johanna uses hers to heal Aaron's wound again. Tiarra puts some more wood on the fire.

After a brief rest, Johanna starts cooking supper. The others set up the three tents. Aaron will sleep alone. They string rope between trees to make several clotheslines, hoping that everything will dry out during the night. They eat what Johanna cooked and discuss the tragedy of losing Tamaranis to the deep chasm. They share their grief.

Johanna says, "This heavy rain and the opening up of that chasm in the road were not ordinary natural happenings. It was supernatural. So is the Red Haze Creature. We are being attacked by something viciously evil. We are lucky to be still alive."

Eridana says, "I agree. The diseased bats and rats also fit into that category. They were sent by something evil, some kind of evil spirit I think. That means that our mission is good, as evil opposes it. Our Gods will help us. We can succeed."

Tiarra says, "We certainly have to try. We can't give up. But we have now lost two of our original group – Tamaranis just now and Amrath at the Forest of Ereba. We don't know if Amrath is dead or alive but Tamaranis is certainly dead. We started with seven, now we are five. That makes each of us who is left that much more important."

Aaron says, "I am not so sure that it is an evil god opposing us. It could be a very powerful magic user creating these obstacles. He could be trying to scare us off, as you suggest, but now he has killed one of us. We are getting closer to our objective. These events are likely to become more and more difficult for us."

Johanna says, "How would a powerful Magic User know where we are and what we are trying to do? We are opposed by something supernatural."

Aaron says, "I am barely more than a neophyte with magic. There is much that I don't know. While I don't know the answer to your questions, that doesn't mean that a very powerful Magic User couldn't do them. I don't like to think that there is an evil God who would be this interested in what we are doing. In the large perspective, our mission is quite insignificant. But a powerful Magic User employed by the Keepers might think that stopping us is worth the effort."

Johanna says, "But the people of the Alliance hate magic. It is not allowed. They burn Magic Users to death at the festival we are going to. They wouldn't employ a Magic User."

Aaron says, "Remember that woman we encountered soon after we started following the ancient paved road toward Derlenen? She was obviously a Magic User and the silver charm she left behind was in the shape of a running wolf, the symbol of the Keepers. She must have been a Keeper, or a Magic User employed by the Keepers."

Tiarra says, "I had almost forgotten about her. Maybe she could have used her magic to follow us all this time and caused these terrible things to happen to us. I said then that she was evil. I wish that I had killed her, but I doubt if I did."

Aaron says, "So do I. I also said then that she was evil but in the sense of being a bad person, not an evil God. I believe that she was a high level Magic User. I won't be surprised if we encounter her again before we complete our mission, and when we do, we will have to do our very best to defeat her. It won't be easy."

Eridana says, "You could be right, Aaron. For all I know she could be responsible for creating the rain and chasm that killed Tamaranis. She probably hoped to kill all of us. If she knows that she didn't, she will probably try again, soon. It could have been her who sent the Red Haze and the Bats and Rats also. She could have given us the bad odor that disturbed Quicksilver. I hate to think that we could be up against such a formidable adversary, but I would rather think that, than that an evil God is opposing us. I would rather think that, than the idea that Quicksilver or Queen Cassia is opposing us. It makes more sense."

Ruby says, "She was able to make herself look like a Dwarf to me, an Elden to Amrath, and a Human to Aaron and Tamaranis. She is a master of disguises. Any time we are with other people we wouldn't know it, but she could have been watching and listening to us. She could have been in Exodus when were there. She could be hiding behind a tree watching us right now, and listening to what we are saying."

Tiarra says, "Then why doesn't she come out and attack us now. Why doesn't she just destroy us and have it over with."

Aaron says, "I think she tried. She looked to us like the Red Mist Creature. But now she may be back at her home resting and meditating. That storm and chasm would have required a lot of spell energy, even for a very powerful Magic User. But she's not a master of disguises, as Ruby said. She's a master of illusion."

Eridana says, "Call it what you will. Maybe she has an Imp of Wishes, like Amrath does. Maybe she doesn't have to meditate."

Aaron says, "Who knows? I don't. This is all speculation anyway. We have very little evidence."

Johanna says, "Now you are talking like Tamaranis."

Aaron says, "I take that as a compliment."

Johanna says, "That is how it was intended."

Being very tired they go to bed early. They would prefer to have two people awake during each watch, but Ruby volunteers to take the first watch alone.

This gives her some time to think without interruption while she combs her long hair. She thinks, *I'm proud of how my hair looks when it's properly combed. I've been doing it every morning, and I'll do it again tomorrow morning, but now it's such a mess. I don't want it to dry out this way.*

Why did Tamaranis have to fall into that chasm? I tried to save him. Maybe I didn't try hard enough. It's my fault. I think I tried as hard as I could, but I was mad at him. Could I have acted more quickly when he jumped out of the wagon? Why did I help Tiarra first? He needed more help than she did. Was it because of that scene we had this morning when Tamaranis was trying to court me as if I was a woman?

Why did I get so angry? I don't usually let myself get angry like that. What was I feeling before that outburst? I didn't have a bad opinion about Tamaranis. I liked Tamaranis. I liked that he helped me with the animals. He liked animals, and liked caring for them. He was wise, well spoken, considerate, brave, and compassionate. He was short, but that doesn't bother me at all. I like short. He was the kind of man I would like a lot if I were, in fact, really a woman. He was the kind of man most women should be attracted to. He was the kind of man a woman could easily fall in love with.

Ruby is crying again, sobbing little crying sounds and jiggling with each sob. Somehow it makes her feel better so she doesn't try to stop.

She thinks, *I wonder why Tiarra didn't pay more attention to Tamaranis. It was obvious from the first night we were together at Sarah's house that Tamaranis was very much attracted to her. Maybe if Tiarra had paid more attention to him, he wouldn't have paid so much attention to me. Strange that someone so wise would pay so much attention to a male Dwarf who only looked like a Human female.*

Why did Tamaranis do that? Did he think I could possibly respond to his advances the way a Human female would? Absurd! He of all people should have known better. Maybe that is why I was so upset. It should make anyone angry to see someone so wise and respected doing something so stupid.

Wait. I don't react like that. My usual reaction to seeing someone smart doing something stupid is to laugh and enjoy it. It feels good to feel smarter than somebody that everyone knows is really smart. That has never made me feel mad before. I must have been upset at something else.

Ruby has stopped crying. Her thoughts drift into other directions, but they always come back to Tamaranis. She feels guilty.

She thinks, *What harm would it have done for me to respond to Tamaranis as if I was a woman? I am, after all, trying to play that role. Tamaranis probably would have appreciated it immensely. It would have given him a pleasure that he was searching for and apparently thought that he could get from me. He is dead now. I might not have given him everything he wanted, but I could have given him something. I could have hugged him. It's too late now.*

Ruby tries to think about something else but she can't do it. She keeps thinking about Tamaranis. Before her watch is over, she realizes that she is really angry with herself instead of Tamaranis.

She thinks, *I was angry because I was beginning to realize that I felt attracted to Tamaranis the way a woman is supposed to be attracted to a man. That must have scared me. I was afraid that I was going to give in to those feelings. I was having feelings. What if I had let go and expressed them? What if I had expressed them in a physical way? I didn't know it then, but I was angry because I didn't know what to do with those feelings. I can see that now. It makes perfect sense that if I have the body of a woman I might have the feelings of a woman, at least in terms of being sexually attracted to a man. I should have understood this all along. Sparrow practically told me that it would happen. She warned me. Tamaranis probably understood that. He probably understood it perfectly, as he did so many things. He probably didn't see any reason why we shouldn't enjoy the pleasure of a male-female relationship. Maybe he was right. Maybe for the time being I really am a woman.*

Something about this thought makes her feel like crying again. She does, but more quietly this time. It does seem to make her feel better.

Later, when the sands of the hourglass have all run down, Ruby wakes Johanna and Aaron for the next watch. She thinks, *Johanna and Aaron are attracted to each other. How does Johanna control her feelings?*

Ruby sleeps – mostly because she is very tired but also because she has put at least partially to rest an emotional issue that was bothering her immensely. Every time she wakes during the night she thinks about it some more. *I am still troubled by this. How can I get rid of it?*

The night passes with no further events.

CHAPTER NINETEEN

A TERRIBLE RAINY DAY

Last Day - Greening Fourteen – Near Tyman

In the morning Nick and Helena get up out of their separate tents in a grove of trees near a small pond part way between Beastgate and Divinity City. It is raining. Their fire has gone out. They eat a cold breakfast. They pack up their gear, and head for Divinity City. The road is muddy so they walk their horses. It is slow going. It is a little after mid-morning when they encounter a group of wagons going toward Beastgate, teamsters cursing the mud and their animals as well.

It is a soaking wet rain. The road gets muddier. They slog on as best they can, sometimes riding off road where the ground is a little firmer. They don't reach Tyman until an hour after noon. They go into one of the inns to get something hot to drink.

Nick says, "If it doesn't stop raining, I think we should spend the night here. We should be able to get from here to Divinity City in one day very easily, but we won't make it before dark tonight. I'd rather sleep in a warm bed than spend another rainy night in the open."

Helena says, "I'm for that. While we're here we can check the inns and try to find out if the other group has been here. You know what they look like."

Nick says, "After it stops raining. We should check right after dark. They might be behind us, planning to stay at one of these inns for the night."

They make arrangements for separate rooms. Then they take their horses to the stable where they are given good rubdowns, some grain, and hay. Back at the inn they change into dry clothes and sit at one of the tables. They sip hot cider, and tell each other stories about past adventures. It doesn't stop raining until late afternoon, nearly suppertime.

After supper Nick and Helena talk with the innkeeper. Nick asks, "Have you seen six people traveling together, one of them being a Dwarf. They might have come through here during the last couple of days."

The innkeeper laughs loudly. When he stops he says, "Are you out of your mind? I haven't seen a Dwarf in my lifetime. If you want to see a Dwarf go to Divinity City. They might have one there waiting for execution during the festival. I presume that's where you're headed."

Nick says, "I should have known better. Come on Helena, let's go outside."

Outside Helena says, "We should have known better than to be looking for a Dwarf. A Dwarf would never get this far into The People's Republic. They would have left him in Eastgate, if he even got that far."

Nick says, "Right. I made a fool of myself asking the innkeeper if he had seen a Dwarf. Let's make the rounds. Look for five young people sitting together: two men and three women, two of the women have Elden pointed ears but that won't show. Their ears will be covered up by long hair. They were wearing ponytails when I saw them, but they won't be now. One of them is a beautiful blonde, about five-feet-three-inches tall. The other has light brown hair. The third woman is taller than the other two, a real Human with long blonde hair. She was wearing a brown cleric's robe but she won't be wearing that now. The two men are Human. The easiest one to recognize will be the short rotund one, about five-feet-three-inches tall, but he's not a Dwarf. He has a bald head but he could now be wearing a wig. The Magic User looks like every man you have ever seen except he has curly black hair. He's about five-feet-ten. He was wearing a Magic User's robe then, but he won't be now. The Dwarf won't be with them."

Nick and Helena make the rounds of the other three inns, looking for five young people sitting together that meet Nick's descriptions. They spend about a half-hour at each place, but with no luck. At each place they order a pint of fine wine. Their last drink is back at the inn where they are spending the night. They are feeling no pain when they go up to their separate rooms.

That same morning another group of people, five of them, who want to rescue Robert Swift start out at another place on their way to Divinity City. They also expect to pass through Tyman on their way.

Aaron, Tiarra, Eridana, Johanna, and Reuben have spent the night at their campsite beside a river on the road between Beastgate and Divinity City in the People's Republic. Ruby did the first watch alone. Aaron and Johanna did the second watch. It has not been raining. But it starts raining hard before Tiarra and Eridana have finished their watch. The fire goes out. To stay as dry as possible they decide to retreat into their tents and wait for daylight. Johanna is in a tent with Ruby. Aaron is sleeping alone in another tent.

When dawn comes, it is still raining and it is still quite dark. Tiarra says to Eridana, "It would be terrible trying to walk in weather like this. We don't need to start now. It should only take about half a day to walk to Tyman from here. We should let the others sleep late."

Eridana says, "I'm tired. Nothing is going to attack us during this storm. I want to sleep too."

Tiarra says, "One of us should stay awake. We can take turns napping. It is your turn to sleep first."

When the others do wake up, on their own, they stay in their tents, munching on whatever cold food they can find from the night before, and try to get some more rest.

When the rain diminishes somewhat, a little before noon, Aaron says, "Let's pack up and walk to Tyman. There we should be able to stay at an inn, get a good meal, and get everything dried out. Tomorrow we can walk from Tyman to Divinity City."

Tiarra says, "I agree. Let's go. But don't be surprised if the inns are full. A lot of people are going to Divinity City right now. We may have to stay in a stable."

Eridana says, "I don't care. I know it sounds unusual for me but I want a roof over my head and some hot food."

They pack up and get moving as quickly as they can. Tiarra makes an effort to apply makeup to Johanna's face and Aaron's face. She hopes that Johanna's bonnet and Aaron's broad brimmed hat will keep the rain from the makeup. But Tiarra is very concerned that the wind may blow rain into their faces while they are walking and the wet might destroy the makeup.

They make a better effort to hide their magic and their weapons than they did the previous afternoon. It seems possible that they will meet other people when they get back on the main road, and certainly when they reach Tyman. They want to look as much as they can like a woodcutter and farming family.

Ruby tries to move her Magic Wristbands further up her arms so they will be out of sight, well hidden by her long-sleeved blouse. She has no trouble getting them past her elbows. They seem quite comfortable there. They look like armbands, but they can't be seen under her sleeves. *I should have thought of this before.* The ring that protects her from fear goes into her shoulder pouch with her garrote and dagger. She tries to balance the weight of her clothes in the two sacks. Her Crossbow and Crossbow Bolts are packed out of sight on the mule. She wears the yellow cloak and puts the shawl on her head. She also wears the Boots of Jumping; it is too cold and wet to go barefoot. Ruby carries Aaron's staff, which somehow seems more appropriate for a woman to carry, while Aaron carries Ruby's magic Battleaxe, which seems quite acceptable for a woodcutter. Aaron wears his old hooded cloak.

Tiarra manages to put her small crossbow and crossbow bolts in her clothing sack such that their shapes cannot be seen from the outside. She loads her Longsword onto the mule. It didn't work well the way it was under her cloak the day before. The tip of the sword was visible below the bottom of her cloak. She borrows Ruby's Short Sword in case she needs a weapon. She puts the belt that is attached to the scabbard around her waist. That doesn't show.

Johanna puts her knife in her pouch, which she carries on her shoulder under her Brown Cloak That Cannot Be Cut or Torn. She carries her mace in her right hand, planning to hold it under her cloak when anyone else is within sight.

Eridana carries her sling, slingstones, and Magic Dagger in her pouch. She carries her scimitar under her cloak; it doesn't seem to show. Everyone but Aaron carries a bedroll and a sack with clothes and a few other things in it. Aaron has the backpack that he has used since leaving Exodus.

It is hard to hide the Longsword on the mule. Ruby completely covers it with tent canvas but its outline still protrudes to the rear. She says to Eridana, "I think its okay. Under the canvas it looks like an axe handle."

196

Eridana says, "We have to find the road that will take us to Divinity City. It was on our left when we started walking on the high ground yesterday after we lost Tamaranis. After a while we didn't see it any more. I'm not sure where we are now."

Aaron gets out the map. Eridana and Tiarra look at it with him.

Aaron says, "This short tributary to the main river on the map must be the one we crossed just before we set up camp last night. We should come to the road pretty quick if we go northeast now. Then we can follow the road to the main branch of the river. That will be the best place to cross it, on the road. There might be a bridge."

That is what they do. They find the road. They follow it northeast for a few miles and use a bridge to cross the river. About a mile past the river it intersects with another road coming from the northwest. They see just a few tracks in the mud.

Aaron gets out the map again.

Tiarra says, "That road doesn't show on the map. Stay on the road we're on. After a while it will turn east. That should take us to Tyman, an inn, and a chance to get completely dried out in a warm place."

Aaron says, "Not many travelers on the road. I like that. Without the wagon, some of our weapons can be seen. Others aren't very well hidden. I don't want to have to answer questions about that."

Tiarra says, "Good point. The fewer questions the better."

Johanna says, "I don't see the Red Mist following us. I think we finally managed to destroy it last night."

Tiarra says, "I just don't think we can see it in this rain. We didn't see it yesterday afternoon either."

Johanna says, "I can see further now than I could then."

Tiarra says, "Not far enough."

Johanna says, "I wish Tamaranis was still with us. I miss him."

Eridana says, "Yes, and he always did his share of the work without complaining."

Aaron says, "Who's complaining? We all do our share. We all complain sometimes, even Tamaranis did. He wanted to play the role of the father because he was older. But he knew he didn't look the part."

Tiarra says, "He was wiser than you, and he wouldn't have made the mistakes you made at Eastgate and Beastgate.

Eridana says, "He liked animals. He was very shy and quiet at first, but that was changing. I think he spent too much of his life in that monastery."

Aaron says, "He was very well educated and had a logical mind. He seemed able to see things in a different way than the rest of us. I don't feel qualified to judge him. I never really understood him. He deserved a longer life. I'm glad I had a chance to get to know him – at least a little."

Eridana says, "He would still be alive if he had jumped sooner. We're having bad luck. Who would think there would be a big hole in the ground as a result of thunder and lightning?"

Tiarra says, "I was thinking about Tamaranis while I was on watch last night. Is it possible that Tamaranis did not die? If some powerful Magic User or evil God caused this to happen, maybe he was Magically Transferred to a safe place as soon as he was out of sight in the pit. Maybe we'll see him again."

Aaron says, "I guess that's possible. It doesn't seem likely though. I doubt if it's an evil God. I'm thinking of Amrath's Imp of Wishes. That is very powerful but it's not a God. Lady Lucy was very anxious to get rid of it. Maybe it has a curse on it that will eventually cause it to do something terrible to its owner. Maybe that curse is what motivated Cassia to ban Amrath from the forest of Ereba. Maybe the Imp is responsible for the Red Haze, the Bats and Rats, and the chasm that swallowed Tamaranis, Toby, and the wagon."

Tiarra says, "I bet you're right."

Johanna says, "If so, I bet the Imp belongs to Quicksilver."

Eridana says, "If Tamaranis were still here, he would tell us that this is pure speculation. We have no evidence to back it up. He would tell us to stay focused on our mission. We are close to Divinity City now, only one day of walking beyond Tyman. He would tell us to keep on going."

Tiarra says, "I wasn't suggesting that we stop. I just think it's good to know what we might be up against. Magic of some kind is against us, and it seems to know where we are."

Eridana says, "The Red Mist is following us. Maybe that is how this mysterious Magic User knows where we are?"

Aaron says, "I suppose it could be."

Eridana says, "Then if we succeeded in killing it last night that Magic User won't know where we are now."

Ruby says, "But we don't really know if we did or not."

Johanna says, "I don't think we did. Anyway, there are other possibilities. We don't know really know why these things are happening to us."

Eridana says, "That's right. Is it an Evil god? Is it an Evil Magic User? We don't know who or how. You brought it up Tiarra. "Do you have a suggestion for what we can do about it?"

Tiarra says, "Not right now, but I thought if I shared my thinking with the rest of you, one of us might think of something."

Aaron says, "That's a good idea. If anybody thinks of something, tell the rest of us."

Ruby thinks, *I'm more confused than ever about what may be causing our bad luck. I think that is all it is, just bad luck. And there isn't anything that we can do about it.* But she doesn't say it out loud. She doesn't think this conversation is helping and doesn't want to add to it.

The road gets more and more muddy. They slog on as best they can, sometimes walking off-road where the ground is firmer. It is slow going.

It is mid-afternoon when a large, fancy looking wagon pulled by a team of fine strong horses catches up to them. The wagon is covered and enclosed so that the rain is kept out. An opening at the front enables the driver to see ahead and hold the reins of the horses, but the forward roof projection seems to keep him and the two women beside him, quite dry. It looks like there are side windows but leather flaps have been rolled down to cover them.

The wagon stops. The driver says, "Its nasty weather. Want a ride? Where are you going?"

Aaron smiles and says, "Right now we're going to Tyman."

The voice says, "That's where we're going. Get in. Throw your things in the back."

The side door opens. The driver, a middle-aged man, jumps out. Another younger man is right behind him. The driver lowers the tailgate. The young man helps the women put their bedrolls and sacks of belongings into the back part of the wagon, tossing them over the tailgate. Aaron ties Jenny's lead rope to an inviting peg, takes off his backpack, and puts that in the back also.

The younger man opens the door and climbs in. Ruby is right behind him. The first step, a small platform about three inches by nine inches, is attached to the wagon just below the door. The second step is the floor of the wagon. They are both high steps. Ruby is at first concerned that she may have a little trouble climbing into the wagon, but she sees a bar beside the door that she can grab with her right hand to help her climb in.

She thinks, *I have longer legs than I had as a dwarf. I can do it.*

The young man puts his hand out to her. "It's a big step. Let me help you."

Ruby says firmly, "I can make it by myself."

She is not used to being helped in this way and considers it an insult for anyone to think that she can't manage getting into a wagon all by her self.

Then she remembers, *I'm wearing a long skirt. That will make it a little harder.*

She uses her left hand, which is also holding Aaron's staff, to hold her long skirt up out of the way while she puts her left foot on the step. She reaches for the bar beside the door with her right hand.

But it isn't that easy. Her staff is almost level with the floor of the door and much too long to go through the door that way. *This isn't going to work.*

So she puts the staff into the hand of the young man who has offered to help her. He takes it and puts it somewhere inside the wagon. Ruby can't see where.

Ruby tries again. When she reaches up to grab for the handhold bar, the young man grabs her hand and assists her. His strong hand feels good and the assist is very helpful. Something about his touch makes her tingle all over. It feels good. It is very helpful. She doesn't need to use the bar beside the door.

When she is safely inside the young man doesn't let go. He keeps Ruby's hand in his, guiding her into the back seat bench, which is empty except for Aaron's staff which is laying across the bench. Ruby picks up the staff, sidles to the far end of the bench, and sits down. The young man sits down right beside her, leaving the older man to help the rest of the hikers climb into the wagon. Eridana soon takes the seat on the bench to the right of the young man. Tiarra, Johanna, and Aaron sit on the bench right in front of them. The driver latches the door from the inside and takes his place at the right end of the front seat beside the two women who are seated to his left.

The wagon has three rows of bench seats inside, all facing toward the front. There would be room for four people to sit on each seat, but that would be a little crowded. It isn't necessary this time. Ruby is wondering what caused that tingling feeling. *Is this young man a MagicUser? Whatever it was, it felt good. He can't be a Magic User. Magic is illegal here in The People's Republic.*

The driver slaps the backs of the horses with the reins and says commandingly, "Giddyup!"

The wagon moves forward.

The young man looks at Ruby with a smile. He has been smiling at Ruby from the time he offered to help put her bedroll into the wagon. He is really quite handsome and well dressed, looking more like a merchant than a peasant, perhaps twenty-five years old.

He says, "My name is Adam."

Responding to his expectant look, Ruby smiles and says, "My name is Ruby."

Eridana says, "My name is Emily. I'm a servant to Ruby's family. Her father and mother, George, and Johanna are sitting right in front of us. That is Ruby's sister, Jessica, sitting to their left."

The people in the front seats all turn around for this introduction even though it was directed to Adam. Then everybody in the back looks toward the front as the male driver introduces himself and the people beside him.

"I am William Tenant. This is my wife, Eleanor, and my daughter Cecily. We are glad to give you a ride. Nobody should have to walk a long distance in hard rain like this."

Adam, still looking at Ruby, asks, "What brings you to Tyman? Do you have relatives there?"

Ruby says, "We are really headed for Divinity City. We want to participate in the Festival."

"That's a long way to walk. Do you live around here?"

Ruby says, "We live north of Exodus, in the Kingdom of Ezrada."

"You have walked a long way already then. You must really want to go to the Festival of Lights. I didn't suppose anybody would walk that far."

Ruby says, "We had a wagon pulled by a horse. Some of us walked. Some of us rode in the wagon. The horse and the wagon fell into a chasm in the road yesterday afternoon during the rainstorm. A big hole opened up right in front of us and we started sliding into it. We were lucky to get away with as many things as we have. Some of what was in the wagon slid into the hole with the horse. My friend who was with us didn't make it. He went right into the hole with the wagon. I'll never see him again."

Ruby involuntarily chokes up when she remembers how Tamaranis was swept into the chasm. Her eyes get watery.

Adam says, "I'm sorry. You must feel terrible. Couldn't he jump out of the wagon?"

"He was the last one to jump out. He jumped out too late. He was dragged into the hole along with the ground and mud he was trying to walk in. He tried to get to higher ground but he couldn't."

Ruby's voice is shaky. The liquid in her eyes overflows, dribbling down both sides of her cheeks. She feels embarrassed. *I'm not supposed to cry like this. I didn't realize that I would become this emotional talking about Tamaranis.*

Adam says, "I'm very sorry. You must have loved your friend a lot."

Ruby doesn't say anything. She doesn't want to talk about something that makes her cry. She can't bring herself to say that she loved Tamaranis. It could mean too many different kinds of things.

Adam says, "I live in Tyman, the next town. We are on our way home. We spent the day yesterday visiting my mother's family, while father was doing some business. He is a merchant, the wealthiest man in our town."

Eridana thinks that this conversation is the riskiest test of their identity cover that they have had so far, and fears that Ruby is not in a stable enough state of mind to handle it well. She says, "My master is a wood cutter. We live near the woods. He cuts trees for the sawmill. We have a fine team of horses. We also have a cow, several pigs, chickens, and some sheep. His son, Harry, is taking care of things at home while we're gone."

Ruby is holding Aaron's staff.

Adam says, "That's a very fine looking staff you're holding. It looks like more than a walking stick. Is it a family heirloom?"

Ruby says, "It's my father's extra weapon. I was carrying it for him."

Aaron turns to face Adam and says, "Ruby likes to carry it. As a matter of fact, it is a family heirloom. It was my father's, my grandfather's, and before that, his father's. I've been told that many long winter nights were consumed with the carving and polishing that you see there. A very fine piece of work, don't you think?"

Adam says, "Yes indeed. May I hold it? I want to get a better look."

Without waiting for a reply, he takes the staff from Ruby's hand. He looks it over very carefully from one end to the other, rotating it slowly back and forth as he does, stopping occasionally to get a better look at a place that attracts his special attention.

Ruby is not wearing her Ring of Protection From Fear. She knows that the staff is not magic but it occurs to her that Adam might think that it is a Magic User type of staff, and that Aaron might be a Magic User, which of course he is. She doesn't know if any of the carvings might tip off someone who knows what to look for – what the staff really is. She is worried.

Adam passes the staff to Aaron, saying, "Here you are, sir. It is indeed a very fine staff. Do you plan to sell it at the Festival? Should you want to sell it, I'm sure my father would like to make an offer."

William says, "Pass it forward to me. I would like to look at it."

Aaron does so, saying, "I'm not interested in selling it."

William looks at the staff even more carefully than Adam did. Then he returns it to Aaron, saying, "A very fine staff indeed."

Adam has already returned his attention to Ruby. He senses that she has recovered from the emotion that she felt when telling about her friend who was recently swallowed up by the earth. "Tell me about yourself."

Ruby says, "I don't know what to say. I live a very ordinary life."

"I see no rings on your fingers. Does that mean that you are not married? Do you still live at home with your father and mother?"

Ruby says, "I live at home."

Ruby likes the sound of Adam's voice. There is something about him that makes her feel as if she wants to be near him, perhaps even touching him. This feeling makes her feel a little frightened of him as well.

Adam says, "I'm surprised that a young woman as attractive as you are has not yet been taken for a wife. Do you have a lover?"

This question frightens Ruby even more. She feels flustered. *I want to say no, that's the truth, but if I say that I'm afraid that he will want to be my lover. I can't think what to say.*

Eridana comes to the rescue. "Pardon me sir, but you shouldn't ask that kind of question! Do you have no sense of propriety?"

Adam turns toward Eridana. With a charming smile he says, "I could say the same thing to you. You are just as beautiful as Ruby is. I see no ring on your finger. Do you have a lover?"

Eridana says, "That is none of your business. If I did, I wouldn't tell you."

Adam says, "Perhaps it doesn't matter after all. I apologize."

He turns his head back in Ruby's direction. "Tell me about your trip, Ruby, before yesterday. You must have been on the road for several days. There must have been some good things that happened."

Ruby tries to think of something good that happened. The first thing she thinks of is their success in destroying the creature that comes from the Red Mist every night. She doesn't want to tell him about that. She can't tell him about Ereba or of the meeting with Sparrow. It seems as if most of the good things that happened were avoiding the bad things.

"Yesterday before the rain we came to a beautiful small pond. We took a break. We were quite dirty from road dust and perspiration so we bathed ourselves in the pond. The water was warm and refreshing. I felt so clean and good that I offered a prayer of thanks to Odin."

Adam says, "So you worship Odin. I've heard several stories about Odin. He is a very interesting god."

Ruby thinks, *I wish I hadn't mentioned Odin by name. I don't know if there are any Humans in The People's Republic who worship Odin or any of the other Gods that relate to Odin. I better not affirm or deny that Odin is my God.*

She asks, "Which is your god? Do you worship Odin?"

Adam laughs. "I worship the One True God, as does the rest of my family, and most of the people in Tyman."

Ruby asks, "Are you a merchant? Do you work in your father's business, or do you have your own?"

Adam says, "I'm the oldest son. Someday my father's business will be mine. He has taught me much, from the time I was a small boy, but right now I'm interested in other things. I'm an adventurer. I've been on several missions, and I want to do more."

Ruby says with enthusiasm, "Tell me about one of your adventures. I love stories of adventure."

Adam is a good storyteller. He tells a story that has a dramatic ending in which he has the key role in the positive outcome and brings home a valuable trophy. Nothing about the story suggests that Adam might be a member of the secret police, a Keeper.

When he is finished, Ruby praises his story and asks him to tell another. She likes the sound of his voice. She also realizes that when he is telling stories he is not asking questions, questions that might be difficult for her to answer.

Eridana listens also. She senses that Adam has selected Ruby as the woman in her group that he is most interested in. She hopes that Ruby will not become visibly upset when and if she realizes that Adam may be courting her, as she did at the young man in the family they had lunch with on the trail two days ago, and as she did with Tamaranis. *She walked away from those situations, but she can't walk away while in this wagon. What will she do? I don't want to have to intervene.*

Tiarra listens also and looks back occasionally. *Adam is quite handsome.* She doesn't say anything. Johanna and Aaron listen but pretend to ignore the situation as best they can. Johanna thinks, *I'm supposed to be her mother. It's my responsibility to see that she doesn't get into trouble. But of course no real trouble can happen right here in the wagon with all of us here.*

At the end of one of his stories, Adam says, "I want you all to stay with us for supper, and then spend the night. I want to show you some of the trophies I've brought back from my adventures, and perhaps some of the other valuable things my father has collected over the years. You would like that, wouldn't you father?"

William says, "Of course, you must stay with us tonight. By the time we get home you won't be able to find rooms at an inn. The inns will be overcrowded with everybody on their way to the festival. I doubt that very many walked from Tyman to Divinity City today, in this rain."

Aaron says, "Thank you. We'd be delighted. After last night our tents will be wet. I wasn't looking forward to camping out again tonight."

By the time they have reached the town of Tyman, it has stopped raining. William Tenant's house is a lot like Robert Swift's house. It has a large, walled courtyard in front with a gate at the entrance from the street. The big house is on the left. The warehouse is on the right. The large stable is against the north wall to the right of the warehouse.

Adam is the second person to step down from the wagon, right behind his father. He helps each of the other passengers negotiate the tricky maneuver to the ground. When it is Ruby's turn Adam helps her by holding her hand, and also putting a hand at her waist. Again, Ruby's entire body tingles. As her foot touches the ground her momentum carries her forward so that she falls right into his arms. She suspects that the pressure of Adam's hand on her waist contributed to this outcome. He holds her there for a moment before he drops his hand from her waist, and she steps back. It felt good being so close to him. It was exciting.

She can't think what to say so she doesn't say anything. She goes to the tailgate of the wagon to help carry their things into the house. She thinks, *I'm glad I didn't have my Short Sword under my cloak. Adam would certainly have felt it.*

Aaron gives her the staff to carry. "You all go right into the house and put your things away. I'll take the mule to the stable and unpack her before I come in. The tents are wet; I'll spread them out in the stable if I can, to dry them during the night."

Eleanor Tenant leads the way into the house. A stable hand leads the team and wagon into the stable. It will no doubt be the stable hand's responsibility to unharness the horses, take care of them, and clean up the wagon. Aaron is faced with the challenge of unloading the mule without revealing the Crossbow, Longsword, and the mace to the stable hand.

Adam carries Ruby's bedroll and sack of clothing into the house. Ruby carries Aaron's staff. Cecily helps by carrying Johanna's bedroll.

Eleanor shows them the rooms where they will stay for the night. Ruby and Eridana will share one. It is the finest room either has ever seen other than the one at Sarah Swift's house. There is a large bed, a low chest of drawers with a large mirror above it, and a small, low cupboard or cabinet. A large bowl and pitcher are sitting on the cabinet. There is a closet with pegs on the wall where clothing can be hung. Adam brings Ruby's bedroll and sack of clothing into the room. He moves to help Ruby remove her cloak.

Eleanor says, "Leave Ruby and Emily alone for a while, Adam. I'm sure they want to have a chance to clean themselves up a little before coming out for supper. You could be more helpful bringing them a jug of fresh warm water so that they can wash themselves."

Turning toward Ruby and Eridana, Eleanor points at the cabinet with the bowl and pitcher on it. She says, "There are wash cloths, towels, and soap in the drawer of the commode. The thunder jug is underneath. If there is anything you need that you don't have, tell Adam when he brings the water."

Eleanor takes Tiarra to another room down the hall. Then she takes Johanna to a room that she will presumably share with Aaron.

As soon as Eleanor and Adam have gone, Eridana closes the door and slides the bolt closed to lock it.

Eridana says, using not much more than a whisper, "Ruby, you did a good job of handling your situation with Adam in the wagon. I was afraid you were going to blow our story at any moment, but you didn't. You let him do most of the talking and played up his masculine vanity by encouraging him to brag about himself. It wasn't perfect, but I don't think he guessed that you are not really a woman, or that there is anything suspicious about our group."

Ruby says, "I was afraid the whole time that he would ask me a question and I wouldn't be able to think up a plausible answer as quickly as I needed to. That's why I tried to keep him talking. I wasn't trying to play up to his masculine vanity, whatever that is."

"Well, I think it worked. It must be really hard to play the role of a woman when you're not, and don't have any experience at it. I didn't think you would have to do it for such a long period of time and with such intensity as you did today. I'm proud of you."

Ruby says, "Neither did I. I didn't expect to ever have to talk with anybody but us for longer than a minute or two."

Eridana says, "It isn't over yet. Soon we'll be eating dinner with Adam, Cecily, and their mother and father. Maybe they have other children. My advice is to pretend that you are shy and let others do most of the talking – like you did this afternoon – but more so if you can. It's very likely that a woodcutter's daughter would be shy. I'll jump into the conversation and help when I can. I don't have to pretend that I'm shy. Don't take offense if I butt in some times. I'll only be trying to help."

Ruby says, "Thanks, I want all the help I can get. I don't want to have to talk. What's a thunder jug?"

Eridana says, "Look in the cabinet and see. It should be a place to put our body wastes so that we won't have to go to an outhouse during the night."

Ruby says, "Oh. We always went to the outhouse in my village."

She leans Aaron's staff in a corner of the room, then opens the drawer of the cabinet that Eleanor called a commode. The washcloths, soap, and towels are right where they are supposed to be. Opening the small door, she sees a very large open-mouthed jug. "This must be the thunder jug."

Eridana looks at it and says, "It is."

They take off their wet cloaks and hang them on pegs. Ruby puts her garrote, knife and sheath in the bottom drawer of the chest of drawers. Eridana puts her scimitar, Magic Dagger, sling, and pouch of sling stones in the same drawer. They take their clothes out of the sacks and hang as many as they can on hooks to dry. The rest they scatter around the room on furniture to dry before putting them into drawers. Ruby puts her wet Dwarven clothes in one of the drawers so that they will be out of sight. No one should see them. They wait for Adam to bring another jug of warm water before removing more of their clothes. While waiting they comb their hair.

Adam comes back with the water, and immediately leaves. Ruby and Eridana take off the rest of their clothes, put warm water in the bowl, and wash themselves thoroughly. Then they put on the driest and cleanest clothes they have left. Eridana seems to have disposed of the concern she had before about showing her naked body to someone who is really a man even though Ruby looks like a woman. Ruby feels self conscious about the experience but doesn't say anything about it. She feels that it is necessary to change into dryer clothes, and does not want to ask Eridana to stand in the hall while she does so. She doesn't feel any sexual attraction to Eridana at all.

But Ruby has a problem. Eridana says, "You can't wear that blouse, Ruby, It's much too wet. The wet cloth clings to your Amulet and it shows. Wear your other one."

"That's wetter than this one. What can I do?"

Eridana says, "I don't have a blouse to lend you. Only this one is dry enough for me to wear. Maybe you can borrow from Tiarra or Johanna. I'll ask on your behalf. You wait here."

208

Only Tiarra has a dry blouse that she can lend, but when Ruby puts it on she finds that it has no ties to keep it closed at the throat. The Amulet and chain Ruby is wearing cannot be covered up.

Ruby says to Eridana, "Look. I can't wear this blouse. My Magic Amulet shows. Let me swap with you."

Eridana says, "I can't do that. I'm wearing a Magic Necklace too. It's the one Cassia gave me to let her know where we are at all times. I have to keep it on, and I have to keep it out of sight. It's more fancy looking than yours is."

Ruby asks, "Then what am I going to do?"

Eridana says, "Wear the blouse that Tiarra gave you. The Tenants won't consider the possibility that your Amulet is magic. Don't worry about it. If anybody asks, say that your grandmother gave it to you. Everything will be okay."

Ruby thinks, *I don't want to lie, but I can't be wearing a wet blouse to supper either. I hope nobody asks about it.*

They do the best they can to wash the dirt out of the wet clothes they wore that day, and the day before. They put them on the floor to dry, all the clothes pegs and furniture already being covered. Then they finish combing their hair. Ruby and Eridana like the large mirror. Eridana is not satisfied with the way Ruby has combed her hair so she re-combs it for her, using the hairpins Johanna had provided to arrange it in a different style.

Eridana says, "Adam liked you before. He will really like the way you look now, hair fluffed out a bit like this and with your collar open, showing your Amulet and some skin."

Ruby says, "I don't want him to like me. Change it back. I'm supposed to look like a peasant girl."

"Lots of peasant girls wear their hair like this. And lots leave their collar open, just as Tiarra does and will be doing tonight. Your Amulet looks very nice, but I think it's okay and there isn't anything you can do about it. Don't worry about Adam. He'll admire you but that's as far as it can go. He isn't going to kiss you with his mother, father, and sister watching. You'll be okay."

Ruby does worry about it. She is afraid that she will not play her role well enough and that somebody will become suspicious. "What if William

Tenant or his wife Eleanor can cast a Perceive Magic spell and discovers that the Amulet is magic? What will I say? What will I do?"

Eridana says, "Neither of them cast Perceive Magic on Aaron's staff. They can't do it. Cecily didn't do it either. It is against their rules to use a Perceive Magic Spell. Don't worry."

Soon Cecily, Adam's sister, arrives to tell them that it is time to eat supper.

"I know it's a bit early for supper but Johanna told us that you haven't had any lunch today. She's hungry. I suppose that you all are."

Eridana says, "I know I am."

Ruby is hungry but she doesn't say anything about it.

When Cecily sees wet clothes all over the room, and the dirty water in the pail, she says, "You need a washtub, more water, a washboard, and a clothesline. I'll help you with that after supper."

CHAPTER TWENTY

AN EVENING
WITH ADAM

Last Day - Greening Fourteen – Early Evening

Cecily leads Eridana, Ruby, Aaron, Johanna, and Tiarra into the parlor instead of the dining room. Adam and his parents are already there. Adam proudly shows them trophies that he has brought back from his adventures. He gives them brief reminders of stories he told about them while in the wagon that relate to his trophies. Then they go into the dining room. No one seems to have noticed the Amulet Ruby is wearing, not even Adam. At least nobody says anything about it.

The table is set and piled high with platters of hot food. The room is not as quite as elegant as the one in Robert Swift's home. The people sit in plain chairs on both sides of the table. No one sits at the ends. Somehow Adam manages to sit directly across from Ruby.

Ruby thinks, *I will have to ask him to tell more stories.*

Aaron is seated to the right of Ruby and Eridana is at her left. The platters of food are passed around in a clockwise direction. Everyone takes what he or she wants to eat and passes the platter to the left. There is still something on each platter when it has gone all the way around the table. There is plenty of food. They all seem to be very hungry, as demonstrated by how vigorously the food is devoured.

William, the head of the household, leads the conversation.

Ruby doesn't say anything. She eats quickly, taking small bites. The food tastes very good, but she stops eating before most of the others do. She sips her wine. It tastes very good and she feels quite nervous so she sips

211

quite often. She keeps listening with interest to Adam's stories. Everybody is listening. Eridana keeps asking him to tell more, and he does. Whether the tales are true or not, they are interesting. Ruby suspects that at least part of what he is telling is made up. Sometimes he says something funny and she laughs, as does everyone else. As he talks, Ruby feels more relaxed and is having a good time.

After the meal when they get up from their chairs, Ruby feels as if she may have consumed a little too much wine. As she heads for her room with Eridana and the others, Adam comes to her side.

He says, "It stopped raining some time ago. I would like to show you around our village. There are some beautiful places. I know you would like to see them. The air is clear. It's early yet but soon the night sky will be full of stars."

Ruby thinks that she will not go, but he takes her hand and guides her to the door. Before she quite realizes what is happening, they are outside and the door is closing behind them. No one else is coming with them.

It is dark already and the sky is indeed full of stars. The courtyard is partially illuminated by a lantern hanging from a tall post near the center. Near the gate she sees the black outline of a large man, casting a long dark shadow against the wall. He is looking right at her, not moving.

"Who's that?"

Adam says, "My grandfather."

"Why is he just standing there? Why doesn't he say something?"

Adam says, "It's a statue."

Ruby wants a closer look. She steps toward it, taking Adam with her because he is still holding her hand. It is a granite statue of a distinguished looking man. The name on the base is Tenant.

Adam says, "He was a very successful merchant."

They stand there for a moment. Ruby wonders why she didn't notice it when she came in. Apparently it was on the other side of the wagon.

Adam opens the gate. They walk through it together into the street, which is also lit by lanterns hanging from posts spaced along the side. There is also moonlight. Sidewalks and buildings line both sides of the narrow way, some of them with courtyards like the one at the Tenant house. Some building fronts are right next to the sidewalk. It seems to be a respectable neighborhood. Some light reflects from scattered curbside puddles left by the recent rain.

They walk slowly along a sidewalk, Ruby's small left hand in Adam's large, strong right hand, which is steadying her a bit. She appreciates a little steadying because she has indeed had too much wine to drink. Her bare feet make no noise on the pavement. Adam's feet make no noise either. He is wearing soft leather boots. Few other people are about but they do see another couple walking on the other side of the street toward them, also hand-in-hand. As they pass, Ruby listens to the sound of their hard leather shoes. The sound soon diminishes into nothing behind her.

Ruby feels quite comfortable. Adam is talking, his voice deep, resonant, and somehow very relaxing. They come to an open area on one side of the street, a park with a fountain, benches, and scattered trees, partly enclosed by a high wall like the courtyard. Only moonlight illuminates this area, its light reflected by a small pond within the park.

Adam says, "This is one of those beautiful places."

Ruby says, "It is beautiful."

She feels happy. He puts his arm around her waist. Her body tingles. It feels good to her. Perhaps her heartbeat is quickening a bit. She thinks, *I don't like this. Tamaranis wanted to do something like this but I wouldn't let him. But what can I do? I've got to play my role. What would a real woman do?* Not able to decide, Ruby doesn't do anything.

Adam keeps talking, almost whispering, in that hypnotic voice of his. Ruby hardly knows what he is saying but it sounds good, very close to her ear. They are no longer moving. She can feel his face pressing into the fluff of her hair and barely touching her cheek. His arm tightens slightly around her waist as he turns gently to face her. He puts his other arm around her, holding her gently at first, then more firmly.

I'm being hugged. Should I be doing this? What would Eridana do?

Ruby puts her arms around Adam's back. Her fingers feel the strong muscles on each side of his spine. It has been a long time since Ruby has hugged or been hugged by anyone. It feels good. She rises up onto her toes and arches her neck backward to look up at his face. He is smiling.

Ruby thinks, *I feel like smiling, maybe I am.*

Adam closes the tiny gap between their faces and kisses her gently on the lips.

Ruby's heart is pounding. She has never been excited in quite this way, not even as Reuben. *Did I kiss him back? I'm not sure.* She does it now – enthusiastically. His hands are stroking her body, caressing it, coaxing it into even greater excitement. She is not thinking about anything, only feeling, feeling something that is close to ecstasy. She tightens her grip on his back – pulling and pressing so that as much of her body as possible is touching his. She feels his tongue between her lips, searching for an opening between her teeth. Feeling afraid of this, she lets the tip of her tongue slide between her own teeth to feel his but she doesn't open them wide enough to allow his tongue to go any further into her mouth. Adam's mouth retreats from Ruby's mouth. He begins to kiss and lick her neck.

Ruby is very excited. His arms behind her waist and back pull her even closer. She tries to pull herself back away from him. *What is happening? I shouldn't be doing this. I'm scared.*

He lets her pull away, but his hands are still on her waist and her hands are on the hard biceps of his upper arms. This kind of touching feels good. *I'm confused. What should I do?*

Now one of his hands is at the front of her waist. Ruby thinks, *He seems to be fiddling with the knot of the drawstring that holds my skirt in place. He must be trying to remove it.*

Suddenly she feels very frightened! *This isn't right! Everything is happening too fast!* She somehow manages to put both of her hands against his chest. She pushes hard, at the same time stepping back. When she does, the bowknot in the string slips loose. She grabs her skirt just in time to keep it from falling below her hips.

Ruby says firmly, "I don't want to <u>do</u> this."

She is free of him. He backs off. He stammers, "I thought you liked..."

"I don't." She pulls her skirt back around her waist and ties the string.

Adam says, "You have been making love to me as much as I have been making love to you. I think you enjoy it. Why should we stop?"

Ruby hesitates. She did like it. She didn't want to stop. She just suddenly got scared. Ruby says, "I wasn't!... I mean, I was enjoying it, but we must stop. Please... I want to go back to...to...my family. I'm scared."

Adam says, "There's no reason to be scared. Kiss me again. I really like how it feels when we kiss. Don't you?"

Ruby kisses him again. She does really like how it feels. Ruby thinks, *Tamaranis wanted me to experience this. Maybe I should have. I'm doing it now. I'm playing the role of a female - and I think I like it.*

Ruby says, "We can do this but you can't take my clothes off."

Adam says, "I should have realized that this isn't the right place to do what we want to do. I let my feelings take over. Let's go back to the stable where we can have some privacy. We can do whatever we want to there."

He gives her another kiss.

Ruby says, "I just like what we are doing here. I don't want to do any more than this."

Adam says, "All right. Let's just do this."

They do. They kiss several times, and do some hugging too. In a little while, without saying anything, they are walking slowly back toward Adam's house. Nobody else is around. Ruby has put her left arm as far as she can around his waist. He has his right arm across her back with his hand on the smallest part of her waist. They say very little. Once in a while they embrace and kiss each other again.

Ruby doesn't want this new exciting feeling to go away. She remembers again that Tamaranis told her she has the unusual opportunity to experience being a female, and can learn from that. She thinks, *This must be what he was thinking about. It certainly is an experience!*

They go into the courtyard, then to the door of the house. When they stop Ruby cuddles up against Adam and they kiss again. Ruby feels good. She likes this kind of play. A moment later she pulls back. Adam opens the door and they both go in.

William, Eleanor, and Cecily are in the dining room to the left of the hall.

Ruby says, "Thank you for the tour, Adam. Good night."

She heads for the hall.

Eleanor says, "Oh there you are, Ruby. Is everything all right?"

Ruby says, "Yes, of course. We just went for a little walk. I think I should join Emily now. We have some things to do before we go to bed."

Eleanor says, "Of course, dear. You must be very tired. If you need anything let us know."

CHAPTER TWENTY-ONE

RUBY AND ERIDANA

Last Day - Greening Fourteen – Late Evening

Ruby goes down the hall to her room. Eridana is there washing clothes. She is using two water buckets, one for soaping and another for rinsing. Several items are already hung on a thin rope that goes all the way across the room at eye level. Some of the clothes are Ruby's.

Eridana asks, "How was your tour?"

"Fine. Let me help."

First you better tell Johanna, Aaron, and Tiarra that you're okay. They're worried about you. I've been worried too. We didn't think you'd be gone so long. Then come right back and help me. I've already washed my own clothes. I'm doing yours now."

Ruby goes to Johanna's room and knocks. Aaron comes to the door. Johanna is washing clothes and Tiarra is hanging them up to dry.

Ruby says, "Hello. I just wanted to let you know I'm back."

Johanna asks, "Is everything okay?"

Ruby says, "Of course."

Tiarra says, "You were gone a long time."

Ruby says, "But everything is fine."

Tiarra says, "Go help Emily wash clothes then."

Aaron says, "Go to bed early. We need to get a very early start tomorrow morning."

Ruby goes back to her own room. She begins hanging clothes on the line, starting with one of her blouses.

Eridana asks, "Did Adam try to kiss you?"

Ruby takes a skirt from the rinse bucket and drapes it over the line. "I don't want to talk about it."

"You know if you get pregnant, you can't change back into a male Dwarf. If you did that you would be destroying your child."

"I don't want to talk about it. I'm not pregnant."

Eridana says, "I'm glad. When you didn't come right back I started to worry. I wished you were wearing my anklet, the one that prevents pregnancy."

Ruby asks, "Are you sure that works? Are you sure you can trust Lady Lucy?"

"Why wouldn't it? The Imp in the Bottle was able to grant wishes. All the magic items that she sold us did exactly what she said they would do. Of course it works."

Ruby says, "My Ring of Protection From Fear works. I believe these things can work. I just don't trust people – sometimes."

Eridana says, "For good reason – sometimes – but most people can be trusted. The Amulet that changed you into a Human female is working the way Sparrow said it would. Isn't it? I don't know everything that she told you."

"Yes. Nothing has happened differently than what she said would happen. And she gave me some warnings. By the way, did anybody tell you where the outhouse is?"

You don't need to use an outhouse. You can use the thunder-jug right here in our room. I've used it already. When you are done, put it outside the door. Somebody will empty it during the night, wash it, and bring it back in case we want to use it in the morning. You do think you could last through the night, don't you? We could wait and put it out in the morning."

Ruby says, "I forgot about that. We Dwarves always go outside – to an outhouse if there is one. That's what I'm used to." She thinks, *I would really like to have more privacy than this.*

Eridana says, "I don't even know if there is an outhouse near this building."

Ruby takes the jug to the other side of the bed, pulls up her skirt, makes sure her split drawers are out of the way, and uses it for a bowel movement. Then she urinates. She doesn't like this method very well.

Eridana says, "When you are done, put it outside the door."

Ruby does. She says, "I wonder where they empty this stuff out to. Would it be the same place the horse manure from the stable goes?

Eridana says, "I suppose so. I see that Sparrow gave you something to help you with your troubles."

"My what?"

"Your troubles. Your female cycle. Something to absorb your bleeding when it comes."

Ruby says, "Oh. Yes. She told me about it. She said it could happen any time and I ought to be prepared."

"I guess you are. Did she tell you that you are most likely to get pregnant when you are midway between your bleeding times?"

Ruby says, "Yes. She warned me about that. She advised me not to get pregnant."

Eridana says, "That means that you shouldn't have sex at all. You don't know where you are in your cycle. You should be very careful. If you get pregnant you should not try to change back into a Dwarf."

Ruby asks, "How will I know?"

"You won't know for a while. Generally women find out when the time for bleeding comes and they don't bleed. That usually means that they are pregnant, but it might not. It might just be a fluke."

Ruby says, "Sparrow told me the cycle is twenty-eight days, a full month. That's a long time to wait."

"If you don't want to wait, you should avoid having sex with a man."

Ruby says, "I don't intend to."

"Good. I just wanted to make sure you understood all of this. I wasn't sure how much a male Dwarf would know about it. Are you sure you didn't have sex with Adam? You were gone a long time. What did you do?"

Ruby says, "We looked at a statue of his grandfather, we walked along a sidewalk to a park. We stayed there for a while, then we came back."

"He kissed you in the park, didn't he, and you kissed back? Don't try to mislead me. I've done this kind of thing and I know what it's like. Sex is fun. Why do you think I bought the anklet? How far did you go? Did you let him take your skirt off? Did you…"

Ruby says, "No. I know what sex is. We didn't do it."

"You wanted to though, didn't you? Reuben, I think you are all woman now. There is no male motivation left in you at all. If you're not careful you will become pregnant, and you will have to be a woman for the rest of your life. That is okay with me, if that's what you want. Is it?"

Ruby says, "No. I'm not going to have sex and get pregnant. I just like feeling kind of aroused, that's all."

"I've heard that before... from girls who soon became pregnant. You are in dangerous territory with Adam. It's a good thing we'll be leaving early in the morning. Just stay away from him until then. I'm telling you this for your own good."

Ruby says, "All right. Thank you. Let's talk about something else."

"There's just one more thing I want to tell you about, then I'll stop. I don't know about Dwarven women, but childbirth is very painful for Human women and for Eldens. Complications can occur. Sometimes Human women bleed very badly and die. Death during childbirth is the most common way for Human women to die before old age. Sometimes the baby comes out feet first instead of headfirst. If that happens both the mother and the baby are more likely to die. Do you want that to happen to you?"

Ruby says, "I never heard of that happening to Dwarves, but that doesn't mean much. We don't talk about it. I never had anything to do with babies being born. It seldom happens in my village, and when it does the women take care of it. My mother never mentioned anyone dying."

"Well, it happens sometimes for Humans, and that is what you are now. I thought you should know about it."

Ruby says, "Well, there's no chance that I'm pregnant, and I'm not going to be. I just sort of enjoyed myself with Adam, but we didn't do anything that could make me pregnant. I know that much."

Eridana says, "You probably won't have another chance with Adam but I don't know what will happen when we get to Divinity City. You may meet some other attractive young man who wants to have sex with you."

Ruby says, "Don't worry about it. I won't do it. I don't like talking about it."

"I won't tell anybody. You shouldn't have gone outside with Adam alone at all, certainly not for such a long time. Tiarra, Johanna and Aaron talked with me about it in Johanna's room. They think it's hilarious that Adam might be trying to make love to a male Dwarf."

Ruby says, "It's not funny."

Eridana says, "We all laughed when Aaron said he'd love to see the reaction on Adam's face if the Amulet inadvertently came off during lovemaking and he found out that he's kissing a male Dwarf."

Ruby says, "That is kind of funny."

Eridana says, "Johanna thinks it was wrong for you to have spent as much time as you did alone with a man. It's contrary to her social customs. But don't worry about that. Tomorrow morning I want you to hold your head up and act normal. Pretty soon no one will think about it any more. Let's finish up with these clothes and get some rest. I'm exhausted."

They do. When all the clothes have been washed and hung up to dry they go to bed.

Ruby can't fall asleep right away. She is thinking about Adam. *How did we manage to get into that embrace and get so excited? It must have been instinct. I don't know if it was right or wrong. It felt awfully good. How could something that feels so good be wrong? Why did I become frightened? Why did I want to stop? Maybe that was instinct too. I guess I've got the instincts of a woman now. I think that must have helped me play the role of a woman. Adam didn't do or say anything to indicate that he might have thought I was anything but a woman. I guess I did well.*

It's a good thing we did stop. I don't want to get pregnant. It doesn't happen every time. Every Dwarf knows that. But maybe Humans are different. They have more children. Could it be that for Humans pregnancy occurs every single time? No it couldn't be. Eridana said it is much more likely to happen at a certain time. So did Sparrow. They must know.

I wonder what it feels like for Humans to really have sex. It must be more fun than what I did tonight and that was wonderful. Is it more fun for humans than it is for Dwarves? Probably. Is it more fun for a Human female to have sex than it is for a male Dwarf? Maybe I just muffed a chance to find out. It would have been better tonight if I had Eridana's anklet that prevents pregnancy. Just in case I lost control of the situation. I didn't expect to be walking alone with Adam. I wasn't sure what to do about it. What would I have done if he had been more aggressive? I'm not sure.

Tamaranis mentioned that I have the unusual opportunity to experience being a female, and can learn from that. Is this what he was thinking about? Am I going to be a better man later because of the experience I had with Adam tonight?

Maybe I should have allowed Tamaranis to hug me and kiss me. I allowed Adam to go where Tamaranis wanted to go. I could have let Tamaranis go a little further than I did. That time when we were on watch and we went into the wagon because it was raining, he asked me to kiss him. That would have been a good time and place to do it. It's too late now.

Finally Ruby falls asleep thinking about what it might have felt like to do with Tamaranis what she did with Adam. She thinks that he would have liked it a lot.

CHAPTER TWENTY-TWO

LEAVING TYMAN

Sun's Day - Greening Fifteen – Very Early Morning

Ruby does not sleep well. She wakes up often, thinking about Adam, sometimes wishing that she could spend more time with him. Kissing and hugging felt so good. Sometimes she wishes that she had not let him do what he did. Again and again she wonders, *What am I? What have I become? What am I becoming? Will there be more? I'm glad we are almost at Divinity City. We should be there tomorrow night. The need for this disguise is almost over. Two days to get back to Eastgate, then I can take this Amulet off for good.*

She has a dream in which her group succeeds in rescuing Robert Swift, taking him back to Eastgate. Then, in her dream, she removes the Amulet. But her body doesn't change back to Reuben as it did when she did it in Sparrow's stable. Nothing happens. Reuben is still in the body of a Human female. This dream repeats itself several times and each time she wakes up in a panic. She also has a dream in which she allows Adam to do whatever he wants to with her body. But when she wakes up she can't remember what they did together, or whether she liked it or not. It is not a restful night.

It is still dark when Johanna knocks on the door of the room where Eridana and Ruby are sleeping. Eridana goes to the door and opens it.

Johanna says, "Get up, get dressed, get packed, and get going! Aaron wants to get an early start. Breakfast will be ready by the time you are ready to go. Aaron says we have a long way to go today and he wants to get there well before dark. He hopes to find Robert Swift during the night, and get away with him. He's already out in the stable packing the mule."

Ruby likes the sound of that. *Maybe only two more days and I can take off the Amulet. Maybe less.* She immediately jumps out of bed.

Johanna leaves. Eridana and Ruby take turns using the thunder jug to eliminate their body wastes. They found a clean empty one right outside the door.

They wash themselves, pouring clean water from the pitcher into the bowl. Then they dress, comb their hair, and pack their extra clothes, magic items, and some of their weapons into their cloth sacks. Ruby wears one of her own blouses, now clean and dry, and which covers the Amulet very well. For now she puts the blouse she borrowed from Tiarra in the sack with her own clothes. Ruby combs her hair very quickly.

Eridana says, "I'm going to lend you my anklet. I want you to put it on now and wear it all the time. Your skirt should hide it from magic perception. I don't want you to get pregnant. It would be a much bigger problem for you than it would be for me. You probably won't need it, but it would be better to be safe than sorry."

Ruby takes it and puts it on. "Thank you, but I don't think I'm going to need it today. Tell me. Have you ever had sex with a man?"

Eridana says, "Yes. It was a wonderful thing to do and we did it several times."

Ruby asks, "Are you going to marry him?"

Eridana says, "I don't think so. It's been a good relationship but it doesn't seem to be heading for marriage. I'll get married someday. It's not uncommon among my people to have a few red-hot affairs before settling down and getting married, but I don't do one-nighters. I want much more of a relationship than that."

"So that's why you bought the anklet."

Eridana says, "I suppose so."

Ruby asks, "How did you keep from getting pregnant when you did it?"

Eridana says, "I avoided having sex at those times when I was fertile. I know that's not a perfect method but it worked for me. I guess I was lucky. I felt confident that if I did get pregnant the baby's father would marry me and we would be all right. I thought it was worth the risk. I only did it two or three times."

Eridana signals the end of this conversation by opening the door and leading the way to the dining room where they join Johanna, Tiarra, Aaron and Eleanor to eat a quick breakfast of bacon, eggs, and biscuits. Ruby is both glad and disappointed that Adam isn't there. There is little conversation. She thinks, *Eleanor will be glad to see me leave. She probably didn't like the idea that Adam might fall in love with a poor peasant girl. What if she knew that I'm really a male Dwarf?*

Everyone has to go back to his or her room after eating breakfast to get weapons, bedrolls, and clothing sacks. Eridana, Tiarra, and Johanna hide their hand weapons under their cloaks as they had before they started walking yesterday. When they get into the courtyard they see that Jenny is packed and ready to go. Her lead rope is tied to a stone post with a large iron ring at its top. In a few more minutes they are in the street headed in the direction of Divinity City. It is not raining.

Aaron says, "I hope everybody slept well."

Eridana says, "I did. You know how I like to sleep outside, but last night I was glad to get all my clothes clean and dry and sleep on a soft dry mattress. I slept very well. How did you sleep? And…why are we leaving so early?"

Aaron says, "We have a long way to go. Ruby, how did your evening with Adam go?"

Ruby says, "The moon was beautiful. I really liked the lampposts and the statue in the courtyard. We had a nice walk. There's a public park; we'll come to it soon."

Ruby expects that one of Aaron's embarrassing jokes will come next, but it doesn't.

Aaron says, "I hope you didn't say anything that might have let Adam know that we are really adventurers carrying magic weapons instead of a woodcutter family. I didn't like it that you were displaying your Magic Amulet right where he could see it so easily. He spent most of the dinner time looking at it."

Ruby says, "I didn't say anything that would let him know who we really are."

Aaron says, "You drank too much wine. Too much alcohol causes loose lips. You may have said something without even knowing it. You shouldn't have left the house with him."

Eridana says, "Don't blame Ruby. She had no choice but to display the Amulet the way she did. All her blouses were soaked. She had to borrow one of Tiarra's, which, as you have noticed, hides very little. Don't you know that the best place to hide something is in plain sight? I don't think Adam was looking at the amulet. He was looking at Ruby. Just like you look at Johanna sometimes and she doesn't have any jewelry at her neck."

Aaron says, "Didn't Sparrow tell us that peasant girls wouldn't have jewelry like that? It's too expensive looking. Of course Adam noticed that it didn't look right. I'm worried. Adam and William examined my staff. They also might have thought it odd that I had such a nice battleaxe. The stableman might have noticed the hammer that used to belong to Tamaranis, your Shortsword, Crossbow, Crossbow Bolts, and Tiarra's Longsword on the mule. Somebody might have noticed the weapons that you, Tiarra, Johanna, and Ruby carry under your cloaks. If anyone sees us carrying so many weapons they are very likely to become suspicious."

Tiarra asks, "What else were we supposed to do? Throw them away?"

Aaron says, "We should have thrown Tamaranis's' hammer down into the chasm. I know we need our weapons, but realizing that someone might have noticed them, we have to be more careful. I want us to be ahead of the crowd of travelers that will be leaving Tyman for Divinity City today. I'm also hoping that if we are well on the way before William and Adam wake up, maybe they won't bother to say anything to the local authorities. I think William likes us."

Tiarra says, "Adam likes Ruby. He wouldn't want her to get in trouble. That could help. I think she did the right thing to spend as much time as she did with Adam last night."

Aaron says, "I hope you're right. Let's keep up a good pace. I want to put distance between us and Tyman as fast as we can."

Now Ruby understands why Aaron is acting so strangely this morning. She says, "I don't think Adam was curious about the Amulet at all. He would have asked me about it. He didn't."

Aaron says, "I suppose he wasn't looking at the Amulet then; he was looking at what was underneath it."

Eridana says, "Probably. He's a man. The time Ruby spent with Adam was probably the best thing that could have happened. He won't want anything bad to happen to Ruby. He won't care whether she's an imposter or not. He likes her."

Aaron says, "Maybe. But that's not the only reason I'm worried. I think the stableman might have seen the weapons I loaded on the mule this morning. If he tells William that we are hiding weapons on the mule, William might tell the constable."

Eridana says, "Let's hope that doesn't happen."

They continue to walk vigorously along the street. They have already passed the public park and are soon near the edge of town on a dirt road, passing farms and farmland.

Ruby thinks, *Aaron and Johanna slept in the same room last night. I wonder if Aaron made advances toward Johanna as Adam did to me. Aaron's wit usually has lots of sexual overtones. He seems to be thinking about sex most of the time. He must certainly have been thinking about it last night. What would Johanna's reaction have been? She has never said much of anything about sex, but she must have feelings about it. I wish somebody would ask, but I'm not going to. Eridana gave me the anklet this morning right after Johanna woke us up. Is it possible that Eridana loaned it to Johanna last night? It seemed like Johanna might have given something to Eridana this morning. Who was it that said 'still water runs deep?'*

Tiarra says, "I hope the Red Mist is not following us this time. We didn't see it yesterday, but the visibility was very poor. Is it possible that we won't have to fight it again?"

Eridana says, "We really beat up on it the last time. It shouldn't want to come back for more of that."

Tiarra says, "I hope not."

Nobody sees it. Ruby says, "The Red Mist has never followed us into a city, but that doesn't mean that it won't be following us today. It might still show up."

Johanna says, "I know you're very worried, Aaron. What do you think might happen if William tells someone in authority that we may not be who we say we are?"

Tiarra says, "I can answer that. If a constable thinks we are hiding our true identity, he may want to search us. If he does, he'll find our weapons. If he can cast Perceive Magic, he'll find our magic items. They may inspect our ears. If they do that, they'll discover that two of us look like Eldens. Then we'll be in real bad trouble. They may discover Johanna's holy symbol."

Tiarra looks at Johanna. "I know you're not wearing it right now. I suppose it's in your pouch. A constable might look there. That might put you in trouble. Someone may suspect that it is the symbol of a religion that casts healing spells. I think William already has enough clues to be suspicious. Did you see the way he looked at Aaron's staff yesterday in the wagon? You can bet he recognized it for a Magic User's staff, not a woodcutter's staff, even if it's not magic. Ruby will be in deep, deep trouble if, during their search, they remove her Amulet. We have to hope that they don't search us. If they do we'll all be arrested and taken to the tower."

Eridana says, "Maybe we should leave the road and find some other route to Divinity City?"

Johanna asks, "What other way is there?"

Eridana says, "We can't go through the fields. We would be noticed. We would have to go through the woods beyond the fields.

Tiarra says, "Let's get going then. In the woods we can carry our weapons in the open. I'll feel better with my Crossbow in my hand where it belongs, and my sword on my belt."

The sun is still out of sight, but the pre-dawn sky is getting lighter. They head for the woods beyond the fields, following a farm road, or lane, between two rows of bushes and trees. Large fields are on both sides of the lane. It looks like tiny sprouts of corn are emerging. They try to avoid walking in muddy places where they would be leaving very obvious tracks.

When they get to the woods beyond the fields, the lane continues straight ahead into the forest, but they are in luck. Another lane follows the edge of the woods between it and the field. A stone wall with brush and trees along it separates the lane from the field. This cover seems substantial enough to hide them from anyone in the road, most of the time. This lane parallels the road and can take them in the direction of Divinity City. They follow it. It is now quite light. There is no sign of the Red Mist.

When they hear the sound of running horses along the main road they stop in place and duck for cover behind bushes. Four horses with riders are galloping toward Divinity City."

Aaron says, "That could be the constable of Tyman and his men, trying to catch up to us."

Tiarra says, "It could be, but it's more likely that their mission has nothing to do with us. Anyway, if they are looking for us on the road, they won't find us."

They hurry along the lane, which is often wet and squishy because of the recent rain. They can't avoid leaving some tracks.

Aaron says, "Don't worry about tracks. Any farmer could make tracks like this."

Eridana says, "If members of his family are with him that have small, female size feet. But that would be unusual. A good tracker might think that these tracks are unusual."

Tiarra says, "Maybe the farmer is taking his children with him. It won't do any good to worry about it. Yes, we're taking a chance, but it's a better chance than if we were walking along the main road. It won't do any good to worry about it."

Eridana says, "It's still a good idea to avoid making tracks whenever we can."

Johanna says, "That's what we're doing."

From time to time Ruby thinks of Adam. *I think he likes me. I like the way he tells stories. It felt good when we were hugging and kissing each other.*

They continue on, stopping for a break when it is near noon, at a small brook in a shady grove.

Eridana says, "This side lane is working out well, but when we get to Divinity City we're going to have to get back on the main road and go through one of the gates. Has anybody figured out what we do if they try to search us then? I wish we had the wagon to hide our weapons in. That worked well when we entered The People's Republic, after crossing the bridge. Has anybody thought about how we get into the tower to find Robert Swift? It's not likely they give guided tours of the tower for woodcutter families."

Aaron says, "Maybe we could climb over the wall."

Tiarra says, "Of course they will have guards watching for that. That's the most likely way for us to get caught."

Ruby says, "I might be able to sneak over the wall using my Cloak of Blending, or just sneak through the gate."

Tiarra says, "We only have one Cloak of Blending. We need to go in as a group. It's too bad Aaron can't cast Invisibility. I bet Amrath's Imp of

Wishes could make us all invisible. If Amrath was with us and did that, we could all just walk in together. We need to make a plan. We have to start by getting a good look at the tower from the outside. There might be a way in other than through the main gate."

Johanna asks, "We also need to plan what to do after we get inside the walls of the city. What will we do? Where will we sleep? All the inns will be full."

Aaron says, "All we need to do is find a place where we can set up our tents."

Eridana says, "A place where we will have some privacy."

Tiarra says, "It was a mistake to disguise ourselves as farmers and give up our horses. All we really needed to do is look like Humans. Some of the people we see on the road don't look like farmers. I want a horse to ride. I want to carry my weapons openly, ready to use them at any time. We've got the wrong disguises."

Aaron says, "I agree with you now. We'll buy horses as soon as we can."

Tiarra asks, "Do we have enough money?"

Aaron says, "I think so."

Tiarra says, "If we can't buy them, we'll have to steal them."

Aaron says, "And we would be caught. It wouldn't be worth the risk. We can buy horses for our trip back."

CHAPTER TWENTY-THREE

APPROACHING DIVINITY CITY

Sun's Day - Greening Fifteen – Mid-afternoon

The lane they are travelling along eventually ends, but they have used it to good advantage for most of the day. It is mid afternoon. It is a fairly warm day. Still wearing their cloaks, they feel quite warm, perspiring to some extent.

Eridana says, "We're almost there. I think I can see the tower of Divinity City in the distance. It's time to return to the main road."

Tiarra says, "All right. Hide your weapons under your cloaks then. Let's go."

Ruby gives her axe to Aaron. She carries his staff. Tiarra puts her one-hand Crossbow and bolts back into her clothing sack. She has Ruby's Shortsword hidden under her yellow cloak. Johanna has her mace under her cloak, jamming it between her belt and her body. Eridana has her scimitar under her cloak and her sling in her pouch. They feel that they can carry their weapons this way without being seen for a little while, and they want to be able to get at them quickly. Ruby's Magic Armbands are on her arms hidden by her blouse. Her Magic Ring that diminishes fear is in the pouch, which she carries openly over her shoulder. The others have their small magic items hidden in pouches as well.

Aaron says, "If they check the mule they'll find Tiarra's Longsword, Tamaranis's' hammer, Ruby's Crossbow and her Crossbow Bolts. The Longsword, Crossbow and Bolts are magic."

Tiarra says, "We don't need the hammer. Let's get rid of it. Leave it here."

Johanna says, "That doesn't seem right. It's valuable. And it's not magic."

Aaron says, "The hammer isn't a problem. The Longsword and Crossbows are the problems."

Tiarra says, "Leave the Crossbows here then."

Ruby says, "No. That's my father's Crossbow and my best weapon. If they search the mule, they'll find your Magic Longsword anyway. Do you want to leave that here?"

Tiarra says, "All right. Let's hope they don't search the mule. Slip the weapons under the tent canvas. If they check, they might not see them anyway."

They repack the mule. The disassembled Crossbow pieces and the hammer are slid within the folds of different tents, but the Longsword, even though it is under canvas, protrudes beyond the rest of what is packed on the mule.

Aaron says, "The Longsword sticks out like a sore thumb."

Ruby says, "Cut some tent poles. We can hide the Longsword in the middle of a bundle of poles. We'll need them if we are going to set up the tents in the city. We can't cut tent poles in the city."

Tiarra says, "Good idea!"

It doesn't take long to cut nine poles of suitable length for the tents, and some smaller sticks to use for stakes. They wrap the poles in cloth using the extra robe that was in Tamaranis's' clothing sack. This covers up the ends of the poles so that no one will be able to see the Longsword unless it is removed. The bundle of poles goes on top of Jenny's load. It doesn't look suspicious, but it is a big load for the mule.

Following another farm lane back to the main road, they turn left toward the city. There are other people on the road going in both directions. Many of them look like local farmers. Most of them have wagons or carts but some have pack animals, and some just seem to be a family group with no animals, walking to or from the city. They might live nearby.

Tiarra and her group walk by themselves. A half-hour later they see a double column of soldiers armed with swords and spears, marching toward them. Tiarra leads her group to the right edge of the road to let the soldiers pass. When the soldiers have passed and are out of hearing Tiarra says, "Those were soldiers of the Alliance. We're in dangerous territory now."

Eridana says, "I'm glad they didn't ask us any questions. Our disguises seem to be working."

Johanna says, "I feel like we fit right in with the other travelers. We're almost there. We're going to make it."

About fifteen minutes later they see a bridge ahead of them that crosses a large brook. The people walking across the bridge are going very slowly in single file. A few uniformed soldiers are standing at the bridge. It looks like one of them is asking questions of everybody that crosses it, but they aren't stopping anybody. The travelers stop for only a moment - then walk right across the bridge and beyond. There are some other soldiers at the other end of the bridge.

Tiarra gets in line behind some others.

Johanna says, "Don't get ahead of your father, Jessica. He should always go first."

Aaron steps in front of Tiarra. When he gets to the soldier with the scroll he says, "My name is George Wood. I'm a woodcutter. I live north of Exodus. This is my family."

The soldier writes something on his paper and nods, signaling for George to move on.

Tiarra says, "My name is Jessica."

Johanna says, "My name is Johanna."

Eridana says, "My name is Emily Herds."

Ruby says, "My name is Ruby Wood. The mule's name is Jenny."

The soldier asks, "What's the mule carrying?"

Ruby says, "Tents, rope, an axe, food, pots and pans, that kind of thing."

The soldier says, "Mister Wood, after you cross the bridge I want you and your family to stand over there near those trees. We may want to have a look at what your mule is carrying. It will only be a few minutes. Then you can move on. It is just a routine check."

They all feel apprehensive. They haven't noticed that anybody else has been asked to go to a designated place and wait.

Aaron thinks, *It may not be routine, but there doesn't seem to be anything else to do.*

As Aaron approaches the soldier at the other end of the bridge the soldier waves his hand to direct Aaron to a place near some trees and bushes on the left side of the road.

Aaron waves back with his left hand in a friendly way as he leads his group to the designated place near the trees and bushes. They stand next to Jenny. The soldier goes with them.

Very soon several armed men and women emerge from the cover of the bushes near the trees and move into positions all around them. The soldier goes to a woman who is carrying a staff, and says something to her in a very low voice that others cannot hear.

Ruby thinks, *We need to run.* She takes a step but no one else moves at all. She stops. She thinks, *If Tiarra and Aaron don't run, I guess I shouldn't.*

The woman who is carrying a staff, says, "I think these may be the ones we are looking for. Eben, take a look at what the mule is carrying."

Aaron says, "Go ahead and look. Would you like me to help?"

He passes the axe to Ruby, saying, "Hold this."

He loosens the rope that holds the tent poles in place and lays them aside. Somehow he manages to keep Tiarra's Longsword in the middle of the poles, out of sight.

He says matter-of-factly, "Tent poles."

Then he does more untying and removes the canvas tent on top, putting it on the ground.

He says, "A tent."

He unloads the other tents one at a time. He lays each tent on the ground trying to keep the hammer and Crossbow hidden in them from being noticed. This reveals packages of food, pots and pans, and the small camp axe. Eben opens every package of food and cooking dishes and finds that it is indeed nothing but food and cooking dishes.

The woman with the staff says, "Spread out the tents. Make sure that nothing is hidden between the layers of canvas. You do it, Eben."

Aaron stands back, right next to Ruby, and unobtrusively takes his staff from her.

Eben unfolds the first tent, the one that was on top of Jenny's load. He says, "There's nothing here."

The leader looks disappointed. She says, "Check the others."

Eben finds the hammer between the folds of the second tent. "Aha. A weapon was hidden here. Is this what we are looking for?"

The leader says, "Maybe, if it's magic. Put it here on the ground. I'll do Perceive Magic on it.

She casts her spell, pointing her right hand at the hammer as if unseen rays of energy are radiating from her hand. The hammer doesn't glow.

Tiarra thinks, *She's a Spellcaster. I didn't think there were supposed to be any Spellcasters in The People's Republic.*

Aaron says, "What's wrong with having an extra weapon on a pack mule? I don't need it any more. I plan to sell it."

Eben is already unfolding the third tent. He pulls out the two pieces of the Crossbow. He says, "Here's a crossbow. Are you planning to sell this too?"

Aaron says, "Of course."

Eben quickly assembles it.

The leader says, "It's a little odd looking. Where's the cocking lever? I think I'll cast Perceive Magic on this too."

The spell is still alive. As she points her right hand at the Crossbow, it glows.

"Aha! A Magic Crossbow! I knew there was magic around here somewhere."

Aaron says, "I didn't know that was magic."

The leader says sarcastically, "Of course not – but I did. I can smell magic. I think there may be some more magic around here."

She directs her spell toward Aaron and Ruby. Nothing visible on Aaron's body glows, but Ruby's boots glow. There is just a little space between the bottom of her skirt and the ground and the glow is barely visible.

"Ohhh! Look at this! Magic on your feet! Look at the glow! Lift up your skirt a bit. I want to see what's causing it."

Ruby has no choice so she lifts her skirt a little. The leader can see her boots.

"Aha! Magic boots. We've hit the jackpot! I must place you all under arrest. Drop your weapons. Theresa, put manacles on these two first."

Tiarra yells, "Grab your weapons and fight for your lives!" As she does she draws the Shortsword from its scabbard under her cloak and thrusts it at the middle of the man nearest to her. He dodges, trying to draw his weapon as he does. Tiarra chops his weapon arm; his sword falls on the ground while he clutches his wound trying to stop the bleeding.

Aaron pokes one end of his staff into Eben's belly. He falls backward onto the ground, screaming in pain.

Ruby takes her axe in both hands and swings it at the leader, hitting the upper part of her right leg with a glancing blow. Ruby is wearing the Wristbands that give her extra strength under her blouse, but she still has a little trouble managing the heavy axe with her weaker muscles. She meant to hit the leader in the chest. Ruby is also wearing the Wristband of Armor Protection. The leader backs away, as a tall fighter moves between her and Ruby.

Eridana casts the spell "Glowing Target" on the female leader. A ring of sparkles dances around the leader's entire body making it easier for her to be hit.

Johanna takes her mace from under her cloak and swings it at the woman closest to her, who has manacles in her hands. The woman dodges, drops the manacles, and draws her own weapon just in time to parry Johanna's second blow.

Ruby swings her axe strongly, hitting the left hip of the tall warrior facing her. He falls down, screaming with pain. But another fighter quickly takes his place.

As soon as Eridana has finished casting, she grabs her scimitar and uses it on the fighter closest to her, an agile young woman. Her first strike misses.

Aaron manages to cast a Magic Beam of Energy spell on the leader. Before he can cast again, a Magic Beam of Energy spell cast by someone else strikes him, interrupting his concentration. He will have to start his spell again. *Who did that? There must be more than one Magic User among them.*

Tiarra's adventurers are outnumbered by more than two to one. There are several archers who form a second line behind those armed with hand weapons. Tiarra and Ruby are each fighting two opponents, both armed with swords. Eridana and Johanna are each facing only one. Each time Ruby swings her axe at one of her two opponents the other one hits her somewhere. She has been hit on her left arm and her right leg. She is bleeding. *I can't fight two at a time.* But there is no one to help her. Tiarra has the same problem.

Aaron has dropped back into a position behind Ruby and Tiarra. He casts the Arrow of Light from his ring, hitting three of their opponents all lined up in a row: a swordsman, the female Magic User, and the archer behind her. None of them seem to be badly hurt. These are very tough fighters.

Arrows are flying. One of them goes right past Ruby's ear. She hears it hit something solid right behind her. She glances back just long enough to see Aaron falling to the ground, an arrow in his chest. She turns back just as an arrow hits her right thigh. She can hear Johanna chanting a prayer in a strange language. This gives her renewed courage. She swings her axe at the face of one of her opponents, then glances at Eridana and Johanna. Each of them has at least one arrow imbedded in their flesh.

A sword strikes Ruby's left leg but she keeps on fighting. From the corner of her eye she sees Tiarra drop limply onto the ground. Then she feels sudden pain at the top of her head and everything goes black.

PART FIVE

DIVINITY CITY

CHAPTER TWENTY-FOUR

THE TOWER

Sun's Day - Greening Fifteen – Late Afternoon

Ruby wakes up slowly and painfully. She is sitting on a hard floor, leaning her back against something that is also hard. She feels groggy. All of her muscles hurt, especially in her stomach and upper torso. It hurts to breathe. She feels manacles digging into her wrists and ankles. Her head hurts, and she feels like vomiting. She opens her eyes. There isn't much light, but at first what there is almost blinds her. When her vision clears, she sees that Tiarra, Eridana, and Johanna are sitting on the floor facing her just a few feet away. They are wearing only short, sleeveless, burlap shifts and are chained to the wall with manacles at their wrists and ankles. The chains are about three feet long, held to the manacles by large padlocks, which also hold the manacles together. They are looking at her.

Ruby realizes that she is wearing only a burlap shift also. *She thinks,* I must be chained to the wall behind me, just as they are. Looking at her legs that protrude from under the burlap in front of her she suddenly realizes that she is back in Reuben's Dwarven body. She feels her neck with her hands. The Amulet is gone. She looks at her bare arms. The Bracelets are gone. She thinks, *No wonder my stomach and chest muscles hurt so much. They have had to do a lot of stretching. My leg and arm muscles had to contract and get thicker. That's why they hurt, but why does my head hurt? The last thing I remembers about the fight is being hit on the head by some kind of weapon – a sword. That's why.*

Reuben feels the top of his head with his right hand. *I feel no wetness; I'm not bleeding. It doesn't even feel a scab. Someone must have used a spell to heal the wound, but it still hurts.* When Reuben moved to feel his head, his muscles hurt even more and the burlap scratched his skin. He settles back into as comfortable a position as he can. He would like to get a look at his male genitals to make sure they are all right but it doesn't seem right to do that in the presence of Johanna, Eridana, and Tiarra. They are all looking at him.

Tiarra is thinking, *He's got awfully large ears. I can see one of them sticking out through his long black hair. But they're not pointed, I guess that goes with being a Dwarf.*

Eridana asks, "Are you all right, Reuben?"

Reuben says, "I guess so. I hurt all over, but I guess I'm alive. Did you heal me?"

His voice is back to normal. It seems almost as strange as when his voice changed from that of a male Dwarf to that of a Human female.

Eridana says, "No. I didn't need to. When I woke up everyone was already healed."

Reuben asks, "Where are we?"

Eridana says, "We are in a prison cell. I suppose we are in the same prison tower that Robert Swift should be in. You were unconscious for a long time, Reuben. I was afraid you might not come to."

Reuben asks, "Where's Aaron?"

Johanna says, "He's right beside you on your left."

Reuben shifts to look and it hurts. Aaron is also wearing a burlap shift. He is manacled and chained to the wall. He is awake. Apparently they all woke up before Reuben did. He looks back at Tiarra, Eridana, and Johanna. Like Aaron's, their shifts cover their legs only down to mid thigh. They are a beautiful trio. He sees no wounds on their bodies, no evidence of the battle at all.

Reuben asks, "How did we get here? I thought we were all going to be killed."

Johanna says, "We all woke up here. Apparently someone healed all of our wounds, not leaving a single scar. We have seen nothing of our captors. We haven't been told anything."

Reuben says, "I thought the Alliance didn't allow magic and spellcasting in their realm. It's obvious that the leader of the group we fought is a Spellcaster. Now we have been magically healed. What's going on?"

Aaron says, "You know as much about that as we do."

Tiarra says, "We were attacked by Keepers, the secret police of the Alliance. The leader of the group was a Magic User. There was at least one other Magic User in the group, and it appears that they also have people who heal wounds like Johanna and Eridana do. They are hypocrites. They do not practice what they preach. They are not opposed to using magic, but they are obviously really opposed to anyone but themselves using magic."

Aaron says, "You are certainly right about that. They are very bad people."

Johanna asks, "Why did they decide to inspect what our mule was carrying? If they didn't do that we would have gone right on into Divinity City without any trouble."

Eridana says, "The soldier might have seen a scar on one of our left hands that indicated to him that we might be allies of Queen Cassia."

Reuben says, "The soldier who checked us when we came across the river into Beastgate didn't seem to pay any attention to the possibility of scars on our hands."

Tiarra says, "I don't think it's likely that the soldier that we gave our names to would have known about those scars either, or much of anything at all about the Erebans, but the woman who led the search of Reuben's mule might know that."

Reuben says, "She didn't ask us to show us what our hands looked like. She did a careful inspection of what my mule was carrying."

Eridana says, "You may be right. Maybe none of the people of the Alliance know about the kind of scars we have on our hands. I didn't know anything about it until Queen Cassia asked us to sign our names in blood."

Johanna says, "There is a lot we don't know about the Keepers and the people who live here."

The walls of the cell are made of stone. There is one strong wooden door to Reuben's right. Sunlight streams through a small window high to his left, striking the opposite wall just above the door. It must be late in the day; the sun should be coming from the west.

Reuben says, "This must be the tower where people are imprisoned until execution on festival day. Did they heal us so that they can burn us at the stake tomorrow?"

Tiarra says, "Probably. We'll be a late addition to the public spectacle that will celebrate the Festival of Light. I don't know when our time will come. I suppose it could be tomorrow."

Reuben sees a white cube, about two inches on a side, sitting in front of Aaron. There is also one in front of Johanna and one in front of Eridana. They are a bit grainy like sugar cubes and just too far away for anyone to touch.

Reuben asks, "What is the meaning of those white cubes? Why don't Tiarra and I have one?"

Aaron says, "You're not Spellcasters. I've already tried to cast a spell. It didn't work. I think it has to do with those white cubes. Johanna and Eridana haven't been able to cast spells either."

Reuben says, "We have to figure out a way to get out of here."

Tiarra says, "We know, but so far we haven't been able to come up with a plan. Maybe you've got a good idea."

Reuben takes a good look at one of the padlocks holding his manacles together. It is about two inches across and about a half-inch thick. The keyhole is a slot in one side big enough for a large key. A quarter inch diameter hole on the other side looks like a place for the end of the key to pivot while moving the catch. It is a simple lock.

Reuben says, "If I had something to use for a pick, I could pick this lock. Does anybody have a lock pick?"

Tiarra says, "Of course not. All we have are these terrible scratchy shifts. They took everything we had away from us."

Reuben says, "I don't need much. If I had a nail I could do it. Look around. Maybe there is something on the floor that would work."

Everybody looks.

Tiarra says, "There's nothing. They wouldn't be so stupid as to leave anything lying around that could be used for a lock pick. We'll have to think of something else.

They hear footsteps in the corridor; the door creaks open. The woman who led the soldiers that captured them is there alone.

She asks, "Do any of you want to join The Keepers?"

No one knows what to say. The idea seems preposterous.

She says, "Don't answer now. I'll leave and give you a chance to think about it. I'll be back in a while."

She leaves. The door slams shut. They can hear her footsteps for a while. Reuben says, "She turned to the left, which should be north."

The woman's words cause the five cellmates to speculate about why they would be offered a chance to join The Keepers.

Tiarra says, "They must want us to join the secret police and do the dirty work of the leaders of the Alliance. I won't do it."

Eridana says, "Neither will I. The Keepers are enemies of my people and yours, Tiarra. We have Elden blood. They are your enemies too, Reuben. Don't do it."

Johanna says, "It would be against my religion."

Everyone looks at Aaron. He says, "I'm not a hypocrite. I'm not going to join The Keepers. I don't see how they could be certain of our loyalty. This offer must be a trick."

Tiarra says, "You're probably right. The Alliance can't be trusted."

In a short time, the door opens again. Four guards bring in two more men wearing burlap shifts and manacles on their wrists and ankles. The guards chain them to the wall beside Reuben and Aaron, then leave, saying nothing.

Tiarra asks, "Who are you, and what have you done to be put in a cell with us?"

One of them has an odd looking tattoo on his right arm. He says, "I'm Richard Drake. I'm a cloth merchant. I have no idea why they brought me here."

The other man says, "I'm David Silverlake. I'm an actor and a singer, the favorite performer of the Duchess. When she finds out I'm here, she'll see to it that I'm quickly released."

He is at least six-feet tall. His dark hair is in ringlets. Apparently the burlap shifts are made in only one size. Because he is so tall, his shift covers very little of his legs, while Reuben's comes down below his knees.

Tiarra says sarcastically, "Good for you."

Eridana says, "Don't trust them. They could be spies. Don't confide in them. We need to be careful what we say, just in case I'm right."

Richard says, "I'm not a spy."

Eridana asks, "Why did they put you in here?"

Richard says, "I don't know. Why did they put you in here?"

Johanna says, "I don't know for sure, but it might be because I'm a Healer. Are you a Healer?"

Tiarra says, "Shut up, Johanna." Then looking at the newcomers, "We wouldn't tell you if we knew. Why are you here, David?"

David says, "Hell if I know. It must be an error. The Duchess is a friend of mine. She'll get me out."

Aaron says, "We've been given a chance to join The Keepers. What should we do?"

Reuben says, "We should not join The Keepers. If I did that, I would be working against the survival of my own people. The Alliance wants to destroy the Dwarves."

Richard asks, "What do you really know about The Keepers? If they intend to kill all Dwarves, why would they let you join?"

Aaron says, "It's obvious that Magic Users are allowed to be a part of The Keepers. They must not really believe Spellcasters are evil. Maybe the Spellcasters they kill are the ones who refuse to join. What does it mean to join The Keepers?"

He looks at Richard and David.

David says, "If I were you I would be more concerned with what it means if you don't join The Keepers. I'm quite certain that if you don't agree to join, you'll be executed tomorrow or the next day. That's what happens. I know that much. I don't know what happens if you agree to join. What do you say, Richard?"

Richard says, "I don't know much about this either, but if they ask me to join, I will. I don't want to be executed tomorrow. One way to find out what it means to be part of The Keepers would be to join. If I don't like it there may be something else I can do to escape from this tower."

David says, "Of course you could ask someone who knows. I don't know. I'm not part of The Keepers. They have never asked me to join. I've been allowed to mingle with them because the Duchess likes me. I don't know why they put me in here with you. It's obviously some mistake. When the Duchess finds out that I'm here, I'll be released."

Tiarra asks, "Who is this Duchess you keep talking about. It sounds like a royal title. I didn't think there were any Dukes or Duchesses in The People's Republic, or in the Alliance. Dukes are hereditary positions of power. Does the Alliance have a King?"

David says, "Oh no. There are no hereditary positions of power here. People with authority are either elected by all the people or appointed by the people who were elected. The Duchess is the term for the Director of Entertainment – you know – theater, music, sculpting, painting, poetry, and fiction. She has been very occupied with getting everything ready for the festival. I have been helping her. She needs me right now. The festival is tomorrow. Several bands will be playing. Even now a musical ensemble should be playing background music for a private ritual for the execution team."

Eridana asks, "What is this execution team?"

David says, "They are the people who chop off heads and burn the heretics and other enemies of the people."

Aaron says, "I don't want my head to be chopped off or be burned as a heretic. It seems like we have been offered an alternative. What are we going to do?"

Tiarra says, "We have two choices. We either agree to join The Keepers or we figure a way to break out of here. So far, I haven't been able to think of a way to break out. Has anybody else?"

Richard says, "There isn't any way to break out of here."

Aaron says, "Then we only have one choice. When she comes back we should tell her that we agree to join The Keepers. Then we'll find out what happens next. Maybe we'll get a chance to find out what The Keepers are really about. Apparently they're not as biased against Spellcasters and other races as we thought. If they were, they wouldn't ask us to join."

Reuben says, "That's easy for you to say. I don't think I can do it. If it's required that I die because I'm a Dwarf, I'm brave enough to die."

Eridana says, "I'll have to think about it."

Johanna says, "I have questions to ask, before I can be sure what to do."

Tiarra says, "So do I."

Eridana says, "We should all do the same thing. We need to stay together."

Aaron says, "While you're thinking about it, I'm going to meditate for an hour. I managed to cast one spell back there in the fight. I might as well get my spell energy back."

Eridana says, "I cast one spell, right at the very beginning. I might as well meditate too.

Johanna says, "I didn't cast any spells. Before I could heal anyone, I was unconscious. Then I woke up here. We all took damage. Somebody else healed us. It is clear that The Keepers have Healers. I don't need to meditate."

Aaron and Eridana meditate.

Reuben rubs and flexes his muscles, trying to get some of the pain out of them. When he, Tiarra, and Johanna talk, they do it quietly to avoid disturbing Aaron and Eridana. They don't say anything that they think would reveal anything important to a spy. They question Richard and David some more, but don't get any useful answers. David seems to be so enamored with his talent and favored relationship with the Duchess that he can't talk about anything else.

Richard is curious. "The five of you seem to know each other. Are you from the same place?"

Tiarra says, "No, but we've been traveling together for several days. We thought it would be safer to travel in a group."

Richard asks, "Who brought you here?"

Tiarra says, "We don't really know. We were attacked on the road by a group of fighters and Spellcasters. They weren't wearing uniforms. We were outnumbered but we fought back anyway. I went unconscious. I don't know if it was because of my wounds or not. Someone might have cast a Snooze Spell. When I woke up I was here. I suppose they carried us here."

Reuben says, "I was knocked unconscious, hit on the head. I don't know how I got here. I was wounded. Somebody healed my wounds. I wonder why they picked on us. It seems like they knew that we were somebody they wanted to arrest before they even talked to us. Do you think somebody told The Keepers something about us that isn't true?"

Tiarra says, "I have none of those answers for you, Reuben, and I don't want to talk about it now. It would just be speculation."

Reuben says, "But she must have known something. How could she –"

Tiarra says, "Don't talk about it. If they want us to know, they'll tell us."

She looks directly at Richard.

Reuben says, "Oh. Uh, okay. I was just wondering."

Reuben, Johanna, and Tiarra try to sleep.

When Eridana and Aaron finish meditating, there is more talk about whether they should join The Keepers. There is no consensus about what to do.

They hear footsteps in the hall near the door. It sounds like only one person. The footfalls stop at the door. It sounds like something was placed on the floor. A key rattles in the keyhole. A guard opens the door and comes in with a tray on which there are seven crude, clay bowls. He puts the tray on the floor and gives one of the bowls to each of the prisoners. The bowls contain thin watery soup. The only way they can eat is by holding it up to their mouths with both hands and drinking. It is not hot, but warmer than the air. It tastes good, but is not very filling. The guard leaves with the tray before anyone has finished drinking.

CHAPTER TWENTY-FIVE

THE MASTER

Sun's Day - Greening Fifteen – Dusk

It is getting dark when the woman who had spoken to them before returns. She has four guards with her.

"Have you decided? Will you join The Keepers?"

Eridana says, "I have questions. What happens to us if we don't?"

"Simple. You spend this night in the tower. Tomorrow you will be executed."

Aaron says, "Yes. I will join."

Richard says, "I want to join."

The woman, looking at Richard, says, "I haven't asked you to join. I will deal with you later."

Johanna says, "If we join, what happens to us? Where will we go? What will we be expected to do?"

"You will live. You will help The Keepers carry out our responsibilities as I do. Where you will go, and what you will do precisely, I wouldn't know."

Tiarra says, "If you accept Eldens, I will join."

Johanna says, "My desire is to help people. My skill is to heal. I will join if healing and helping people is what I will be expected to do."

Rueben says, "I'll join with the others, but I'll never do anything to harm other Dwarves. Is that understood?"

"Understood. You will come with me now, one at a time. Bring the male magic user first."

Aaron

One of the guards uses a large key to detach Reuben's chains from the wall. The ankle and wrist manacles are kept on. The guards lead him along a corridor down some stairs, along a corridor, around a corner to the right, and along another corridor. There are usually closed doors on both sides of the corridors. They go down some more stairs, through an intersection of corridors, and finally outside through a door. They are in an open area near a forest glade. The sun has just gone down. The light is dim. Reuben's eyes are facing red streaks of sunlight reflected on the underbelly of low gray clouds. About three feet in front of him is a small table.

A man comes from behind Aaron to a place beside the table, turns and faces him. He is a Human who looks to be at about the same age as Robert Swift looked to be in picture that Sarah had shown him, but his hair looks quite different. He is dressed in a very nice looking robe which may or may not have armor under it. He has a wooden staff in his right hand. He says, "I am The Master of The Keepers. I am told that you have volunteered to join The Keepers. You look like you could be useful, but before I can decide; I must ask you some questions. How you answer is very important. I know that you are a magic user because I was told that you cast a magic spell during the fighting that took place when you tried to enter our city. I expect that you knew that magic users are not allowed among the general populace of The People's Republic. Did you know that?"

Aaron says, "Yes. But I wanted to be at the Festival of Lights and did not intend to use any magic while here. I wouldn't have if my group had not been attacked by your soldiers. By the way the woman who was leading the group that attacked us used magic against us before I cast a magic spell. Why was it all right for her to use magic, but not for me cast a magic spell?"

The Master says, "She is one of The Keepers. She is allowed to use magic, just as I am allowed to do. And if you decide to join us you will be allowed to cast magic as well. You appear to be a Human but I am told that some of your companions are not of the Human Race. They were disguised as Humans, I suppose because they knew they were not supposed to be here. Did you know that?"

Aaron says, "To tell the truth, I did. But I knew that they wanted to see the Festival of Light just as I did. I thought it would be all right. One of them is a Human."

The Master says, "I know. I will talk with her later. Show me the palm of your left hand."

Aaron holds out his hand. Some light from the setting sun falls upon it.

The Master says, "I see that you have a scar on your hand. Is that a battle wound?"

Aaron says, "It was an accident. I expect that it will heal soon."

The Master says, "I am told that each of your companions has a similar scar on their left hands. Did you all have the same kind of accident at the same time? Or is this really something else?"

Aarons says, "I didn't notice that they all had scars like mine."

The Master says, "I know that almost everybody that enters the Forest of Ereba and then leaves have scars just like yours. Have you been inside the Forest of Ereba? Is that where you got your scar?"

Aaron had not expected The Master to know anything about this. He doesn't want The Master to think that he ever had any conversation with Queen Cassia of Ereba. He says, "Maybe the others did."

The Master says, "I think that you did too. Did you make any promises to Queen Cassia? Are you on a mission to help her here in the People's Republic? Tell me the truth. If you don't tell me the truth you cannot join me as a member of The Keepers organization."

Aaron says. "Of course not, I came to the Divinity City to see the Festival of Lights.

The Master says to the soldiers, "Take this man away. Put him in a different prison cell from the one you brought him from. You know where I mean."

Aaron says, "Wait. I don't want to be in prison. I want to be a member of The Keepers. I have very good skills, just the kind you are looking for."

The Master says, "Take him away."

The guards take Aaron away. They seem to be retracing their steps, but Aaron is soon chained to the wall in a different prison cell. No one else is there. He hears boots tapping steadily against the floor as the guards march into the distance. Soon the footsteps can no longer be heard. He is alone in the dark. He wonders if he will have another chance to talk with the master about joining The Keepers.

Johanna

Johanna is the next person taken to see The Master. She is taken down some stairs, along a corridor, around a corner to the right, and along another corridor. There are usually closed doors on both sides of the corridors. They go down some more stairs, through an intersection of corridors, and finally outside through a door into an open area near a forest glade. About three feet in front of her is a very small chest-high table. The lamp on the table provides a limited amount of light.

A man comes from behind Johanna to a place beside the table, turns and faces her. He is a Human who looks a lot like the picture of Robert Swift that Sarah had shown him, but in some ways different. He is dressed in a very nice looking robe which may or may not have armor under it. He has a wooden staff in his right hand. He says, "I am The Master of The Keepers. I am told that you have volunteered to join The Keepers. You look like you could be useful, but before I can decide; I must ask you some questions. How you answer is very important."

"Johanna says, "I was told that you wanted me to join The Keepers, but I am a woman. I didn't know that women could join The Keepers. What would I do?"

The Master asks, "What are your skills? Do you fight? Do you cast magic spells?"

Johanna says, "I have done some fighting but my best skill is to heal people who have been wounded while fighting. I am a healer."

The Master says, "And you appear to be of the Human race. Like Aaron, but not like your other companions. We don't very much like Dwarves and Eldens. I think that your healing ability would be very useful to us. But I want to be assured that you will be absolutely loyal to me. Where were you born?"

Johnna says, "I am a Human. I was born in Domus. Domus is not in the People's Republic but it is very close.

The Master says, "I have been told that you have a special scar on you hand which might mean that you have been in the Forest of Ereba. Will you let me see it?"

Johanna shows him.

The Master says, "I have been told that this scar is a symbol of loyalty to the Queen of Ereba. Have you promised loyalty to the Queen of Ereba?"

Johanna says, "No. But I have been in the Forest of Ereba and promised to her that I will not tell anyone anything about the people who live there."

So you did talk with her. Tell me about her. Has she remarried? Does she have any children?"

Johanna says, "I don't know anything about that."

The Master asks, "Why did you come into The People's Republic?"

Johanna says, "I want to see the Festival of Light. It is supposed to begin tomorrow. Will I be allowed to see it?"

The Master says, "That depends. Will you swear loyalty to me as The Master of the Keepers? You must promise to be absolutely loyal and faithful to me and do whatever I tell you to do without question. Will you do that?"

Johanna says, "I will be loyal and do what I am asked to do as long as it is not contrary to what my God wants me to do. If what I am told to do is evil I will not do it. I would like to reserve the right to resign from the Keepers if my God tells me that it would be evil. I might want to do it for a while. But at some time I might want to go back to where I was born, get married, and raise a family. Is that all right with you?"

The Master says, "No. If you become a member of the Keepers you are committed for the rest of your life unless I decide that I don't want you anymore, or my successor decides that he doesn't want you anymore. Is that acceptable to you?"

Johanna says, "Let me think about it. I don't think so. If I decide not to will you let me go back to my home in Daring?

The Master says, "I will let you think about it for a while. I will send someone to your prison cell to ask you. If you don't decide to do so you will be executed tomorrow during the Festival of Light. Remember, you must also tell me what you know about Queen Cassia. Has she remarried? Does she have any children?"

The Master turns to the four soldiers and says, "Take her now to the same prison cell that you took the man a little while ago."

The guards take Johanna to the same cell that Aaron was taken to. She sees Aaron chained to the wall. Soon she is also chained to the wall, facing him.

When the guards leave, she says, "Is that you, Aaron? Where is everybody else?"

Aaron says, "I think they've put us in a different cell. Did you agree to join The Keepers?"

Johanna says, "No. I don't know what to do. I don't what to commit the rest of my life to doing whatever The Master tells me to do."

Aaron says, "I don't either. But it might be better than to be killed tomorrow.

Johanna says, "He told me that I will be executed tomorrow unless I agree to his conditions for being a member of The Keepers.

Aaron says, "I think you better do it.

Eridana

Eridana is the third person to be taken to see The Master. She is taken down some stairs, along a corridor, around a corner to the right, and along another corridor. There are usually closed doors on both sides of the corridors. They go down some more stairs, through an intersection of corridors, and finally outside through a door into an open area near a forest glade. A lamp resting on a very small chest-high table partially overcomes the darkness.

A man is sitting at the table. He is a Human who looks a lot like the picture of Robert Swift that Sarah had shown her, but in some ways different. He is dressed in a very nice looking robe which may or may not have armor under it. He has a wooden staff in his right hand. He says, "I am The Master of The Keepers. I am told that you have volunteered to join The Keepers. If you want to do this you must promise to be absolutely loyal to me. I have some questions for you. How you answer is very important. Absolute loyalty to me, personally, is of course required. You must always do as I instruct you, without question. Is that understood?"

Eridana asks, "What kind of things will I be asked to do?"

The handsome Druid says, "You must do whatever I ask you to do, but of course I would never ask you to be insensitive to wild creatures or the blessed sanctity of the natural environment. You do understand?"

Eridana says, "I think so."

The Master says, "Good. I know that you have recently been with Cassia in Ereba. Tell me about her. I suppose that Cassia is now Queen of Ereba. Has she remarried?"

Eridana says, "I cannot answer that question."

The Master says, "You must give me an answer. Don't say that you don't know. I know that you know."

Eridana says, "I have a good reason for not answering. You must respect me for that."

"I know about the scar on your left hand and what that means. Maybe you have made a promise to Cassia. Don't worry about that. She has authorized me to release you of that vow. You may tell me anything you wish about what you learned in the Forest of Ereba. Cassia and I are close friends. I would never do anything that would harm her or any of the Erebans. When you help me, you are helping her as well."

Eridana says, "Can you show me some proof of your friendship with Cassia? Show me the palm of your left hand."

"It is not for you to question or doubt me. I am the Master. Let me remind you that you have agreed to join The Keepers. When you so agreed, you bound yourself to me. You must do as I tell you, and you must respond to my questions. You must always answer truthfully. If you do not do this, you are of no use to me or to the Alliance. Do you understand?"

Eridana says, "I understand what you are saying. I only need some evidence that tells me that you are a friend of Cassia. I want to trust you. Please help me."

"I have given you my word. No other proof is needed. I am losing my patience with you. Has Cassia remarried? Does she have any children?"

Eridana says, "My father told me that the people of the Alliance are Humans, not Eldens or Half-Eldens. I have been led to believe that Eldens are not welcome in the territories of the Alliance. I'm trying to understand."

"Why did you come here if you thought you would not be welcome here? What is the true purpose of your visit? It was not simply to experience the Festival of Light, was it? Why did you come here?"

Eridana says, "I'm here for the Festival of Light."

You have not answered any of my questions. You dispute my authority. I will give you one more chance. Answer me now or you must bear the fate of all outsiders who threaten the Alliance. Why did you come here?"

The Master peers directly at Eridana for a full minute, and she stares right back at him, not saying a word.

"You don't want to talk with me. You are useless. Soldiers, take her back to the tower. She will be executed tomorrow."

The guards take her away. They take her back into the tower and to the same cell now occupied by Aaron and Johanna. She is chained to the wall beside Johanna. The only light is that which is carried by one of the four guards. It is gone when they close the door.

Johanna asks, "Is that you, Eridana?"

Eridana says, "Yes, Johanna. I failed the Master's test. How did it go for you?"

Johanna says, "I will probably be executed tomorrow. But I'm not sure."

Aaron says, "I was told that I will be executed tomorrow. Johanna still has a decision to make. Is that what you mean? Were you told that you will be executed tomorrow?"

Eridana says, "Yes, Aaron. I thought it might be you over there but I wasn't sure. The Master seemed to be very friendly at first, but when I wouldn't answer some of his questions, he got nasty. He asked me why I came here, but I wouldn't tell him."

Aaron says, "He knows about the scars on the palms of our left hands. They seem to know what it means. That is how they know that we have been in the Forest of Ereba and talked with Cassia."

Eridana says, "I wonder how it will go for Tiarra and Reuben."

Johanna says, "I can't believe either of them would reveal anything that we learned in Ereba."

Aaron says, "If they don't, they will probably join us in a few minutes."

Eridana says, "Let's make a plan for how to get out of here before we are burned at the stake. We have to figure out a way to get free of these manacles."

Johanna says, "That sounds like a job for Nick Blackwood. I'm sure that he would know how to do that."

Aaron says, "Only if he still had his lock picks. I wish Amrath were with us. He could wish us right away from here using his Imp of Wishes."

Johanna says, "He wouldn't have his Imp in a Bottle if he were with us. That would have taken away from him."

Aaron says, "Maybe he doesn't have to be with it to make it work for him."

Eridana says, "It doesn't matter, does it? He's not here. He has no idea where we are or that we're in trouble."

Aaron says, "We are in trouble. We need to be rescued. We came here to rescue someone else, but now we are in prison. Do you think we'll be tortured?

Eridana says, "I was told that I would be executed tomorrow. If we are to be tortured, it will have to be tonight."

Aaron says, "I don't want to be tortured."

Reuben

One of the guards uses a large key to detach Reuben's chains from the wall. The ankle and wrist manacles are kept on. The guards lead him along corridors and eventually outside through a door. They are in an open area near a forest glade. It is quite dark but there is a lamp sitting on the table. A man is sitting at the table. He is a Human who appears to be a little more than middle aged. He is dressed in a robe which may or may not have armor under it. He has a wooden staff in his right hand. He says, "I am The Master of The Keepers. I am told that you have volunteered to join The Keepers. If you want to do this you must promise to be absolutely loyal to me. I have some questions for you. How you answer is very important. Absolute loyalty to me, personally, is of course required. You must always do as I instruct you, without question. Is that understood?"

Reuben asks, "What kind of things will I be asked to do?"

The Master says, "You will do whatever I ask you to do without question."

There is a long period of silence.

Finally the Master says, "I take your silence to mean yes. Let us move on. I know about the scar on the palm of your left hand. I believe you have recently been with Cassia. I suppose that Cassia Gydeen is now Queen of Ereba. Has she remarried?"

Reuben says, "I cannot answer your question."

The Master says, "You cannot – or will not? You **must** answer my question."

Silence.

"Is it because you don't know, or is it because you have made some foolish promise? Believe me when I tell you that if you have made a promise to Cassia, that promise is meaningless. She has no ability to enforce anything outside the Forest of Ereba. No promise made in the Forest of Ereba has any meaning at all here."

Silence.

"Does that help? Will you answer my question now?"

Silence.

"No? Let me remind you that you have agreed to join The Keepers. When you agreed you bound yourself to me. I am your master. You must do as I tell you. You must respond to my questions. You must always answer truthfully. If you do not do this, you are of no use to The Keepers. Do you understand?"

Reuben doesn't say anything.

The Master waits several minutes for a reply, peering directly into Reuben's eyes. Reuben does not flinch or say a word.

The Master says, "I will give you one last chance to tell me about Cassia. Speak now or take the consequences. There are consequences. By the way, they tell me that you had a very interesting disguise when you were brought into the tower. You appeared to be a Human female instead of a male Dwarf. Can you explain that? Why did you come into The People's Republic wearing a disguise? Why are you here?"

Silence.

"You don't want to talk with me. You are useless. Take him to the prison cell with the others I have talked with tonight. He will be executed tomorrow."

The guards take Reuben away. He is taken to the same prison cell that Aaron, Johanna, Eridana were taken to. He is chained to the wall beside Aaron, looking at Johanna and Tiarra.

Aaron asks, "How did it go for you Reuben?" I suppose you will be executed tomorrow just like the rest of us, except maybe Johanna."

Johanna says, "I still have a chance to tell The Master that I agree to his terms for being a member of The Keepers early in the morning. I don't know what I am going to do. Aaron tells me that it would be better living a while longer even if I don't like what I am doing and don't have very much respect for my leader."

Eridana says, "That will be your decision to make. I suppose Tiarra will join us pretty soon."

Aaron says, "Unless she makes the promises that The Master tells her to make."

Tiarra

The guards use their keys to detach Tiarra's chains from the wall. The ankle and wrist manacles are kept on. Richard and David are still chained in place. The guards lead Tiarra a long way to a door that takes them outside to a place near a forest glade. She is facing a lamp resting atop a very small table.

A Human man is sitting at the table. He appears to be a little more than middle aged and is dressed in a long heavy robe. He has a wooden staff in his right hand. He says, "I am The Master of The Keepers. I am told that you have volunteered to join The Keepers. If you want to do this you must promise to be absolutely loyal to me. I have some questions for you. How you answer is very important. Absolute loyalty to me, personally, is of course required. You must always do as I instruct you, without question. Is that understood?"

Tiarra asks, "What kind of things will I be asked to do?"

The Master says, "Whatever I tell you to do. You should understand that. I believe you are of noble blood. I expect no less from you than you expect from your servants. In fact, your nobility prepares you well for the tasks I will assign to you. You have that spark of leadership ability that will enable you to be promoted rapidly to positions of greater and greater responsibility. You will do well here, and your achievements will be appropriately rewarded. You will grow in wealth and power; in fact, one day you may even be promoted to the position that I hold today. You see, the Alliance promotes and rewards ability and accomplishment instead of the accident of birth. Yes, I foresee that you will do very well here. You will one day have far greater power than any member of your royal family has ever had. Do exactly as I tell you to do and your rise to power will be very swift."

Tiarra says, "Thank you sir, for sharing this vision with me. I feel greatly honored."

The Master says, "I believe you have recently been with Cassia Gydeen. I suppose that Cassia is now Queen of Ereba. Has she remarried?"

Tiarra says, "I cannot answer that question. I have made a promise with blood not to tell anyone anything about Cassis. Surely you would not want me to break such a promise."

The Master says, "Of course I know about your promise. I have been told of the scar on your left hand. I know what that means. I would not have asked you the question if it were inappropriate for you to answer it honestly. I know a lot about the people of the Forest of Ereba. I am asking to find out if you will tell me the truth. So tell me. I know that her former husband was killed. I want to know if she has remarried. Please tell me."

Tiarra says, "According to my code of honor only Queen Cassia herself can release me of my vow. Perhaps you have a letter signed and sealed by her that will show me that she has authorized you to release me of the vow that I made directly to her."

The Master says, "Aah – yes – but I don't have it with me. I keep it in a very secure place. But surely I would not lie to you. You must trust me. Tell me, has she remarried? Does she have any children?"

Tiarra says, "May I ask you a question?"

The Master says, "Normally I ask the questions, but I will accord you the courtesy of one question, which I will answer if I choose to do so."

Tiarra says, "Thank you. I have understood that there is extreme hostility between the people of the Alliance and the people of Ereba. How is it that you, The Master of The Keepers, the secret police of the Alliance know so much about the Queen of Ereba. Tell me. How many fingers does she have on each hand?"

The Master says, "Three of course. All Erebans have three fingers and a thumb, not like you and me."

Tiarra asks, "How do you know this? Have you been in Ereaba?"

"That is a question I choose not to answer. Now, you tell me, has Cassia remarried and does she have any children?"

Tiarra says, "I cannot answer that question for the same reason that you cannot answer mine. If I did, you would not be able to trust me with your secrets. I'm sure you understand."

The Master frowns. He says, "I have one more question for you, then. You must answer this. Why did you come to Divinity City at the time of the Festival of Light when you know that Eldens, if discovered and apprehended here, will be executed just because of being Eldens?"

Tiarra says, "I cannot answer this question either and for the same reason."

The Master says, "I am very sorry to hear you say that. I commend you for your sense of honor but if you are to serve me you cannot hold any secrets from me. You understand. I have no choice but to have you executed tomorrow during the Festival of Light. Unless you change your mind here and now, that will be your fate. Think carefully. I would hate to see such a promising career as yours – lost – for so little a reason. Your death would be a great loss to the people of the Alliance. Duty calls. Think about it."

Tiarra pauses, creating a very long silence. Then The Master says, "Your time is up. What is your answer?"

Tiarra says firmly. My answer is the same. I cannot answer your questions."

"I am sorry, but you give me only one choice. Soldiers, take this woman away. She is to be executed tomorrow. Take her to the execution cell with the others, but treat her with respect."

The guards take her away. They retrace their steps. She joins the others in the dark cell, being chained to the wall near Johanna and Eridana. The guards leave.

Reuben says, "Tiarra? I suppose you are to be executed also. Did you talk to the Master? What happened."

Tiarra says, "Yes. I think he sincerely wanted me to join his secret police, but I could not answer most of his questions. It would have been against my honor to do so. If I die tomorrow, I will die with my honor intact. I will not dishonor the House of Galadrin. I think he respects that. What about the rest of you?"

Johanna says, "The Master asked me to promise absolute loyalty to him for the rest of my life. I don't want to do that because I don't want to spend the rest of my life being a Keeper. What if sometime the Keepers attacked Domus, where my family lives? I couldn't do that. But Aaron thinks that it might be better for me to save my life. I have to decide before tomorrow morning."

Tiarra says, "I refused to answer his questions about Queen Cassia. I can't break that promise. Did he ask the rest of you that question?"

Johanna says, "He asked me but I didn't answer it. He did say that he would ask me again tomorrow morning. What is the answer?"

Tiarra says, "She has not remarried and of course wouldn't have any children. We all know that. But I wouldn't tell him. It would be against my sense of honor."

Johanna says, "I wasn't sure about that. I was going to say I didn't know. I can't tell a lie. My God wouldn't like that. I guess I will be executed like the rest of you. I won't be able to pass his loyalty test."

Aaron says, "None of us passed his loyalty test. We are all sentenced to be executed tomorrow, burned at the stake I expect."

Tiarra says, "Unless he changes his mind. He could do that, you know."

Eridana says, "I'm not going to hold my breath. We have to think of a way to escape. Make a plan now. I don't trust Richard and David. One of them might show up any minute. Don't tell them anything."

Reuben says, "I think whoever who called himself The Master is aware that we each have the scars on our hands that indicate that we have had communication with the government of Ereba. I thought He wanted me to pledge allegiance to him to help me fight against the Erebans. I think he thought I might have no respect at all for Cassia, the Ereban leader. But you, Tiarra, saw the Master in the form of a Ereban person. Do you think he thought you might believe he was an Ereban rebel who no longer respected the Ereban leaders? The Ereban government doesn't seem to have an cooperative relationship with the leaders of any of the other governments on our Island. I don't like the Master at all, but he might have thought that we would like him better than we might like Queen Cassia."

Eridana says, "He doesn't like any of us now. He doesn't like any of us now. He intends to have us killed as part of the annual ceremony. We need to spend our time now making a plan to avoid that, and then try to find Robert Swift and help him escape also."

Reuben says, "I agree. Do you have a plan?"

Before Eridana can answer they all hear sounds of footsteps right outside their door.

CHAPTER TWENTY-SIX

A WAY OUT

Sun's Day - Greening Fifteen – After Dark

A guard unlocks the door of the prison room and opens it. Another guard comes into the room and places three white cubes on the floor, one in front of Aaron, one in front of Johanna, and one in front of Eridana."

Eridana asks him, "What are these white cubes for?"

He says, "I don't know. I was just told where to put them."

"How do you know which one to put in front of me?"

He says, "They are marked on the bottom. Yours is a "D". His is an "M"; hers is a "C". Any more questions?"

Reuben says, "I need to use an outhouse."

The soldier says, "That's your problem, not mine. Do it on the floor."

Reuben says, "It may be your problem tomorrow when I'm dead and you have to clean up this cell. You must have a place that you use. Can't you take me there? A condemned man shouldn't have to sit in his own wastes on the last day of his life."

Eridana says, "That's right. The least you could do is provide us with a decent place to eliminate our wastes, and something to wipe ourselves with."

The soldier says, "You've got a point there. Here in the tower we call it the garderobe or toilet. I'll talk to the sergeant about it."

Eridana says, "Ask him about giving us some decent clothes too. It isn't right for us to be dressed like this in a prison cell in the presence of these men."

The guard says, "I'll ask, but it won't do any good. It's a matter of security."

Reuben says, "Please hurry."

The soldier says, "Don't try to hold it in too long. I won't be back if he says no." He laughs.

The soldiers leave. The only light in the cell is the moonlight that comes for the time being through the high window in the wall opposite the door.

As soon as she can no longer hear their footsteps in the corridor, Tiarra says, "A brilliant plan, Reuben! When he comes back to take you to the toilet, after he has detached your chains from the wall, you must overpower him, take the keys, and toss them to me. I'll get myself free and give the keys to Johanna. I'll help you subdue any other guards he may have brought with him. Then we'll be on our way."

Aaron says, "It could work. Let's hope he comes back <u>alone</u>."

Reuben says, "I'll try."

About ten minutes later when they hear footsteps, it sounds like only one person. They stop right in front of the door. A voice says, "The sergeant said no. Like I said, it's your problem, not mine. He said no to the clothes too."

They hear the sound of his footsteps going back the way they came.

Johanna says, "Don't feel too bad, Reuben. It's unlikely that he would have come in to get you alone. There would probably have been too many guards for you to overpower by yourself."

Reuben says, "I would have tried. I would rather die fighting than be burned at the stake."

Tiarra says, "If they killed you here in the cell they would bring you back to life. They wouldn't want to deprive the crowd of the chance to watch you burn."

Reuben asks, "Do you think they would resurrect us so that we can be burned at the stake?"

Tiarra says, "I don't know. They might. Resurrection is possible, you know. Eridana had a Chalice of Resurrection. Maybe some of us were killed when we fought The Keepers, yet we are all here."

Reuben says, "You mean you think we were killed when we fought The Keepers and resurrected so that we can be burned at the stake? I assumed that we were healed, not resurrected. Why do you think we were killed?"

Tiarra says, "I don't know. It seems like it could be. If we were resurrected, maybe they did it because they wanted to recruit us to join The Keepers."

Aaron says, "Or question us."

Eridana says, "I don't think they killed any of us. I think we were badly wounded, and might have died from our wounds if not quickly healed, but I don't think we were dead."

Aaron says, "I don't think it matters now. We are alive and stuck in prison. I wonder what happened to Richard and David. There has been more than enough time for them to see the Master and be brought here."

Tiarra says, "They probably answered all of the Master's questions to his satisfaction. They probably have good clothes on by now."

Eridana says, "I don't think David would have done that. It's more likely the Grand Dame has used her influence to get him free. Maybe he will convince her to use her influence to get us free, too."

Aaron says, "That's extremely unlikely, even if he convinces her to try. We have to figure out a way to escape without her help. Does anyone have an idea?"

Tiarra says, "We have a plan. First we need to get free of these terrible chains. Then, the next time a guard gets close we jump him by surprise, subdue him, and go out the door."

Aaron says, "The door might be locked."

Tiarra says, "If so, we take the keys, unlock and leave."

Aaron says, "Then what do we do? We have no weapons. Our clothes are just swatches of burlap that mark us as prisoners."

Tiarra says, "All right. We stay here until some more guards come in. We kill them and take the weapons that they have. We can use their clothes, too, until we find our own. We are going to get out of here."

Johanna says, "Yes. God will answer our prayers. We are not going to be executed. We don't deserve that."

Aaron says, "Sometimes bad things happen to good people. God may help us, but we have to do our part. We can't just wait for the guards to come and take us out for execution. We have to do something now."

Johanna asks, "What? What can we do now?"

Aaron says, "I don't know. We have to think of something."

Tiarra says, "I'm thinking. We've got to get loose from these chains. There has to be a way."

Reuben says, "I could pick the locks on our chains if I had a nail or something to do it with. I can't do it with my fingers. Somebody must have something."

Tiarra says, "We don't – and we won't find anything on the floor. It's too dark in here.

Johanna asks, "What did you do with the hairpins I gave you, Reuben? Are they still in your hair? Maybe we could use those for lock picks."

Reuben says, "I forgot about those. They might not have noticed them in my hair. Yes. Here's one. There should be two. Here's the other one."

Tiarra says, "Give one to me."

Reuben says, "I can't see you. It's too dark. I can't toss it to you. We would lose it. Wait until I get myself free. Then I'll give one to you."

Eridana says, "I bet it won't work. The hairpins are probably too flimsy."

Johanna says, "These are pretty strong. It's worth a try."

Click!

Reuben says, "I've got one. My left hand is loose. Now I'm working on my right hand. This is harder. I can't see what I'm doing."

Eventually there is another click.

Reuben says, "Right hand's free. Now my legs."

He unlocks his leg irons more quickly.

Click! Click!

"Where are you, Tiarra? I'll give you a hairpin."

Tiarra says, "I'm here – here – here. Okay. I've got it. Let go."

Reuben says, "I'll undo you next, Aaron. The guards may come back at any time. If they do, we have to look like we're still chained to the wall. When you get free, put the manacles on your legs and wrists but don't lock them."

He starts picking the locks of Aaron's manacles and has Aaron free before Tiarra can get herself free. He does Johanna. Tiarra does Eridana. As soon as Johanna is free, Reuben goes to a corner. He pulls up his shift and eliminates his wastes there. He tears off a piece of burlap to wipe himself with.

Tiarra says, "I smell it. You shouldn't have done it there, Reuben. When the guards come in they will know that you are free of your chains."

Reuben says, "It's dark in the corner. By the time they notice that, we will already have overpowered them. I don't want to sit in my own waste. Would you?"

Tiarra doesn't respond.

Reuben puts his hairpin back into his long black hair. Tiarra notices. She puts the hairpin she has into her light colored hair in a way that it is not noticeable.

Aaron tries the door of the cell.

He says, "It's locked on the outside. I can't budge it."

Tiarra asks, "What about the window?"

Aaron says, "It's too high and it's barred. It is much too small for escape anyway."

Tiarra says, "I want to look out. Lift me up."

Aaron says, "It's too high."

Tiarra says, "No. Johanna can stand on Reuben's shoulders. I'll stand on her shoulders. Help me."

Tiarra and Aaron help Johanna stand on Reuben's shoulders. Then Aaron and Johanna help Tiarra climb up on Johanna's shoulders. Tiarra looks out, observing what she can by moonlight. They are high above the stone courtyard below. There are no other buildings or trees nearby.

Tiarra says, "Okay. Help me down. The window won't help. It's too far down to the ground. We have to go out through the door."

Eridana says, "Sooner or later a guard will come with food and water. We must make it appear that we are still constrained by the manacles. When the guards are fully inside, we must all attack them together and subdue them. The door will be unlocked. We'll be able to go."

Reuben says, "That was my plan all along."

Eridana asks, "Which way do we go when we get out?"

Reuben says, "Turn left. That's the way to the place outside where I saw the Master."

Tiarra says, "That's a good start, but before we go outside we have to get our weapons, and our clothes."

Aaron says, "We won't have time. There will be soldiers all over the place. We have to get out first. Our lives are more important than the things they took from us. We have no idea where they are."

Tiarra says, "We have to try to find them, and we can't leave without Robert Swift, the person we came here to help. I would rather die fighting than abandon our mission."

Aaron says, "Even if being killed means being resurrected so that you can be burned at the stake? That's what you said would happen. The people of the Alliance want to watch you burn. It's a terrible way to die."

Tiarra says, "My honor is at stake."

Reuben says, "I will fight and die with you if necessary, Tiarra. I have given my word. My honor is also at stake."

Aaron says, "Your pride and sense of honor go too far. You know I am brave. You saw me fight the bats and rats. There is a time to be brave, but - he who fights and runs away lives to fight another day – and pride goes before a fall. We must use our wits, not our sense of honor, to succeed in our mission."

Eridana says, "I agree with Aaron. I am committed to completing our mission, but we have to be smart about this. We need to escape and regroup first."

Tiarra says, "We don't have time. The person we came for will be executed tomorrow, burned to death to please a crowd of bigots, even though he doesn't deserve it."

Johanna says, "Nobody deserves it. Do we have to talk about this now? I'm trying not to think about it. None of us deserves to die a painful death to entertain a crowd of bigots who think they believe in God but don't understand that God is not a bigot. They must think that praying is all talking to God. At least half of it is supposed to be listening. Why do they always say Amen as soon as they stop talking? Isn't it possible that God has something to say? God loves everybody. He gives me the gift to heal people who need healing. Is that something I should die for?"

Eridana says, "Of course not. I agree with you. God loves all of us, including those of us who have pointed ears and very long lives." She looks first at Tiarra, then at Reuben.

Aaron says, "And what about people who cast magic spells? Does God love us too, or are we left out?"

Eridana says, "Yes, God loves you too, Aaron, and other Magic Users, whether you pray or not."

Aaron says, "I do sometimes."

Eridana asks, "Who do you pray to?"

Aaron says, "I pray to Hecate, Goddess of magic. Who is your God?"

Eridana says, "I should have known your God would be a beautiful and sexy Goddess. I pray to Kia, ancient Goddess of nature. Many Druids pray to Kia, and we listen also. She tells us that all forms of life are important, and instructs us to respect all Gods and Goddesses."

Johanna says, "That is what God tells us, too, respect all life and treat others as we ourselves would wish to be treated. God is not a list of rules. God is a way of living. God comes to us in different forms but if we listen well enough the message is the same."

Tiarra asks, "Does your God have a name? I have never heard it mentioned."

Johanna says, "My God doesn't need a name. God is enough."

Tiarra says, "A God should have a name. I respect all the Gods and Goddesses. Mine is a very ancient race. My family worships all of the old Gods. My own favorite is Elanna, Goddess of love, beauty, and war, but I respect the Gods you worship as well, even though I don't pray to them."

Reuben says, "My God is Odin. I guess you know that, but I respect all of you and the Gods and Goddesses that you worship just as I respect you."

Aaron says, "Odin is a Human God. I would have thought you would have a Dwarven God."

Reuben says, "In a way I do. You probably wouldn't know much about that. Much of my belief stems from the teachings of Fror Ingren. He is a prophet of Odin and as far as we know his only Dwarven child, a son. His teachings seem to be much like those of your God, Johanna. He tells us to pray to Odin and to treat all others as we would wish to be treated. Fror Ingren died many hundreds of years ago, but his teachings remain. Odin is a God who loves all races, not just Humans and Dwarves. You could all pray to Odin if you wanted to."

Eridana says, "I was wondering – when you were a Human female did you consider Odin to be your God, or did some other God or Goddess seem more appropriate? I would have thought you would have been more interested in having the guidance and help of a Goddess."

Reuben says, "Odin is a God for women as well as for men. I never even thought about the possibly of worshiping a different God when I was a woman. Why do you think I needed the guidance of a Goddess."

Eridana says, "Well, Odin's wife is Frigga, Goddess of the atmosphere and weather. I was told that many Dwarven wives worship Frigga while their husbands worship Odin. When we were in Tyman and you went out walking with Adam, I thought you might be under the influence of Freya, Goddess of love and fertility, or perhaps a Human Goddess of passion and love."

Reuben blushes. "You are teasing me now. I'm serious about my religion. I know about those Goddesses and I respect them, but Odin is the father of the Gods. He will always have my greatest respect."

Johanna says, "Your prophet, Fror Ingren, seems to be very much like our most important prophet, who is also the Son of God. It seems remarkable that they would have the same concept, that we should both worship the father God and treat all people, regardless of race, as we would wish to be treated ourselves. This must be more than a coincidence."

Aaron says, "Perhaps you would like to lead us in a short prayer, Johanna. Then we can get some sleep, or each meditate and pray in our own way. We certainly are in need of help."

Johanna says, "Thank you. Be quiet then. Father, we praise your glory, your goodness, and your interest in our seemingly petty affairs. We all seek to do as we should do – with your guidance. We ask for your help in the hours ahead of us now. If it is your will, allow us to succeed in our mission. You know what it is. Help those who persecute us to understand their errors. We forgive them for the harm they have done to our people. It is not for our pleasure that we pray, but for you to help us accomplish your will."

She pauses.

Aaron says, "Thank you."

Johanna says, "Wait. Don't say anything now. Try to listen to what God may be trying to tell you. If it doesn't come now, maybe it will come in your dreams. Let us have a short period of silence."

No one says anything until Johanna again speaks. "I believe that God has heard us. A successful plan will emerge and I am confident that we will be successful."

Tiarra says, "We already have a plan. All we need to do is carry it out."

Eridana says, "We know that the first thing we have to do is get out of this cell. From there we will have to just do the best we can. In the meantime we ought to get some rest. We will need all our strength when we try to fight our way out of here."

Tiarra says, "Of course. Make it look like we are still chained to the walls while we sleep."

They arrange their manacles and chains so that it looks as if they are still attached, being careful not to let the locks snap shut. Reuben doesn't even put the locks on his manacles. He doesn't want to have to remove them before attacking the guards.

Tiarra says, "Take turns sleeping. At least two of us should always be awake. If you hear somebody coming, wake the rest of us up."

Reuben says, "I can't sleep. The rest of you can. I'll be awake."

Eridana says, "I'll stay awake with you."

Reuben says, "Thank you. I don't want to be awake alone. It makes me feel lonely."

Eridana says, "I know. I feel that way too."

The cell becomes very quiet. Reuben changes position, flexes, and rubs his muscles. They still hurt. They are not yet accustomed to their reconfiguration into the shape of a male Dwarf. It is dark; no one can see him. He checks his genitals by feeling them with his right hand. Yes, they are still there and they feel normal. He hears others muttering; they must be praying. It doesn't sound as if anyone is sleeping. Reuben prays to Odin, also thinking of Frigga and Freya. He never thought very much about it, but his mother did often pray to Frigga.

The sound of muttering eventually stops. It is very quiet. Reuben thinks, *I know that I'm not alone but I feel alone. I'm scared. I don't want to die.* He is also getting sleepy. He jiggles himself from time to time to stay awake, and tries to relieve the pain in his muscles. He stands up once in a while, and jogs in place. After what he believes to be several hours, he wakes up Aaron and tries to sleep.

CHAPTER TWENTY-SEVEN

NICK AND HELENA

Sun's Day - Greening Fifteen - Mid Morning

Nick and Helena sleep late after their big night in the town of Tyman. They start their day slowly. They both have headaches as a result of drinking so much alcohol. They eat a big breakfast. Most of the other travelers are already well on the way from Tyman to Divinity City by the time they saddle the horses and get on their way. They alternate trotting for a while, then walking for a while. By late morning they are passing those travelers who are walking on foot. By late afternoon they are approaching the walls and gate of Divinity City. Many people are passing through the gate. Uniformed soldiers are watching but no people are having identities checked. Nick and Helena pass though with the rest of the crowd. This is a huge city, much bigger than Beastgate.

They easily find their way to the spot where executions take place. It is a large raised stone platform in the center of a very large arena. Stone steps on each side provide access to several tall stone pillars that protrude upward out of the platform. The pillars have dry sticks of various sizes heaped around them. The viewing area for spectators surrounds the platform. The ground slopes gradually upward providing places where crowds of people can stand to watch; those behind looking over the heads of those in front of them. It is an amphitheater.

They see a long stone tunnel that extends about three hundred feet from the base of a large tall tower to a place about sixty feet from the platform at the center of the amphitheater. A very open lattice-type fence made of rope goes from the end of the tunnel to the platform. This will allow people in the amphitheater to see who is walking between the tunnel and the platform. Very tall poles display the blue and white flags that are the symbol of The People's Republic. A number of other people are also viewing this ceremonial center of the Festival of Lights. Some of them seem to be picking out places where they want to stand and watch tomorrow's spectacle.

Nick says, "This is the place. It looks like they bring the condemned prisoners from the tower through that long tunnel to this place of execution. There is nothing we can do here now. We'd better find a place to stay for the night."

Helena says, "If there are any places left."

Most places to sleep have been taken. Inns have signs on their doors saying **NO VACANCY** or **FULL UP**. They see signs on houses that say **GUEST ROOMS BY THE NIGHT** or **BED AND BREAKFAST**. Many of these also have **NO VACANCY** signs attached.

Nick says, "Let's try this Bed and Breakfast."

They can have a single room together with one bed but there are no places for their horses.

Helena says, "Let's look for a stable. We could sleep in a stable or almost anywhere; but we've got to feed and water the horses. They have to be somewhere safe."

They finally find a place for their horses to stay, but the price seems exorbitant. They take it anyway. It is a corral next to a stable.

Helena says, "Now let's find a place where we can set up the Magic Eye before it gets dark."

Nick says, "We don't need Leander and Amrath to be here now. We haven't found Robert Swift."

Helena says, "We should let them know that we are here in Divinity City. They can decide if they want to go right back to Eastgate or stay here and help us find Swift. We need to find him <u>tonight</u>. They may burn him tomorrow. That's the opening day of the festival."

Nick says, "All right. Let's try to find someplace near that big tower. That must be where the prisoners are kept."

They can see the tall main tower from almost any place in the city. They head in that direction. When they get close they circle the tower examining each gate or door trying to figure out how to sneak in without being noticed. Prospects seem abysmal. It is very secure. Near the west side is a public park. Much of it is neatly clipped lawn; part of it is wooded. The wooded area seems to be surrounded by a seven-foot-high stone wall. When no one is looking Nick boosts Helena over it. Then Helena throws a rope over the wall which she has tied to nearby tree to help Nick get over the wall. They find a small forest glade within which is a clear space with park benches. Nobody else is there. It seems to be an ideal place to actuate the Magic Eye.

Nick stands in a secluded spot from which he watches Helena uncase the Magic Eye and place it on one of the benches. It slowly revolves in a clockwise direction. Helena steps back a few feet near a tree trunk. They both wait and watch. The sun is setting. Orangy-red sunlight is reflected from the underbelly of the distant clouds.

Five minutes pass. Nothing happens.

Nearly ten minutes have passed when Leander and Amrath suddenly materialize in the middle of the clearing about ten feet from the Magic Eye. They look around. They are not wearing their normal Magic User robes. They are wearing merchant's clothes with colorful turbans that cover their ears. Leander goes to the Magic Eye and picks it up. Helena gives him the egg-shaped case in which to put it.

Leander asks, "Where is Robert Swift?"

Helena says, "We haven't found him yet. That's the tower right over there. We haven't figured out how to get inside. We wanted you to know that we are here. We want you to help us make a plan. Our horses are being kept in a corral next to a stable, but we have no place to stay for ourselves or for you. The city is overcrowded."

Amrath asks, "What have you learned about Tiarra and her group?"

Nick says, "Not a thing. We spent last evening in Tyman, checking every inn, but I didn't see them. We have no idea where they are."

Leander says, "All right. You have done well. We are here on time. You keep the Magic Eye for now, Helena. If we get separated you may need to use it again to bring us together. Nick, how are you going to find Robert Swift? Sneaking into the tower and finding him is your responsibility."

Nick says, "I thought you might have some kind of magic that would help me get in there. The tower is very secure and heavily guarded."

Leander says, "We have the darkness of this night in which to find him. He may be incinerated tomorrow."

Nick says, "Maybe we should plan to keep a close watch on every person brought out to be executed tomorrow. When we see Robert Swift, you can magically Transfer him to his home in Althen, then get the rest of us away to a safe place. How close do you have to be to Transfer him?"

Leander says, "I have to be able to touch him. I don't think they'll let me do that. We have to think of another way. You have to bring him out of the castle to a place where I can touch him. This would be a good place."

Amrath says, "I don't have to touch people to Transfer them when I use my Imp of Wishes to do it."

Leander says, "You said you have already tried to wish Robert Swift to Althen and it didn't work."

Amrath says, "Yes. I tried that. I don't think the Imp knows where he is, but if I can see him it should work. I have magically Transferred you and your horse without touching you. I might be able to Transfer Robert Swift from the place of execution to Althen if I can see him."

Leander says, "That would be good. I wonder how close you might have to be for it to work. Nick, how close do you think we can get to the prisoners when they are brought out for execution?"

Nick says, "I'm not sure. Probably no closer than fifty feet."

Leander says, "Stand over there then, Nick, about fifty feet away. I want to find out if Amrath's Imp of Wishes can Transfer you from there to here if he can see you."

Nick says, "I don't much like the idea of being used for a test of magic."

Leander says, "Go ahead. It's just magical Transference. Amrath has done that to us several times."

Nick paces off a distance of about fifty feet, stands, and looks at Amrath, Leander, and Helena.

Leander asks, "Do you think we can get this close?"

Nick says, "Just about."

Leander says, "All right, Amrath. Transfer Nick back to us."

Amrath says, "I wish Nick was standing here beside me."

It doesn't work. Amrath looks at the Imp in the Bottle. It sticks its tongue out at him.

Leander says, "I think you must have to be less than fifty feet from whoever you are going to Transfer, maybe closer. We won't be able to get that close. Let's try it a little closer, about half this distance."

Nick walks closer. Amrath makes the wish and Nick instantly moves to within five feet.

Leander says, "All right. Now we have a better idea what your Imp of Wishes can do. I don't think we will be able to get close enough to do it at the festival. We should try to find Robert Swift in the tower tonight. That's your job, Nick."

Nick says, "That is much easier said than done. This tower was designed to prevent it."

Leander says, "And I'm sure the people will be heavily guarded when they are brought out to be burned. We may not be able to save Robert Swift."

Nick says, "We don't know if he's in the tower, and if he is, we don't have any idea where. I need a lot more to go on before I can do anything. As a minimum I need a plan of the castle that tells me where the prisoners are kept, and where the corridors are. I need to know where the guard stations are. Get me that information and I might have a chance at finding him and getting him out. Otherwise it's a fool's game."

Amrath says, "I wish I had a detailed plan of the tower that shows where the prisoners are kept, where the corridors are, and where the guard stations are located."

He is holding the bottle with the Imp of Wishes in his hand. A large rolled up paper suddenly appears in his other hand.

Amrath unrolls the paper. It looks like the floor plans of a tower, with different maps for each level. It is labeled **COBRA TOWER – KINGDOM OF SERPENTINE**.

Nick is looking at the map upside down. He says, "This is no help. It's the wrong tower. Try to get a map of this tower."

Amrath says, "I wish this map to be where it was before I asked for it." The map disappears.

Amrath says, "I wish I had a detailed plan of this tower in Divinity City showing where Robert Swift is being kept, where the corridors are, and where the guard stations are located."

Another large roll of paper appears in his hand. He unrolls it. Nick is craning his neck trying to get a good look at it.

The legend says **The Tower – Divinity City**. The drawing shows the plan of one of the levels of the tower. It shows a large rectangular space marked **Torture Room** with smaller rooms that must be prison cells around it. One of the smaller rooms might be a guard's ready room, but none of them are labeled. A circle near the center of the torture rooms looks like it might be circular stairway. It seems to be the only entrance or exit.

Nick says, "Robert Swift must be in one of these cells. I wish I knew how to get to it."

Amrath says, "I do the wishing around here. I wish Nick knew how to get to the torture room in the Divinity City Tower."

After about a minute Amrath asks, "Did you get it? Do you know how to get into the torture room now?"

Nick says, "No."

Leander says, "Nice try. I guess that kind of wish doesn't work. At least we know that Robert Swift is in this tower, either in the torture room or one of these smaller ones. It would help if we knew which level this is. It is probably below ground. That's where most torture rooms are. This may or may not show everything at that level either. It may just be showing the part where Robert Swift is."

Amrath looks at Nick. "Does this help?"

Nick says, "It's a lot more than we had before; I think it tells us where Robert Swift is but it doesn't tell me how to get there."

Helena says, "I'm not so sure that Robert Swift is in the torture room of this tower. I know it's highly likely, but we have no definite information that it is so."

Leander says, "Thank you. I stand corrected. But I think we must proceed as if it is so. I see no other way to proceed. Right now I'm hungry. Let's get something to eat. I don't think anyone will realize that Amrath and I are Eldens."

The sun has gone down. As they leave the forest glade Nick says, "Wait. I see a light over there close to the castle. It's not moving. Wait here. I'm going to get a closer look."

When Nick comes back he says, "I saw a man talking to a woman who was almost naked, wearing a short burlap shift; the man was wearing a white robe. I couldn't make out what they were talking about. It might have been a superior talking to a new initiate. I don't know much of anything about what they do. Right near them is an open door in the tower wall. It might be a good way to go in but I don't think we should try right now. I saw four soldiers just outside the door and there may be more right inside. I'm sure they would keep it heavily guarded whenever the door is open. I might come back later. It might be a good way for me to get in if I can pick the lock, when nobody is around to guard it."

Leander says, "All right. Let's give the man and woman some time to do what they are doing. We can come back later. Hopefully no one will be here then, and we can use this door to get into the tower. Right now, let's see if we can find a good place to eat. "

By moonlight they follow a pathway from the glade to a gate in the wall. It is locked on the inside. Nick picks the lock so that they can use the gate. They go to the part of town where the inns are full of guests and wait in line for a chance to sit down and order a meal.

After eating they go back to the forest glade, using the gate that Nick unlocked earlier. Leander and Amrath stay at the bench where the Magic Eye was. Nick and Helena go to where Nick saw the light. It is no longer lit. By moonlight they see the small table upon which the lamp must have been resting.

Nick whispers, "Wait here and watch. I'm going to try the door."

He heads for the door, staying in shadow as much as he can and moving very quietly. This is why he wears black. When he gets to the door he finds that it is a very small heavy wooden door that opens inward. He would have to duck his head a bit to enter. He pushes gently, then harder. He can't push it in. It must be locked or barred on the inside. He looks for a keyhole. There is none. He can't see the hinges; they must be on the inside.

Nick goes to where Helena is waiting. He whispers, "I can't force my way in and there's no keyhole. I'm going to try to get someone inside to open it for us. Come with me. Flatten yourself against the wall on one side of the door. It opens inward. I'm going to kick the door to make some noise. If someone comes out to investigate, we jump him. If we succeed, we're going in. If it's more than three people, we just wait. If they capture me, run and tell Leander what has happened."

When Helena is in position Nick kicks the door as hard as he can, making a loud thump. He moves about six feet along the wall and flattens his back against it. He listens and waits.

Nothing happens. He kicks the door twice, making as much noise as he can, then again flattens his back against the wall and waits.

Still nothing happens. Nick whispers, "I'm going to kick it again. Right after I do, make a loud scream as if you are terrified. That should get somebody out here if they can hear us at all."

Nick kicks the door. Helena screams. Nick is against the wall. They hear running footsteps getting louder. Somebody seems to be removing the bar on the inside of the door. Helena screams again. The door opens inward. Two soldiers come running out, looking around. One of them has a lantern.

Nick jumps behind that one, puts his garrote around his neck, pulls it tight, and holds it. Helena hits the other one on the head with her hammer. He falls unconscious, or possibly dead, on the ground. When Nick's adversary goes limp, he waits another full minute, then lets him too, drop on the ground. By this time Helena has slit the other soldier's throat just in case he wasn't dead. They drag the bodies away from the doorway to the edge of the wall, confident that they have not made enough noise to alert anybody else inside.

Nick leads the way in, using the lantern that was carried by one of the guards to light the way. The corridor is quite dark at the near end, with light coming from the other end. He moves slowly and quietly, pleased that Helena isn't making any noise either. When several more soldiers appear in the corridor, between him and the light, Nick hisses, "Go back."

They both run back, hoping the soldiers don't see them, and prepare another ambush just outside the door.

Nick and Helena stretch a rawhide strip between them across the door a few inches below knee height. The first soldier, running through, trips and falls forward, dropping his sword and hitting his head on his shield. The second is coming so fast that he falls forward on top of him, yelling loudly. Before he can get up, Helena hits him on the head with her hammer. He drops limply full across the first soldier's body.

Nick plunges his Longsword into the torso of the third soldier, striking the heart and producing almost instant death. Two darts of magic energy from the direction of the forest glade strike the fourth one. He falls down on top of the others.

The sound from the corridor indicates that several more soldiers are running toward the open door. Helena slits the throat of the soldier at the bottom of the pile while he is trying to pull himself out from under the others.

Leander's voice from the glade yells, "Stand back."

Nick and Helena get away from the door, one to either side. An explosion of fire ignites in the corridor and spreads in both directions, some of it coming out through the open door. This is followed by yells of pain and the smell of burning flesh. The flame puts light on Leander standing at the small high table. He casts a flash of lightning straight through the door and out of sight. The yells of pain end abruptly.

Nick and Helena look in at the motionless and charred bodies inside.

Leander says, "Let's get away from here while we can. This place will soon be swarming with soldiers. Run for the gate."

Nick, Helena, Amrath, and Leander run. They run through the gate and along the wall away from the tower, Nick in the lead, until Leander gasps, "Far enough. I need to rest."

They huddle beside the wall. Nick says, "I guess I won't be sneaking through that door into the torture room tonight."

Still gasping, Leander says, "Nor through any other door. The guards will be especially alert at every door for the rest of the night. It was a good try though."

Amrath says, "If you had asked, I would have wished the door open for you. You might have sneaked in without being noticed."

Nick says, "That would have been a better idea."

Leander says, "But your idea could have worked, Nick. Why don't we have Amrath transport us all back to Eastgate where we can get a good night's sleep? There's nothing else we can do here now. We'll come back to this spot in the morning."

PART SEVEN
ESCAPE

CHAPTER TWENTY-EIGHT

A MAZE OF CORRIDORS AND DOORS

Moon's Day - Greening Sixteen – Dawn

The sun rises. Aaron, Johanna, Eridana, Tiarra, and Reuben think that this could be the last day of their lives. It could be the last day of Robert Swift's life too. If they are to survive – they must escape today. If they are to complete the mission for which they have risked their lives, rescuing Robert Swift, they must do it today. They have a plan for getting out of their prison cell. They have no plan for how to rescue Robert Swift. They don't know where he is. They presume that he is in another cell in the same tower. They have no weapons. They have no clothes other than scanty burlap tunics. They have each spent part of the night praying to their respective Gods for help.

They are free from their manacles and chains, having picked the locks that hold the manacles at their wrists and ankles, and also the locks that hold the chains to the wall. Their plan for getting out of the cell is to overpower the prison guards the next time they open the door. Reuben has made a garrote from a strip of burlap cloth he tore from the bottom of his shift.

He gives it to Aaron to use saying, "I'm not tall enough to reach a guard's neck."

Others plan to use their manacles and chains as weapons. They have been waiting for hours.

Reuben asks, "What if no one comes to bring us food? What if no one comes until it is a large group of guards to take us to our place of execution?"

Tiarra says, "We attack them anyway, no matter how many of them there are. I would rather die fighting than be marched meekly to my slaughter. I'm not a sheep."

Johanna says, "Quiet. I think I hear someone coming."

They each make sure that their chains and manacles look as if they are still attached to their wrists and ankles. The chains are attached to the walls by open locks so that they can be quickly removed. It sounds as if there is more than one guard, but not many. They hear the jangling of keys, and a key turning in the lock. The door opens. Two guards enter carrying trays of food.

The first one laughs and says, "Eat hearty. This will be your last meal. You will be executed today."

Both guards laugh.

The second guard says, "I feel a little sorry for you, Dwarf. You have to be killed because you happened to be born a Dwarf. It doesn't seem fair, does it?"

The first guard says, "Don't feel sorry for him. He should have known better than to enter the territory of the People's Alliance."

They place the trays on the floor. The five bowls appear to contain the same thin watery soup as before.

When one of the guards brings a bowl to Eridana, she slashes him hard across the face with a loose manacle and its chain. He slumps to the floor with a grunt. Tiarra grabs the guard's dagger and uses it to slit his throat. When the other guard turns that way to look, Aaron garrotes him from behind using the strip of burlap that Reuben gave him.

Reuben tussles with the one struggling to get Aaron's garrote off his neck, which helps Aaron immensely. Tiarra turns on him with the dagger and plunges it into his chest, hoping to reach his heart. Blood spurts from the wound. Aaron keeps the garrote tight until the guard's body slumps to the floor. Then Tiarra slits his throat also, just to make doubly sure that he is dead.

Tiarra says, "We did well. We killed them both without allowing them to call for help or warn other guards." She speaks with a very low voice so as not to alert any other guards who might be nearby.

Eridana takes the blue-and-white tabard off one of the guards, puts it on over her burlap shift, and uses his belt to hold it close around her waist. She doesn't bother with the armor. Tiarra gives her the dagger she took from one of the guards. Johanna takes the tabard, belt, and dagger of the other guard. Tiarra and Reuben take the swords. Aaron grabs the ring of keys.

Tiarra says, not very loudly, "Hurry. Follow me."

Reuben glances at the hot food on the floor. "But I'm hungry."

Tiarra whispers, "We can't waste time eating, Reuben, come on!"

They all rush out through the open door, Tiarra leading.

Reuben is whispering, "That watery soup probably isn't very good anyway."

They turn left, the direction from which they have heard the footsteps of the guards coming and going. The corridor is fairly dark. They go down the stairs and along the corridor until they see light coming from an open door on the left.

They move forward more slowly and quietly. Aaron peeks in. He sees two guards playing checkers. There may be others out of sight, or possibly in the room beyond this one. He can see light through the open door. The others peek in also, one at a time. Aaron tries to cast a spell into the room but his spell doesn't work. They all duck back into the hall out of sight.

Eridana whispers, "It must be the cubes. They are still preventing us from casting spells. We left them in the prison cell. We've got to destroy them."

Eridana and Tiarra run back to the cell while Aaron, Reuben, and Johanna wait near the door. Tiarra smashes one of the large, dice-shaped objects with her sword –the one marked with a D. At that instant Eridana feels sharp pain throughout her body. Several small wounds open up and she bleeds. She casts a healing spell on herself. It works. The bleeding stops. Tiarra smashes the other two – one marked with an M and the other with a C.

Aaron and Johanna also feel a jolt of sudden pain and bleed. They don't know why. Johanna rips strips of burlap from the bottom of Reuben's shift to bind the wounds. Then Johanna tries to cast healing on Aaron, hoping that her power has returned. It works. She then heals herself.

Eridana and Tiarra race back down to where their friends are waiting, slowing when they get near, to avoid making excessive noise with their bare feet.

Eridana whispers, "We can cast spells now. We destroyed the cubes. When I did that, cuts appeared on my body. I started to bleed, but I was able to heal them."

Johanna whispers, "I know. Aaron and I started bleeding. I've done healing on us already."

Aaron again peeks into the room. The guards are still playing checkers. He casts the spell, Frighten, on one of them, a short man, who immediately stands and looks nervously around. He does not see Aaron, who has ducked back behind the door. When Aaron peeks in again he sees the agitated guard is walking into the other room and is soon out of sight.

The other guard stands and looks that way. "What's wrong, Enoch, aren't you going to take your turn?"

Enoch says, "Something's wrong."

Aaron casts another spell, Influence Person, on the closest guard, who turns and looks at Aaron.

He smiles and says, "What do you want?" The 'Influence' spell seems to be working.

Aaron smiles and says, "Come here."

The man walks toward Aaron, saying, "What can I do to help you?"

Aaron says, "Show me where you keep the clothes and weapons of your prisoners."

The guard points to the adjoining room where the other guard went a moment ago.

Tiarra and Reuben hurry to it and look in. It seems to be a storage chamber with many clusters of personal belongings piled on the floor in several rows. The guard who was given the 'Frighten' spell is alone there nervously walking around between the rows. Tiarra and Reuben rush in to overpower him before he can think what to do. When the guard sees them, he yells, "Help!" He draws his sword and turns to face Tiarra, who is closest to him. They jab and parry. Reuben gets behind the 'Frightened' man and strangles him with the burlap garrote.

Tiarra wants to plunge her sword into the man's heart, but if it goes too far it could wound Reuben. So she doesn't.

When the guard slumps to the floor she does it and says softly, "Well done, Reuben, quiet and quick."

Then Aaron, Johanna, Eridana, and the guard who has been 'Influenced' come into the room.

Aaron sees his staff, knapsack, and clothes in one of the piles of things he sees on the floor. The others see cloth sacks like the ones they were carrying when they were captured. Their weapons are on top of the sacks. The tents and other things that were on the mule are in another pile, but there is no sign of Jenny. When they look inside the sacks they see the rest of their clothes and belongings. Reuben finds his Wristband of Strength, Wristband of Protection, and Ring of Protection From Fear in one of the pouches. He puts them on first. He feels a lot better. The Amulet that Sparrow gave him and the Anklet that Eridana loaned him are also in the pouch. He gives the Anklet back to Eridana. He keeps the Amulet.

Johanna says, "We women need a little privacy. While we are changing our clothes, you three men must look in the other direction. We promise not to look at you while you're dressing either. Look at the open door. Let us know if you see anybody."

Instead of looking at the open door, Reuben, Aaron, and the 'Influenced' guard go into the other room, taking Aaron's knapsack and the bag that has Reuben's clothes with them. Reuben puts on the off-white linen shirt and wool trousers that he put in his sack at Exodus. Then he puts on the Boots of Jumping. He attaches the quiver of Crossbow Bolts to his belt, and straps the Shortsword around his waist. Then he adds his Cloak of Blending, which makes him barely visible. He then divides his remaining belongings, mostly Ruby's clothes, into two sacks to balance the weight, ties them together, and slings them over his shoulder. He grabs his Crossbow in his left hand and his battleaxe in his right hand. He flexes his muscles with satisfaction and says, "I'm ready!"

Aaron has put on the woodcutter clothes he wore on the road from Exodus to Divinity City, having left the blue Magic User smock at Sparrow's house. For almost the first time he is wearing his Red Cloak of Protection from Fire. He is wearing his backpack and holding his staff.

Meanwhile, the magically Influenced guard has, a bit nervously, watched Aaron and Reuben change their clothes and pick up weapons.

Aaron says, "I'm ready too."

Johanna says, "So are we."

The men turn to look. Johanna comes through the door wearing tight fitting tan trousers, the white blouse from her disguise, soft leather boots, and the 'Brown Cloak That Cannot Be Cut, Stained, or Ripped'. Two pouches are attached to her belt. She does not have her helmet or chainmail. Her Holy Symbol is clearly visible, hanging from a gold chain against the bare skin revealed by the open collar of her blouse. She has her mace in her right hand.

Aaron thinks, *She has never looked this beautiful before.*

Tiarra is wearing a white blouse, yellow hose, and plain leather boots. She doesn't have her helmet, chain armor, or the leather jacket she usually wears under it. Those were left with Sparrow. She has not taken the time to comb her hair but it is tied back in a ponytail. Her pointed ears are clearly visible. Her Magic Longsword, dagger, pouch, and quiver of crossbow bolts are strapped to her waist and she is holding her Crossbow. She looks ready for action.

Eridana is wearing a white blouse, light green skirt that comes to her knees, soft leather brown boots, and a wide leather belt secured with her Magic Silver Buckle of Protection. Over these is her dull green hooded cloak, but the hood is down. Her pointed ears are still covered by her hair. She has two pouches. Her scimitar is attached to her belt and her sling is in her hand.

They are carrying some of their other belongings in the cloth sacks Sparrow gave them. Tiarra found her Longsword and scabbard in the pile of loose tent poles that were being carried by Jenny. They can only carry so much, so they leave their bedrolls, tents, poles, food, and cooking pots in the big pile. They have their clothes, weapons, and magic. That seems to be enough.

Aaron says to the guard, "Show us how to get out of the tower."

The guard says, "Come with me." He takes them into the corridor, around a corner to the right, and down more stairs. He leads them to a door on the right hand side of the corridor that opens into a large circular room. The room looks empty but the guard points to a door on the other side.

He says, "Go that way."

CHAPTER TWENTY-NINE

GOING AROUND
IN CIRCLES

Moon's Day -Greening Sixteen – Morning

Reuben enters the circular room first, followed by Tiarra, Eridana, Aaron, and Johanna.

They see five doors equally spaced around the perimeter. Each door has a number over it: 1, 2, 3, 4, and 5.

Aaron asks, "Which door leads out?"

The guard doesn't answer. He is nowhere to be seen. The door through which they just entered has disappeared.

Tiarra says, "Your spell must have expired. The guard has probably gone to tell someone that five prisoners have escaped. More guards will probably arrive soon. We need to get out of here quick!"

Eridana asks, "Which door goes out?"

Tiarra says, "They all do!"

Aaron says, "Wait! We need to be careful here. We are in the presence of magic. The door we came in through has disappeared. We can't go back that way. Probably all five doors lead out, but they probably lead out to different places. We must pick one door and all go through it one right after the other, so that we don't get split up. We must stay together. We will probably have to fight some guards as soon as we get out. Follow me."

Aaron goes to door number one, which is the one he thinks the guard pointed to. He goes through and the others follow him. They find themselves in what appears to be a small village. It can't possibly be Divinity City; it's much too small.

Reuben asks, "Does anyone recognize this place? I don't."

Aaron says, "I don't either. I think we came here by magic. We might be miles from Divinity City. This is not where we want to be. We won't find Robert Swift here. Let's try another door."

They go back through the door into the circular room.

Reuben tries door number two. They find themselves in a forest where all the trees are dead.

Eridana groans. She says, "This is a terrible place. We don't want to be here."

They go back into the circular room.

They try door number three. They see nothing but sand dunes. The air is hot. It is a desert.

Tiarra says, "Go back. We have to try another door. None of these doors seem to bring us to a good place."

They go back into the circular room.

Reuben says, "Let's go back to the village, door number one. That seems like the best place. Maybe we can walk to Divinity City from there."

They try door number one again. They find themselves at the entrance to a castle on a high hill with trees and fields all around it.

Reuben says, "This is strange. This castle wasn't here before. It's not the tower in Divinity City. I can't see the village anywhere."

Aaron says, "We are in a different place. Go back. We need to go through one of the doors we haven't tried yet."

They go back into the circular room. Aaron leads them through door number five. They are at the top of a mountain.

Tiarra says, "This won't help. We should have tried door number four first. We shouldn't have skipped one."

They go back into the circular room.

Tiarra leads the way through door number four. They are in a garden of herbs and flowers.

Eridana says, "Oh good! Let's take some of these herbs."

Tiarra says, "Have you been here before? Do you know where we are?"

Eridana says, "No. But it seems like a good place."

Tiarra says, "We have to go back into the circular room and try again. We need to come out into some place where we will know where we are. It would be a waste of time to gather herbs and flowers."

Eridana says, "Maybe one of these herbs is the key to finding our way home."

Aaron says, "I doubt it very much. Let's go back now. I agree with Tiarra."

They go back into the circular room.

Tiarra says, "I want to try door number four again. I think we might have to use the same door twice. The first time is an illusion. The second time will be a real place."

This time it is an abandoned village. It is not Derlenen. None of them has ever seen this place before.

They go back into the circular room, feeling very frustrated.

Reuben says, "This just isn't working."

Johanna says, "Let me choose a door."

She leads them through door number three. It leads to a field where a battle is raging between two large armies.

They go back into the circular room.

Johanna leads them through door number two. It's a green bedroom. The bed is covered with green velvet. A naked lady is reclining on the bed.

Aaron says, "Let's stay here for a little while. I'll ask this woman for directions." He starts for the bed.

Tiarra says, "I know what you're going to ask her! We don't have time for that!"

She grabs him and pulls him back into the circular room. As soon as Tiarra releases him, Aaron goes right back in.

The woman is gone. This time door number two is an orchard with purple pomegranate trees. Aaron goes back into the circular room. He says, "The woman is gone. It's an orchard now."

They try door number one again. It is a bedroom of green velvet with a naked man on the bed.

Aaron says, "I suppose you want to ask this man for directions, Tiarra. Well, go ahead. I'm not going to hold you back just because you spoiled my fun. We'll look the other way and wait."

Johanna says, "No we won't. We're going back right now. This isn't going to help."

Tiarra says, "Right. Back we go."

They go back into the circular room.

They try door number five again. It is a tropical island with nymphs.

Johanna says, "Don't even think about it, Aaron. It's an island. If we stay here too long we may get stuck here. Go back now."

They go back into the circular room.

They try door number three again. It is a feasting hall with good looking and good smelling hot food on the table.

Aaron says, "I'm hungry." He walks toward the table.

Eridana says, "Don't eat any of it. If we do that, we may be trapped here."

Aaron eats some of the food anyway. Eridana grabs him and stops him, but he instantly turns into an orang-u-tan. He scrambles out of her grasp and eats some more, making strange, ape-like sounds between bites.

Tiarra and Eridana together grab him and drag him from the room. He changes back into his normal self when they are back in the circular room.

Reuben asks, "Do your muscles hurt?"

Aaron says, "Not at all. It was fun, and the food tasted great."

Johanna says, "You've got to take this more seriously, Aaron. We are dealing with magic here. You are the magic user. You should be figuring this out for us. We are wasting time."

Aaron says, "Try door number four."

It is a forest in winter. Evergreen trees are covered with snow. The snow looks deep. They just look. They don't go in.

They try door number two. They are at a lake shore. They go back into the circular room.

They try door number one. It is an old house. No one recognizes it. Aaron knocks on the front door. This small amount of force seems to be all that is necessary to open the door. Apparently it wasn't latched. It is a one-room house. There is no one inside. Everything is covered with thick dust. It must have been abandoned long ago.

They go back into the circular room.

They try door number five again. Reuben says, "It's a Dwarven village." He leads the way in.

Eridana asks, "Is this your village, Reuben?"

Reuben says, "No, but it's the best place we have come to so far. I'm going to find out what village it is. Somebody here will help us."

Eridana says, "Wait. It is probably an illusion, like the other places were."

Aaron says, "These places are not illusions. The food I ate was good."

Eridana says, "That was probably an illusion too."

Reuben says, "Before we leave I want to talk to somebody."

Johanna says, "There's nobody here to talk to. There's no smoke from any chimney. It's another abandoned place."

Tiarra and Johanna grab Reuben and pull him back through the door into the circular room.

They try door number four again. This time it is a treasure room. They scoop up some of the gold and jewels. The only way out of the room is the way they came in. When they start to go back out, a loud voice says, "Leave the treasure."

They throw it back and leave.

They try door number one again. It is a bazaar. There are lots of people present, but when they try to talk with them, no one seems to notice. It is as if no one can see or hear them. They can't buy anything. They go back into the circular room.

Eridana says, "We are just frantically opening doors at random accomplishing nothing. We are wasting time."

Johanna says, "I'm frustrated. Do you have a better idea?"

Eridana says, "There must be some pattern to this that we are not seeing. This is a puzzle to solve."

Aaron says, "All right. You choose the next door."

She chooses door number three. They find a vegetable garden, a pasture with cows, the shore of a river, and an apple orchard. Aaron eats an apple. Nothing happens to him, so they all eat apples. They are terribly hungry. Then they go back into the circular room.

Reuben says, "Stop. This isn't working. It doesn't seem to matter which door we try, which of us is the first person to go through first, or which order we choose. We have to think of something else."

Aaron says, "All right. Do you have something in mind?"

Reuben says, "Let's each go through a different door at the same time. I was the first one into the room, so I will choose door number one. Each of you go through a door in the order of when you came into this room."

They easily remember who was right in front of them when they entered the circular room and position themselves in front of a door as Reuben suggested.

Reuben says, "Everybody, open your door and go through when I say three."

Reuben counts, "One, two, three." On three, they each open their door and walk through. They find themselves in a hallway, all in the same place. The hall is dimly lit. It is the kind of hallway they were in when they approached the circular room. They must be somewhere in the tower. There is no sign of the guard that led them to the circular room.

Aaron says, "That guard tricked us. He put us into a magical trap. We could have been there for the rest of our lives."

Eridana says, "I wonder what it would have been like if we had stayed in one of those places. I liked the herb garden. We should have stayed there. After picking some herbs we could have found our way home, safe."

Tiarra says, "This is better. I think we are still in the tower. We have a chance to find Robert Swift and take him out with us."

Aaron says, "Maybe. I don't know where we are. Maybe the next door we open we'll find ourselves back in that circular room."

Chapter Thirty

A Crazy Old Man

Moon's Day - Greening Sixteen – Still morning

The only light comes from both ends of the hall. The atmosphere is slightly cold and laden with moisture.

Reuben says, "We need to find Robert Swift and get out of this tower. Which way should we go?"

Tiarra says, "I don't know. Let's go this way." She heads to the right."

Around the corner is a stairway.

"Let's go down these stairs."

They follow Tiarra down the stairs and along another hallway. They hear voices ahead.

Tiarra holds up her hand to signal stop. She whispers, "Guards."

She moves forward, more slowly and quietly. They come to an intersection of hallways. They could go straight ahead, to the left, or to the right. Tiarra peeks around the corner to the right. This hall has more stairs going down. The voices are coming from the left.

Eridana peeks around that corner. She sees several guards standing only a few yards away. For the moment, they are looking in the other direction. Eridana pulls her head back. She thinks, *Surely one or more of these guards will notice us if we try to go through the intersection of corridors. We should deal with them now, when they can take them by surprise. I think we can win if we do that.*

Eridana whispers to the others, telling them what she has seen. "There are several guards around the left corner. We need to deal with them before we go any further. They are looking the other way. I think we can take them by surprise. Aaron, the spell you cast on the guards in the guardroom worked well. Let's do it again. I can cast a Hesitation Spell on one of them. What can you do?"

Aaron whispers, "I'll cast another Influence Person Spell. You do the closest one, I'll do the next one."

Eridana casts a Hesitation Spell on the closest guard. Aaron casts "Influence Person" on the one next to him, then whispers, "Come here."

The guard walks toward the corner where Aaron is peeking, right past the guard who is 'Hesitating'. Aaron ducks back out of sight. When the guard with the Influence Person Spell comes around the corner, Eridana slits his throat and takes his tabard. She puts it on over her regular clothes. In the dim light she almost looks as if she could be a guard.

The other guards don't seem to have noticed anything.

Aaron peeks around the corner again and casts the 'Sticky Net' spell from the Ring of Spell Storing that Cassia gave him.

A huge web, like a spider web with strands of half-inch diameter sticky rope, spreads across the hallway right where the guards are standing. The ones entangled in it are unable to free themselves from the sticky goo or break the strands. Two of the three guards not trapped by the web on the near side use their swords to try to hack free those who are entangled. The one who was subdued by the Hesitation spell, is looking at Aaron, but not doing anything.

Reuben leaps forward, using the magic of his Boots of Jumping, and kills him with a single blow to the neck with his axe.

Tiarra with her longsword, Johanna with her mace, and Eridana with her scimitar, rush forward to help Reuben kill the other two guards, who try in vain to defend themselves. Then, despite screams for mercy, they kill the five still entangled in the web. The two guards still free on the other side run away.

Only Reuben and Johanna of Tiarra's group are wounded. Neither Eridana nor Johanna has much healing energy left. They quickly bandage the wounds to stop the bleeding. Reuben seems to have been hurt the most so Eridana spends one healing spell on him.

Quickly they each put on a tabard taken from the guards so they will resemble guards. Eridana picks up a gold ring and ten gold pieces, from one of the men, probably the leader. The ring has a tiny image of a running wolf engraved on its flat circular face. This is the symbol of the Keepers, the secret police of the People's Alliance. She also takes his sword; it looks as if it could be magical. The rest salvage other valuable items, consisting mostly of copper and silver pieces and a few trinkets that can easily be carried in small pouches. Johanna puts them all into one of the pouches and attaches it to her belt. Aaron doesn't use a Perceive Magic Spell to determine if anything is magic; he doesn't want to spend his magical energy on that. He will probably need it for fighting.

Ahead of them, beyond the guards they have just killed, is a large door.

Reuben says, "I think we are at ground level. That door probably leads outside."

Tiarra points in the opposite direction. She says, "That hall has stairs going down. They should lead to the dungeon. That is probably where Robert Swift is. We need to find him before we try to go outside."

They go the way that Tiarra has pointed At the bottom of the staircase is a short corridor leading to a spiral staircase made of stone that goes both up and down. As they go down they hear moans and snapping sounds. The stairs descend one level to a large room.

A large man dressed in blue and white is flogging an almost naked thin man tied to a rack. Another man, also dressed in blue and white, is watching.

Tiarra yells, "Get the guards!" She leads the way, Magic Sword held high. The others follow at a run.

The two guards run toward a closed door in the far wall. When they reach it they remove the bar that keeps it from opening, open it, scamper through, and close it behind them.

When Tiarra and the others get there they find that it is locked or barred from the other side. They can't open it. Tiarra and Johanna replace the bar on the inside so that no one will be able to come back through it.

Then they look around. Several torture machines can be seen. Individual prison cells defined by iron bars adjoin the room. The man who was being flogged is yelling at them. "Cut me loose. Get me out of here."

When the five adventurers get closer they see that it is David Silverlake, the tall thin man who had been brought into their cell the night before. Red welts on his back are oozing blood.

Eridana and Johanna untie him from the rack. Eridana is saying, "How is it that we find you here? I thought the Duchess was going to set you free."

David says, "She should have. She must not know what has happened to me."

Eridana asks, "Why were they whipping you?"

David says, "They think I know something that I won't tell them. Their questions were completely unreasonable. I don't know the answers. There was nothing I could do."

Eridana casts a Heal Minor Wounds spell to stop the bleeding. The red welts remain visible.

Tiarra asks, "Is there anybody else down here?"

David says, "I heard someone jabbering in one of the cells over there." He points. "I don't know what he was saying."

Everyone looks, then all but David run in that direction. David, apparently still suffering from torture, moves more slowly. An old man dressed in rags is lying on his back in one of the cells. He looks as if he has been badly treated.

Johanna speaks to him. "Who are you?"

The old man tries to answer, but his words are weak and difficult to understand. What he says doesn't make sense.

Reuben sees a ring of keys hanging on a peg nearby. He takes them and one by one he places a key in the lock hoping that one of them will unlock the cell door. Finally one of them does.

Other questions produce no better result. The old man is incoherent and seems to have lost his sanity. He has a scar on his left hand like the ones Johanna and the others have.

Johanna says, "He must have made the promise to Cassia. That means he is probably Robert Swift."

Tiarra says, "Maybe, maybe not."

Johanna gives him some water.

Aaron, who has been looking around, reports, "There are no other prisoners in any of the other cells. Nobody at all."

Tiarra says, "Let's take this old man out with us whoever he is."

Reuben and Tiarra carry the old man, who is too weak to walk. David has found a rough and ragged robe hanging on a hook. He puts it on and follows behind them. They go back up the circular stairs, then the straight stairs, and straight across the intersection of corridors to the place where they fought the guards just a short time ago. The spider web made of rope that resulted from Aaron's spell is no longer there. The bodies of the dead guards remain. Ahead is the large door that Reuben speculated might lead to the outside. It has a heavy bar across it. The guards they killed must have been assigned to guard this entrance to the tower.

Johanna and Aaron remove the bar. Very slowly Eridana pulls the door inward. They see daylight. The opening leads into a walled courtyard with large heavy gates in an opposite wall. The gates are closed. Straight ahead beyond the wall they see the tops of trees.

Eridana says, "If we can get into the trees we might find a place to hide, or get to the edge of the city without being noticed."

A few wagons are scattered about the courtyard perhaps waiting to be loaded or unloaded. No horses are hitched to any of them, but a team in harness is drinking water from a trough. They don't see any people.

Johanna says, "Let's hitch those horses to one of the wagons, put the old man in the wagon, and go out through the gate. I'll get the horses."

She darts away. The others run toward a wagon. Reuben and Tiarra move as fast as they can, but more slowly, encumbered as they are by carrying the old man. David lags behind. When they get to the wagon, a shower of arrows comes down at their backs from the direction of the tower, hitting Johanna, Eridana, and Aaron.

Looking back, they see blue-and-white uniformed archers standing behind the crenellated wall above the door. They are getting ready to shoot another volley. The gate at the opposite side of the courtyard opens. Guards armed with hand weapons rush through toward them.

Tiarra yells, "Run back into the tower!"

Everybody speeds back through the open door, Aaron and Johanna taking wounds from the second shower of arrows that comes down at them.

Tiarra shouts, "Quick! Close the door!"

Johanna and Aaron push the door shut and replace the bar. They hear the sound of guards outside yelling and pounding.

Panting, they rip clothing from the sacks into bandages and bind each other's wounds. Eridana and Johanna each expend another healing spell, one for Johanna and one for Aaron.

Tiarra says, "We must get away from here! Word is certainly passing throughout the tower that we are loose and trying to escape!"

She leads the way, running directly away from the door toward the intersection of the four corridors. They hear running footsteps from the corridor on the right, the one they were in after they left the circular room.

Tiarra yells, "When you get to the corner, go left!"

But the guards in the other corridor get to the intersection first.

Tiarra and Reuben put the old man on the floor.

Tiarra yells, "Charge!" and leads them directly into the mass of guards, holding her Magic Sword high and ready. Reuben and Johanna catch up, one on either side. Reuben has his battleaxe ready and Johanna has her mace ready. Aaron and Eridana are right behind them. The old man sits up and looks around. He seems to be trying to figure out what is happening. David Silverlake doesn't have a weapon. He runs behind Aaron and Eridana.

Four of the guards with swords form a line to receive the charge. The others stand behind them at the intersection of the four corridors. Tiarra wants to engage the two guards in the center, leaving the ones on the ends of their line to Reuben and Johanna, but without her shield she can't do it. She slashes at the one on the right. He parries her blow with his longsword.

Reuben, on her left, swings horizontally with his axe at the knees of the two guards in front of him. This is his favorite method of attack against taller opponents. He tries to make it look as if he will hit them in the chest, then shifts his aim lower where they don't expect it and where they have less armor to protect themselves. He hits the first one so hard that his axe never gets to the knees of the second. The first one falls screaming to the floor, but the other hits him a glancing blow on the left shoulder. It hurts terribly.

Johanna feints at the head of the guard facing her and instead hits his longsword close to the hilt as hard as she can with her mace. This deflects his attempt to plunge it into her chest. He also loses his grip on the longsword, which clatters to the stone floor. When he reaches to pick it up she smashes him on the head, knocking him down into a motionless heap.

300

Eridana and Aaron are casting spells. Eridana casts Glowing Target on the guard she thinks is the leader, the one Tiarra is fighting. Aaron casts a Magic Beam of Energy spell on the one who hit Reuben in the shoulder. David seems to be casting a spell, but the result is not evident.

Two of the guards behind the first line aim crossbows at Johanna. She tries to dodge, but is hit by one of them. Two more aim at Reuben. He dodges to the left behind the guard still standing in front of him. Both crossbow bolts miss. They skitter down the corridor past the old man and thump into the barred door.

Other soldiers with longswords take the places of the two fallen guards.

Tiarra continues to plunge and parry against the lead guard, who seems to be as adept with his weapon as she is with hers. Reuben feints at the shins of the guard right in front of him, then uses his axe to parry the blow of his new opponent.

Johanna tries to hit the hilt of the sword of her new opponent with her mace but he steps back, avoiding contact completely. She had been hoping to knock the weapon out of his hand.

Eridana has finished with her Glowing Target spell on the leader. She would like to do them all but it takes too much time. Her friends are heavily outnumbered. They need help now. She takes her scimitar and plugs the hole between Tiarra and Reuben, taking that soldier by surprise and slicing deeply into his weapon arm. Bleeding badly, he falls back.

Aaron casts another Magic Beam of Energy spell, this time at the leader.

Johanna and Eridana are both hit by crossbow bolts. Johanna falls back behind Tiarra to heal herself. The guard she was fighting advances and manages to slash Tiarra's right forearm with his blade. Tiarra shifts her Longsword into her left hand.

Reuben, still facing a much taller man, tries to slam him in the belly with his battleaxe. He succeeds in chopping him hard on his right thigh. At the same time his foe strikes him on his left arm. Now Reuben will have to use his battleaxe with only one hand.

Johanna heals herself. Aaron casts Blazing Hands, steps forward into the gap left by Johanna, and directs it at both the leader and the guard beside him. They both fall back, badly burned, unwilling to continue to stand in range of the searing flame.

Eridana slashes the neck of the guard fighting Reuben. This guard falls back. All of the swordsmen have been wounded by weapons or by Aaron's fire. One of them is behind the crossbow men, encouraging them, and trying to apply first aid to stop his bleeding. Three are retreating, trying to stay away from Aaron's fire as he continues to advance toward them. Two have already ducked around the corner out of sight.

Tiarra yells, "Quick! Run down the corridor to the left! It might be another way out."

But before any of them can get around the corner, a flurry of crossbow bolts flies into them. Tiarra, Reuben, Eridana, Aaron, and David are all hit. Johanna is missed only because she is still behind Tiarra. Reuben and Tiarra fall. Aaron is still holding his hands forward, emanating flame toward the swordsmen, but none of them are in range. He rushes forward in pursuit.

Johanna picks up Tiarra. Eridana tries to pick up Reuben but, because of her wounds, she can't lift him. The five men with crossbows cock their bowstrings and place bolts in the channels of their crossbows, getting ready for another volley. The other guards get out of the line of fire of the crossbow bolts. Aaron runs at the crossbow men, hoping to burn them before they can release another volley, but he doesn't make it. When the bolts come, he falls on his face; five of them lodged in his body.

Eridana and Johanna gasp. They realize now that escape is impossible. Even if they were to run down the hall to the left, they would not be able to escape this devastating volley of crossbow bolts.

Eridana looks for the old man. He has somehow managed to struggle back to the big door that goes outside. He is trying to lift the bar but can't do it. He is much too weak. She has more important things to worry about right now. Taking a firm grip on her scimitar she screams and runs forward toward the crossbow men. David picks up Reuben's axe and follows. Johanna puts Tiarra's body on the floor, grabs her mace, and runs forward also, screaming a high pitched battle cry, "Aaggghh!" But they are not quick enough. Another volley of crossbow bolts comes at them before they can close. They are struck, and fall to the floor, their screams of anger changing into low sobs of frustration and pain.

CHAPTER THIRTY-ONE

TESTING THE IMP OF WISHES

Moon's Day - Greening Sixteen – Morning

Leander, Amrath, Nick, and Helena are up at dawn. Leander and Amrath put on the turbans that hide their pointed ears before leaving their rooms at the inn they are using in Eastgate. They eat quickly. Leander uses his Transference Spell to move them to the same place in the forest glade near the tower where the Magic Eye was placed the previous day.

Leander says, "Let's take a look at the place where they do their executions. I want to see for myself how close we can get to where the prisoners will be."

They leave the walled-in part of the park through the same gate they used the night before. Nick and Helena lead the way to the amphitheater and the platform with the stone pillars. A great many people are already there, apparently reserving places for themselves in the front rows of the spectator area.

Leander takes his time examining the space. As he walks from the platform to the underground passageway he says, "I wonder why they call it the Festival of Lights. I don't see any places for lights, unless they are referring to the platforms where people will be burned alive. Could that be the light they are referring to? How macabre."

Several armed soldiers are standing near the entrance to the tunnel, if that is what it is. Its double doors are closed. It is only about sixty feet from here to the nearest edge of the stone platform. The rope fence will make it extremely unlikely for a spectator to get within twenty-five feet of a prisoner being led to the platform.

Leander says, "I've seen enough. Let's go back to where we were."

When they are again in the wooded park, away from other ears, Leander says, "Amrath won't be able to get close enough to use a Transference Spell to move Robert Swift anywhere if we wait until he is brought to the amphitheater. Let's see if we can find him in the tower. We must hurry. We'll go in the same door you and Helena opened last night, Nick. This time we'll have Amrath try to wish the door open. Many soldiers are now at the amphitheater. Maybe there aren't as many left to guard the tower as last night."

They walk swiftly to the small table and the door in the wall of the castle.

Leander says, "Wish it open. You, Nick and Helena, will have the privilege of leading the way in. Amrath and I will be right behind you.

Amrath holds the Imp in the Bottle in his right hand and says, "I wish that the door right in front of me were open right now."

The door opens inward without making a sound.

Nick and Helena jog into the opening, stepping lightly and making hardly any noise at all. Nick ducks under the low lintel of the portal. Leander and Amrath follow, making only a little more noise. A few yards into the corridor Nick and Helena suddenly stop.

Nick whispers, "Look. Soldiers of the Alliance."

They all see a line of five guards, wearing blue-and-white uniforms, about sixty feet in front of them facing to their right, apparently toward another corridor. They are loading crossbows and aiming at something straight ahead of them. Several swordsmen are nearby.

Leander says, "Get out of my way."

Nick and Helena fall back. Leander starts casting a spell.

The crossbow men let their bolts fly.

A great ball of fire suddenly appears at the very spot where the crossbow men are standing. It fills the width of the corridor; some of the flame shooting back a few feet towards Leander. Screams of pain join the wooshing sound of expanding fire.

When the flame and smoke clear, no one is standing where the guards had been. They see several men running away from the intersection in the opposite direction, some with burning clothing. The screams continue. Charred bodies lie prone in the intersection, some of them still burning.

Nick shoots at one of the retreating guards with his longbow. He hits one of them but they are all soon out of sight around another corner.

Nick, Helena, Amrath, and Leander run forward. The badly burned bodies of six guards, four of them with crossbows, sprawl at the intersection of the four corridors.

When the heat of the fireball has sufficiently dissipated, they walk into the intersection and look to the right to see what the crossbow men were shooting at. They see the bodies of seven blue-and-white uniformed guards lying on the floor. Two of them are trying to get up. Another is not wearing a tabard, he has a ragged old robe. They also see someone else, not wearing a blue-and-white tabard, at the far end of the corridor near a large door.

Leander says loudly, "Everyone stand back!"

Amrath says, "Wait! It's my turn!"

Leander, Nick, and Helena fall back behind Amrath, anxious to see what he will do.

Still holding the Imp in the Bottle in his right hand, Amrath says, "I wish everyone in the corridor in front of me would instantly fall into a deep sleep."

The three guards who were trying to get up collapse onto the floor of the corridor.

Amrath says, "I want to see who they were fighting before we destroy everything in this area. There may still be somebody here for us to save."

Nick says, "There's nobody else here except the one in the robe and the old man sleeping next to the door. The crossbow men must have been trying to kill them."

Helena says, "They must have been fighting each other. These six have crossbow bolts sticking into them."

Amrath says, "This body is wearing a blue-and-white tabard, but it looks like a Dwarf."

Nick says, "He's not wearing chainmail under the tabard like the guards armed with crossbows. He's wearing civilian clothes. It could be Reuben."

Helena says, "Only two of these are wearing chainmail. They were armed with longswords and have no crossbow bolts in them."

Amrath says, "This one I just put to sleep is a woman wearing a blue-and-white tabard but under it is the kind of green dress Eridana liked to wear."

Helena says, "Here is another woman, wearing civilian clothes under her tabard. Could she be one of your group?"

Amrath says, "She could be. This man doesn't have a sword. I think it could be Aaron, but he's not wearing a mage's robe."

Nick says, "I think I've found Tiarra. It looks like she was holding a magic Longsword in her hand when she fell."

Amrath says, "That leaves Tamaranis. He's a short little guy with a bald head, kind of overweight. That can't be him at the end of the corridor."

Leander says, "Nick and Helena, keep an eye out on the other two corridors. More guards will probably be coming. Amrath, see if you can wake up your friends. I'm going to find out who the old man is."

Nick says, "Don't dally. We have to find Robert Swift. One of these corridors must lead to him. We need to find the circular stairway."

Leander strides quickly toward the door.

Amrath tries to wake Tiarra but he can't.

Leander says, loudly, "I hear pounding on the other side of the door. Some people are trying to force their way in."

Leander wakes up the old man. "Who are you?"

The old man looks frightened. He says tremulously, "I'm nobody, nobody at all. I'm thirsty and tired. Give me water, please."

Leander asks, "Who are these people with you?"

The old man says, "Good people. All good people. I know nothing."

Nick and Helena stand nervously at the intersection of hallways looking to see if anyone else might be headed their way along the other two corridors.

Amrath, moving as quickly as he can, rouses Eridana. She comes into consciousness slowly.

He says, "We found you!"

Eridana smiles as she tries to get up, saying weakly, "Amrath? Where did you come from?"

Amrath says, "I'll explain later. Where's Tamaranis?"

Eridana says, "Tamaranis is dead."

"Who is this tall guy wearing a robe?"

Eridana says, "His name is David Sliverlake. We found him in the torture room. He was being whipped."

Amrath turns to wake up Johanna.

Eridana crawls to Reuben's motionless body and nudges it. She can see him breathe. She says, "Reuben's alive, but I can't wake him up. I'm going to heal him."

Amrath says, "Be quick."

She casts a Heal Minor Wounds spell on Reuben, not because he has minor wounds but because that is the only healing spell she has energy to cast. She is bleeding quite badly herself, as is Johanna. She drinks a healing potion from her pouch, the one she bought from Lady Lucy.

Reuben moves. He opens his eyes.

Eridana says, "Good. Drink a healing potion if you have one. You're still in pretty bad shape."

Reuben, moving painfully, manages to find the one he bought from Lady Lucy and drinks it.

Johanna heals herself. Then she goes to Aaron. Amrath goes to Tiarra.

Johanna says, "Aaron is dead. He's not breathing at all."

Amrath says, "Tiarra's not breathing either."

Leander is half-carrying and half dragging the old man toward the intersection of hallways.

The weapons and sacks of clothing are scattered about the floor.

Helena says, "Stop talking and do something. I think I hear someone else coming down this hall."

Leander asks, "Does anybody know who this old fellow is?"

Johanna says, "We think he might be Robert Swift. We found him in a torture room."

Nick asks, "Did the torture room have a spiral stair?"

Johanna says, "Yes. How are we going to get away from here?"

Helena yells, "Guards are coming!"

Nick turns to look. He shoots an arrow at the leader of a large group dressed in blue and white running toward them. The leader falls to the floor, but the rest keep coming. Helena does not throw her hammer because the ceiling seems too low for the arc it would have to take to reach the guards. Nick aims an arrow and lets it fly, hitting a guard in the middle of the chest. The man sprawls forward onto the floor.

Leander says, "Get us out of here, Amrath! Wish us all to the stable at Tarek! Quickly!"

Amrath tries not to panic. He moves as quickly as he can to a place where everyone, including Nick and Helena as well as the bodies of Tiarra and Aaron, are within twenty-five feet of him. What should he tell the Imp in the Bottle to do? There is no room or time for error.

Helena holds her hammer ready. Nick nocks another arrow. Down the corridor several archers dressed in blue and white come to the front of their group, raise their crossbows, and aim.

"I wish… I wish that Nick, Helena, Leander, Tiarra, Aaron, Eridana, Johanna, and Reuben – and this old man – and I, all of us that are here together with the weapons and sacks on the floor, are all in the stable of my father's house in Tarek – Now!"

In a flash the stone corridors of the tower disappear and Amrath finds himself standing under the sunlight in the walled-in courtyard next to his father's house. Tense and nervous, he looks around. He sees his father, the old man, Nick Blackwood, and Helena Heath all looking at him. The tall young man in the ragged cloak is looking all around. Amrath sees Eridana kneeling and looking at Reuben who is sitting on the dirt of the yard. He sees Johanna kneeling and looking at Aaron's prone body. He sees Tiarra's body lying at his feet. These five are still wearing blue and white tabards. He sees two other bodies on the ground wearing blue and white tabards. Like Aaron and Tiarra, they are either dead or dying. He also sees several sacks and some weapons on the ground.

Amrath takes in a very deep breath and lets it out. He points at the two bodies he doesn't recognize and says, "Eridana, can you tell me who these two people are?"

Eridana says, "They are guards. They were trying to keep us in the tower."

Leander says, "I'll take care of them."

He kneels next to them and casts a spell. They disappear. He says, "I Transferred them back to the Tower. They won't know they ever left it."

Eridana says, "I think they were dead."

Amrath says, "I did it then! I got everybody out to a safe place!"

Leander says, "I am very proud of how you worded that last wish. You were under extreme pressure and you got it right."

Reuben struggles to his feet and asks, "Where in Odin's realm are we? Are we in Divinity City?"

Leander says, "We are in the courtyard next to my stable in Tarek. We are no longer in The People's Republic. You can breathe easy."

CHAPTER THIRTY-TWO

THE AFTERMATH

Moon's Day - Greening Sixteen – Before Noon

Eridana is examining Tiarra's body. She says, sadly, "Tiarra is dead."

Johanna says, mournfully, "Aaron is dead too. I'm glad we have the bodies here. It would have been too bad to leave them behind."

Eridana looks at Amrath and says, "It was vital that you brought the bodies here. I should be able to resurrect them."

Amrath looks at Eridana with awe. "Resurrect is a very high level spell. How could you possibly do that?"

Eridana says, "I don't have the spell. I have a magic chalice that does it. It can resurrect two people per week. I've never used it before. I'm going to use it now."

Leander says, "The quicker the better. The longer bodies lie dead, the more difficult it is to resurrect them, and the more likely that there will be some lingering impairment. A resurrected person's mind is most likely to be affected. I don't have the power to resurrect. Neither does Ephraim. That's a clerical spell."

Johanna says, "I know, and it will be a very long time before I will be able to learn it."

Eridana has located her sack of clothing and is searching among the things in it. She pulls out the Silver Chalice of Resurrection that Cassia gave her.

She says, "Reuben, I'll need water. Do you have your Bottle of Endless Water? We know it is pure water. It seems like that would be the best to use."

Reuben finds the Bottle of Endless Water he purchased from Lady Lucy and gives it to Eridana."

She puts some water from the bottle into the chalice, crouches beside Tiarra, and says, "I ask the power of this chalice to resurrect Tiarra Galadrin." She lifts Tiarra's head slightly and tries to put a little bit of the water into her mouth. It at least wets her lips.

Nothing changes. Eridana says, "Please help me. I have never done this before. I think we should all pray."

Johanna says, "I am praying. Help me. Add your prayers to mine."

Eridana says, "Pray to your own God and to Tiarra's God, Elanna."

If anyone is praying, it is silent prayer. Reuben can see Johanna's lips moving slightly. Eridana drips some more water onto Tiarra's lips, this time touching the chalice to them. She says, "I ask the power of this chalice to resurrect Tiarra Galadrin."

Tiarra's lips appear to move a bit. Eridana wonders, *Did the chalice move them, or did Tiarra do it?* Eridana says it again. "I ask the power of this chalice to resurrect Tiarra Galadrin."

Tiarra's lips are definitely moving; they open a little. Eridana tips the chalice slightly to allow a little more water to enter her mouth. Tiarra swallows.

Eridana is elated. "It's going to work! She's swallowing!"

In less than two minutes Tiarra is standing with them, a little shakily, but her wounds are healed and she is able to talk. "Where am I?"

Leander says, "I am Leander Darkriver. You are at my home in Tarek. Amrath brought you here from the tower in Divinity City. You were dead. Eridana has just resurrected you using her Silver Chalice of Resurrection. You are safe now."

Tiarra says, "Thank you, Eridana and you, Elanna, my guardian Goddess. Thanks to all of you. I see that you are all here, except that Aaron looks pretty bad. Can you…?"

Eridana says, "I am going to resurrect him now. I can do it twice per week. Your resurrection was the first."

Eridana resurrects Aaron the same way that she did Tiarra, this time with more confidence. Everyone is quiet.

Eventually Aaron stands. When told what happened to him, he thanks Eridana and the others.

Helena says, "You have done well, Eridana, but you look as if you could use some healing yourself."

Eridana says, "I could, but I'm exhausted. I can't do any more healing until I rest and meditate for at least an hour. I'm afraid Johanna is in the same situation."

Helena says, "I can help. I have a Magic Ring of Regeneration. I can help you by holding you firmly for a few minutes, if you want me to."

Eridana says, "Please do."

Helena stands close to Eridana. She places one hand on her forehead and the other at the back of her head. "Please stand still and think about healing yourself. You might feel warm; that means that it is working."

Eridana feels warm; in fact, perspiration rolls down her face and that of Helena as well. She feels an itch at each of her several wounds. When Helena pulls away, her wounds are fully healed and she feels much better. "Thank you."

Helena does the same kind of healing for Johanna, Reuben, and David Silverlake. When she is finished, she seems to be quite tired.

Leander says, "What a splendid demonstration of resurrection and regeneration. You must all be tired. Come into my house and sit. We could all use something to drink. If you are hungry, you can have food. I believe we have nearly completed our mission. This old man is probably Robert Swift. All we have to do is…"

The old man looks around as if wondering who Leander could be talking about. He sees that everyone is looking at him. Suddenly he says, "I am not Robert Swift! I am Robin Wanders!"

Leander looks directly at the old man and says, "You are safe now, among friends. Don't you remember me? I am Leander Darkriver, your old friend."

The old man says, "I am Robin Wanders."

Leander says, "Once we are comfortably settled in my dining room, we can compare stories and fit the pieces together. You must all know Amrath. I am Leander Darkriver, his father. These two are Nick Blackwood and Helena Heath. We were hired by Sarah Swift to find her father and bring him home. The rest of you should introduce yourselves."

"I'm Tiarra Galadrin."

"I'm Aaron Ivey."

"I'm Eridana Silverdean"

"I'm Johanna Morningstar"

"I'm Reuben Huskins."

"I'm David Sliverlake."

The old man says, "I'm Robin Wanders."

Leander says, "Come. Let's go into the house." He leads the way. Ephraim Darkriver comes out to meet them. Leander introduces Ephraim to those who don't know him at the door as they go in. They are soon all seated around the large Darkriver dining table. Ephraim is at its head. He says, "Welcome, all of you. I'm Leander's brother, Amrath's uncle. Leander has told me that you have succeeded in your mission."

Leander says, "I think so, but that really depends on whether this man who calls himself Robin Wanders is really Robert Swift. I think he is. Either he doesn't realize that he is, or he does - but he is afraid of telling us the truth because he doesn't trust us. I think he may have been treated so badly that he doesn't remember."

Ephraim says, "That seems like a possibility. Amrath, do you think you might be able to use your Imp of Wishes to restore some health and coherence to his being so that we can know for certain who he is?"

Amrath takes his Imp of Wishes again into his right hand. "I wish that the old man who called himself Robin Wanders be restored to good health in mind and body, as he was before he was captured by the Alliance and taken to Divinity City, and so that he will tell us who he really is and what happened to him after he left home last month."

Gradually, as everyone watches during the course of approximately two minutes, the old man's appearance changes to that of Robert Swift, much as they had seen him in the portrait in the Swift dining room, but possibly a little older.

The old man says, "Where am I?"

Leander says, "I am Leander Darkriver. You are in my house in Tarek. We have rescued you from the torture room of the tower in Divinity City. When you are ready to tell us, we would like to learn how you managed to get there."

Robert says, "Leander! My old friend! It's so good to see you, but why am I here? How did I get here? What day is it?"

Leander says, "Hello, Robert. Today's date is Greening Sixteen. You left on your annual journey with goods to sell more than a month ago. Your wagon train was attacked near Derlenen by Keepers or soldiers of the Alliance or both. You were captured and taken to Divinity City in The People's Republic for questioning. We rescued you from the torture room in the tower and brought you here today. I was hoping you would tell us what happened after you started your journey."

Robert says, "I don't remember much about that. I remember being captured and taken to a prison cell somewhere. Not much else. I guess I owe you a huge debt of gratitude. Thank you."

Leander says, "I didn't do it alone, and others contributed far more than I did, but we can tell you about that later. First let me get you some proper clothes. Come with me."

When out of hearing of the others Robert asks, "What happened to my wagon train? It was carrying some valuable things. Was it destroyed? Did the people who captured me burn it? I remember seeing the village on fire."

Leander says, "I believe the wagons survived, but some of what was in them may have been taken. I was told that your daughter, Sarah, sent teamsters to bring them home. We will soon take you there and she can tell you what was salvaged."

Robert doesn't tell Leander that he is most concerned about Michael Abner's book and the other things he was returning to Queen Cassia because that is something that is supposed to be a secret. He can easily see that there is no scar on either palm of Leander's hands. Robert and Leander talk about other experiences that they have had together.

Leander and Robert must have enjoyed this brief time together because they are both chuckling as they return. A male waiter has brought sparkling glass goblets and filled them with wine for each person around the table. Robert is wearing one of Leander's good quality robes so he looks as if he is a Magic User.

Ephraim stands and says, "Raise your goblets and drink a toast to Robert Swift and the success of your mission. You are heroes!"

Everyone stands, cheers, and drinks. Then Reuben raises his goblet and says, "Let us drink also in remembrance of Tamaranis Ri-ekm, who gave his life for our success. He was the bravest of us all!" Some of the others see tears welling up in his eyes.

All raise goblets again. Tiarra says, "To Tamaranis!" Others repeat his name and everyone drinks.

Leander says, "We are hungry, but I am sure that Sarah Swift is very anxious to see her father. We have stories to tell each other, but we can do that while eating dinner at Robert Swift's home in Althen. Amrath, can you use your Imp of Wishes to get us there, or do you think you have already reached your limit?"

Amrath says, "I have not, so I can." He takes the Imp in a Bottle out of his pocket and declares with a flourish, "I wish for all of us that are seated around this table to be standing in the courtyard of Robert Swift's mansion in Althen."

And there they are, excepting the male waiter who is still standing in the Darkriver dining room. Robert Swift shouts with glee, "I'm home! I'm home! Where's Sarah?"

Sarah must have heard him. She comes running out the front door calling, "Father! Father! I was afraid that I would never see you again!"

Robert responds, "Sarah! My beloved daughter! I'm so glad to be home!"

They hug each other for a long time, tears streaming down their cheeks.

Then Sarah says to the others, "Thank you for bringing my father home! It took so long! I was beginning to give up hope of ever seeing him again. I thought I would probably not see any of you either. Where is Tamaranis?"

There is a moment of silence. Then Johanna says, "Tamaranis is dead. He fell into a chasm that suddenly opened up in the road right in front of us. He fell in with a horse and wagon that we were using. It's a miracle that the rest of us managed to escape. He died bravely, trying to salvage the weapons we would need to succeed in our mission. Let us pray for his soul."

They bow their heads. Johanna says, "We pray that the soul of Tamaranis Ri-ekm is with you in heaven, dwelling in your house of many mansions. We remember his wisdom, courage, and devotion to duty. He will have a place in our hearts forever. Amen."

The others say Amen in chorus. Then Robert Swift says quietly, "We are very hungry."

Sarah says, "Of course. It is well before noon but I have wine, bread, and cheese. I will tell the cook to make hot food for all of us. Come into the dining room. You can tell me all about what happened."

Ephraim says, "I don't think we have met before, Sarah. I am Ephraim Darkriver, Amrath's uncle. I didn't go to Divinity City to rescue your father but I did make some minor contributions to the mission, not really worth mentioning. I am glad that they were able to rescue your father."

Sarah says, "I'm glad to meet you. Your great reputation as a Magic User precedes you. But there is still one of you that I don't know. Who is this tall man in the ragged robe? What's he doing here?"

Tiarra says, "His name is David Silverlake. We found him in the torture room in the tower at Divinity City. We rescued him along with your father. That's all I really know about him. He'll have to explain the rest."

Sarah says, "Later. I want to hear about what you did first."

Relaxing, feeling safe at last, each person has a piece of the story to tell, but no one reveals anything about Cassia and the Forest of Ereba. Ephraim has little to say about anything except praise for the heroic deeds of the adventurers. David just says, "I was helping provide entertainment in the castle at Divinity City. I don't know why they were questioning me."

Everybody assumes that he lives in Divinity City.

Smiling and bowing Sarah gives each of her hired rescuers their reward. It consists of gems and gold valued at two hundred gold pieces each for Tiarra, Aaron, Eridana, Johanna, Reuben, Amrath, Leander, Nick, and Helena. Leander is the only one who doesn't accept a reward, saying, "I don't want it. I did what I did for my friend, Robert, not for money."

Of course David Silverlake and Ephraim receive no reward.

Johanna says, "Tamaranis died in his effort to carry out our mission. He told us that he intended to give the two hundred gold pieces that were promised to him to his monastery. I think that this should happen."

Sarah says, "That seems fair to me, Johanna. Would you be willing to deliver his gold to his monastery? I know that your home is quite close to it."

Johanna says, "I will if you want me to, but I would like it if someone would go with me. Would you be willing to do that, Aaron? Your home is in Ezrada, which is also to the east. You could escort me all the way home, then go north to Ezrada. I would rather not have to travel alone."

Aaron says, "I will be glad to travel with you, Johanna."

By now Robert has noticed that Tiarra, Eridana, Johanna, Aaron, Amrath, and Reuben all have scars on their hands that indicate to him that they have communicated with residents of Ereba and have sworn to keep secret anything that they know about the Forest of Ereba and its people.

He manages to get Amrath alone and asks him about it. "What is the origin of the scar on your left hand? I assume that you have been in Ereba and have vowed in your own blood that you will never communicate to any outsider anything you learn in the Forest of Ereba."

Amrath says, "That's just a scar. It has nothing to do with Ereba."

Robert says, "Look at my hand. I have a scar just like it. You can tell me about it."

Amrath says, "I don't think I should."

Robert says, "You can trust me."

Amrath says, "I don't want to talk about this." He leaves Robert and joins a conversation involving Sarah, Tiarra, and Aaron.

When Robert talks with Eridana about it she looks at the scar on his hand.

Robert tells her. "You can trust me. I know by your scar that you have made the same promise that I did. I had with me, hidden in one of the wagons, one of Michael Abner's books, a crown, a pendant, and a banner. I need to know what happened to these things. Can you tell me about them? I tried to talk with Amrath about it. He refused to talk about it. Will you?"

Eridana says, "I see your scar and I trust you. But I think it would be better if you talk to Queen Cassia about it. I will tell you that she told us that you had been captured by the Keepers and wanted us to try to save you. She promised a reward. Maybe you should go with us when we go to collect it from her."

Robert says, "Thank you. I want to go with you. I want to talk with Queen Cassia. I know the way."

Eridana says, "I think we may need our horses, saddles, and the other things that we left in Exodus when we put on the disguises that we used to get into The People's Republic. We should do that first. I am hoping that Amrath may be able to use his Imp of Wishes to Transfer us there and Transfer us back here. You won't need to go there with us.

Eridana leaves Robert to talk with Tiarra and Aaron about a trip to Exodus. They agree that it would be best to ask Amrath instead of Leander to magically Transfer them to Exodus and back. He can Transfer all of us at once instead of just one or two at a time. He demonstrated that when he transported us from the tower to his home in Tarek. They speak to Amrath and he agrees to do it in the morning.

Tiarra then says to Amrath, "Our next trip will be to Ereba City. We need to report to Cassia and let her know that Robert Swift has been saved and collect the reward that Cassia promised to give us. I feel certain that she would like to talk with Robert. I see that you have a scar on your palm. Will you be able to come with us?"

Amrath says, "No, I can't because I have never been there. I can Transfer you to the white bridge near Derlenen. I can't go with you into Ereba because, despite the scar on my palm, I am not allowed to enter the Forest of Ereba. They still don't trust me."

Eridana says, "We can't tell everybody here where we are going or why. It would probably be best if Sarah thinks that you are helping us to go home. I don't think we should leave directly from here. Maybe we should go to your house first. I don't know what Robert Swift will tell his daughter about where he is going and why, but I know that he wants to go."

Amrath says, "I guess I should spend the night here then, if I can. I don't know if my father and Uncle Ephraim will want to do that or not."

At supper Robert Swift invites all of the guests to stay overnight. Nick and Helena decline. Soon after supper they go to find accommodations at an inn. Leander wants to stay but Ephraim does not. After supper Ephraim magically Transfers himself home to Tarek. The others talk about the adventure well into the evening. Sarah finds a place for everyone to sleep for the night, even though some of the guests have to sleep two in one bed. Aaron and Reuben sleep together, as do Johanna and Eridana.

The next morning, David is given serviceable clothes, basic weapons of his choice, some money and a horse. He leaves Althen headed east toward The People's Republic.

Amrath uses his Imp in a Bottle to move Tiarra, Aaron, Johanna, Reuben, Eridana, and himself to Exodus to get the things that were left there. They appear at a place outside the city near the gate that goes directly to Eastgate but out of sight from the gate and road. It is near the pool where his companions fought the Red Haze creature. Amrath remembers seeing this place when he, his father Leander, Nick, and Helena left Exodus on their way to Eastgate.

Tiarra leads the way to Sparrow's house. The gate in the wall is closed so Reuben pulls the rope to ring the bell, hoping that Sparrow will hear it right away. She does.

Tiarra smiles and says, "Hello Sparrow. I want to introduce you to Amrath Darkriver. He was with us when we first started to search for Robert Swift. I'm glad to tell you that we did manage to find Robert Swift in the Tower at Divinity City. It was Amrath who found us there and used his Imp of Wishes magic to magically transfer all of us from the Divinity City tower to his home at Tarek in Sudelden."

Sparrow smiles. She says, "I am so glad to hear this. Where is Robert Swift now?"

Tiarra says, He is with his daughter at his home in Althen. He was in very poor physical condition when we found him but his health has been restored. He looks very good now. We have come back here to get our things that we left here under your care."

Sparrow asks, "Where are my horse and wagon? Did you bring those back to me? Where is Tamaranis? Why isn't he with you?"

Aaron speaks up. He says, "We lost Tamaranis, your horse, and your wagon while on the road from Eastgate to Tyman. We were going along the road when suddenly a huge thunder and lightning rainstorm happened that created a very mushy road. I never saw anything like it before. Then huge lightning strike or an earthquake or something happened that made a big deep hole right in front of us. I tried to lead your horse away from it but the oozing mud was going right into the hole. I couldn't. We took our most valuable things out of the back of the wagon and put them on an outcropping of ledge, using a rope held by Reuben's mule while it was standing on the ledge to keep us from drifting into the big hole. Tamaranis was just about to grab the rope when the wagon went down the hole and Tamaranis went in with the wagon. We never saw him again."

Eridana says, "I never saw anything like this happen before. I wonder if maybe some magic user did this to us. I mean someone who could use magic to see where we were and could cast a spell to make such a big rainstorm and make a big hole in the road. It doesn't seem to me that this could have been a natural event.

Johanna says, "We didn't wait around at all. We walked away as soon as we could, carrying the things we had managed to salvage from the wagon, which was magic and clothes. We lost all the kegs of wine. We walked on the ledge well beside the road until we got a long way from where the big chasm in the road and the sloppy mud was. We camped out that night right beside a river. It made me, it made all of us, feel really bad to lose Tamaranis."

Tiarra says, "And your horse and wagon. Losing them took a lot away from being able to look like an ordinary farmer family when we tried to enter Divinity City."

Sparrow says, "Tell me about that. Did you get in okay? How did you find Robert Swift?"

Tiarra says the next day was a rainy day. We started walking to Tyman. Luckily we were given a ride by a merchant family that let us spend the night in their house. Early in the morning we walked to Divinity City. We had a lot to carry. We used a farm road that went parallel to the main road from Tyman to the city. We went back to the main road when we got close to the city. There were other people walking without wagons. We got in a line of people who seemed to be checked by a few soldiers at a small bridge. Everybody ahead of us was allowed to go through, but when we got there we were told to go aside and have some soldiers examine our pack mule to see if it was carrying something that we shouldn't be bringing into divinity city. They discovered my longsword among the tent poles on Jenny's back. That was it. They attacked us. We fought back but they outnumbered us. We lost."

Reuben speaks up. "I woke up in a prison cell in the big tower. My hands and legs were chained to the stone wall behind me. I was not wearing the amulet that made me look like a woman so I looked like myself again. All that I was wearing was a piece of burlap. I looked around. Tiarra, Eridan, Johanna, and Aaron were also wearing burlap and chained to the wall. We figured that we were simply waiting to be executed at the Festival of Light.

Aaron says, "We tried to figure out a way to escape. But we couldn't. I was surprised when a woman came in and told us that the Master of the Keepers wanted to talk with each of us alone and give us a chance to work for him, as a keeper. One by one we each did this."

Aaron says, "The Master is a tall strong looking man maybe a little older than middle age. He was wearing a long robe and had a staff in his hand. I thought he might be a magic user like me. He told me that I needed to pledge my complete loyalty to him. Hs asked me some things about Queen Cassia. I wouldn't answer him. He soon told me that I would soon be executed at the Festival. Soldiers escorted me to a different prison cell than the one that Reuben, Johanna, Tiarra and Eridana were in."

Johanna says, "The Master seemed to like it that I am a Human instead of a Dwarf or an Elden. I told him that I could cast healing spells. He seemed to like that. He thought I would fit very well into his group of Keepers. He asked me some things about Queen Cassia that I didn't answer. He gave me a chance to think about it overnight. His soldiers escorted me to the same prison cell that Aaron was in. Soon the rest of our group was with us. After talking it over with them I decided that my answer would be no.

Eridana says, "The Master told me that to be a member of the Keepers I must be absolutely loyal to him and no one else. He asked me some questions about Queen Cassia that I wouldn't answer. I didn't trust him. He soon told me that I would soon be executed at the Festival. Soldiers escorted me to the same prison cell that Aaron and Johanna were in."

Reuben says, "When I saw The Master he told me that I must give him absolute loyalty. It was like he wanted me to worship him like a God. He asked questions about Queen Cassia that I couldn't answer. I didn't trust him. He soon told me that I would soon be executed at the Festival. He sent me to the same prison cell that Aaron, Johanna, and Eridana were already in."

Tiarra says, "I saw the Master as a pretty good looking middle aged man. He behaved like a pretty dictatorial leader. Not the kind of leader that I am, or that Aaron is. He asked me about Queen Cassia also. I couldn't possibly accept him to be the leader of the Keepers. He told me that I would soon be executed at the Festival. He sent me to a prison cell where Reuben, Johanna, Eridana and Aaron were already chained to the wall. We talked it over. We knew that we had to figure out a way to escape. We did."

Reuben says, "I used a hairpin that was in my hair to pick the locks so that I was no longer attached to the wall.

Tiarra says, "The rest of us did the same thing. We shared the use the two hairpins that Reuben had in his hair. In the morning when two guards came to bring us breakfast we killed them, took their weapons and left the cell. Going down the hall we found a room that had all our clothes, weapons, and magic items. We managed to find the cell in the bottom floor where Robert Swift was being kept. We killed a couple of guards and led Mr Swift upstairs into a hallway. Before we could get out we were attacked by a large number of soldiers. We were losing, but Amrath, his father, Nick and Helena showed up just in time to rescue us and get us out of there."

Amrath finally gets a chance to say something. He says, "My father used his magic to do a lot of damage to the soldiers. I used my Imp of wishes to transfer all of us, including Robert Swift, to my father's house in Tarek. Tiarra and Aaron were dead. Eridana used her Silver Chalice of Resurrection that Cassia gave her to bring them back to life. I used the Imp of Wishes to transfer us all to Robert Swift's house. Sarah was very glad to see her father again. So now I have transferred us all here."

Eridana says, "I'm very sorry that we can't return your horse and wagon. Sarah Swift has paid each of us the two hundred gold pieces for rescuing her father. We have enough money to give you so that you can buy a new wagon and a nice young horse. We will also pay you for the kegs of wine that we lost. How much do you need?"

Sparrow says, "I admire all of you for what you have done. You don't need to give me any gold. Have you told Queen Cassia that you have rescued Robert Swift?"

Aaron says, "Not yet. But we will soon. We wanted to tell you first. We have no one who can use a Transfer spell to take us into the Forest of Ereba. We want to use the horses that we left here to get there. Amrath doesn't want to go into the Forest of Ereba. He and Cassia don't like each other very well. He can transfer us to the entrance bridge but then he will go back to his home.

Sparrow says. "I suppose that makes sense. Do you mind if I use my special communication ability to let Queen Cassia know?"

Tiarra says, "That seems okay to me. Does anyone object?" She looks toward Aaron.

Aaron says, "Fine with me. Let her know."

Nobody else says anything about it.

They bring back their riding horses, two packhorses, and all the other things they had left with Sparrow, returning to the Swift courtyard in less than an hour. Reuben keeps the Amulet that disguises. Sparrow didn't ask for it. He regrets that his pack mule, Jenny, was lost at Divinity City. All of their tents and bedrolls were also left behind in the storage room in the Divinity City tower where they found their clothes and weapons. They expect to replace them at some future time.

Back at the Swift home, Johanna and Aaron offer to buy the horses they were using that belong to Robert Swift. They have developed a liking for them. But Robert and Sarah insist on giving the horses and the saddles to them so that they can ride home on them. Robert and Sarah also give them tents and bedrolls to use if by chance they have to sleep but can't find an inn.

Robert doesn't want to tell Sarah that he is going to Ereba so he tells her that he wants to spend a few days with Leander in Tarek. He promises to return home in four days, or less. Sarah doesn't want her father to go but he insists.

Amrath Transfers Tiarra, Johanna, Aaron, Eridana, Reuben, Leander, Robert and himself to the courtyard of his home in Tarek. All the horses and baggage go with them. Then Amrath Transfers Tiarra, Eridana, Johanna, Aaron, Reuben, and Robert to Derlenen, close to the white bridge.

The five adventurers and Robert Swift are soon riding their horses north across the bridge into the Forest of Ereba. Rangers escort them to Ereba City. After a wait of about two hours a few palace dignitaries escort them into the presence of Queen Cassia and Ander. Quicksilver, and surprisingly, David Silverlake are with them. When he gets a chance he explains that Quicksilver is his sister. This I a big surprise to Reuben, Eridana, Tiarra, Aaron, and Johanna.

Queen Cassia says, "I am very pleased to see you, Robert. I am pleased to observe that there is no indication that you were tortured. I am pleased to see all of you. Thank you for rescuing Robert. I see that Tamaranis, the young monk, is not with you. What happened to him?"

Reuben says, "Tamaranis was killed when we were in The People's Republic, on the way to Divinity City. He fell into a huge chasm that opened up right in front of our wagon. He went in with the wagon."

Queen Cassia says, "I am very sorry. I am very glad that the rest of you are alive and seem to be in good health."

Tiarra says, "Robert Swift looks good now, and seems to be in good health, but when we found him in the dungeon at Divinity City he was in a terrible condition. He had been tortured to the point of near insanity and physical exhaustion. He didn't even seem to know who he was. We could see that he had been treated very badly. Amrath was able to use his magic to restore his physical condition and mental capacity, but did not bring back his memory of what happened while he was a prisoner. I think he thought it better if he can't remember much of it. His mental condition is now much better."

Cassia asks, "Is this true, Robert? Were you tortured? Did you tell the Keepers anything of what you know about Ereba?"

Robert says, "I can't remember much at all about my capture or what happened when I was in the dungeon. I was in a very stressful situation. I was tortured but I don't know if I told anybody something that I shouldn't have or not."

Cassia says, "I hope not. I am sorry that such a terrible thing happened to you. I'm glad that you have recovered so well. I suppose that this Amrath that you speak of is the same one who was with you, Tiarra, when you first came into the Forest of Ereba, the one who kept writing in his little book."

Tiarra says, "That is true. He is also the one who came to Divinity City, separate from us, and who used his magic to Transfer all of us out of the tower to his home in Tarek, including Robert Swift and Quicksilver's brother, David Silverlake, He saved us all from certain death."

Cassia says, "David told me about that. It sounds like a good thing, but I still do not fully trust Amrath. He is still not welcome in the Forest of Ereba. I suppose you are here to collect the reward that I promised for rescuing Robert Swift. You have earned it. It will give it to you in the morning."

Aaron says, "I was hoping to be able to start for my home today."

Cassia says, "I have a very busy schedule today. I will have it ready for you in the morning. This will give you all an opportunity to have a tour of Ereba City. There are very good things for you to see that you didn't see the last time you were here.

Robert says, "Good Queen Cassia, I had the things I had found for you in the wagon train, Michael Abner's book, the crown, the necklace, and the banner. I don't know what happened to them. I'm sorry that I wasn't able to get them to you."

Cassia says, "Those things were given to me by the people your daughter hired to rescue you. I have the gold and jewels that I agreed to give you for them. I will give them to you in the morning. It will be up to you to decide if you want to share some of them with those who rescued you."

They all spend much of the day on another tour of Ereba City and the night in the Forest of Ereba guesthouses. David Silverlake is with them for the tour. He is also staying in one of these guesthouses. As before, Eridana stays in her own tent in a nearby grove of trees. David and Eridana seem to be paying a lot of attention to each other. Something must be sparking between them.

They see Cassia fairly early in the morning when one of her staff asks them to come to her large office room.

Cassia says, "Before I give you your reward I want to ask some questions. I have communicated with Sparrow and she told me that some of you had communication in Divinity City with someone called "The Master" What she said seemed somewhat confusing so I want to ask you about it. Who is this "Master?" Is it "The Master" of the Keepers, those terrible people who keep trying to take things away from me? He seems to want to destroy me and my people. Tell me about it."

Tiarra says, "We were captured by soldiers of the People's Republic when we tried to enter Divinity City. We were taken to a prison cell, all in the same room. A female soldier came to us and asked us if we would like to join "The Keepers", those soldiers who use magic, which is contrary to the rules of the government of the People's Republic, but are encouraged to do it anyway. The soldier told us that the "Master" wanted to talk with us one at a time. It seemed like it would be an interview. If "The Master" was well enough impressed he would give us a chance to become a member of the Keepers instead of be executed at the Festival of Light, probably that day or the next day. I didn't think it would be very likely that he would want me to be a member of "The Keepers" but it seemed like a good idea to talk to "The Master" and find out what might happen. At least we could learn something about "The Master". We all asked to see "The Keeper". Aaron was the first to be taken to see him. He was still dressed in only a burlap bag. Aaron, tell Queen Cassis what happened to you."

Aaron says, "Four soldiers escorted me along a few corridors and down some stairs to a door that took me outside where there was a small table. It was dark out there not very well lit by the lamp on the table. The man standing next to the table was holding a wooden staff. He looked to me like a magic user. He seemed glad that I wanted to be a member of the Keepers group. He wanted me to know that as a Keeper I would be expected to be absolutely loyal to him. That didn't surprise me. Then he asked me questions about you, Queen Cassia, and I refused to answer. He wanted to know if you had remarried. I refused to answer. He said that he knew that I was a magic user and said that he was a magic user also. He said that the Alliance needed more magic users. I knew that quite a few of The Keepers were magic users. I thought that if they really wanted more magic users to fight for the Alliance they should make it legal for all of their citizens to be magic users and encourage them to join The Keepers. But I didn't say that. He asked me to tell him if you, Queen Cassia had remarried and had any children. I said that I didn't know. Then he asked me what you had asked me to do for you in Divinity City. I told him that I didn't come to Divinity City because of you. He didn't believe me. He told the soldiers to take me back into the tower and into a prison cell. I was all alone there."

Queen Cassia says, "Thank you, Aaron. It is pretty obvious that He wanted to find out how loyal you might be to me. I don't think you would have been allowed to join The Keepers no matter what you said.

Johanna says, "I was the second one to be escorted outside to see "The Master". The four soldiers took me a very short distance outside the tower where I saw him wearing a very nice robe. He started talking to me in a friendly way. He seemed to like it that I am a Human who can heal people's wounds. He said that these abilitys would be very helpful to the Keepers. But he soon demanded absolute loyalty to him personally. I don't think he liked it that I felt more loyalty to my God than to him. He asked me if you, Queen Cassia, had remarried. I said that I could not answer that question. He seemed to understand that the scar on my hand meant that I had been with you in the Forest of Ereba. He told me that if I had made a promise to you I didn't need to keep it. I told him that I would like to help him and the Keepers for a while, but at some time I might want to leave and do something else. He didn't seem to like that. He asked me again if you, Queen Cassia, have any children. I refused to answer. He gave me a chance to think it over until the next morning. I understood that if I didn't answer his questions about you I would be executed. I was taken to the prison cell where Aaron was. We were both chained to the wall.

Cassia says, "Thank you Johanna. What happened with you, Eridana, when you saw "The Master"?

Eridana says, "The four soldiers took me to the table outside where the Master was. I saw the same man that Aaron and Johanna described. He looked good to me. I felt embarrassed because I was dressed in a single piece of burlap. He told me that to be one of the Keepers I must give him absolute loyalty. It seemed like he wanted me to consider him to be a God. When he asked me questions about you I refused to answer. He said that he knew you as a good friend and that it would be all right for me to tell him what I know about you. But I didn't believe him. Since I wouldn't cooperate he told his soldiers to take me away. I was taken to the same prison cell that Aaron and Johanna were.

Queen Cassi says, "Thank you Erudana."

Tiarra says, "Reuben. It is your turn to tell Queen Cassia what happened when you were with the Master."

Reuben says, "When I saw The Master he told me that I must give him absolute loyalty. It was like he wanted me to worship him like a God. He asked questions about Queen Cassia that I couldn't answer. I didn't trust him. It was a lot like what the others have already told you. I consider the Keepers and their Master to be enemies of you that live in the Forest of Ereba and enemies of the Dwarves but I didn't tell him that. He soon told me that I would soon be executed at the Festival. He sent me to the same prison cell that Aaron, Johanna, and Eridana were already in."

Queen Cassia says, "That was quick but very well said. Now it is your turn, Tiarra, to tell us what happened when you talked with The Master."

Tiarra says, "I saw the Master as a pretty good looking middle aged man. He behaved like a pretty dictatorial leader. Not the kind of leader that I am, or that Aaron is. He asked me about you, Queen Cassia, also. I couldn't possibly accept him to be the leader of the Keepers. He told me that I would soon be executed at the Festival. He sent me to a prison cell where Reuben, Johanna, Eridana and Aaron were already chained to the wall. We talked it over. We knew that we had to figure out a way to escape. We did. Reuben took a couple of hairpins out of his black hair and we used them to pick the locks that held our chains to us and to the wall. We ambushed the next two soldiers who came into our cell in the morning and escaped. We found the rest of the things that we had brought with us to Divinity City, found Robert Swift and David Silverlake in the Dungeon and brought them up to the ground floor. Before we could get outside we were attacked by a large group of soldiers wearing the uniform of the People's Republic. Amrath, his father Leander, Nick and Helena showed up just in time. Amrath used his Imp of Wishes to transfer us all to his father's house in Tarek."

Eridana says, "Aaron and Tiarra were dead when they were transported to the outdoor courtyard at Amrath's home. I had to use the Silver Chalice of Resurrection that you gave to me to bring them back to life. Thank you, Queen Cassia for that."

Tiarra says, Now you know what we learned about The Master of the Keepers when we were prisoners in the tower at Divinity City. Do you have any questions?"

Queen Cassia says, "Not right now. I will think about it. If I do I will contact one or more of you and ask about it. I think you all did very well to rescue Robert Swift. I am glad that he seems to be in very good health now.

Robert Swift says, "And I thank you again. You risked a lot to get me away from the tower at Divinity City. I didn't expect that I would be rescued. I feel lucky that you did it before I was killed.

Cassia gives them the reward that she promised; a pouch of gems valued at one hundred and fifty gold pieces for each. Aaron and Johanna volunteer to carry Tamaranis's share of the reward to the monastery which is fairly near to Johanna's home at Domus.

Cassia also gives Robert Swift a pouch with the ten large rubies and fifteen very large pieces of gold she had promised him. The total value is about the same as five hundred normal pieces of gold. Robert gives each of the five people with him one ruby and one large gold coin. He also gives

Johanna a ruby and a large gold piece for her to deliver to the monastery that Tamaranis was a part of. Four rubies and nine large gold coins are left for himself.

This calculates to an additional forty-six normal gold pieces in value for each of the six helpers, including Tamaranis, and two hundred and sixty-four normal gold pieces for Robert Swift. He plans to give Amrath a share the next time he sees him.

It is still early in the day when Queen Cassia uses her Transference Spell to Transfer them all, two at a time, back to Derlenen, just on the southern side of the white bridge. From there, they go their separate ways along the roads that take each back to their own homes. Eridana and David Silverlake almost immediately separate from the others, heading west on the trail that appears to be a shortcut toward Eridana's home, Daring. Tiarra, Reuben, Johanna, Aaron and Robert Swift go south on the narrow road toward Althen.

Johanna and Aaron head east from Althen. Aaron intends to accompany Johanna to her home at Domus, east of Jen. From there he will go alone to his home at Ezrada. On the way, they will deliver Tamaranis's share of Sarah's reward and Cassia's reward to his monastery.

From Althen, Tiarra and Reuben will go west to Tiarra's home at Galadrin. Reuben will continue alone from there the rest of the way to Tarek, then north to his home at Springbrook. He may try to find the Darkriver home as a place to spend the night in Tarek.

The End

Printed in the United States
By Bookmasters